CW00344690

THE DAUGHTER OF THE FENS

ELENA COLLINS

Boldwood

First published in Great Britain in 2023 by Boldwood Books Ltd.

Cover Design by Alice Moore Design

Cover Photography: Shutterstock

A CIP catalogue record for this book is available from the British Library.

Paperback ISBN 978-1-78513-171-4

Large Print ISBN 978-1-78513-167-7

Hardback ISBN 978-1-78513-166-0

Ebook ISBN 978-1-78513-164-6

Kindle ISBN 978-1-78513-165-3

Audio CD ISBN 978-1-78513-172-1

MP3 CD ISBN 978-1-78513-169-1

Digital audio download ISBN 978-1-78513-163-9

Boldwood Books Ltd
23 Bowerdean Street
London SW6 3TN
www.boldwoodbooks.com

To Big G and the amazing journey...

Roman Britannia (AD 60)

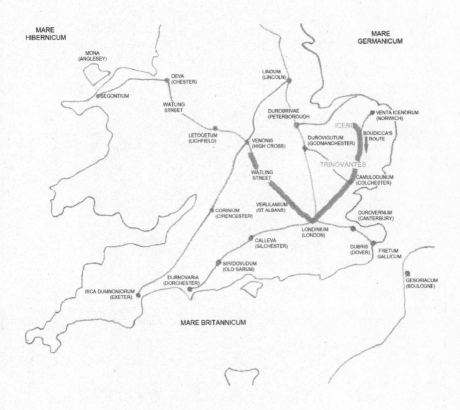

MARE
HIBERNICUM

MARE
GERMANICUM

MONA
(ANGLESEY)

DEVA
(CHESTER)

LINDUM
(LINCOLN)

SEGONTIUM

WATLING
STREET

DUROBRIVAE
(PETERBOROUGH)

VENTA ICENORUM
(NORWICH)

ICENI

LETOCETUM
(LICHFIELD)

VENONIS
(HIGH CROSS)

DUROVIGUTUM
(GODMANCHESTER)

BOUDICCA'S
ROUTE

TRINOVANTES

WATLING
STREET

CAMULODUNUM
(COLCHESTER)

CORINIUM
(CIRENCESTER)

VERULAMIUM
(ST ALBANS)

DUROVERNUM
(CANTERBURY)

LONDINIUM
(LONDON)

CALLEVA
(SILCHESTER)

DUBRIS
(DOVER)

FRETUM
GALLICUM

SIRIDOVUDUM
(OLD SARUM)

DURNOVARIA
(DORCHESTER)

GESORIACUM
(BOULOGNE)

ISCA DUMNONIORUM
(EXETER)

MARE BRITANNICUM

Roman Villa

DOMUS (HOME)

CUTAWAY DRAWING

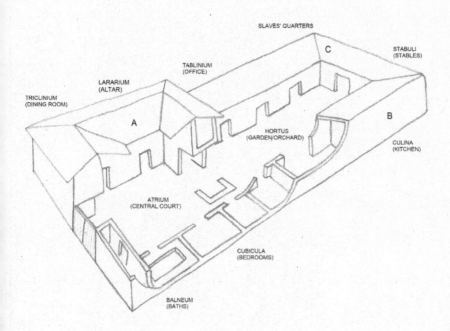

SLAVES' QUARTERS

STABULI
(STABLES)

C

TABLINIUM
(OFFICE)

LARARIUM
(ALTAR)

TRICLINIUM
(DINING ROOM)

B

A

HORTUS
(GARDEN/ORCHARD)

CULINA
(KITCHEN)

ATRIUM
(CENTRAL COURT)

CUBICULA
(BEDROOMS)

BALNEUM
(BATHS)

A PARS URBANA (OWNERS' SECTION)
B PARS RUSTICA (SLAVES' SECTION)
C VILLA FRUTUARA (STORAGE)

PROLOGUE
NORWICH, 2006

The instant her head hit the floor, something changed forever. Seconds passed. It took moments for Hanna to open her eyes again and when she did, she had no recollection of what had happened. Another life flashed before her eyes, a life she didn't recognise as her own, but one that would never leave her.

She'd been standing in a line in the gym, waiting her turn, her shoulders relaxed, arms by her sides, chin raised. In her black leotard, she looked exactly the same as any other thirteen-year-old girl in the competition, lean, muscled, hair neatly tied back. This was the East Anglia area competition; the reward was a place in the finals in London for the best three competitors. Hanna had closed her eyes, concentrating. She was ready for this – she had trained hard, perfected every move.

An authoritative voice had called out the name of the gymnast before her, a girl with a mass of curly hair who'd hesitated before leaping forward in a sprint, light as air as her body arced on the trampette, flipping over, landing firmly on the trampoline. She began her display with a perfectly executed pike, a straddle, a precise front and back drop. She was good, Hanna had conceded, a strong rival. Hanna had watched as the girl bounced higher, a slick twist in each somersault, landing confidently, legs slightly bent, arms in the air, finishing an impressive sequence. Hanna took a breath. If she was focused and calm, if she gave her best performance, she could beat her.

Hanna knew her mother was watching from the other side of the gym, seated on a bench, nervous fingers folded on her lap, waiting. Stephanie Frampton had driven her all over East Anglia and beyond to gymnastic competitions since Hanna was nine years old. Her mother was as keen and committed as she was. She'd been divorced since Hanna was seven, there were no other children: her mother's life revolved entirely around her daughter. Everything was about practising, eating properly, dedication. Their lives ran like clockwork, a perfect busy timetable of school, training and competitions. Hanna didn't look across. She had to keep her mind on what she was doing.

Then someone had called out her name in a crisp voice, 'Hanna Frampton.'

She had waited a second, controlling her breathing, slowing it down, then she leaped forward.

Hanna had no idea how it happened. One moment she was sailing onto the trampette, then her foot had slipped or she'd placed it clumsily, she wasn't sure. The trampette hurtled backwards while she was in mid-air and an ankle became tangled in the rope of the trampoline. Her body twisted and fell. Her head cracked against the floor.

Time passed. Hanna had no idea how long she'd been unconscious. She lay, unmoving. But it was as if she had stood up and entered a dream. Something had changed – she was somewhere else, a place she had never been to before. Yet there was an uncanny familiarity about the surroundings, the open space, the damp grass beneath her feet.

Hanna looked around; she was standing in a village, a cluster of smoky huts, tethered animals. Then she was no longer herself – she was another girl. Her clothes were different: she seemed to be dressed in a long tunic, bronze jewellery, her hair was loose. Over her shoulder, people she recognised were anxious. Faces twisted in shock; angry mouths shouted in warning – an advancing army were snaking across the field towards her. Then there was a noise in her head, the thunder of roars and cries and clashing of metal.

For a moment, she was aware of her feet sinking into soft ground, then a man she instinctively knew she trusted pushed a sword into her hand and shouted in a strange language. Hanna understood in an instant what he meant – he'd told her to stay close, he would protect her. He'd called her another name, not her own. She was shaking, afraid, not listening. The next minute, she was running among a crowd of stampeding tribespeople who were screaming and yelling. A man in steel armour hurled himself towards her and Hanna's heart churned. She ran the other way, dodging a snarling soldier with a shield. Then a young soldier hovered; he lurched towards her, grabbing her arm.

Her eyelids flickered and her mouth was dry as she spoke. Her lips moved numbly and she heard her own voice, but the words were mangled. '*Dwek... bwe... Eceni...*'

Hanna glanced up. Faces loomed over her and swirled as she lay twisted on the gym floor.

'*Eceni...*' She felt a low twinge grip the back of her head and she closed her eyes again.

* * *

Later, Hanna sat in the changing room with her mother, who clutched her hand. Hanna was wearing tracksuit bottoms over the leotard now, a sweatshirt wrapped around her shoulders for comfort and warmth. She was confused. 'Mum?'

Her mother's face was anxious. 'Your foot slipped. Apparently there's not a mark on you. But you were out cold for a few seconds.'

'I don't remember.' Hanna had been left with a strange feeling, her emotions bruised, the sense of a devastating change having happened.

'You said something – but it made no sense. And you still seem to be in shock. I'm sure you're fine, Hanna, but I want to take you to A&E to get you checked over.'

Hanna put a hand to her head. 'I'm not sure where I am...' She recalled the thunder of battle, soldiers with raised swords rushing around her, the scent of the grass as she fell.

'I think we should take you to see a doctor.'

Hanna stood on shaky legs. 'I was somewhere else – I was trying to run away.'

Hanna's mother smiled, reassuring. 'Let's get you home via the hospital, shall we?'

For a moment, Hanna didn't move. The word *home* was a difficult word to process. She wasn't sure where home was. She knew the name Little Rymer, the village where she lived, not far from King's Lynn, number 32, Mawkin Close, but it wasn't home. She closed her eyes and saw fields, mist, wide skies. The smell of something burning was in her nostrils, the smoky hut, the cooking pot over the fire. She moved her lips but no words came.

Then her mother was helping her to stand, an arm beneath hers, guiding her to the doorway, clutching her sports bag. Hanna couldn't feel her trainers touch the floor but her feet moved by themselves. Her mind wasn't her own. There was still a humming behind her eyes, the sound of people shouting, a sense of panic, and she shook her head to see if the noise would go away. But the worst thing was the turbulent emotions hammering inside – the anxiety, the fretfulness, the sense that she should be trying to escape, fighting for her life, not following her mother to the car, not passively allowing herself to be strapped into the passenger seat, not leaning back against the headrest, eyes closed, listening to the skirmish raging inside her head.

Her mother was calling her name. 'Hanna? Hanna, can you hear me?'

'Sorry,' Hanna mumbled. Strangely, she still thought of herself as the girl in her dream. She saw the concern etched around her mother's eyes and tried to respond. 'I'm fine.' Hanna took a deep breath and exhaled slowly. 'Fine, really.'

'We'll pop in to A&E. I want to make sure you're all right. After all, there's another competition next month and I don't want you taking part if you're not well enough. That was quite a tumble you took. You gave us all a scare. It's not like you, Hanna. I'm wondering if you're coming down with something, a bug perhaps. I was sure you'd win today. You've worked so hard for this. Everyone said...'

Hanna wasn't listening but she was aware of the disappointment in her mother's tone. She closed her eyes again. An image had frozen itself in her imagination, the teenage girl who was her, but yet not her. She wore a brightly coloured woollen tunic, a bronze torc – she knew the word although she'd never heard it before – around her neck. Her hair was loose and tangled, the way she moved was wilder, free. It was Hanna, but it was someone else too, someone desperate. The young woman was running, although Hanna wasn't sure whether she was dodging away from someone or hurtling towards them. She felt so many emotions as strongly as if they were happening to her now – the lurch of her heart, the squeeze of fear, the crushing rush of shock that someone was chasing her, hurling her to the earth, dragging her arm, lifting her over a wide shoulder as she watched the earth spin.

Although her mother was still talking, Hanna couldn't hear. She was in the car; her mother was stopping, speaking loudly, clambering out, tugging her arm. They were walking towards a white building, a brick hospital behind it, and into a waiting room, where Hanna stared at blank walls.

Time passed, but the voices continued to repeat in her brain. She could still see people throwing themselves forward, sounds of clashing and shouting, screams, more people falling. Then a woman in a white coat was talking to her and Hanna was replying, her mouth was moving, and the woman was shining a light in her eyes, speaking to Hanna's mother. It was all very vague, as if Hanna wasn't yet awake.

Then she was back in the car again, staring at her hands. Her shoulders ached, as if something heavy was lodged between them.

Her mother muttered, 'That's good news, just mild concussion, apparently. Nothing to worry too much about, but I'll keep an eye, like the doctor said...'

Hanna nodded. She wanted to stop the buzz of her mother's voice. There was too much going on inside her own head for her to reply.

Then her mother touched her cheek gently, a gesture of affection and concern, and said, 'You need to rest. The doctor said you should lie down for a while. Let's get you home, love. You'll be better after a good night's sleep.'

Hanna sighed, offering a single mumbled word. But her mother was wrong. Sleep wouldn't make things better. From this moment onwards, the dreams would start.

Nothing would ever be the same.

* * *

Norfolk, AD 47

It was a day like any other, a wide bright sky spanning the Iceni village. Wood smoke curled from the little huts and the villagers busied themselves with their crops and animals. Brea was in her thirteenth summer. She'd been helping her mother, Cartimandua, to weave cloth inside the hut. The coarse fabric was to be dyed blue, a new tunic for her father, Esico. She was excited about making it; Brea loved him especially, and she knew that he'd hug her when she presented it to him, he'd swing her high in his arms and laugh behind his huge beard.

Her father was outside in the sunshine now, fashioning a sword; he was the best metal worker in the village. Brea made an excuse to leave the smoke-filled hut to sit outside in the sharp air and watch him at work. She loved the way he hammered metal with such skill. It would be a good sword with a fine handle. Brea hoped he was making it for her – she was thirteen now, she'd learned to wield a sword as well as anyone, and she needed one of her own.

She frowned as she recalled the conversations she'd heard around the fireside during the evenings. Brea did not fully understand what the adults were talking about, but everyone agreed that the Iceni king, Antedios, was right to be suspicious of the Romans, the strange invaders who'd arrived years ago with their emperor, Claudius. They were people who thought about things differently, people from far away, with their own language and new ways, building settlements of their own. Her father had said they wanted to change everything, to take away the traditions of the Iceni people. Their king did not trust them; he did not want to trade with them and he had no intention of meeting their recent demand to throw away their weapons. Esico's expression had been determined as he'd swigged mead flavoured with meadowsweet: they must make more arms, not less, for when the inevitable happened: the Romans would come to the villages with their armour and their swords, and they, the Iceni tribe, would be ready to protect their families and their homes.

Brea thought about her father's words again as she stared over the flat-lands into the distance. Several people were working in the fields, digging up cabbages for tonight's broth. There would be chicken for dinner too, Brea's favourite.

Her mother's voice reached her ears, calling her back to work. There were vegetables to prepare in the hut.

Brea called cheerily, 'I'm on my way.'

She stood up, stretching her lean limbs, then something caught her eye. It was a wink of light, metal gleaming in the sunshine. She gazed towards a distant clump of trees beyond the fields and saw a square formation of men marching towards them. It took Brea a moment to take it in before she gasped. Then her feet were moving towards her father, she was shaking his arm and pointing. She saw her father's expression change, his eyes widen, and he raised the sword and called a warning to the other families.

The scurrying started almost immediately – the Iceni were moving, ready to fight. Children were hurried into huts, while men and women reached for swords, sticks, anything they could use to defend the village.

Brea watched as the Roman soldiers pushed forwards across a field; at first, small in the distance, then she could see details, the close formation as if they were one body of many men, their steps rhythmic. Bronze helmets encased their faces, row upon row of impenetrable masks, each man with a gleaming red and yellow shield on his arm. The soldiers seemed to grow larger, like giants, and Brea watched them, frozen. Iceni tribesmen and women shouted fierce cries of warning. Then her father pushed a sword into her hand and said, 'Stay close to me, Brea. I'll protect you.'

Her mother was standing tall on the other side of her, breathing heavily, clutching a sword, muttering a prayer to Andred, the warrior goddess. Brea noticed the wild look in her mother's eyes: anger and fear. The Iceni people from the village had gathered round them. They began to stamp their feet, warriors preparing for battle, and Brea did the same, her teeth bared, her eyes narrowed.

There was a huge roar, then a clash of metal. Brea rushed forward, screaming as loudly as she could, her feet running on the muddy ground.

There were harsh cries, the crashing of sword against armour, the sickening lurch of bodies sinking to the ground. Seconds later, she was hurled onto the earth, dragged by her arm, lifted over a wide shoulder and she watched the earth spin beneath her. She hit her head and was dazed for a moment.

A young soldier raised her in his arms; she was his prize. He shouted at her in a strange language. She leaped up at him, trying to kick and bite. He shoved her down roughly and turned away as if she was of no consequence. There were others of her tribe huddled next to her, men, women, children; they were surrounded by soldiers who pointed swords, guarding them, herding them to their feet. They were prisoners now, slaves of the Romans. Nothing would ever be the same.

1

THE PRESENT DAY

Hanna stood at the entrance to Guangzhou Baiyun International airport, a heavy backpack between her shoulders, a bulky case at her feet. She moved forward to gaze up at the arrivals and departures board. After four years of teaching in the international school, her contract had ended, and she needed something new: she was going home to Little Rymer in Norfolk.

Above her, a tannoy echoed, a nasal voice giving new departure information: passengers were urged to go to gate sixteen. There was the bustle of busy people, the hubbub of chattering, but Hanna felt calm. Being in China had meant that the voices in her head had quietened over the past few years, the dreams were less frequent. The rushing images that had been her constant companions as a teenager and at university, and afterwards when she had taught modern languages in a secondary school in Thetford, had almost stopped now. Working in Guangzhou had been a good idea. It had been fascinating, all-consuming, but now, at almost thirty years of age, Hanna was ready for change. She had no idea what she'd do, but she'd take her time. She had savings. Perhaps she'd go back to education, do a master's, or maybe she'd take a job as a waitress in a café in King's Lynn and just settle for a quiet life for a while. After all, she'd need something routine now things were going to be so different back home.

Her mother's wedding was scheduled for three weeks' time. She hadn't even met her mother's fiancé yet. Patrick Palmer, he was called. Hanna couldn't help her grin. Her mum was going to marry Farmer Palmer who owned a big farm just outside Little Rymer, with acres of arable land and droves of British Saddleback pigs.

Hanna's mum was almost sixty now. She'd found it difficult being on her own once Hanna left the UK. She'd been lonely at first, texting every day, but after much coaxing from Hanna, she'd sorted herself out with a dating app and started to meet new people. Then she'd met the love of her life almost on her own doorstep. In the video calls, she talked of very little else but wedding plans and how she baked apple pies in the farmhouse kitchen and coaxed the hens to lay. Her mum deserved some happiness. She and Hanna's father had divorced over twenty years ago and she'd devoted herself to Hanna ever since.

Hanna recalled sadly how her father had always been focused on his career. A captain in the navy, he'd had little time for family. He sent money, visited on occasions, but he lived in Bangkok with a new wife and daughter; he and Hanna hardly spoke now. It was Hanna's mum who'd always been there for her. Stephanie Frampton had shared her passion for gymnastics. Then, after Hanna gave up at thirteen, her mother had quickly adapted to her fascination for learning languages, even though she didn't speak a word of French or German or Spanish herself. When Hanna had achieved a languages degree at the University of East Anglia, her mother had been so proud. She'd rarely put herself first for all the years of Hanna's growing up, then two years ago she'd met Patrick Palmer. Hanna was looking forward to getting to know him properly – saying hello on a video call had told her nothing except that he seemed jolly and pleasant, his arm protectively around his wife-to-be.

Hanna's eyes flickered to the information board. The flight to Heathrow would leave in two hours; she'd get back late tomorrow night. She'd meet her mum at the station and they'd drive back to Bramble Wood Farm, where there would be a room for her as long as she needed one.

Hanna made her way forwards. She planned to check in, go through security, then she'd grab a coffee and relax for a while. It felt good to be going home. It was a new chapter of her life, and she was ready to embrace it.

* * *

Two hours later, Hanna flopped down in the window seat on the plane and stretched her legs. She pushed a hand through her short blonde hair, wondering what her mother would make of the new cut. Her mother had always loved brushing her hair, plaiting it or putting it in a ponytail. The pixie style was neat and suited her. It was practical, no-nonsense, cute and a little bit sassy. She liked it.

Hanna gazed through the window and wondered what in-flight film she should choose. She closed her eyes and imagined arriving in Little Rymer, if much had changed over the last four years. Her mother had said in their last video call that lots of new houses were going up, expensive red-brick ones with gravel drives – she'd commented that she didn't know where all the money was coming from. Hanna couldn't help smiling – her mum had moved from the three-up two-down terrace to a grand seven-bedroom farmhouse just outside the village. And the wedding was going to be lavish, no expense spared. Hanna was looking forward to it.

She felt someone take a seat next to her, the light sinking of another body into the adjoining seat. Hanna kept her eyes closed and, at that instant, an image of a terrified girl running across marshland flashed across her mind. She was there again, clutching a sword, dodging soldiers, the sound of fighting all around her, the intense feeling of panic, of needing to find safety.

Hanna opened her eyes and caught her breath. She'd experienced the dreams and flashbacks much less frequently since she'd arrived in China. Yet the image was back again, the moment she sat on the plane to go home.

She turned to see a small woman watching her. She was dark-haired, greying, tiny inside a pale coat, the twist of an enigmatic smile on her face. Hanna couldn't have guessed her age – her skin was smooth, there was wisdom and calmness in her eyes. She might be forty, she might be seventy, it was hard to tell.

The woman's gaze was level. 'You are travelling back home?'

'I am.' Hanna wasn't sure how to reply.

'I have a son in London, in Soho. He owns a restaurant. The Zen Café. Have you heard of it?'

'I haven't.'

'My name is Song Yue. You may call me Yue. My name means moon.' The woman inclined her head. 'What may I call you?'

'Hanna.' Hanna wasn't really in the mood for talking.

'*Hana* is a name that travels throughout many different cultures. To me, it means flower,' Yue said quietly. 'It's a good name for you, a blue flower, like the ones that grow in the English woodlands every year in spring.'

'Bluebells?' Hanna wondered if she should say something polite, take out her book and immerse herself in reading. She didn't want to be rude but she wasn't feeling like a conversation with another passenger who had her cornered. Yue seemed to know her thoughts.

'It is many hours until we reach Heathrow. I am glad of your company. This will be a long journey, but it will be an interesting one,' Yue said. 'Exactly as your life will be.' Then she closed her eyes, just at the point that she had Hanna's full attention.

Yue meditated for several minutes as the plane accelerated along the runway and heaved into the air. Hanna's head was buzzing with thoughts about what Yue had said to her, about her life, her journey. She told herself it was just a flippant throw-away remark that anyone could have said about anyone. But she recalled Yue's intense eyes, the wisdom that lay behind them. She gazed out at the ground below, the small houses, the diminishing squares of fields. Then she relaxed in her seat and closed her eyes as a dream tugged her...

Hanna was in a building with columns, tall white posts that were decorated ornately. It was a temple, a place of worship – she could smell incense, something sweet hanging in the air. There was a feeling of nervousness, her hands shaking; she had the strong sense that she shouldn't be there. Then she saw the reason why. Many men were lifting stones, ironstone or flint, and building the steps, the floors. While they worked, they were goaded and scourged with whips. Other men with harsh voices urged them on, sometimes with a kick to the stomach if they stopped to catch their breath. Hanna was looking for someone she loved, someone she'd known all her life, and the feeling of loss and loneliness became more intense.

The heavy scent of incense was replaced by something stronger, burning, the smell of destruction. She saw orange flames leaping and heard rising screams. People were trapped, their voices rising with the curling smoke.

Hanna opened her eyes to see Yue watching her again.

'You were dreaming?'

Hanna nodded.

'These dreams have stayed with you for a long time?'

'Some of them.' Hanna was mystified by the question, but she searched for the right words. 'While I was working in Guangzhou, they stopped for a while, but now they've started again.'

'You are going home, to the place where they began.'

Hanna nodded again, wondering how Yue knew so much. Then she said, 'I don't know why I have them. But it's like I am somewhere else – as if I'm somebody else.'

'The visions began when you allowed them to come in. They will end when you find what you must find.'

'And what is that?' Hanna asked without thinking.

'You are connected to someone who is now in the shadows.' Yue's expression was serious but without emotion, as if what she was saying was quite normal.

Hanna shuddered. 'What does that mean?'

'Someone else is searching, just as you search. She has long been gone, but she is not at rest. And you are not able to rest, until it is finally resolved.'

Hanna hugged herself. Yue's words had unsettled her. 'What do I need to resolve?'

'You will know when it is time. Until then, you and she remain connected.'

Hanna heard the desperation in her own voice. 'Who is she?'

Yue did not answer.

Hanna was unsure if she had heard her speak. She thought about asking again. Instead, she said, 'What shall I do?'

This time, Yue smiled. 'She will let you know.'

She turned away, staring at the space in front of her.

Hanna had the impression that Yue did not wish to be asked anything more, but she couldn't help herself. 'Why me? Why do I have these dreams?

I mean – is it reincarnation? Is this person me, in a former life? The dreams are very vivid, so it could be. Or am I being haunted? I've often wondered about it.'

'So many questions, Hanna, but the answer is simple.' Yue put her hands to her ears. 'You must be patient. The understanding will come, in time.'

Hanna pressed her lips together to stem further questions. She did not want to be rude, but she was fascinated to know more.

She gazed out of the window at the sunlight glinting on the edges of clouds, the vast blue expanse of the sky. There was so much that people couldn't explain. Most likely, her recurring dreams had been caused by the accident she'd had on the trampoline setting in motion a new activity in her brain, opening the possibility of the vivid imaginings. That was it, imagination.

Of course, she'd never told her mother about the dreams. After her initial disappointment that Hanna had given up gymnastics, Stephanie had been delighted that her daughter was becoming a talented linguist; she'd enjoyed fussing about trips abroad, exchange visits and extra classes. Hanna saw no point upsetting her. Her mother would only worry, and she had no idea how to explain the strange changes that were happening.

Hanna's lids were heavy. She was suddenly tired, her limbs leaden. Sleep took her quickly and this time, she did not dream. Behind her eyes, the azure sky buffeted clouds along as if they were curled lambs, and she slept sweetly.

When she woke, a middle-aged man was sitting beside her, squashed in the seat, sipping tea. She could smell the stale tweed of his jacket, a slight whiff of aftershave.

Hanna was confused. 'Where's Yue?'

The man shook his head and adjusted large-framed glasses, a brief dismissal of her question. 'Who?'

'The woman who was in the seat next to me?'

'Oh.' The man waved a hand. 'She had the wrong seat. I can't stand sitting at the back of the plane. I told the attendant I'd booked this seat and I jolly well intend to have it.'

'Ah...' There was little point Hanna continuing the conversation. Yue had gone and, with her, any chance of further questions. She'd content herself with her book now.

The aroma in her nostrils told her an in-flight meal was being served. Then she'd watch a film. It would all help to pass the time.

Hanna pushed the conversation with Yue from her mind. Soon she'd be home.

2

The plane journey had been tiring. Hanna slept fitfully, but by the time she clambered on the train from King's Cross to King's Lynn, she was beginning to feel excited. In less than two hours, she'd be standing on the platform in Little Rymer, hugging her mum. Hanna's head was buzzing with questions about her own new life as she sat in the lurching carriage. How would she feel to be back home? After the daily bustle of China, she'd grind to a halt in the little Norfolk village, but that might not be unpleasant. Hanna had savings: a few months off while she rethought her plans would be a good idea. She'd take up cycling again – the roads were flat and she could bike to King's Lynn, find a temporary job there until she worked out what to do. It was still August; she might research the master's programmes at the University of East Anglia in Norwich. Or she could help her mother settle into the daily routine as a farmer's wife. They could share the chores: cooking, keeping the house tidy, feeding the chickens. Maybe there would be a horse she could befriend – she was sure her mother had said there were one or two at the farm. The idea of riding a sweet-natured mare every morning appealed to her.

Hanna gazed out of the window at the flatlands beyond, feeling the soothing rattle of the carriage. The sun was setting and a mist was rising over the fens. Water-filled irrigation ditches flashed by, followed by wide fields, shadows lurking over scrubby grasses. She couldn't wait to see her mother again. They'd always been close; they understood each other. Stephanie Frampton seemed to realise that Hanna's choices didn't always need discussing and Hanna was grateful for her mother's calm acceptance. The day Hanna had left for the teaching job in Guangzhou, tears had gleamed in her mother's eyes, but she'd hugged her and murmured encouragement.

The train shuffled into a small country station that was dark and deserted; a few fuzzy lights illuminated the tracks and the exit. Little Rymer would be next. Hanna felt a little guilty that she'd never mentioned the vivid recurring dreams to her mother, although Stephanie's sharp eyes seemed to notice when she hadn't slept well.

The train teetered forwards agan. Hanna couldn't wait to see her mum's smile. She wondered what sort of car her mother was driving now she was engaged to Patrick Palmer. What would a farmer's wife drive? The old blue Citroën surely must have been replaced. Stephanie's life had completely changed. There would be an early September wedding. Hanna was excited about sharing plans, being a part of a new family, enjoying her mother's happiness. She'd visited her mother only once throughout the whole time she'd been in China, and suddenly it felt too long. She couldn't wait.

Hanna gazed around the carriage. There were just a few people now, single travellers in random seats dotted around. One woman was talking quietly on her phone; another was tapping the keys of a laptop. A man wearing a waistcoat over a striped shirt was almost asleep, his mouth open. Hanna felt the carriage begin to slow – it was drawing into Little Rymer station. She couldn't help the lightness that lifted in her chest, happy anticipation, a buzz of energy. She stood up, conscious of the aches in her legs – she'd been stuck on a plane since yesterday. She swung her handbag onto one shoulder, heaved her backpack on to the other and collected her case. The train slowed, grinding to a halt and Hanna stepped into the Norfolk fresh night air.

She gazed around at the old station as the train shuddered away towards King's Lynn. The place was deserted. A hazy light glowed from a single lamp. Night had fallen now, and Hanna could smell sweetness in the air, honeysuckle. The brick-built station was a murky, mottled colour.

Everywhere was closed – the ticket office, the waiting room. A sign hung over a padlocked door, Serenity's Café, with a design of a lotus flower. In the half-light, shadows clung to every corner and the drop to the tracks below was filled with darkness.

Hanna dragged her luggage along towards the bridge and climbed the steps. The only sound was the wheels of her case thrumming on the ground. Overhead, a slice of moon hung in a starless sky. She began to descend the steps to the exit gate, scanning the road ahead for a waiting car. There was none.

Hanna caught a slight movement of a woman sitting on a far bench, her head tilted forward. It was past ten o'clock – there were no more trains tonight. She stared harder. The woman was young, was wearing a thin dress, her hands folded on her knee. It was hard to see the colour of her hair in the darkness, but there was a sheen to it, so it may have been fair. Hanna thought she must feel the cold of the night chill – although it was summer, the air from the fens was damp. The young woman seemed sad; perhaps there had been a family tiff, a break-up with a boyfriend. A sense of solitude surrounded her, an acute loneliness. Hanna wondered if she was in trouble or homeless; she'd go over and ask if she needed a lift somewhere. Her mum wouldn't mind.

She reached the bottom step and the sound of an engine caught her attention. Beyond the gate, bright headlights swerved. A large square car was pulling in, coming to a stop. Hanna glanced back to the bench, but the woman had gone. She looked around, hoping the woman hadn't approached the tracks, but she had disappeared.

Suddenly tired, Hanna pushed through the gate towards a large Range Rover and saw her mother's smiling face appear as she wound the window down. She called cheerily, 'I brought the biggest car. I thought it would be better for all your luggage. Paddy's busy with paperwork, so it's just me.'

Then Stephanie slid from the car door and Hanna was in her arms, inhaling floral perfume, feeling the silkiness of her hair against her cheek, hugging her in a tight squeeze.

Her mother held her away. 'You're looking well. But oh, the short hair, Hanna. I can't believe it's so short. I always loved it long.' There was a mistiness in Stephanie Frampton's eyes, quickly replaced by a smile. 'But it suits you. It's good to see you.'

Hanna hugged her mother again, conscious that the woman in her arms was a little leaner, her hair lighter and her clothes very different – she was wearing a wax jacket, jeans, a bright floral scarf. There was a casual smartness to her clothes that had replaced the sensible skirt and blouse she'd always worn.

Hanna spoke into her mother's hair. 'It's good to see you, Mum.' Then she remembered. 'Did you see a girl on your way in – a young woman? She was all on her own at the station...'

'No, no one passed me.' Stephanie gripped the handle of her case. 'Come on, let's get you home. Have you eaten? I saved some quiche that we had earlier. Paddy hates quiche – he thinks it's a yuppy dish. Of course, there are no yuppies now – Paddy's stuck in the eighties. He likes proper farmer's grub, lots of carbs, like potatoes and pies – I have to watch his waistline for him! I've got him eating pasta for a change, not so heavy – a nice pesto or a mushroom linguine. That's our compromise, a few healthy carbs and plenty of flavour...'

Hanna stared at her mother as she heaved Hanna's case into the Range Rover; she was newly galvanised, a sense of purpose to her movements. She'd become a no-nonsense farmer's wife already. A smile on her lips, Hanna wondered briefly if she skinned rabbits for a pot roast.

Stephanie was patting her cheek, urging her into the car. 'Let's get you home, love. Bramble Wood Farm is your home as long as you need a roof over your head. And Paddy's just dying to meet you. Of course, Oliver is away – he's not back until the weekend.'

'Oliver?' Hanna was aware Patrick Palmer had a son, but she'd forgotten he lived in the farmhouse.

'He does most of the heavy farm work now, all the long hours. Not that Paddy will ever give up farming. He's sixty-seven – you'd never think it to look at him. But the farm will go to Oliver. Abby won't want it, although she's the oldest child – Paddy's not at all sexist, of course, but Abby's in Australia. She won't even be back for the wedding. She likes the lifestyle out there too much, hairdressing by day and parties and pools in the evening. No, Ollie is the sensible one.'

Hanna clambered into the passenger seat as the engine revved, remembering all the information shared on video calls. 'Oliver is Paddy's son... and Abby's his daughter in Melbourne...'

Her mother nodded. 'Abby's thirty-five now, living with an Australian called Holden. Ollie's not married, although he almost was, then it all went a bit wrong, I think. He lives in the cottage just beyond the farmhouse. You won't see much of him. He works all the time. Paddy suggested he ought to take a few days off, so he's gone to Cambridge for a long weekend at an eco-show. It's one of these environmental things. He's very much the eco-warrior, Ollie. He's trying to bring the farm into the modern age.'

Hanna closed her eyes, listening to the babble of her mum's voice. It was good to hear her sounding so immersed in her new life, but Hanna was tired. It had been a long journey. And suddenly it felt like another new journey was unfolding. She yawned. 'Mum, if it's all right with you, I'll just say a quick hi to Patrick – Paddy – and then I'll go to bed. I'm shattered.' She stared through the window at the open farmlands in the dark, the low mist.

'Of course, you must be absolutely worn out,' Stephanie agreed. 'Coming all that way from China. Oh, I do hope you'll be able to settle down here, Hanna. Life will be much slower, of course. But on the farm, no two days are the same. And it all changes with the seasons. Ploughing and harvesting, then there are all the pigs...'

Hanna rested her head against the glass of the window, her eyelids heavy as the car bumped along the road. She listened to the soothing lilt of her mother's voice talking about the wedding dress she'd ordered and the ideas she had for what Hanna might wear to the ceremony – they'd go shopping together to pick something nice out – and the reception in The Sprowston Manor Hotel in Little Rymer was going to be wonderful and there would be twenty-five guests for the sit-down meal and loads more for the dancing afterwards...

Hanna grunted contentedly. 'Sounds great, Mum.' Then she was asleep.

* * *

An hour later, after smiles, shaking Paddy's hand several times, drinking a scalding cup of tea and refusing any help with her cases, Hanna dragged her luggage upstairs. She fell asleep again almost immediately in her new bedroom beneath a down-filled duvet, surrounded by fresh yellow wallpaper. She drifted into dreams like sinking into a pillow...

She was standing in the servants' quarters of an ancient building, timber and stone capped with a tiled roof, a wide hall with many rooms leading off: courtyards, baths, storage rooms, exercise rooms, orchards and gardens. Her clothes were different and yet, somehow, they were her own.

She wandered into a large dining room with a tiled mosaic floor and a man wearing a long robe beckoned to her. He was old with a white beard; his face wasn't unkind, but she was cautious of him – he was powerful. She approached him and he spoke in Latin, but Hanna could understand him. *Volo te epistolam accipere.* I want you to take a message.

Then Hanna was rushing through an old town, past a river. On one side was a temple – a pale building with tall steps and magnificent pillars. She inhaled the scent of incense; there was someone inside, offering a prayer. There was a tightening ache in her chest, an old anxiety. Then she heard the crack of a whip and looked into the face of a tall man who she recognised. His name was Marcus Rubrius Memnon and she knew instantly that she didn't trust him. He lived in some sort of training ground, and Hanna knew she needed to go in there. She met his eyes boldly and he leered back with a mouth blighted with missing teeth.

Then she woke up, hot and fretful, staring into absolute darkness, and remembered that she was at Bramble Wood Farm.

But her heart was thudding hard. She'd left part of herself in the dream and it would take her a while to become calm again and to remember who she really was.

3

CAMULODUNUM, AD 60

Brea was working in the *culina*, the large kitchen close to the servants' quarters, preparing the master's breakfast. Now he was older, his appetite had changed from ravenously hungry to fussy and demanding. Each morning, Publius Julius Silvanus would request a wheat pancake with dates and honey. Brea was expected to cut it into small pieces and bring it to him in the *triclinium*, and he would eat with his fingers, chewing slowly, relishing each mouthful, telling her she was the only slave in the household who knew how to cook a pancake.

She hummed quietly, happy in her work, despite the difficulties she faced each day. She was the only Iceni in a villa of Greek and Gallic slaves, although there was Addedomaros, a slave from the Trinovantes tribe who worked in the orchards and gardens, whom she often spoke to when she was passing.

Brea had been working in the villa since she was thirteen and now, at almost twenty-six, she looked exactly the same as all of the other slave women. They had taken away her Iceni clothes, tamed the wild hair, replaced the colourful tunics and thick mantles and thrown away her jewellery. She was made to wear her hair pinned up; she wore a simple pale tunic tied at the waist, just as the others did, and she moved on silent feet, her eyes cast down, hoping not to draw attention to herself. It was the only way to survive – Brea's father, Esico, had told her this often as a child. 'These are hard times,' he'd say. 'The Romans are never far from our village, with their eyes on what is ours.' And he'd repeat that, come what may, her first duty was to make sure she stayed alive. The chance to fight would come again, and she'd know when it was the right time to take it. The goddess Andred would whisper it in her ear, and she'd be sure. For now, she'd bide her time, go about her duties and say nothing. But the memory of her mother, her father, the village where she'd grown up stayed with her like a constant ache. Each waking morning, she longed for her tribe. One day, she was sure, her family would be together again.

She spooned honey onto the pancake, singing quietly.

Someone behind her said, 'You're chirpy today, Brea. Don't let everyone know it – Galyna will find even more work for us to do if she thinks we're too happy.'

Brea glanced at Daphne, a house slave around her own age, with dark hair and a bony frame. She smiled. 'I've just made the master's breakfast. It'll keep him sweet today.'

'Old Alba Barba isn't the biggest problem.' Daphne groaned, using the master's nickname, referring to his white beard. 'He's an old goat now. Thank the gods for all the retired soldiers in Camulodunum. All they want is to doze, drink wine and have someone oil their back in the baths. They won't cause us any trouble. Oh no, it's the younger ones that we need to watch.'

'He's a fair man, the master,' Brea said. Publius Julius, with his white beard and his red-rimmed eyes, treated his slaves with an ambivalent lack of interest, as long as he could relax in the bath or sleep for most of the day. Being a slave in his house wasn't too arduous unless rules were broken. The same could not be said for his daughter, Julia. It was best to work hard and avoid any confrontation.

Daphne was chattering. 'I was talking to another slave at the marketplace the other day and her mistress beats her every day. She has a terrible temper, apparently. She treats her poor slave so badly, calling her names. And her husband just looks on, as if nothing is happening. These women seem to enjoy making slaves' lives miserable and some of the men are worse. They think their slave women are – you know...' she lowered her voice, '*meretrices*... prostitutes simply for the taking. I wouldn't like to live like that.'

'I'd better give the master his breakfast.' Brea was never interested in slave gossip. She knew it could lead to being overheard and then beaten.

Daphne picked up a bowl. 'I have fish to prepare for tonight's meal. It's just the master by himself for a few days. It's hard to persuade him to eat more than a morsel. If there's any left over, we can share it. But, mark my words, the hard work will start soon enough. I can't say I'm looking forward to it.'

'Why, what's amiss?' Brea asked, hesitating. 'Are we expecting guests?'

Daphne beamed, putting the bowl down distractedly, delighted to be passing on news. 'The master's son, Marcellus, is on his way home and there will be feasting. The gods have watched over him. Apparently, he's taken a small kingdom from some wild Britons for Nero, although I don't know what it all means, to be honest. It certainly won't be of any use to us slaves – whatever Nero gets Nero keeps for himself. He's a nasty piece of work. They say the nice old Emperor Claudius was killed by his wife, Agrippina, so that she could crown her own son, Nero—'

'What kingdom?' Brea interrupted her.

'I don't know – some land belonging to one tribe or another. It doesn't affect me.' Daphne poured water into a jug. 'I'd better get on with my work. And the master's breakfast is getting cold – you'll save yourself a beating if you take it now.'

Brea hadn't moved. Her heart thumped. 'What kingdom has the master's son taken?'

'Who cares? He's always off fighting some Briton tribe. I just pick up bits and pieces from what the master says when I pour his wine. Marcellus is coming back and then there will be a big wedding. A bride's coming from Rome. She'll live here while her husband is away.'

'Oh?' Brea was still desperate to find out the name of the conquered kingdom. But Daphne wanted to talk about the new mistress.

'Old Alba Barba's daughter doesn't like the idea – the mistress Julia's furious. She's mean enough without having a rival for her brother's attention. But she'll be round here every opportunity she gets, ruling the roost, feasting with her husband and her father and her brother. She'll want to get to know his new wife, seek out her weak places.'

Brea was momentarily sad. 'I remember the master's son's first wife. I was sorry when she died in her childbed.'

'That was years ago. A man has to marry again, especially one who is a legate in the Roman army. He's left it long enough – he must be thirty now and he needs sons.' Daphne arranged fruit in a dish. 'I wonder what the new mistress is like. She can't be any worse than Julia. She's a water snake if ever I met one.'

Brea caught Daphne's eye, a silent communication to keep her voice down.

A tall woman walked into the kitchen, staring around with a stony face. Brea and Daphne immediately sprang into action, Brea spooning more honey onto the pancake, Daphne gouging at the fish. Galyna pressed her lips together. 'I hope you're not gossiping.'

'Not us.' Daphne increased her efforts.

Galyna turned on Brea. 'There are vegetables to prepare.'

Brea lifted the pancake. 'I'm off to sweeten the master.'

'Give old White Beard a kiss from me – and tell him there's a tasty fish or two for supper.' Daphne cackled.

'I will.' Brea was on her way, a smile on her face.

Galyna reached for two small fish in the bowl, grumbling. 'These should have been done already, Daphne.'

Brea fled for the steps. There was always a beating to be had when Galyna was there. Many years older than the other women, she considered herself chief kitchen slave. Daphne was a good sort, though; she meant no harm. She'd always accepted Brea – not everyone trusted people from the Iceni tribe. Brea understood why.

Not a day passed that she didn't whisper a prayer to Andred for her father and her mother. She hadn't heard any news of them since the Romans' attack on their village. Yet each day, she prayed silently to the warrior goddess, begging to see her parents once more. And if the worst had happened, if they were dead, Brea entreated Andred to allow her to find those who had killed them and avenge their lost lives. For now she was a slave, but it wouldn't always be that way. Her first duty was as an Iceni daughter. And the chance would come, she was sure of it.

She reached the *triclinium*, where Publius Julius was stretched languidly on a couch waiting for breakfast. He glanced in her direction.

'Ah, *ancilla*.' He called all the slave women by that name; it meant *slave* and was deliberately impersonal. 'You have my pancake? I hope it's smothered in honey.'

'It is.' Brea deposited the food on the couch in front of him and turned to go.

'*Ancilla*.' Publius Julius waved an arm. 'I hadn't dismissed you.'

Brea turned back and glanced at her feet.

She watched him, despite her head being down, as he pushed a piece of pancake into his mouth. He chewed for a while, and then he said, 'Most delicious, praise the goddess Ceres. The bounty of the earth and the fertility of the growing fields combine in this wonderful pancake. And dates, too? I am blessed indeed.'

'Master,' Brea said quietly. She wanted to return to the *culina*, to help Daphne prepare the next meal. She was also thinking about going outside; it was a fine day. She could make an excuse to walk through the gardens and talk to Addedomaros. He was good company and he understood her well. Unlike the slaves who had been shipped from Rome, Addedomaros had been brought to Camulodunum in the same way as Brea after his people had been attacked. He'd always said he was lucky not to have been sent to build the Temple of the Divine Claudius, where he would have surely died from the hard work, as many had done. Brea suspected that was where her father had been taken.

'*Ancilla*.' Publius Julius stopped chewing and wiped his beard on the long sleeve of his tunic. Brea knew she'd have to wash out another stain later. '*Ancilla*, I want you to take a message into Camulodunum.'

'Very well.' Brea was secretly pleased. It would be a chance to go outside the villa.

'I want you to ask Canipectus the potter to come here. I need him to make some special pots on his wheel for a great banquet.'

'I will.' Brea recalled what Daphne had told her.

'My son, Marcellus, is getting married. His wife will be here from Rome in a few days. I knew her father, Lucius Aurelius. A fine man, an excellent brain and a great writer of satire too.' He glanced at Brea, not expecting her to have understood. 'Go now, *ancilla*. Tell Canipectus I wish to see him after lunch, and not to tarry. I wish to buy the finest pottery for my son's wedding and only the best of everything will do.' Publius Julius waved a hand. 'What are you waiting for, *ancilla*? Go.'

'I am on my way,' Brea said quickly and was hurrying across the mosaic floor towards the atrium, a smile on her face. Being outside in Camulo-dunum was the nearest she came to freedom.

4

Brea found Addedomaros among a group of slaves working in the *hortus*, the walled garden of the villa that led to a vast orchard, where he was tending ornamental plants. Nearby, a cherry tree was in flower and Brea scooped up a handful of petals, holding them in front of her nose. 'The scent is wonderful.'

'Lady Julia asked me to collect them. She wants them dried and placed in the bedrooms in her *domus*.' Addedomaros was tall and lean. His dark hair had been shaved but it had started to grow back, and his head was a mass of black prickles. 'She told me I should deliver them myself. She said I'd find her in the bedroom and to come on a day when her husband was out.' His face was unhappy. 'I think she likes to use young slave men as a cat does a mouse.'

'I hear Julia isn't a dutiful wife.' Brea kept her voice low. 'I shouldn't speak of it, but it worries me if she has set her sights on you.'

'I'm afraid too. I don't want anything to do with her,' Addedomaros said. 'Her father and her husband are both powerful men. Just imagine what would happen.'

'Then you mustn't go, Adde,' Brea said. 'You're too busy. The master will not let you go. Tell her that.'

'How can I tell her anything? She sees life as a game.' Addedomaros sighed. 'I wish I was free to marry a good woman. We'd have the most wonderful garden, full of fruits and vegetables – peas, leeks, cucumbers, artichokes.' His eyes shone at the thought of it.

'Do you think one day you'll buy your freedom? Maybe the master will give it freely – although it is not often that a master grants a slave liberty while he's still alive. And White Beard may live for ten years, more.'

'I'm too useful here,' Addedomaros said sadly. 'What about you, Brea? Do you dream of freedom too?'

'I'm sure it will happen one day.' Brea's hand moved to her hip as if an imaginary sword was there. 'I'll go home, back to my tribe and search for my family. I'd find a village, speak to King Prasutagus, tell him what happened.'

'Prasutagus is dead – did you not hear?' Addedomaros said quietly. 'In his will, he left instructions for his kingdom – half to be given to his two daughters and half to Rome, to appease the emperor. That's where the master's son has gone now. He's led an attack to take the Iceni lands.'

Brea moved closer to him. 'How do you know?'

'There's been talk, but I do not want to speak of it to you, Brea. It's best not to know – don't think of it again for your own safety.'

'Queen Boudicca won't allow her land to be taken.' Brea couldn't help the sudden anger that flared.

'She'll find it hard to stand against the Roman army.'

Brea's hand clutched an imaginary sword. 'But half of it rightly belongs to the king's daughters.'

'The Romans don't recognise that women can own land. These people are not like us. Most Roman women are the property of their fathers or husbands. While others...' Addedomaros shuddered. 'Think of Julia. She takes lovers, goes to the amphitheatre, makes her husband look like a foolish old man when they are in company.'

'Adde, we shouldn't talk – we might be overheard.' They had already said too much. Brea looked around, changing the subject deliberately. 'The garden's exceedingly beautiful. You make it look and smell like a place where gods might live.'

'Then, one evening, when your tasks are completed, would you come here to walk with me for a while?'

'I seldom finish before nightfall.' Brea gave him a kindly smile. 'But if I can, I will. It is always pleasant to share your company.'

'We could talk about the future...' Addedomaros ventured.

'I don't think about it,' Brea replied honestly. 'Now I must go. I have a message to take.' Other slaves had noticed them talking together; someone might report them.

Soon, Brea was on her way into Camulodunum. As she hurried past the Temple of the Divine Claudius, she paused momentarily to look at the alabaster-smooth pillars, the tall stone steps. She could not read, but something had been engraved in beautiful letters beneath the roof. She took a deep breath, recalling how she had passed the temple many times when it was being built, pausing to hear the cry of slaves, the swish of whips, the harsh yell of the guards who urged the men to work harder, lifting stones, building pillars.

Brea wondered again if one of the slaves might have been her father. She believed the Romans had brought him here to Camulodunum because he was a strong man. They would have thought him capable. And dispensable. She'd always noticed the men as they bent over, their backs scarred and scourged, a simple loincloth to keep out the cold. She'd wanted to call out 'Father,' but there were so many fathers there. Would she have even recognised Esico? Would she recognise him if she met him now? She pushed the thought away; she would be reunited with her father one day, her mother too. She was sure of it.

Brea walked onwards towards the potter's shop passing the small theatre and the *ludus gladiatorius* where the gladiators were trained. Brea had never seen a gladiator fight, although she had seen their trainer, a large man called Marcus Rubrius, who fed his men on barley, beans and dried fruit. He carried a whip and a lucky charm – an image of Minerva the Roman goddess of wisdom. Brea didn't like the way he looked at her. Even now, she was scurrying down the road as quickly as possible in case Marcus Rubrius came out to heckle and shout lewd words.

Brea reached the potter's shop. Canipectus was a pleasant man who sat calmly at his wheel, whistling happily to himself as his palms made beautiful smooth pots grow from between them. She liked to watch him work, but today she had an important message.

'You need to visit my master Publius Julius Silvanus this afternoon. He will speak with you urgently about some pottery.'

'Oh?' Canipectus lifted an eyebrow. 'Do you know what he wants? Old White Beard expects things to be done before I've had chance to clean my wheel.'

'His son is getting married again.'

'I hadn't heard.' Canipectus frowned. 'I usually know everything that's going on in Camulodunum. I'm surprised, I must say. Marcellus Julius spends most of his time on the battlefield. Why does he need a wife?' He shrugged. 'The usual reason, I suppose. To get sons. Someone in his line to leave everything to when he dies, but I never thought he'd marry, not after the lady Claudia.'

Brea remembered her, a slight woman who was so delicate that it seemed a strong breeze might blow her over. 'There's a woman coming from Rome. The daughter of a friend of the master.'

'It's been arranged then? Claudia and Marcellus had known of each other since they were children. I can't see the new wife ever managing to edge herself into his favours.'

'Perhaps she'll be good-natured,' Brea said hopefully. 'A pleasant mistress means an easier life for us all.'

'Then she'll be easily hurt.' Canipectus shrugged. 'The best thing would be for her to be self-centred, like Julia. They can keep each other happy trying to seduce noblemen or slaves when their husbands are drinking wine in their baths.' He raised an eyebrow. 'I hear Julia likes to watch the gladiators in the arena.'

Brea shook her head. 'I feel sorry for those poor men, fighting for others' entertainment. A battle should be fierce and harsh, but it should be for the right reasons.'

Canipectus gave a short laugh. 'You are Iceni – I forgot. The Roman ways must still be strange.'

'Not at all,' Brea said quietly. 'I understand them too well.'

'You lost your parents to the Romans?' Canipectus asked gently.

'They aren't lost.' Brea tilted her chin. 'I haven't found them yet, that's all.'

Canipectus leaned forward, lifting his hands that were crusted in dried clay. 'Did you know that I'm a Briton, from a long line of potters.'

'I didn't know that, no. Many of the people in my village were potters too.'

'I'll give you some advice,' Canipectus said quietly. 'The Roman army is a rolling wave of destruction, and it will flatten everything that stands against it. But the Romans have done some good. Their roads, their houses...' He grinned. 'The way they heat their rooms when the cold weather comes. It's not without merit. So, my advice is...' He took a breath. 'Forget your tribe. Let the past go. Instead, concentrate on pleasing your masters and one day you'll get your freedom and live happily.' He met her eyes. 'That's all we can hope for.'

'Perhaps some things are greater than life – family, honour, love,' Brea suggested. 'And what if we have more than one life? I believe the gods can bring us back again. My father told me.'

'The Romans would not like to hear you speak this way.' The potter shook his head gravely. 'Leave those notions in the past.' He offered a warm smile. 'Trust me, life will be easier if you embrace Rome. You're a woman. It is the same for you whatever happens, you must bear the yoke of marriage or the yoke of slavery.'

'Iceni women are not like Roman ones. We stand side by side, father, husband, wife, daughter. We are strongest together.' Brea raised her chin defiantly.

'Go now. Tell your master I'll come directly to talk about pots. I'll make fine pitchers, wine goblets in the curved shape of a woman, bowls deep as thirsty Roman throats. I will not fail him. And you,' Canipectus said gently, 'forget your Iceni ways.'

'Fare you well,' Brea said quietly, then she was gone from his shop.

She hurried through the streets, past the *ludus*, where shouts of men clanging swords and fighting echoed loudly. She rushed by as quickly as she could and was soon level with the Temple of the Divine Claudius. A beggar woman was huddled on the steps, her matted hair over her face like a mass of cobwebs. She held out a skinny hand. 'Pray you – bring me food and I will grant a favour—'

'I have nothing,' Brea said kindly. 'I'm just a slave.'

'I'll be here later. Bring me something from your kitchen or I'll be dead by morning. Come from your *culina* with a morsel and I'll have something for you, by the grace of the gods.' The woman's eyes were glassy with hunger and her voice was almost unearthly. 'I will be on these temple steps, waiting.'

'I'll try my best,' Brea promised.

'You'll not be sorry. I have a gift that will change your days.' The woman lifted a skinny finger and pressed it against Brea's cheek. 'My name is Luna.'

'Then farewell, Luna.' Brea rushed towards the villa. She had already been away too long. She glanced over her shoulder and saw the woman watching her, a bundle of tattered rags beneath tangled hair and glittering eyes.

Brea hurried on. There would be a beating waiting for her from Galyna back in the kitchen, but she'd find the chance and slip out again. The beggar woman had promised a gift that would change her life and Brea was intrigued.

5

It was past nine when Hanna woke. Although, at first, her sleep had been haunted by strange dreams, she sat up in bed feeling refreshed and energetic: she was home. She rushed to the window, flinging back the curtain. Below, a man was driving an enormous farm vehicle across a field. She stared harder – it was Paddy, and there was a black and white Border collie sitting in the cab seat beside him. Hanna wondered if she ought to learn more about farm life – what each vehicle was for, when the time was for ploughing and harvesting and what farmers did in between. Farming probably had a language all of its own. Then there were all those pigs.

Hanna smiled – her mother was adapting well to the new way of life, so perhaps Hanna could too. Fleetingly, she remembered it was Friday. She decided to hurry downstairs and see what her mother was doing: she could smell cooking.

Stephanie was standing at the Aga, poaching eggs and pouring coffee. Hanna sat down at the table. 'I don't usually have breakfast, Mum.'

'What, not at all?'

'Not really – I never have time.'

Stephanie smiled fondly. 'You have time now. So, two eggs or three?'

'One's enough,' Hanna gasped. 'And one piece of toast.'

'I'll cook two – you're living on a farm now and my chickens lay the best eggs. You'll taste the difference.' Stephanie turned her back, waving a spoon. 'And I make all my own bread.'

'You must adore living here, Mum.' Hanna loved how her mother appeared to be queen of the kitchen, creating breakfast as if she was making magic.

'Oh, it's a fantastic way of life,' Stephanie agreed. 'I'm sure you'll settle in.' She indicated the coffee and Hanna took a sip.

'Mmm. I think I will.'

Stephanie's eyes softened. 'Is it good to be back?' She placed a plate of toast and two perfectly poached eggs in front of Hanna. 'I hope it feels like home.'

'It's wonderful,' Hanna said. 'It will be lovely to have some time to work out what to do next.'

'There may be jobs in the schools in King's Lynn – they are always looking for languages teachers.'

'Maybe.' Hanna nodded, her mouth full.

'Or you said you might go back to uni and do a master's.'

'It feels so nice to have choices, Mum.' Hanna was suddenly filled with new enthusiasm. 'I've always been interested in jewellery – I could take a course and learn to design it.'

'That sounds like fun.'

'Or I could just work on the farm,' Hanna teased.

'Oh, I'm not sure Paddy and Oliver need—' Stephanie realised the joke. 'Ah, yes, you could help Paddy with all those lovely smelly pigs.' She sat down opposite Hanna, cradling a cup between her palms. 'You can stay here as long as you like. Something is sure to come along and grab your interest and you'll be off like a tornado again. But perhaps you'll stay this time...'

'You mean find *the one* and settle down?' Hanna grinned, tucking into the second egg. 'Maybe when I'm your age, Mum – that might be soon enough.'

'You don't think that I've been a bad influence?' Stephanie's expression changed to one of anxiety. 'I mean – I brought you up by myself – there was never a man in the house. Even when I was married to your father, he was always away. We were just like friends, Hanna, not mother and daughter.

We went everywhere together and I sometimes worry that I made you too independent.'

'No one can be too independent.' Hanna squeezed her mother's hand across the table. 'You're the best mum – you always have been.'

'But you had no father figure and now...' Stephanie sighed. 'You don't seem to want a partner.'

'You're right.' Hanna pushed her plate away along with the idea. 'You know there have been boyfriends along the way, but I've never looked to settle for one in particular. I suppose I've never found anyone who interests me enough.'

'It happens when it happens,' Stephanie said philosophically. 'I mean, I'm fifty-nine, and it's taken this long for me to find Mr Right.'

Hanna grinned. 'That will be soon enough for me.'

'But you'll be thirty years old in November.' Stephanie was shocked. 'Don't you want a home, a family? I suppose I shouldn't ask—'

'Of course you can ask, Mum.' Hanna pushed a hand through her hair. 'It might be nice one day. I don't know. How would anyone put up with someone as independent as me? Besides, I'm not sure any man could stay in the same bed as me all night. I'm such a lousy sleeper.'

'Oh?' Stephanie's brow furrowed. 'I didn't know.'

Hanna pressed her lips together. She'd said too much. 'Breakfast was delish, Mum. Any more coffee in the pot?'

'Of course.' Stephanie stood up and moved to the Aga just as the kitchen door opened and Paddy came in. 'Did I hear the mention of coffee?'

A black and white Border collie bounced into the kitchen behind him and leaped playfully up at Hanna. She ruffled the dog's fur. 'You're a real sweetie.'

'Down, Roy,' Paddy commanded, taking a mug from Stephanie, kissing her cheek. Roy squatted on the tiled floor next to Hanna's feet.

'He's very obedient,' Hanna said, fondling the dog's velvet ears.

Paddy plonked himself heavily at the table, glanced at the wall clock and gulped coffee. 'His mother was a good sheepdog. Roy was the runt of the litter, a rum scrawny ole thing. I sold the rest. A farmer mate of mine said I should shoot him – that he'd never make a working dog. But there was something about him, a look in his eyes, so I kept him.' Paddy took another swig of coffee, clearly in a hurry. 'He's all right, Roy. I'd better be off in a minute, Steph love.'

Stephanie smoothed Paddy's hair and Hanna felt warmed by the easy affection between them. She looked down and saw Roy gazing at her, his eyes round and pleading. She reached out a hand. 'He's adorable.'

Roy licked her fingers and Paddy grunted. 'Now don't you go making him all soppy. He's the best dog I ever had for rounding up pigs.'

'Really?' Hanna couldn't pull her gaze from the begging eyes. 'I think you're gorgeous, Roy.'

Roy barked once and Paddy laughed. 'It's been a long time since I ever heard anyone in this house call a working dog gorgeous.' He stood up abruptly, draining his mug. 'Well, Roy, we can't afford to hang around – it's back to the grind.'

Roy sprang up immediately and stood by Paddy's side, waiting.

Paddy kissed Stephanie's cheek. 'Right, I'll be back at half one for lunch.'

'See you then.' Stephanie smiled as she watched him go, then she turned to Hanna. 'What are you up to today?'

'I'll just potter about, find my bearings,' Hanna said. 'Is that all right?'

'It's fine. You can always help me here if you want, but...' An idea occurred to Stephanie. 'There's an old bicycle of Abby's in the shed outside. It's a sit-up-and-beg and she'll never use it now she's in Australia. You could ride into Little Rymer and see if anyone you know still lives there. Or you could bike into King's Lynn and look up some old school friends.'

'Most of them are married with kids,' Hanna mused. 'But yes, I'll take the bike out. I've missed the exercise of cycling along the lanes. It's a beautiful day. Thanks, Mum. Can I help you wash up first?'

'No, get on with you.' Stephanie's eyes were misty as she hugged her daughter. 'Oh, it's so good to have you home.'

* * *

An hour later, Hanna was cycling down the narrow road, a mile and a half ride towards Little Rymer. On one side, open fields of wheat belonging to Bramble Wood Farm stretched to the horizon, and to the left, there was an litch and a scrubby field. The sky was a wide, deep blue, but for a ... of clouds. It was a perfect August day, and Hanna pushed the ...nd effortlessly.

The timber and iron village sign for Little Rymer appeared by the side of the road, surrounded by tall flowers. Hanna glanced to her left at the railway station where her mother had collected her. She slowed the bicycle down and looked around. There were several cars in the car park, a few people standing on the platforms, sitting on benches. Hanna noticed the bench where she'd seen the young woman and frowned at the recollection, hoping she hadn't come to any harm. She half expected to see her there again, head down, looking lost, but she was nowhere to be seen.

Hanna pushed the bicycle down the ramp towards the platform, leaning it against the brick wall near the waiting room. The sign for Sereni-ty's Café caught her eye. She'd pop in for a drink.

The café was half full: a woman with two lively toddlers sat at a table strewn with crisp packets; two men in paint-spattered overalls slurped tea and chomped biscuits; four teenage girls chatted over milkshakes. Hanna approached the counter, watching a woman around her own age in a green apron bustling about, wiping a surface, rearranging a display of chocolate. She offered Hanna a wide smile and tucked a dark curl behind her ear. 'What can I get you?'

Hanna inspected the chalk board. 'Can I get a chai latte please?'

'Oat milk, soya or cow?' the woman asked.

Hanna shrugged. 'Oat.'

'Take a seat – I'll bring it over. Anything else?'

'No, thanks.' Hanna tapped her card in payment and made her way to an empty table near the window, gazing outside. A train had just arrived and people were shambling away tugging cases, as a guard marched along the platform slamming doors.

Hanna shook her head slowly, almost in disbelief. Just a matter of days ago, she'd been living in busy Guangzhou, so many people bustling around her. She'd work long days and stroll home each evening among the young movers and shakers shouting energetically into mobile phones, passing the older people in the park doing tai chi, their faces serene. There was an ancient man she'd see each night sitting on a bench playing an erhu, a strange two-stringed instrument with a bow. Most evenings, she'd eat with teacher friends from the international school in restaurants with circular tables, watching alligators swimming in tanks. They'd drink tea and strong baijiu until the late hours. Now here she was in a small café in East Anglia, watching a train pull slowly away while she wondered what to do with her life.

The young woman placed a mug in front of Hanna and smiled. 'Chai latte?'

'Thanks.' Hanna picked up the mug, inhaling sweet cinnamon. 'Ah, I've missed this.'

'I'm guessing you're Stephanie's daughter who's just back from China?'

'That's right.' Hanna smiled.

'Everyone knows everything about everyone around here. I'm Serenity Hobbs. This is my café.'

Hanna held out a hand. 'Hanna Frampton.' She thought for a moment. 'Did you go to school round here?'

'King Edward VII in King's Lynn,' Serenity said. 'I left ten years ago.'

'I went to King's Lynn Academy – we probably wouldn't have met.'

'I've heard about you, though.' Serenity smiled. 'Apparently you're staying in Little Rymer for a while.'

'I suppose so, yes.' Hanna was taken aback – she'd been living in an anonymous city for so long, she'd forgotten how villages were such close communities. She decided to change the subject. 'This is a nice café.'

'It may be stuck on the station platform, but it's the only café in Little Rymer. I've put a lot of work into it over the last two years.' Serenity was proud of herself. 'It was just an instant coffee and snacks kind of place when I took over. I bake all my own food from scratch and I've added milkshakes and lattes. It's busy – I can hardly keep up.'

'That's good, though,' Hanna commented, sipping from the mug.

'Well, it's nice to meet you.' Serenity turned to go. 'What's your favourite sweet treat?'

Hanna answered without thinking, 'I love flapjacks – with raisins. My mum used to make them.'

'Drop in for a latte tomorrow and I'll have a batch,' Serenity promised as she made her way back to the counter, where the two men in overalls were waiting to pay.

Hanna finished her drink and stood up. She decided to ride into Little Rymer and see if it brought back memories – the primary school, the church, the village green and the little terraced house with flowers in the front garden where she and her mother used to live. It had been sold very recently; while she'd been in China, her mother had already moved to Bramble Wood Farm; it would be strange to see it again with new residents.

She was at the door of the café, about to go out onto the platform, when a man filled the space. He was dark, tall, sinewy in jeans. He stood back to let her through. Their eyes met and the darkness of his gaze seemed to burn into hers. Hanna felt the jolt like an electric shock and stood back a moment, stunned.

The man waited, the same look of recognition on his face. For a moment, they didn't move, their eyes welded, then Hanna blundered forward. She was still transfixed by his stare as she paused on the busy platform, grasping the handles of her bicycle. She quickly threw a leg over and pedalled up the ramp towards the road.

Hanna could still feel the scorch of his eyes as she rode through Little Rymer. The image of him was rooted in her mind, dark hair, deep-set eyes glimmering as he stood in the doorway. She couldn't stop thinking about him – it had been impossible to look away. And there was something else about him, an aura of sadness. It unsettled her more than she could understand.

6

It was late now, the sky starless. The kitchen slaves were mostly asleep in their quarters, a tiny room sparsely furnished, just four small hard beds crowded together, a chamber pot and a wooden chest. Daphne was already snoring, exhausted. Chloe, the youngest at only seventeen, was curled in her bed sucking her forefinger, a habit she always clung to before she fell asleep. Galyna was still in the kitchen, finishing chores. The master had long since retired to his bed. Brea stood in the atrium, holding a folded cloth containing the evening meal's leftovers. She'd collected bread, scraps of meat, figs and a small flagon of wine. She knew if she was discovered, Galyna would tell the master and she would be punished with a severe beating.

Brea looked around and made a dash for the door. She scurried through the garden, past a few slave men who were working. She wondered briefly if Addedomaros was still busy, or if he was asleep in the male quarters: it would be an early start again in the morning; slaves rose before dawn to begin their chores.

Brea made her way towards the road through Camulodunum. Many people still moved around. Three men in heavy togas rushed past without noticing her, talking about literature in excited voices. A woman wearing a colourful tunic that exposed her shoulder hissed and waved Brea away, thinking she might be competition for men's attention. Two more men passed, their voices slurred from an excess of wine. Brea watched them stagger by, then she ran towards the temple.

The beggar woman was sitting on the steps, wrapped in a tattered rag. She recognised Brea immediately. 'What have you brought?'

Brea passed her the cloth and the woman unwrapped the contents, her thin fingers reaching for the scraps of meat, pushing them into her mouth. Her eyelids closed with the ecstasy of pacifying her hunger. She swigged the wine, tearing hunks of bread, chewing toothlessly. Then she made a low sound of satisfaction.

'It is good to eat.'

'I hope you feel better,' Brea said kindly, sitting beside her on the cold step.

'My name is Luna,' the beggar woman reminded her. 'And you are Brea.'

'How do you know that?'

The woman gobbled the fruit. 'I have lived a long time. I know much of life and the ways of the world.'

'What do you know of me?' Brea asked.

'That you are searching now. That you will search forever.' Luna carried on chewing roundly, wiping her wet lips. Then she said, 'You seek your parents. You should follow your heart. Your father is alive. He is not far from you now, at this moment...'

'Where is he? How can I find him?' Brea leaned forwards.

'When you discover the answer, you will still be searching. One day you will be offered love, Brea, the chance of complete happiness. You may accept it with no hesitation, but it comes at a price.' Luna's eyes were fierce. 'There are risks. I can see hatred following you, and danger. You will know love and sadness. I see that you will give away your heart. And if something slips through your fingers, you will be searching forever.'

'What will I search for?' Brea asked, troubled.

'Ask no more. It is time for me to leave this place.' Luna glanced around, her face full of disdain. 'A temple for a dead emperor who people think is a god?' She sighed. 'But it is of no consequence. It will not be here long.'

'What do you mean?'

'You will know soon enough.' Luna shook her rags. She was tiny inside the tatters.

Brea could not take her eyes from the beggar woman, who clambered to her feet. She reached out to touch her skinny arm. 'Please – what more of my parents?'

'I see a man with a sword. More than one man.'

'My father?'

'I see a battle. I see gold jewellery.'

'Jewellery?' Brea was astonished. 'Iceni jewellery? My mother? Tell me, is it my family – will I be reunited with them?'

'I can tell you no more.' Luna frowned, her face creased as a walnut. 'But for one thing...'

'What is it?' Brea clutched her arm, desperate to know more.

The beggar woman cackled. 'The Greek slave is thinking of retiring to her bed at this moment. She has almost finished her work for the day. She'll notice you aren't there. Go quickly – save yourself a thrashing. And remember well what I have said.'

'I will.' Brea ran, almost colliding with an old man who paused and called after her with lewd entreaties. She hurried on, turning once to gaze over her shoulder at the Temple of the Divine Claudius. There was no one on the steps: Luna had gone.

Back in the slaves' quarters, Brea huddled on the hard bed, listening to Chloe sucking her fingers and Daphne's intermittent snuffling. She closed her eyes tightly as Galyna padded in on bare feet and lay down, groaning that her bones ached, then she was silent. But Brea couldn't sleep. Her mind was filled with the beggar woman's prophecies: she would give her heart away, she would find her father, she would be reunited with her people. She was sure of it.

* * *

The next morning, the clouds hung heavy over Camulodunum, the rain dripping outside the shuttered windows of the villa. Brea took the master's breakfast into the *triclinium*, retiring to the *culina* to help prepare the meals for the rest of the day. She occupied herself with honey biscuits, one of the master's favourite sweets. Daphne was her usual chatty self as she prepared garum, a salty condiment sauce made from fermented fish guts, which the master would pour on all his savoury foods. Daphne wrinkled her nose. 'This stuff stinks like a sewer,' she declared.

'It makes my stomach turn,' Chloe agreed as she shelled peas.

'Can you imagine kissing someone who has just eaten this?' Daphne guffawed at the thought of it. 'His tongue would taste like a dead eel.'

'Oh stop – I might be sick,' Chloe yelped, laughing.

'Don't worry – no man will want to kiss you,' Daphne scoffed good-naturedly.

'Nor you,' Chloe retorted. Then she stood up straight and sighed. 'We'll never be kissed, either of us. Who'd want to be caressed by a slave girl with hands that smell of a *sterculinum publicum*...'

'Can we help it if we work so hard that we smell no better than all the public toilets in Camulodunum?' Daphne pushed the garum to one side. 'But just imagine if a handsome slave came along and turned his gaze upon me, or a gladiator perhaps...'

'Most gladiators are fat – they eat too much grain. Or too thin, because there is no food left for them. And there would be no point falling in love with one – they are always training and they think about nothing other than their next fight,' Chloe said. 'I must admit, if I were to choose a man for his looks, I think Addedomaros is handsome.'

Brea smiled quietly. She preferred to avoid such conversations, but she understood that sharing chatter somehow made the other slaves' lives lighter.

'Oh, he's most kind and good-natured,' Daphne agreed. 'He gave me a plum once and it tasted juicy, like a kiss. And I always make an excuse to see him, to ask for flowers for the *triclinium*.'

'I think he likes Brea best,' Chloe said pointedly but Brea worked on, her head down. Chloe raised her voice. 'What do you think, Brea? Does Addedomaros like you most of all of the slave girls here?'

'I don't think of it.' Brea pushed the biscuits into the clay oven.

'You're quiet today.' Daphne was suddenly concerned. 'Are you all right? Has Galyna given you a beating?'

'No – all's well.' Brea forced a smile and went to Chloe's side to help her finish shelling peas. She wanted to be allowed to be quiet, to think about what Luna had said to her last night. She was trying to make sense of it all and it worried her as the words returned to her in an echo. *'Your father is alive. He is not far from you now, at this moment.'* Brea wondered if it was true. There were other strange mutterings – that she'd give her heart away. Brea frowned – that wasn't likely, she was far too wise. And Luna had mentioned jewellery. Brea thought of the Iceni torcs, brooches and bracelets. She longed for a time when she would be free to return to her people and wear them again.

But Luna's words troubled her. *'If something slips through your fingers, you will be searching forever.'* The thought took her breath away. Did that mean she would never find her parents, she'd never be reunited with her own people? Brea could not shake the words from her thoughts, so she reached for the flour to begin making flatbread.

The sound of footfall on the steps made the three women look up as Galyna rushed into the room. She was out of breath. 'Julia is here to see her father. She wants wine and fruit in the *triclinium*. She has her *ornatrix* with her – she can be a nasty piece of work. If Balbina comes down here to gossip, we won't get any work done. She'll be complaining all day about her aching feet and how she has to stand from morning until bedtime.'

Chloe's mouth was open. 'Is it true that an *ornatrix* will use a mixture of pigeon droppings on a lady's hair to make it look beautiful?'

'I'd rather be a kitchen slave than have to put urine and decomposed leeches on my mistress's hair all day before perfuming it. It must make your hands smell worse than garum,' Daphne remarked.

'Never mind that,' Galyna snapped. 'Wine and fruit are needed urgently. Brea – can you do it?'

'I can.' Brea shook the flour from her hands, collected an urn of wine and placed grapes, figs, olives, nuts and honey on a platter.

'And be quick about it,' Galyna commanded. 'Julia's not known for her patience.'

Brea carried the tray up the stairs to the *triclinium*, and paused until the master lifted a hand for her to move forward. She placed the wine and fruit on the table, filling goblets, then she stood back, waiting to be dismissed. The master was lying on a couch, his legs sprawled in front of him, as his

daughter walked up and down, talking angrily. Her *ornatrix* hovered in the
background, meeting Brea's eyes and smiling slyly.

'It is ridiculous – he's a soldier. He has no need of a wife. I'm his sister. I
know this. I've no idea why Marcellus agreed to it.' Julia flicked a hand
impatiently, smoothing the skirts of her stola, fastened over her tunic with
an ornate brooch.

'It will be good for Marcellus to have a wife again, and I decided that it
was time.' Publius Julius sighed patiently. 'They've been promised to one
another for long enough now, since his first wife died. Her father is an old
soldier friend of mine, so she comes from a good family.'

'And what if she has children, sons? What of me then?'

'You will have sons too,' Publius Julius said gently.

'I have been married to Caius Fabius for six years.' Julia turned wild
eyes on her father.

'When the gods look kindly—' Publius Julius began.

'*The gods*?' Julia was furious. 'Someone has placed a *defixio* on me, a
curse, what with my useless husband who sits all day sweating on his couch
drinking wine, and my perfect soldier brother, away making war against
some tribe of foolish Britons for our wonderful emperor, Nero, while I wait
here with nothing to occupy me. At least when Marcellus is here, I have
some lively company. My life will be even worse when this woman arrives
from Rome, the virgin bride, the centre of everyone's attention, and there
will be a big wedding. For what? Marcellus will never care for her. His heart
was buried with his first wife. And as for me, wedded to fat impotent old
Caius Fabius whom I hate as much as I hate fanged serpents...'

Brea glanced up and saw Balbina cover a smile. She lowered her head
again as Publius Julius spoke.

'You are rash, Julia, and you speak out of turn. But for my fondness for
you, I would forbid it. Your place is here at home, to watch and wait. That is
what a wife must do.' Publius Julius reached for his wine. 'Nero will reward
Marcellus for capturing land for Rome. The Iceni king who died was a fool
– we can't allow him to leave half of his property to women. That is just
Briton folly. Marcellus had to show these people that the law of Rome is
strong.'

'Marcellus was just having some fun. I can imagine how I'd enjoy it in his place. How exciting it must be to be an important soldier.' Julia laughed. 'I hear he had the dead king's women publicly humiliated, which is no more than they deserved. I've no doubt that Nero will be delighted.'

Brea kept her head low, willing herself not to speak. Her eyes filled with tears and she swallowed the anger rising in her throat.

Publius Julius sniffed. 'It's what any Roman officer would have done. Perhaps now the Iceni will do as they are told.'

Brea caught her breath; when she looked up, Balbina was smiling.

'They are nothing more than savages. And tomorrow my brother will be here, thank the gods, and I'll no longer be bored in this dreadful place. What I'd give to be in Rome, where the entertainment is good and there are interesting people, not all these old retired soldiers.' Julia ignored her father's pained glance. 'When Marcellus is home, we'll feast and celebrate his triumph in the name of Rome.' Julia's eyes glittered. 'Why is the slave girl still here?'

Publius Julius had forgotten about Brea. He waved a finger. '*Ancilla*, you may go.'

'Master,' Brea muttered and walked slowly to the steps, trying to keep her face calm. Then she was running, her eyes full of tears, gasping sobs and trying to catch her breath. So it was true, the Iceni tribe had been attacked, Boudicca and her daughters punished, their lands taken. Brea was far from home; she could do nothing. Sobs came again, then she took a deep breath and wiped her face quickly. She recalled Luna's words: *you will search forever.*

Brea stood tall, placing a hand at her hip as if she had a sword there. Determination swept through her. She didn't care how long it took, or how hard the search. She'd find her parents, and she'd return to the tribe to live as her family wanted her to live. A chance would come for revenge against the Roman soldiers who had denied her freedom. She promised herself as she stood outside the kitchen stemming the flood of tears, she'd wait quietly until the time came.

Brea was Iceni; she was loyal, strong, determined. She could be patient.

7

Hanna sighed good-naturedly as she sat in a wine bar in King's Lynn, watching her mother downing a second cocktail. She'd driven her into town after Stephanie had insisted on putting her on the insurance for the Range Rover. She said it would be useful and now, as they perched on stools at the bar holding stemmed glasses, Stephanie was delighted with the idea. She was already tipsy, speaking too loudly. 'I love mojitos. Oh, Hanna, this is the life. Mother and daughter out shopping together on a Saturday, spending quality time.' Her eyes shone with happiness and the impact of the alcohol. 'It wasn't like this before you came home. I'm making up for lost time.'

'It's so nice to be able to do this.' Hanna smiled indulgently, glad that her mother was having fun. She glanced at the mocktail she was drinking, a virgin piña colada. It wasn't too bad. 'Have you had a good time?'

'Oh, it's been absolutely wonderful – lunch was delicious, and coming here is the icing on the cake,' Stephanie said excitedly. 'It's a pity we couldn't find you a dress though. I thought you'd look lovely in that cream one.'

'It was expensive.' Hanna grinned. 'And very beige, Mum. It wasn't really me.'

'The red dress you liked would have been a bit garish next to me at the ceremony. My dress is such a delicate shade of ivory. You'd have stuck out on the photos.'

'I would.'

'Ah.' Stephanie sighed. 'We'll just have to do the same thing again next week, but we'll go somewhere else – Norwich perhaps.'

'Or I could look online?' Hanna suggested hopefully.

'Oh, but I want to see you in it before we buy it.'

'I suppose so,' Hanna conceded with an affectionate smile. Her mother was so excited about her wedding. Hanna knew it was the least that she could do, shopping and then lunch. Stephanie clearly hadn't enjoyed herself so much in ages.

She finished the mojito and held out her glass. 'I'll just order one more, shall I?'

'If you like.' Hanna smiled. 'I'm still drinking this one—'

'But you'll join me in another – I can't drink by myself,' Stephanie insisted, ignoring Hanna's almost-full glass. 'Sandro?' She called the mixologist over. Hanna was impressed that she'd read his name tag and remembered it. 'Two more please – thanks, that's so kind of you.'

Hanna noticed her mother leaning forward, swaying a little as she watched him stride away in tight trousers. She suppressed a grin – this was a side of her mother she'd rarely seen, but it was a good opportunity to bond.

'You didn't say...' Stephanie began, '...how did you get on in Little Rymer yesterday? Did you meet any of your old school friends?'

'No, but I cycled past our old house. It looks very different now, doesn't it. There's a new gate, a metal one. I went into the station café before that. I chatted to Serenity.' Hanna paused as she recalled the man she'd met in the doorway. She wondered how she could find out who he was without drawing attention to the fact that she wanted to know. She'd ask Serenity, perhaps, if she could find a subtle way.

'I've been to the café a few times. She does nice cakes there but—oh, thank you, Sandro.' Stephanie gave the mixologist her most effusive smile as he placed two glasses on the bar. 'The station's a cold place for a café. I don't know, there's something about Little Rymer station...'

'What about it?' Hanna was interested.

'It's hard to say.' Stephanie reached for her glass. 'It's a station, I suppose, so it's bound to be chilly, but I've always felt it's a bit of a creepy place.'

'I know what you mean.' Hanna was thinking of the darkness, the young woman seated by herself.

'But then this is the fens.' Stephanie wriggled in her seat. 'It's an eerie place.'

Hanna was surprised. 'I've lived here most of my life – you've never said that before.'

'Little Rymer itself is all right – it's a pretty village and a close community.' Stephanie took a glug from her glass. 'It's the old road from the station up to the farm that puts my teeth on edge. I hate driving along it at night, especially when I'm by myself.'

Hanna gave an involuntary shiver. Her mother's words had struck a chord: she knew what she meant. 'It's very dark along that piece of road, Mum. I mean, there are no street lights there. It feels desolate.'

'There's a lot of history in these parts.'

'The Romans?'

'You must have studied it?'

Hanna put a hand to her head, remembering. 'We did the Roman invasion in primary school – Boudicca came from round here. We had to do a project about whether she was a heroine or a terrorist.' She remembered the sense of unease she'd had as a child working on it. It had given her a particularly vivid nightmare. At ten years old, she'd been the only child in the class who'd opted for Boudicca as a heroine. She reached for her glass and was surprised that her hand was shaking. 'We'll finish these and go, shall we?'

'Mmm.' Stephanie gulped from her glass. 'You should talk to Paddy – or Ollie. Ollie found a Roman coin in one of the fields when he was a boy. I think it was taken to a university in Cambridge to be looked at. Nero, I think, was on it – no, it was Claudius.'

'That sounds fascinating.' Hanna hadn't started the virgin piña colada.

'And as for Paddy, he's the last person you'd expect to believe in such things, but he was driving back from somewhere one night – Wisbech, I think he said – and he had Roy in the car and suddenly Roy started whining. Paddy said the temperature in the car dropped and he felt something touch the back of his neck and he went cold as death.' She glanced at Hanna's mocktail as she emptied her glass. 'He probably imagined it. Drink up – we should go.'

'That's just made me shiver.' Hanna took a quick sip. 'Come on then, Mum.' She was secretly glad that it was daylight. Her mother's story of Paddy's late-night experience had shaken her a little.

'It's almost three. Paddy will be wanting his afternoon cuppa,' Stephanie said, reaching for her handbag to pay with her card.

'Oh,' Hanna remembered. 'Serenity's made some flapjacks. I'll pop down for a chat, I think.'

'That's nice, love.' Stephanie was inadvertently watching Sandro's tight trousers walking away again.

Hanna smiled; her mother was sweetly tipsy. She'd get her into the car and drive her home. Then she'd make a pot of tea and leave her mother and Paddy to it. Perhaps they'd lend her the Range Rover to drive into Little Rymer.

* * *

It was past four when Hanna arrived at the station. She parked in the car park and rushed down the ramp. A voice rattled through speakers that the 15:47 from King's Cross to King's Lynn was delayed by twenty minutes due to problems on the line. Several passengers groaned audibly and turned their attention to the café for sustenance. Hanna joined the queue, waiting while people bought coffee in cardboard cups.

Serenity was pleased to see her. She popped a flapjack on a small plate. 'Oat chai latte? The flapjack is on the house – I've sold lots of them today – they are going fast, but I saved you one.'

'Business is good,' Hanna observed.

'Always.' Serenity grinned. 'I'll bring your drink over.'

Hanna found the same table by the window and peered out. Passengers had started to line up expectantly for the train. It was windy; the breeze rearranged hair and buffeted coats. Hanna shivered.

Serenity took the seat opposite and placed a mug and a flapjack in front of her. 'I've got a couple of minutes before the London train gets in. It's all go here by myself. Enjoy.'

'Thanks.'

Serenity pushed a curl behind her ear. 'So – how's life in Little Rymer? Quiet, I'm guessing.'

'I took my mum to King's Lynn this morning to find a dress for me, for her wedding. Then we hit the cocktails.'

'Oh?'

'I think she'll lie down for the rest of the afternoon.' Hanna smiled. 'I was designated driver on mocktails.'

'When's your mum getting married?'

'September the second.' Hanna counted on her fingers. 'Three weeks away. My goodness, I'd better get that dress sorted out.'

'Is it going to be a big wedding?'

'I think so – my mum and Paddy both know lots of people.'

'Have you met Oliver yet, Paddy's son?'

'No – he's away for the weekend at an eco-convention.'

'Ah, that will be Ollie.'

'Do you know him well?' Hanna asked.

'No. I met him once in the pub.' Serenity grinned at the memory. 'I don't think anyone knows Ollie that well. I've heard he's the independent sort. What's the expression? He ploughs his own furrow.'

'That's appropriate for a farmer's son.'

'It is.' Serenity laughed. 'I was hoping you'd come in, Hanna. I wanted a quick word.'

'Oh?'

'I don't suppose you've found a job yet?'

'I haven't been looking.' Hanna ran fingers through her hair.

'Would you like to work here? I need part-time help, Thursdays, Fridays, Saturdays – odd hours, just serving behind the counter.'

Hanna frowned. 'I hadn't considered getting a job so quickly.'

'Well, give it some thought.' Serenity grinned. 'It's yours if you want it. Your mum told me before you came home that you wanted some temporary work. I just get the feeling that you'll be great with the customers. And

I'm really pushed on busy days during the summer.' She handed Hanna a business card. 'Let me know.'

'I will.' Hanna reached for her mug. 'It would get me out of Mum's hair, and I'd meet local people.'

Serenity stood up. 'How's the flapjack?'

'Scrumptious.' Hanna wiped a crumb from her lips. 'With raisins. My favourite.'

'I remembered,' Serenity said. 'Oh, there's someone at the counter. See what I mean? I'm busy as.' She winked. 'I'd better get back. Give it some thought though. It would be fun.'

'I'll let you know, definitely,' Hanna said, cupping her hands around the mug. It felt warm, somehow comforting, as she stared through the window.

The wind whipped up dust and moved it around the platform. Then a train came in sluggishly and people clambered aboard. Hanna examined each one of them carefully and realised that she was looking for the man she'd encountered yesterday. He'd made an impact; she could remember every detail of his face, the hair over dark brown eyes, the imperceptible recognition in his gaze. It unnerved her a little just to think of it and Hanna knew that the next time they met she'd find it very difficult to appear calm.

She sipped her creamy chai latte and thought about working in the café. Of course, if the mystery man was a regular, she'd meet him again. She imagined him standing at the counter asking for an espresso as she fumbled at the coffee machine, their hands touching as he passed money across the counter. She smiled and pushed the thought away – she was being silly.

* * *

Minutes later, Hanna steered the Range Rover towards the farm. It was a mile and a half back to Bramble Woods and she drove slowly. She'd passed her driving test at eighteen and, for a few years, she'd owned a small Fiat, but it had been years since she'd driven regularly and the Range Rover was larger than she was used to. The radio was on; a female voice talking about politics. Hanna pressed a button to change the channel, and a strange whining came from the speaker. She turned the radio off, her eyes on the road ahead.

The sky was a wash of grey overhead and the wind was still blustering, flattening the grasses and tugging at trees and hedgerows. The farm was only a mile away now. There was no traffic, but still she drove carefully.

Something scuttled in front of the car and stopped in the middle of the road. Hanna braked suddenly. A hare squatted stubbornly, staring at her, unblinking. Hanna stared back. She spoke aloud. 'Come on, little one – don't just sit there.'

The hare remained, stone-like, watching her. Hanna revved the car engine, but the animal stayed. They gazed at each other for a moment, as if waiting for the other to move, then the hare sprang across the road and disappeared into an irrigation ditch.

Hanna felt her body go cold. She shuddered, reaching out, turning the heating up, pressing the accelerator, moving the car forwards quickly. The wind buffeted the door, making a low whining sound like a sigh. Hanna remembered the story her mother had told her about Paddy's experience while driving home at night and, without meaning to, she increased her speed.

8

Brea shivered as she stood in the centre of Camulodunum. The wind shuffled between the buildings, lifting the skirt of her tunic, chilling her bare legs. She was glad of the opportunity to be away from the villa. It was busier than ever now Marcellus was expected home and, soon, his new wife-to-be would arrive. Brea didn't know her name yet, but she'd overheard Julia say that Marcellus would never love her, that his heart had been buried with his first wife. Brea felt sorry for the new Roman woman. In truth, she would be almost as much a prisoner as Brea, confined inside the villa with little chance of warmth in her life.

She pushed the thought away. She was expected back at the villa. She'd been sent into the town to request an order of salt, which was brought regularly from the marshes outside the town. She'd never ventured beyond the river, but now she stood, gazing at the road that stretched out of town. She could simply run as fast as she could, never stopping to look back. But she knew what would happen if she did. Slaves were told from their first hour: if they tried to escape, they would be hunted down and caught, then their skin would be scourged. They'd be an example to others, the cost of disobedience: she'd seen it before once, as a child. A slave had tried to run away and was flogged until he could not stand. She had never forgotten the look on his face, subdued, broken. As she stared into the distance where the river curved into flatlands, Brea knew there would be another way, in time.

She began the walk back to the villa. Passing the *ludus*, she paused for a moment to listen to the clash of swords, the yells of men practising combat. She had never been to a contest in the arena, although she knew that Publius Julius went often and that his daughter Julia loved to watch one man pit his strength against another. Brea listened to the roars inside and imagined the men fighting, dressed in their *subligaculum*, simple loincloths offering no protection to the skin. Images of the slicing of flesh and the awful moment when one man triumphed over another came to her and Brea shuddered.

A gruff voice behind her called out, 'Has someone sent me a slut? Well, you'd better come inside.'

Brea whirled round. 'I'm on my way to the villa of Julius—'

'You can come in anyway.' It was the gladiator trainer, Marcus Rubrius Memnon. He folded his arms, standing in her pathway, leering, his mouth covered in spittle. 'I'm in need of a young woman.'

Brea stood up straight and took a breath. 'Please, would you kindly stand aside and let me pass.'

'I will.' Marcus Rubrius was toying with her. 'But only if you give me a kiss first.'

'I can't be late.' Brea avoided his eyes. 'I'm expected.'

'A kiss takes just one moment. Two if my tongue is down your throat.' Marcus Rubrius laughed. 'Minerva has been kind to me. She has sent me a *meretrix*, a slave girl for my pleasure so that I can end the working day happily in my bed.' He spread his feet wide so that she could not pass. 'So, just a kiss first – a taster.'

Brea looked at him from head to toe. In one hand, he clutched a whip, which he used to taunt and provoke his fighters. In the other, there was the lucky charm carved from wood in the shape of the goddess. He waved it in her direction. 'I deserve a little luck. Minerva always sends gifts to me.' He was bragging now. 'I was a gladiator, then I was attached to the Thirtieth Legion, and Minerva helped me to buy my freedom. Now all I want is a kiss and maybe some firm young flesh beneath my fingers.'

Brea made a move to pass him and he caught her by the elbow. She smelled the sourness of his breath.

'One kiss.' He made a grab for her waist and for a moment she thought he held her too fast for her to escape. Then she kicked his shin hard and he doubled over, yelping in pain.

Brea ran as fast as she could and his voice followed her, cursing, calling foul names. She didn't stop, although when she reached the Temple of the Divine Claudius, she glanced towards the steps to see if she could see Luna. The old beggar woman was not there.

Minutes later, she was back in the *domus*. She had regained her composure as if nothing had happened as she stood in the garden, where Addedomaros held an enormous bunch of fragrant flowers, his expression nervous. 'I must take these to Julia. She demands more than I can grow.'

Brea noticed that his head was newly shaved. 'I'll take them.'

'Thank you. I'd be glad if you would. I don't like being inside the house when Julia is there. She tells me that her husband cannot satisfy her and that a lusty slave might do much to earn his freedom. I don't trust her, and if she accuses me of accosting her, I'd have no chance, my word against hers. She terrifies me, Brea.'

Brea placed a gentle hand on his arm. 'She'll find another plaything and forget you.'

'I pray that she will.' Addedomaros was breathless with fear. 'My life would be over with one word. Her husband, Caius Fabius, is an old soldier, much respected. He rarely accompanies her anywhere.'

'I think he prefers his own company and to drink wine. It's not a respectful marriage.' Brea remembered the conversation she had overheard in the *triclinium*. 'Adde, have you heard anything about the master Marcellus's business with the Iceni? I believe he's captured land for Rome.'

'It's sad news. I told you King Prasutagus died. I knew of him only by name, but his reputation was as a peaceful man.'

'And now he's gone, the Romans are taking advantage.' Brea's face was strained with worry. 'I heard that the master Marcellus has taken our land for the emperor in Rome.'

'You're right. He will come home victorious. Queen Boudicca was beaten.'

Brea felt tears spring to her eyes. 'My tribe won't tolerate that. We are proud people.'

'You mustn't think of it.' Addedomaros was suddenly afraid again. 'Put the Iceni out of your mind. They're not your concern any more.' He saw the flash of anger in her eyes. 'I worry when I see you look that way. It can only lead to trouble. Brea, you'll be missed. Go – now.'

'You're right. I will.' Brea hugged the flowers, trying hard to calm her thumping heart. 'I'll give these to Julia for you, Adde. I wish you well.'

She rushed through the atrium into the villa, her mind in turmoil. Voices came from the *triclinium*, males and a female laughing, talking excitedly at once. Brea watched Publius Julius, who was offering wine to several guests, Julia and a dark man in a richly coloured toga. She recognised him as Marcellus, the soldier who had returned from claiming land. He had come back somehow broader, taller. The *ornatrix* Balbina hovered in the background, a smirk on her face.

Brea stood at the entrance, her head bowed, waiting to be summoned.

Julia was in full flow. 'It is dull here without you, Marcellus. My ridiculous husband is no company. But now you're back home, we can go to the arena together, watch gladiators and have some excitement. Maybe we can go to the theatre. Oh, I long for the time when the amphitheatre is built properly. I hear the one in Rome is so huge that men's voices echo from one wall to another. Why do I have to live in this tedious place?'

Marcellus smiled. He was clearly fond of his sister. 'Perhaps when my new wife arrives, she'll be a friend for you.'

'But will she be company for you, Marcellus?' Julia placed a hand on his arm.

Publius Julius spoke in a thin voice. 'Marcellus needs someone to comfort him when he comes back from his duties. And, of course, he needs sons.'

Marcellus nodded. 'Perhaps I do, Father. I'm honoured that you think of me with kindness.'

'Nonsense.' Julia laughed. 'You don't need a wife. There is plenty of entertainment to be had without a permanent woman, I'm sure. What about the Briton women you punished in front of their tribe? I would have found that most exciting.'

'I think not, Julia.' Marcellus's face was sad. 'The soldiers saw the women as spoils – but the daughters were only children, and I didn't like to see it, nor did I enjoy the flogging of the queen. I was acting on instructions. My own feelings are that making an enemy of the Iceni won't come to good.'

'It's a good thing indeed,' Publius Julius protested. 'You quashed the armed tribes, showed them who is in charge.' He rubbed his hands together. 'More wine, I think.'

'For me too.' Julia held up her goblet, then she saw Brea watching and listening. 'What's she doing here?'

Publius Julius lifted a hand. 'What brings you, *ancilla*?'

'I have flowers for this room. I was asked to bring them from the garden.'

Julia approached, her glass to her lips. 'I asked the slave to bring them. I like to see him. He is well-toned and easy on the eye.'

'I brought them for him.' Brea stood her ground. 'He's busy, growing more flowers to perfume this room, at your request—'

Julia slapped her face hard. 'I didn't say you could speak.' She whirled round to her father. 'I demand this slave is flogged for her insolence.'

Julius lifted an indulgent hand. 'I don't usually flog slaves, but if you feel she spoke out of turn—'

'She did.'

Brea stared at her feet. She had made an enemy. She felt her body shaking and forced herself to stand still even though it was her instinct to fight or to run.

Julia tugged the flowers from her hands. 'I will not be spoken to this way by a slave, Father.'

Publius Julius sighed. 'Very well, Julia, if you insist, then I'll have her flogged in the orchard.'

'I'll deal with it, Father,' Marcellus interrupted. 'I have a suitable punishment in mind for her.' He looked directly at his sister. 'With your indulgence, Julia.'

'Whatever you wish.' Julia was already bored. She thrust the flowers into Balbina's arms. 'Here – arrange these well in water. I'll refill my own cup.'

Marcellus waved a hand. 'Follow me, *ancilla*.'

He strode from the room and Brea scuttled after him, head down, breathing rapidly. She had no idea what would happen next, and she was terrified: this was the Roman who'd overseen the Iceni queen's thrashing. Brea thought for a moment that he was going to take her through the atrium and out into the garden, that he might speak to Addedomaros and accuse him of disobeying his sister and punish them both. She hoped not; she'd intended to save Addedomaros, not bring him more trouble.

Brea held her breath as Marcellus paused at one of the *cubicula*, a small bedroom with beautifully detailed wall paintings, a small wooden chest and a comfortable sleeping couch. He gestured that Brea should follow him, and she hesitated, unsure. She understood the punishment that had been inflicted on Prasutagus's daughters: the young princesses were raped, thrown aside.

Marcellus ushered her inside, his eyes blazing. 'What do you think of this room, *ancilla*?'

Brea found her voice. 'I don't think anything of it, Master.'

His eyes glinted and flickered to the couch. 'I ask you again. Do you think it a nice room? Pleasant?'

'It is well enough.' Brea met his gaze boldly. Her heart thudded. She gazed at Marcellus's hands as he rubbed them together, huge hands that were used to holding a sword, that were capable of great strength. He intended to assault her – that was to be her punishment. She looked around the room for something to use as a weapon. There was an ornate mirror. If he lurched towards her, she'd smash it into fragments and use it to fight for her life. Then she'd have to run as fast as she could. She'd be caught, of course, but there was no other choice: she would not submit to the desires of a Roman soldier.

Brea stood absolutely still, breathing hard, waiting for his next move.

9

Hanna woke feeling something wet against her face, hot breath. Roy had leaped onto her bed and was licking her skin with his rough tongue. She put out a hand and stroked his fur. 'What time is it, boy? Have you been sent to get me up for breakfast?' She could smell baking below and something frying. She stretched her limbs happily. 'Come on, Roy. Let's go downstairs. It's Sunday morning – we can do as we please.'

Hanna had slept reasonably well and was feeling refreshed. She threw back the duvet and swished the curtains wide. Outside, a low mist hovered over the field. She rushed downstairs in pyjamas and bare feet to find her mother making pancakes, brewing coffee, lifting a crusty loaf from the oven.

Hanna kissed Stephanie's cheek and smiled. 'The smells are gorgeous.'

'I used to be happy with a wrapped white sliced from the Co-op.' Stephanie turned to Paddy as if he was a fresh loaf. 'Not any more – it's strictly home baking now.'

'And I'm very happy too.' Paddy grinned as Stephanie slid a pancake onto his plate. He covered it with lashings of runny honey. 'Delicious.'

Stephanie moved from the Aga to lean on one of his broad shoulders, kissing his cheek. 'Not too many pancakes, though, or you won't fit into that wedding suit.'

'I thought you liked the generously proportioned man, Steph.' Paddy rubbed his stomach. 'It's all muscle from working on the land.'

'I just want you to stay healthy.' Stephanie kissed his cheek again. 'Pancakes, Hanna?'

Hanna was beaming, pleased to see her mother so happy. 'I should be making you breakfast, Mum.'

'Oh, there will be plenty of time for that. Let me make a fuss of you. I'm enjoying it.'

'Thanks.' Hanna sat and poured coffee into a mug. Roy settled by her feet.

'Roy's taken a liking to you,' Paddy commented. 'I sent him up to get you for breakfast and off he went. "Fetch Hanna, Roy," I said and he was up the stairs like a shot.'

Roy gave a single bark of agreement.

'He's a good boy,' Hanna crooned, trailing a hand, feeling the wet nose and twisting his fur gently between her fingers. She felt him lick her fingers.

'What are you planning for today?' Stephanie asked.

Hanna looked down at Roy, smiling into the begging eyes. 'I wondered if I could borrow Roy, take him for a walk around the farm.'

Roy barked again, happy approval.

'You'll need wellies,' Paddy grunted, his mouth full. 'It's misty as hell over yonder. Early mist well before autumn sets in, I reckon, means a rum ole winter will come.'

'It's still August, for goodness' sake. It had better be sunny for our wedding day,' Stephanie said, dropping a pancake onto Hanna's plate. 'We've got some bits and pieces to go through for the wedding, Paddy. I thought we could talk about the flowers.'

Paddy rolled his eyes good-naturedly. 'If you like, Steph. Flowers are all the same to me – they smell nice and look nice. You choose and I'll be happy.'

'But we should do it together,' Stephanie insisted gently.

Paddy's eyes crinkled with affection. 'Whatever you want.'

'And we still need to find you a dress,' Stephanie said to Hanna. 'I haven't asked you yet but – Paddy and I want you and Oliver to be our witnesses.'

'That's as it should be,' Paddy agreed.

'I'm honoured.' Hanna grinned. 'Definitely. It will be a pleasure.'

'And the dress?' Stephanie's face held an anxious look.

'We'll pick something together,' Hanna promised, kindly. 'I promise not to choose anything you won't like.'

'As long as you don't both go drinking cocktails again.' Paddy chortled. 'Steph was fair pickled when she got home.'

'I was not.' Stephanie feigned outrage. 'Oh, Hanna – Ollie will be home tonight.'

'Will he come here for dinner?' Hanna asked. She was looking forward to meeting her new stepbrother. She'd never had a sibling, not really: although her father had another daughter, she had never felt part of his new family. No, the thought of a brother was exciting.

'Knowing our Ollie, he'll be back late. I've been looking after his horses while he's away. They need taking out of the fields. He usually makes his meals in his own cottage. He doesn't eat what we eat – he's saving the plan-et.' Paddy lifted his fork proudly. Hanna wasn't sure if Paddy was impressed with Oliver's dietary choice or Stephanie's honey-soaked pancakes.

'I made him breakfast with Quorn sausages once. He was very polite, but he wouldn't eat them,' Stephanie said. 'I'm not sure what he eats.'

'Grass,' Paddy offered and guffawed at his own joke.

Hanna finished her breakfast, arranging her knife and fork neatly on the plate. Her mother swept it away towards the dishwasher. 'That was lovely, Mum. I think I'll grab a quick shower then and take Roy out.' Roy barked his approval.

'Don't you get lost out there in the mist,' Paddy joked.

'Hanna, you'll need to be careful – there are irrigation ditches you might fall in,' Stephanie said seriously.

'Roy will look after her,' Paddy remarked cheerily.

'I'm a Norfolk girl, Mum, I'll be fine.' Hanna bent over and kissed Roy's nose. 'Stay here, boy – I won't be ten minutes. Then you and I will go for a nice long walk.'

* * *

By eleven o'clock, the sun was pushing through, but the mist was still drifting over the fields in straggly clumps as Hanna left her mother in the kitchen. She crossed the farmyard, feeling toasty warm, wearing wellingtons and a borrowed jacket, Roy scampering at her side.

As she passed the outbuildings, her feet squelched in shallow mud and she glanced briefly towards Oliver's farm cottage. It was a cosy little stone building with white windows and a slate roof, tubs of plants growing outside. Hanna looked more closely; there were chillies and strawberries, lavender, mint. Next to the house was a stable block with three stalls; she noticed a copper-coloured horse lift his head and sniff the air.

She wondered what Ollie was like, if they'd become friends. She imagined them at their parents' wedding together, toasting them, sharing a friendly hug, he a handsome, younger version of Paddy. Hanna decided that Christmases might be even nicer now she had a bigger family. Maybe Abby could come back from Australia with her partner – what was his name? Holden, that was it. In her imagination, they were both tall, bronzed and exuded good health. They'd share bottles of sparkling wine and the conversation would sparkle even more, the Christmas tree lights winking from the corner of the room. There would be a roast turkey and something else for Oliver and plenty of scraps for Roy.

Hanna stopped herself. She'd only just arrived at the farmhouse and already she was planning events. But last Christmas had almost passed unnoticed in Guangzhou. She'd received apples from her friends and they'd all dined out on dumplings and spring rolls. She'd enjoyed it, but, in truth, she longed for a traditional family Christmas.

Hanna crossed the road, Roy running ahead, leading the way towards an open field cloaked in low mist. Grass and mud clung to her boots as she followed Roy across the rough field. He headed over to a clump of trees and beyond, a field of bare dirt, dotted with animal arks and what seemed like a huge number of pigs snuffling in the soil. Hanna turned to Roy. 'You've brought me to see the pigs?'

Roy jumped up excitedly, leaving a paw mark on the wax coat. Hanna smoothed it away with her hand.

'Shall we go and look at the pigs, Roy?'

Roy barked again as Hanna pushed the gate open, making a curve in a mound of mud, closing it carefully behind her. She blinked through the coils of mist, gazing at the rows of pigs as they snuffled in the mud. A pig began to trot towards her, then another, followed by several pigs who surrounded her.

Hanna scratched the rough back of a broad porker tentatively. 'I haven't brought you food – I'm sorry.'

The pigs soon lost interest, trundling away to snuffle in the mud, their snouts grubbing at pebbles. Hanna looked into the distance; the pigs had completely destroyed the field. All vegetation had been devoured, apart from a few feathery plants with tiny white flowers that looked like wild chamomile. One pig was demolishing a plant, chewing it with a slobbering mouth.

Roy barked proudly and Hanna patted his head. 'Shall we leave the pigs and have a walk across the field? Look, Roy – there's a gate and some woodland beyond. Shall we go and take a look?'

Roy jumped ahead excitedly and Hanna followed him. The field was a mud bath, wetter than she'd first thought, and she felt her wellington-clad feet sink deeper. She decided it might be easier to skirt the field, so she headed for a clump of neat hedges, Roy by her side. She kept her eyes on the slippery earth, putting one foot tentatively in front of the other. The soil was completely destroyed by the pigs' rooting. Hanna vaguely remembered the expression *pig sick*. Someone had once told her it referred to a field after a drove of pigs had eaten and trampled everything in it. If that was so, then this place was certainly pig sick.

Hanna had almost reached the hedge when she noticed Roy pawing the ground, making a hole. As she approached, Roy was digging deeper, flicking mud high in the air, then he paused and turned to Hanna, waiting. Something glinting, buried deeply beneath the earth, caught her eye and Roy barked, gazing at Hanna with excited eyes. Hanna bent down and dug further with eager fingers, until she pulled at a dirty piece of metal and examined it carefully. It was clogged with mud, a pendant on a gold and beaded chain. She stared at it, the tarnished disc dull, almost brown. The stones between the gold links of the chain were a dark blood red, the same as the large stone in the centre of the disc.

'What have you found here?' Hanna crouched next to Roy, who sniffed her hand. She rubbed the necklace between her fingers. 'This looks really old. I wonder how long it's been there. Clever boy.'

Roy was suddenly alert, his eyes wide, then he squatted low on his haunches, putting his head down on his paws. He made a low whining sound and flattened himself against the ground. His fur bristled as he cowered, genuinely afraid.

Hanna reached out a hand. 'What's wrong, Roy?' Then she looked up.

A few metres away through the mist, a figure was watching them, a young woman. She stood perfectly still, with cascading hair, a long green dress, a pale face, melancholy eyes.

Hanna caught her breath, the jewellery in one hand, the other touching Roy's head to calm him. 'It's all right…'

She glanced up quickly. The mist hovered and the woman was gone. Hanna had seen her before; she'd been sitting on the bench in the railway station when she'd first arrived, the same sadness surrounding her.

She pushed the jewellery in her pocket and a cold shudder went through her. 'Come on, Roy – let's get back.'

Hanna trudged the way she had come, heading for the farmhouse. The fog was patchy, damp against her face. Roy trotted at her side, looking up anxiously as Hanna tugged her collar up and increased her speed. She'd be happy to get back to the warmth of the kitchen and take another look at the necklace. Her fingers touched it in her pocket, and she felt a warm tingle. She felt sure it held an interesting story in its gold metal and stones.

10

Brea faced Marcellus, meeting his icy eyes, her own narrowed like a trapped animal's. She wouldn't look away; it would be a sign of submission. He was waiting, plotting his move. They were alone in the room and his presence was unsettling.

Marcellus's voice was low when he finally spoke. 'I've brought you here, *ancilla*, because I didn't want my sister to have you flogged. I have a much better use for you.'

Brea's instinct was to run away, or to lurch for the delicate mirror, smash it and push the shards against his neck. She forced herself to stand still, although her legs shook beneath her tunic. 'Master?' she mumbled, just to break the silence.

'I asked you what you thought of this room.'

'It's pleasant.' Brea wondered what to say next; she had nothing to lose. 'I sleep on a hard bed next to three other slaves, where it is cold each night. It's much nicer here.'

Marcellus sighed. 'This is the room we'll give to my new wife. She arrives tomorrow.'

'I've heard you are to be married,' Brea said, trying to recover her composure. She was still shaking. She'd expected something completely different at Marcellus's hands.

'Do you think she'll like it here?'

'Any woman would be glad of a space that is so clean and private,' Brea muttered, relieved by the normality of their conversation. 'Why do you ask me?'

'I can't ask my sister. She's not interested in my new wife's well-being. And I'm a soldier – I know nothing of what comforts make a woman happy. I had a wife once and she slept here when I was away. She liked it well enough. Besides...' He glanced at his feet. 'I want you to put flowers here and... anything that will make my new wife comfortable.'

Brea didn't understand. 'Is that to be my punishment?'

'Not at all.' Marcellus smiled. 'I don't want you punished. I want you to help her to settle. She'll be in a strange country and everything will be unfamiliar. I'll tell my father that I've asked you to do this. She'll be lonely – she'll need someone to look after her while I am away.'

Brea couldn't help herself. 'Are you going to fight more Iceni people and take their land?'

Marcellus was taken aback. Brea covered her mouth. She had spoken out of turn and this time she would certainly get a beating. Marcellus was watching her, his expression puzzled. 'I will go to fight the Druids soon on the Island of Mona.' He studied her carefully. 'You're not a Greek or a Gaul. You're an Iceni slave.'

'I am.' Brea lifted her chin. 'I was taken from my tribe at thirteen years of age. I haven't seen my parents...' She closed her eyes. The memory behind them was as fresh and real as ever, marauding Roman soldiers advancing towards her in heavy armour, her father on one side, her mother on the other, both breathing heavily, clutching their swords.

'I remember it.' Marcellus exhaled. 'I'm a legate, a commander, but my duty is to Nero and to Suetonius, our governor general. I do as he orders. But it's not something I like to see, people's lands stolen, their livelihoods drained away.' He spoke quietly. 'In truth, I'm sorry for what we did to Prasutagus's queen. And the treatment of her young daughters fills me with shame.'

Brea kept her gaze fixed on his. 'You could have given a different order.'

Marcellus shook his head. 'You don't understand.'

'I understand how it was to be fighting for my life as a child and being taken by a soldier who threw me on the floor as if I was nothing. Do you think that's what my people are – nothing?' Brea's tongue had run away with her. 'I'm sorry, Master,' she said quickly. 'I speak only what is in my heart. And from fear.'

'Fear?' Marcellus raised an eyebrow. 'Do I frighten you?'

'I thought you brought me here to do me harm,' Brea spoke up. 'As you ordered your men to do to King Prasutagus's daughters.'

'Not I.' Marcellus was thoughtful for a moment. 'What's your name?'

'Brea – that is the name my parents called me.'

'Then, Brea, I will speak to my father and ask that you be given a new job in the villa. You'll be a personal slave to my wife, Aurelia. I want her to be as comfortable here as she can be.' He examined her face for a reaction. 'How does that sound?'

'It sounds as if you have decided what I will do, Master,' Brea replied. 'Of course, I'll do my best to make the lady happy.'

'How old are you, Brea?'

'Twenty-six years.'

'The same age as Claudia when she died. A year older than Aurelia is now. But she seems such a child, so untutored in the real world. Of course, I haven't met her, but we have corresponded in letters, politely, as strangers. Our fathers knew each other in the army long ago and they promised us to each other. Her father is a landowner in Rome.' Marcellus looked at Brea for a moment. 'I thank you for looking after her.'

'A slave needs no thanks,' Brea replied. 'I'll do my best, Master, as I do in all things.'

'I can see that.' Marcellus seemed unhappy. 'You may go, Brea. I'll talk to my father about what we have spoken of.'

'Thank you, Master.' Brea hurried away towards the servants' quarters. She wasn't sure exactly what had happened. At first, she had been in fear of her life, then the master's son had offered her the chance of a new position as Aurelia's slave, although she knew she'd still have to help out in the kitchen, where they were always too busy. But if the lady was pleasant and kind, Brea's life would be easier. However, if she was unpredictable and discontented, like Julia, Brea's daily existence would be a misery.

Brea muttered a quiet prayer to Andred, the warrior goddess, as she hurried back to the kitchen. She hoped that the new mistress was not capricious and fickle.

Brea rushed into the *culina* where Daphne and Chloe were preparing the midday meal, the *prandium*, for the master, Julia and Marcellus.

Galyna was making flatbread. She watched as Brea walked in on light feet and her face was pinched and angry as she snapped, 'Where have you been?'

'I had to arrange flowers in the *triclinium*.'

'Old White Beard loves his flowers.' Daphne groaned. 'He also loves his stinking salty garum. I have done nothing this morning but make more of the foul fishy sauce.'

'Let me help you,' Brea offered. She was glad to find something to do. Her mind was buzzing after her meeting with Marcellus, but she would not mention his promise of a possible new role as lady Aurelia's personal slave. Often, things were promised and then the masters forgot – after all, a promise to a slave meant nothing.

* * *

The next day, there was a bustle in the kitchen as the slaves gathered to make the morning meal.

Galyna was full of herself as she broke the news. 'Two guests arrived last night – the bride-to-be and her brother, a young soldier. The men are in the *balneum*, enjoying the warmth of the bath, being oiled and purified. We must take the pancakes to the *triclinium*. Chloe, you're to take water to wash everyone's hands and then we are to prepare a feast for the *cena*. It is to be a special supper – venison, hares, pheasants, dormice stuffed with minced pork, dipped in honey and rolled in poppy seeds. And the master says there is to be as much wine as they can drink. It must flow like a river. Julia and her husband, Caius Fabius, will join the master and Marcellus and his new bride-to-be. And Brea –when everyone has broken their fast, you are to go straight to the new lady and serve her as she wishes. Do you all understand?'

'We understand,' Daphne said, her face serious. 'A new mistress. Is she beautiful? Does she wear all the gorgeous fashions from Rome?'

'I haven't laid eyes on her yet. For all I know, she could be a three-headed *strix*, a witch come to do us mischief and eat us alive in our beds.' Galyna groaned at the thought of the extra work. 'I must be cursed. How am I supposed to manage with one less pair of hands? If Brea is helping the new lady, then who will do her share? I asked the master for another kitchen slave – we can't do everything by ourselves – but he told me Brea would have time to help out in the kitchens as usual.'

'I'll do my best to do both,' Brea said quickly. She didn't want to let the other slaves down, but she was intrigued by the idea of helping Marcellus's bride to settle into her new home and baffled by his kind treatment of her. She'd do her best as a favour to him. He seemed pleasant yet, she reminded herself with a jot, he had committed atrocities to her tribe. It was hard to connect this gentle man with the one who had overseen the whipping of Queen Boudicca.

'Perhaps if we make the breakfast rather than talk about it?' Chloe said without thinking and she received a sharp slap to the head from Galyna for her troubles. Chloe scuttled behind Brea, who was spooning honey and filling jugs with water and wine. 'I'm sorry – I didn't mean to offend.'

Galyna put her hands on her hips. 'Let's just get the work done, shall we? We'll all be given a flogging if the breakfast is late.'

* * *

Brea took a plate of pancakes up to the *triclinium*, where Publius Julius was reclining on one of the three couches with Caius Fabius, laughing and drinking wine. Caius Fabius was an older, balding man with a large paunch and pouched eyes that he wiped constantly, water streaming down his chubby face. He and Publius Julius were clearly old soldier friends, and were deep in conversation to the exclusion of everyone else.

Julia was bored, strutting around as if the walls were holding her back. Balbina watched Julia's every movement, her face placid. Marcellus stood behind another couch where a striking woman with auburn hair was resting, her eyes cast down, her hands neatly folded. Brea thought she looked awkward and tired. Next to Marcellus, a handsome young man stood stiffly as if duty and dedication were all that mattered in the world.

Brea placed the dish of pancakes down, aware that Chloe was behind her, holding the water urn and bowl that would be used to wash their sticky fingers. Publius Julius reached for a pancake and Caius Fabius copied, oblivious of everyone else around them, pushing the sweet mixture into their mouths as they chatted. Brea waited to be dismissed.

'Can I entreat you to eat?' Marcellus said gallantly to the young woman.

She gazed around as if only half aware of her surroundings. 'I have no appetite.'

Julia rolled her eyes impatiently. 'A woman needs a good appetite to live in Camulodunum. A shrinking flower will soon be blown over in this cold, comfortless country.'

The auburn-haired woman, whom Brea took to be Aurelia, looked as if she might cry.

The handsome soldier's face changed to one of concern.

Marcellus spoke to his fiancée again. 'I'm sure you'll quickly learn our ways of life in Britannia. It's not so bad. We have many of the comforts of home – imported food, good heating, luxurious baths. And we keep our traditions, just as we would at home.'

'You could come to the arena with me and pick out a champion, Aurelia,' Julia muttered. 'I enjoy nothing more than seeing two men in loincloths sweating it out, swords clashing, blood staining the sand red.'

Aurelia looked as if she would faint.

The soldier spoke, his voice calm. 'My sister has had a long journey. The water was very rough, the winds too, and the ride from the boat to Camulodunum was over bumpy ground.'

'A nice, honeyed pancake will settle your stomach, then,' Julia said emphatically. 'Tuck in, Aurelia. Why don't you have some wine? I always find an abundance of it goes with everything. And it improves my mood. Based on that, you look as if you need a drink right now.'

'Thank you, no.' Aurelia's voice was a whisper. 'I'd like a glass of water.'

Brea was at her side, pouring fresh water into a cup. Aurelia took it, nodding her head in thanks as if it was too difficult to speak.

'I hope you will find your room to your taste,' Marcellus said.

'My son has just returned from quelling the Britons, seizing land for the emperor,' Publius Julius said to Caius Fabius, his face flushed with pride. 'He put their queen in her place – he had her whipped like a dog.'

'I heard it. And the two daughters had their bellies filled with plenty of fresh Roman seed.' Caius Fabius chortled. 'Bravo, Marcellus. A job well executed.'

Julia snorted, glancing from Caius Fabius to the young soldier, and muttered beneath her breath, 'Better a lusty tribune than a fat old general, any night of the week.'

'Marcellus is going to put the Druids to the sword next. He'll come back here the greatest hero, as great as Suetonius Paulinus, the governor of Britannia.' Publius Julius turned to Aurelia. 'Your husband is a fine soldier; his hands are thick with enemy blood. May the gods bless you to bear many strong sons just like him.'

Aurelia wobbled to her feet. 'I wish to retire.' She glanced nervously towards Marcellus. 'Where is my *cubiculum*?'

'Of course – at once.' Marcellus turned to Brea and she saw the relief in his eyes. 'Will you show my lady the way to her room?'

Brea nodded her head once and waved a hand. 'This way, if you please...'

Aurelia followed her quickly from the *triclinium*, down the steps to the bedroom.

Brea stood back to allow Aurelia to enter. 'Is there anything I can get you? Food, water?'

'No thank you – there is nothing you can do. No one can help me,' Aurelia said.

Then her face crumpled, she threw herself on the bed and immediately burst into tears.

11

Brea watched in disbelief as the Roman woman lay on the bed sobbing. Aurelia's body shook and the sounds that came from her were intermittent wails, the like of which Brea had never heard. The Iceni didn't behave this way – Aurelia was like a child, allowing her emotions to run uninhibited. Brea didn't know what to say, so she waited for the sounds to subside. Then she said kindly, 'How can I help you, my lady?'

Aurelia sat up, her face blotched, contorted with surprise as if she had forgotten Brea was there. 'What shall I do?'

'Do?' Brea wasn't sure Roman women did anything but please their husbands or please themselves. They bathed, drank wine, ate when they felt like it, made demands on their slaves. She tried again. 'You may do as you wish.'

'But I may not. I'm here in this cold, windy country. I have left my father and my dear mother in Rome, where I was happy, to come here and marry a man I don't know.'

'The master's son seems pleasant,' Brea answered honestly. She thought of Julia's husband, Caius Fabius, and the slave trainer, Marcus Rubrius Memnon. 'There are worse men to have as a husband.'

'But I don't want one at all. My father tells me it's time for me to make a good match with a great soldier and have many sons.' Aurelia lowered her voice. 'His first wife died in her childbed, did she not? The child with her? My mother told me it was only a girl child. In Rome, many husbands demand that girl babies are discarded – they want only sons.' She burst into tears again. 'Oh, what shall I do?'

Brea felt sorry for Aurelia. She knew nothing of the world. Brea approached the bed. 'How can I help?'

'No one can help,' Aurelia snivelled, wiping her face.

'But you have this wonderful house.' Brea felt she was clutching at straws as she said, 'Your husband will be away fighting much of the time and you will command your own home.' She thought of Publius Julius, of his daughter who visited whenever she wished, and for a moment, she wondered how this vulnerable young woman would manage to live in a house where they both behaved as they pleased. Brea said quietly, 'You may feel better once you have slept. You're weary.'

'At least Lucius is here with me.' Aurelia sighed. 'But soon he'll have to leave.'

For a moment, Brea wondered if Lucius was a Roman god she had never heard of, then she remembered the soldier standing behind the couch. 'He's your brother?'

'Yes, he was my travelling companion. I had a slave woman too, but she spent the voyage talking to a sailor and when we arrived at the port, she disappeared.' Aurelia shuddered. 'My brother will go to his legion, the Ninth, after my wedding – and I shall be all alone.'

'The master Marcellus is a kind man,' Brea said, wondering at her own words; she had no idea she thought that way, particularly after the assault he'd led against her tribe, but Brea decided she'd do her best to help this lonely woman who seemed not to have the strength to cope by herself. 'I'll help you prepare for bed, my lady. If you sleep now, you'll be ready to join the household for supper and all may be well then.'

Aurelia stared at her. She seemed almost glad to have someone on her side. 'Please – if you would help me, I'd be most grateful.'

Brea wondered at the politeness of her tone. It might be pleasant working for such a lady. Unlike Julia, Aurelia didn't seem the type to make unreasonable demands, to slap her or order her to be flogged.

Aurelia stood up. 'Yes, I will sleep. Please – will you help me with my jewellery?' She held out a hand. 'I will keep the ring on my finger, because it's to be worn at all times. Marcellus gave it to me.'

Brea gazed at the wide band of gold adorned with engravings. 'It means you are to be married.' She rolled a snake bracelet from her mistress's wrist, placing it on the wooden chest, then Aurelia lifted her hair for the necklace to be taken off. Brea held up the chain of gold and carnelian stone, admiring the shining disc in the middle with a gleaming red gem in the centre. 'This is beautiful.' She placed it carefully on the chest.

Aurelia looked sad. 'It belonged to Marcellus's mother and he gave it to his first wife. I believe his sister thinks it should be hers.' She was momentarily alarmed. 'Do you think there is a *defixio* placed on the necklace? My life feels cursed already – and Marcellus's first wife died in her childbed and his mother did not live a long life.' Aurelia looked terrified. 'Perhaps a *strix* watches this house, flying over us at night, feeding on the blood and flesh of small children.'

'I do not believe in flying night owl monsters and curses and such things,' Brea replied.

Aurelia perched on the end of her bed. 'What people are you from?'

'I am Iceni.'

'Then what do you believe?'

'We believe that a good life is important and that once we die, we may come back to this earth again. My people love metalware and horses, loyalty, family and hard work. That is why it is important to bury food, weapons and ornaments with the dead.'

'Such strange beliefs.' Aurelia was puzzled. 'Why are you not with your family? Why are you a slave here?'

'It's a long story, and not one you might wish to hear before sleep,' Brea said quietly. She picked up an ornate comb made from a single piece of bone with hand-cut teeth and began to brush Aurelia's hair. Her mistress's shoulders relaxed. 'Perhaps you might like to take a bath before supper?'

'Oh, I would.' Aurelia clasped her hands. 'Back in Rome, I used to bathe each day and someone would read poetry to me. Would you do that?'

'I cannot read,' Brea admitted. 'The people of my tribe don't write things down.'

'A bath would be wonderful.' Aurelia took Brea's hand lightly and Brea was reminded how vulnerable she was. 'Will you sit with me while I sleep?'

'If you wish,' Brea said. 'Although I would be more useful in the *culina* making supper.'

'Stay.' Aurelia stretched out on the bed and Brea covered her lightly with a wool blanket.

'I will.' Brea watched as Aurelia's eyes flickered. Within minutes, she was asleep.

Brea moved to the corner and sat quietly on a chair, thinking about her conversation with Aurelia. They were both far from home, isolated, wishing they were somewhere else. The difference was that Aurelia was an important Roman woman about to be married to a great soldier while Brea was a simple slave, although she had more wit than Aurelia. It kept her alive. But she, too, dreamed of being elsewhere and in her heart, she believed that one day she would be free.

She felt someone watching her and turned abruptly. A shadowy figure was loitering outside the bedroom, not far from the *impluvium*, the sunken part of the atrium, designed to carry away the rainwater falling from the roof.

Brea walked quietly from the bedroom and found Marcellus standing alone, looking anxious.

'How is the lady Aurelia?'

'She sleeps now, Master,' Brea whispered. 'It has been a long journey. She's weary. I've suggested she rests and, before supper, perhaps she can bathe. She'll feel better then.'

Marcellus was unsure. 'She's been brought here from Rome against her will. I fear she'd be happier had she stayed there.'

'She'll get used to the changes in time.' Brea met his eyes. 'We all must.'

'Indeed, we must,' Marcellus said sadly. He thought about her words for a moment. 'I'll remain here for several weeks after my wedding – perhaps I'll get to know her better that way. Then I must go and deal with the Druids.'

'Master.' Brea glanced back into the bedroom where she could hear the sound of Aurelia breathing deep and regularly.

'I thank you for the care you have shown her, Brea,' Marcellus muttered.

Brea was surprised that Marcellus remembered her name, that he'd spoken it instead of the customary *ancilla*. She shrugged. 'It's what you asked of me. I'm happy to do it.'

'At least her brother is here to keep her company before he goes north. I wish I had him with me in my legion, but he has been sent elsewhere. He appears to be very like his sister, delicate and not worldly-wise.'

Brea did not comment. It was not her place.

Marcellus placed a hand on her arm. 'I'm glad to be able to talk with you.'

'I do but listen.' Brea almost smiled.

Marcellus removed his hand quickly. 'I fear I'll be missed. My father and Caius Fabius wish for us to meet in the *balneum*. There's much for us to talk about – my father enjoys hearing about battles and army life.'

'Master.' Brea nodded. Then she added, 'Do you find it a hard life, being a commander of men?'

'Often. It is lonely at night-time, looking at the stars, so far from home. And I have to make decisions I don't like. I follow the emperor's orders and Nero is not known for his kindness and patience...' Marcellus stopped himself. 'I've said too much. It's something that I speak of rarely, and never to a slave.'

Brea wondered if her tongue had got her into trouble. 'I'm sorry, Master.'

'No, I'm sorry to burden you with it. I thank you for your kindness to the woman I will marry, Brea. I will not forget it.' Marcellus turned abruptly and walked away, his feet resounding on the mosaic floor.

Brea frowned as she considered his words. She had never heard anyone speak about their feelings that way. Despite herself, she was warming to Marcellus; he seemed kind, generous-hearted, vulnerable even. She returned to the bedroom quietly where Aurelia was still slumbering. Brea walked over to the chest and picked up the gold and carnelian necklace, holding it up to the light, watching the metal gleam and the stone shine. It was beautiful.

* * *

Hanna examined the necklace in the light of her bedroom, wondering if it was real gold. The blood red stones were dark, the metal grey and dull. She picked up a tissue and began to rub the gold disc carefully. It must have been a beautiful piece of jewellery once. She wondered how old it was and who might have worn it. It was certainly an antiquated design. For a second, she closed her eyes and the sound of panic, scurrying feet and high screams filled her ears. She shook her head and the sound stopped.

Hanna gazed at the necklace again, wondering what to do with it. She would have mentioned it to her mother and Paddy when she came in, but they were sitting by the fireside, drinking coffee and talking about flower arrangements, and Roy had skittered around the room to settle at Paddy's feet. Hanna had left them to it. She wrapped the necklace in another tissue and slipped it into the drawer of a tall chest by the window. She'd return to it later, talk to her mother about it and ask her what she should do. There must be regulations about finding things in fields – she assumed it belonged to Paddy, as it was on his land.

Hanna picked up her phone and thumbed a message to Serenity saying thanks, she'd be glad of part-time work – she'd pop into the café in a day or two, and they'd discuss terms. She pressed *send* and felt suddenly tired, so she flopped back on the bed, her head colliding with the pillow. But Hanna's thoughts raced. The image of the woman she'd seen in the mist floated back to her; there was a sadness that seemed to surround her. Hanna was unsure now if her mind had played a trick, if it had simply been a momentary confusion of colour and light. But she doubted it. She was sure she'd seen a person in the field, the same woman she'd seen at the railway station. And hadn't Paddy said he'd felt something once, in the car? That was something else she'd talk to her mother about.

Or perhaps she wouldn't – she'd wait and see. She wasn't sure how she felt: she had seen a ghost, and her skin tingled at the thought. She didn't want to worry her mother. In time, she'd know what to do for the best. She'd only been at Bramble Wood Farm for a few days – she hadn't even met Oliver yet. She was looking forward to meeting him. It would be nice to have someone her own age living nearby – she hoped they'd get on.

12

Hanna stretched out on the bed and closed her eyes. Straight away, a dream lifted her. She was standing in a field, a wide-open space, and there was no sound. She looked around. A light breeze made the grass tremble. The trees bent one way, then the other: the silence was everywhere, an eerie stillness. Overhead, the sky was low, dark grey across the flatlands, the clouds brooding. In the distance, a heavy mist rolled in; it was early morning.

Hanna looked down – she was wearing a long green robe and a blue woollen cloak. Her feet were spattered with mud; the hem of her dress was soiled. The wind blew a sudden gust and she shivered. She was herself but she was also someone else – she wasn't Hanna, she didn't look like Hanna. She was in someone else's body, feeling as they felt, cold, edgy – something else. Her heart was warm, expanding, a feeling of unwavering trust.

A man stood next to her; he was broad, dark, a determined expression on his face. He was wearing a red cloak fastened at one shoulder. Being close to him made Hanna's breath quicken. He held out a necklace and placed it in Hanna's hands. She gazed at the bright gold links of the chain, the shining carnelian stones like huge droplets of blood. The pendant was ornate gold, a large stone set in the centre. She held it up, then he placed the necklace over her head and she felt the weight of it as it settled against her skin beneath her dress.

Hanna looked into the man's eyes and recognised his scorching stare. It reminded her of the man she had encountered in the café, the same expressive, dark gaze, the electric shock of their eyes meeting. He spoke anxiously – something was wrong. His lips moved, but Hanna couldn't make out the words. Around her, everything was deathly silent, a graveyard. She placed a hand against his arm and saw the glint of a gold snake bracelet on her wrist.

Then she was alone, gazing around, troubled. The man had gone. The silence was replaced now by the low moan of the wind. Hanna's blood thudded in her ears like a drumbeat. Then she saw the man rushing towards her; figures behind him were ominous silhouettes in the mist. He grabbed her hand – she had to hurry – they were running out of time.

In her dream, Hanna caught her breath as a group of men surrounded her. One of them said something, a threat; she scrambled up and began to run. The men chased behind her as she dodged towards a clump of trees, a forest beyond. They were quickly closing in – twigs snapped beneath Hanna's feet as she spurred herself forward. They were so near, she could hear their breathing; a soldier put out a hand to snatch at her arm. Then another threw something that hit her hard in the back and she fell. She could taste soil in her mouth, the bitterness of wet grass, and she couldn't breathe.

Hanna woke up. The dream was so vivid, so intense, that it could have been real, and now she was lying on the top of the bed shivering. She gazed at the little alarm clock on the bedside cupboard. It was almost six. She could smell cooking from the kitchen. Hanna tried to get her bearings. She was Hanna Frampton; she lived at Bramble Wood Farm, Norfolk. Her mother was downstairs cooking supper. But her senses tingled; a part of her still wore the necklace, the green dress, and she was lying on her face in a field struggling to catch her breath. She stood up slowly and took a few moments to come down to earth.

Hanna wandered into the warmth of the kitchen and Roy raised himself from where he slumbered at Paddy's feet and moved to sit beneath the table on top of Hanna's toes.

Her mother placed a steaming bowl of pasta in the centre. 'I was just about to call you.'

Paddy was already digging in, forking linguine onto his plate. 'Your mother and I have been busy checking the details of the wedding. You've been flat out asleep.'

'I popped up at two to see if you wanted a bite of lunch,' Stephanie explained. 'You were so peaceful, I didn't have the heart to wake you. I said to Paddy, all the travelling from China has caught up with you.'

'Jet lag.' Paddy poured some water from a jug. 'I always tell Oliver, you may think you can burn the candle at both ends, but it catches up with you in the end,' he grunted. 'He texted earlier to say he'd be back around midnight. He's up at five tomorrow – we've plenty to do on the farm.'

Stephanie smiled. 'They are young, our children. They just bounce back. It's when you get to our age that we need time to recover.'

'Too right – nice pasta, this. What sauce have you got on it?'

'Pesto – basil leaves, cheese, pine nuts,' Stephanie said, her eyes brimming with affection.

'Proper home cooking.' Paddy laughed. 'Before your mother moved in, I'd be eating out of packets from the freezer.' He rubbed the jumper that stretched across his belly. 'I used to microwave a family-size lasagne most nights and get that down me when I came back in from work. I'm spoiled for choice now.' He glanced at Stephanie and winked. 'And oh, the puddings your mother cooks are wonderful – she makes pastry light as angel's wings. Of course, when Wendy was alive, she'd burn most things.' Paddy paused, examining Stephanie's face. He left the rest of his comment in the air.

Stephanie said quietly, 'Wendy was Paddy's first wife. She died when Ollie was a teenager. He and Paddy managed by themselves for years.'

'Abby had just moved to Australia.' Paddy exhaled. 'Ollie would take himself off to school, get on with things without so much as a word. He learned to be independent. His mother was one for having clean clothes ready in the morning, making sure she'd attend parents' meetings and read his school reports, say all the right things to encourage him. I didn't have time for it – I was out working most hours. Then Oliver went to agricultural college in Norfolk and learned all the modern ways before coming back here and moving into the cottage. He's all for bringing the farm up to date.' His tone was affectionate, proud. 'He's done it by himself really.'

'That's impressive.' Hanna pushed a fork into the pasta. She'd hardly eaten anything.

'You still seem half asleep, love.' Stephanie was concerned. 'The flight must have taken it out of you.'

'Oh, I'll be fine.' Hanna blinked, bringing herself round. 'In fact, I've got myself a part-time job in Serenity's café. Just a couple of days a week to help out.'

'In a café?' Stephanie looked a little disappointed. 'Is that what you want to do, Hanna?'

'Only while I find my bearings. I thought it would get me out from under your feet and I'd meet some new people. Then, after the wedding, I'll give my future some serious thought.'

Paddy pushed his empty plate away. 'I need to give those horses' future some serious thought right now – I promised Ollie I'd see to them. They'll need bringing in from the fields and some hay to munch.'

Hanna hauled herself from her thoughts – she was standing in a field, wearing the gold necklace. 'I've seen horses in the stables.'

'Nutmeg's the mare and Hunter is her foal, although he's a lively stallion now – he's five years old. That must make Nutmeg eight or nine.' Paddy grinned. 'Oliver loves those two horses.'

'Hanna used to ride when she was younger,' Stephanie said pointedly.

Hanna recalled the years she'd taken lessons at a local stable, from the age of four to seven. Then her passion for gymnastics had kicked in and she'd done nothing but train. The horses had been forgotten. She hadn't been on one for well over twenty years.

Stephanie wasn't going to give up. 'You could go out riding with Ollie into Bramble Woods. I'm sure it's just like riding a bike.'

'I could.' Hanna chewed half-heartedly. 'I don't have any of the right gear – I'd need a hat, boots—'

'There's some of Abby's old stuff in the boot room – she's got riding boots, hats, jodhpurs, you could try them all for size.' Paddy stood up. 'Well, those horses won't sort themselves out.' He gave Stephanie a quick peck on the cheek. 'I won't be long.'

Roy leaped up from Hanna's feet and followed Paddy to the door.

Stephanie watched them go, then she turned concerned eyes on Hanna. 'Are you sure you're all right?'

'I'm just still a bit tired,' Hanna said, shaking her head. She placed her fork on her plate – she had eaten enough. 'I might have a bath, Mum, then get some more sleep. I'll be right as rain tomorrow.'

'All right, love.'

Hanna watched her mother collect the dishes. She felt a pang of selfishness. 'Oh, I should be helping you do the washing up, Mum, I've hardly done a thing since I've been home.'

'There's plenty of time,' Stephanie said kindly. 'You go and have a long soak.'

'If you're sure – thanks,' Hanna muttered. 'I will.'

'There's some lovely relaxing bath oil upstairs – chamomile and lavender,' Stephanie called as Hanna made for the door to the stairs. 'Help yourself.'

'Thanks, Mum.' Hanna rushed back and pecked her mother's cheek. 'I'll see you in the morning.'

She headed upstairs, the muscles in her legs spongy and tired. As she opened the bathroom door and turned on the taps, watching the bath fill, Hanna thought again about the gold jewellery wrapped in tissue in the tall chest.

She wondered why she hadn't mentioned it to her mother. It felt like a secret, something she couldn't share, not yet.

* * *

Brea and Balbina sat at the edge of the baths holding pots of oils and lotions, carrying folded towels. Balbina slipped into the water beside Julia and began massaging oil into her back, scraping it off with a strigil, a metal scraper with a dull blade and a handle. Brea copied her movements, sliding next to Aurelia, pouring oil and rubbing it in with a firm, soothing touch.

'Oh, this is heaven.' Julia closed her eyes. 'Of course, you'd have had beautiful baths in Rome, more slaves to tend to you, more companions to talk with. How I wish we had such luxury here.'

Brea felt Aurelia's muscles tense beneath her fingers – her new mistress was intimidated by Julia.

Aurelia said, 'In Rome, we had poetry read to us, and several slaves to cleanse us. My mother used the waters to relieve her suffering – she was plagued by aches in her fingers and hands, and she swore that regular baths helped her.'

Julia was uninterested. 'I prefer the *balneum* in my own house – or the public ones in Camulodunum, where I meet my friends and...' She smiled and leaned towards Aurelia. 'There is a young man who often comes to see me there. He is my lover, one of several I choose to spend time with.'

Aurelia was shocked. 'Do wives take lovers as many men do in Rome? I have heard such things happen. I had no idea it was allowed here in Britannia?'

'Of course it isn't allowed – you are such a silly thing.' Julia laughed. 'But Caius Fabius has no idea what I do when I'm not playing the compliant wife.' She turned angrily towards Balbina. 'Pay attention to your work, *ancilla*. Your nails are pinching my flesh.'

'I am sorry, Mistress,' Balbina replied, her expression unchanged.

'I will do my best to be the most dutiful wife.' Aurelia was still thinking of Julia's remark. 'My mother spoke to me about my duties. I am to run the house efficiently, please my husband in every way, bear sons. I will support him in his every decision and make him as comfortable as I can. I will dress modestly, I will appear chaste and obedient at all times, I am—'

Julia's laughter bubbled. 'Are you reciting a list?' She waved a hand in disgust. 'If you believe that rubbish, Aurelia, your life here will be unspeakably dull. My brother is a great soldier – he'll be away fighting more often than he'll be at home.'

'In his absence, I'll raise his children and supervise their education. I will maintain the smooth day-to-day running of the household.'

Julia snorted. 'It didn't work for Claudia. She suffered for days trying to bring a child into the world and it killed her. Who knows? You may have many children, or perhaps you'll go the same way she did.'

Aurelia trembled: Julia's comment had hit the mark. 'I heard about his wife's death. It was not long afterwards that I was promised to him. My father said that Marcellus was not ready to take another wife, so I waited until I was called.' Her shoulders tensed and Brea massaged in more oil.

'Well, now you are here, maybe I'll take you under my wing. I need some entertainment.' Julia smiled. 'We can go to the theatre, we can attend the gladiator fights in the arena.'

Aurelia was troubled. 'Oh, I don't think I'd like to see fighting.'

'The sight of a man in a loincloth, his muscles gleaming as he pits himself against another?' Julia shuddered with delight. 'I cannot think of anything that pleases me more... except for the strong arms of a lover. Never mind. I am sure that in time you'll see the light. I'll leave my invitation open – and I want to talk to you, to find out more about that handsome brother of yours. He intrigues me. What's his name?'

Aurelia was alarmed. 'Lucius. But he's only twenty-two years old.'

'His age is not important. A new handsome man is always a challenge I intend to rise to.' Julia glanced over her shoulder. 'I'm ready to leave now, *ancilla*. Fetch my towel.'

Brea was not surprised by Julia's affairs but she felt sorry for her mistress, who was clearly out of her depth. She whispered to Aurelia, 'You grow cold, my lady. Shall we return to your room?'

Aurelia nodded. She was shivering.

Brea helped her from the baths and wrapped her in a towel. Julia and Balbina had moved away and Balbina was dressing Julia, who was complaining that her hair needed to be done again.

Aurelia murmured, 'This place is very different to my father's *domus* in Rome. I doubt that I shall like it here.'

'Give it time,' Brea said quietly. 'The master is kind and you will be cared for well. His father, Publius, Julius is an old man now – they call him Alba Barba, White Beard, but he is not a hard master as some are. You will become the lady of the house and when your husband is absent, you may find that you have much happiness and independence.'

'I don't want independence.' Aurelia sounded unconvinced. 'I wish I could go home. I wish I'd never come here.'

'But you would not have met Marcellus.' Brea frowned. 'Do you not think he will make a fine husband?'

Aurelia was mystified. 'How would I know? It does not matter what I think of him. I just have to do my duty.'

Brea helped Aurelia into her robe, wrapping a cloak around her. She imagined herself in Aurelia's position, privileged, protected, about to become the wife of a handsome legate. She couldn't help thinking that, in her mistress's place, she'd be looking forward to being Marcellus's wife.

13

The next morning, Hanna opened the curtains to her room, the sunlight a stream of hazy lemon. In the field, a man was driving a tractor. He was fair-haired, wearing ear defenders. Hanna assumed that it was Oliver; he'd come home late last night and had started work early, just as Paddy had said. Hanna peered closer; she couldn't see his expression from the vantage point of her room, but there was something independent about his demeanour and she was intrigued to meet him. Perhaps she was imagining too much; it was typical of her to be impetuous.

Nevertheless, Hanna felt energised this morning: she had slept well after a luxurious bath and today was the beginning of a new week.

The kitchen was empty downstairs, a note on the table explaining that Stephanie had gone into King's Lynn for a wedding-dress fitting. Hanna made herself toast and tea and sat munching thoughtfully. Roy was out with Paddy, presumably; she imagined them in the pig field, rounding up the drove of hogs, Roy barking excitedly. She remembered the gold and carnelian stone necklace and reminded herself to mention it to her mother and Paddy tonight.

Hanna wondered what to do with herself for the rest of the day. She decided to head outside. In the farmyard there was a car parked by Oliver's cottage, a blue Peugeot 208 electric car, just the sort of car she'd expected him to drive. Glancing towards the neighbouring field, she saw a chestnut horse and a bay horse grazing, Nutmeg and Hunter. She wandered over to the field and held out a hand, calling their names. The chestnut mare raised her head for a moment and then went back to nibbling grass.

Hanna checked her phone for a reply from Serenity about the job in the café, but there wasn't one. In an instant, she made up her mind. She'd borrow Abby's old bike, cycle into Little Rymer and pay her a visit, talk through the hours she'd work and decide when she'd start.

It was an easy ride to the station, less than two miles on flat roads. The wind had almost subsided and it was a beautiful summer's day. Hanna glanced over the farm fields, wheat and barley waving in a light breeze, past the Little Rymer sign. She thought momentarily about the village, steeped in history. At primary school, there had been a Roman day each year when the children dressed up in sheets for togas and waved wooden swords. There had been a tribal settlement centuries ago on the Peddars Way, east of Thetford, and Hanna had been there for a school trip aged nine, eating sandwiches on the grass in the sunshine with her friends, secretly dreaming of being a great gymnast.

She pushed her bicycle down the ramp towards the station. A train had pulled in and was rumbling on the platform. Hanna crossed the bridge just as it shuddered away and walked over to the café. The doors were bolted and locked and there were no lights on inside. A notice on the window said that Serenity's café was closed on Mondays – opening hours Tuesday until Saturday. Hanna checked her phone, but there were still no messages. She decided not to interrupt Serenity on her day off – she clearly had precious little free time, running the busy café.

Hanna pushed her bicycle back to the road and clambered on. She wanted to visit the post office and buy a few postcards to send to friends in China. They'd love the quaint English village. It was such a gorgeous day and gardens were crammed with flowers: sweet peas, roses, geraniums.

She cycled down a narrow road, turning the corner past the village pub, The Dribbling Duck. The name always made her smile. She and her friends had got tipsy on bottled cider there on Saturday nights as sixth formers. She rounded the corner, over the small bridge that crossed the gurgling river Nar. Hanna had taken picnics there as a teenager; she recalled sharing a special picnic one day with a boy called Kyle who'd been in all her A level languages classes; she'd been unable to eat the sandwiches because she was so in love with him. He was tall, gangly, sporting the beginnings of a beard. It made her laugh to think back on it now: he'd been a rugby player, always complaining about his sore back and pain from the dislocated shoulder he'd received in a match. She wasn't sure she'd have the patience for Kyle now.

She continued past The Sprowston Manor Hotel, the Tudor-fronted building where her mother's wedding reception was to be held. She passed the church, the sweet scent of blooms drifting towards her. Hanna slowed the bicycle down and paused at the post office, wandering in, selecting cards from a tall stand. She grabbed a bottle of water from the glass-fronted refrigerator, taking it to the counter, rummaging in her pockets for money.

'Hanna – how nice to see you.' A smiling woman with smooth grey hair took the coins from her. 'I thought you were in China.'

'I just got back.' Hanna grinned, lifting the top from the water and taking a sip. 'How are you, Mary? How is Lisa?'

'We're all doing fine, thank you.' Mary leaned forward. There was no one in the post office and Hanna remembered Mary always liked to chat. 'Lisa's a mum now – two kids, Sophie and Jake. She'll be delighted to hear you're back home in Norfolk.'

Hanna, and Mary's daughter Lisa had been classmates since primary school, then later in the same French A level class, but Lisa was dreamy-eyed, already planning a future with her boyfriend.

'And how about you?' Mary asked, interested. 'Married? Engaged?' She glanced at Hanna's finger to check.

Hanna shook her head. 'There's no one special.'

'But your mum's getting married, isn't she, to Paddy Palmer?' Mary said excitedly. 'The wedding must be soon.'

'The second of September,' Hanna said. 'I can't wait...'

'Oh, I'm sure you'll find someone,' Mary soothed, misunderstanding. 'You'll be thirty years old now, same as Lisa. But that's not too late – there's someone out there for all of us.'

'I'm in no rush,' Hanna said, swigging the water. 'I can't make my mind up about what I want to do yet.'

'So what are you up to today?'

'Just taking a bike ride, looking at the old place.'

'Have you seen the house you used to live in? The flower beds that your mother kept so lovely are a bit neglected. I expect the new owner's too busy. He's a professional.'

'I've cycled past it.' Hanna thought about the house she grew up in, everywhere kept so tidy, everything in its place.

'Have you met him?' Mary was keen to chat.

'No.'

'He's been there a few months now. Nice chap. I forget his name. He comes in here sometimes with his girlfriend on a Saturday for the paper. I think she lives in London, but he's bought a house here. *Guardian* reader, but I won't hold that against him.'

Hanna grinned. 'Right, I'll be off. Give my best to Lisa, will you?'

'I will. She lives over in Shouldham – if you ever find yourself over there, drop in...'

'I will,' Hanna called on her way out.

She reached the bicycle and finished the water, pushing the empty bottle into a bin.

The ride past the silent, shuttered primary school brought back fond memories, but she doubted that there were any teachers still there who'd remember her. Her feet pressed the pedals, negotiating a corner into a narrow road that led to Mawkin Close, the three-bedroomed terrace where she'd lived with her mother and father, then just her mum, before she left home at eighteen. She'd cycled down it several days ago, but now she paid particular attention to number thirty-two, with the green door and the new iron gates. There was an old Land Rover parked outside.

Hanna slowed down, intending to peer at the house, to see what had changed. Then a man came out in a hurry, a case under his arm, closing the door crisply behind him, and Hanna pushed hard on the pedals and took off as fast as she could, almost cannoning into him as he drew level with the car.

'Sorry,' she mumbled and raced off down the road, determined to escape as quickly as possible.

For a second, their eyes had met and it had happened again, the inability to look away as an immediate electricity passed between them.

Hanna sped down the road, reaching the end of the terrace, before turning around and coasting aimlessly back towards number thirty-two, watching the Land Rover pull away. Hanna braked, taking deep breaths. It was him, the man she'd seen in the café. He owned their old house.

* * *

The man was still on her mind as Hanna, her mother and Paddy shared a meal. She said, 'I cycled past our old house, Mum. There are new blinds up.'

Paddy grunted disinterestedly, reaching down to ruffle Roy's fur. The dog promptly eased himself up onto his legs and moved to sit on Hanna's foot. 'I'm not keen on blinds. Give me good thick curtains any day. Blinds are too modern for me.'

'You can get some nice ones though,' Stephanie suggested. 'There are blinds that insulate rooms against heat and cold, and save energy.'

'I bet Oliver would approve of those.' Paddy laughed.

Hanna tried again. 'So – who bought the old house, Mum?'

'The estate agent dealt with it – I never met the new owner, but he's from London, he's picked up work down here.'

'I've heard of the chap – Wright, I think his name is – or White. It might be White.' Paddy stopped, as a thought occurred to him. 'Oh, that reminds me – I wanted to tell Oliver about Nutmeg. She needs her wolf teeth looked at.'

'What are those?' Stephanie had never heard of wolf teeth. 'Are they like wisdom teeth?'

'They can make the soft tissue in her mouth a bit sore, and I thought she looked like she might be having a bit of bother with them when I went in to tend her and Hunter last night.' Paddy sighed. 'That's a vet's visit to organise. I need the pigs looked at anyway. They are coming up for their annual review and Oliver always reminds me when it's time for them to get checked over.'

'I hoped Oliver would be here for supper tonight...' Hanna remarked.

Stephanie looked at Paddy. 'Did you ask him? I reminded you to ask him to come over and meet Hanna.'

'I hardly had a moment today – I was going to ask about the eco-show thing he went to in Cambridge but—'

Stephanie protested, 'I got some sausages in specially for him from the supermarket – those ones that are made from beetroot, carrot and sunflower seeds and are high in fibre.'

'And taste like cardboard, I should think.' Paddy laughed. 'You can't replace proper meat with sunflower seeds.'

Hanna stood up. 'I'll go and ask him to come over for dinner, shall I?' She was desperate to meet him. 'Perhaps he can come tomorrow or Wednesday?'

'Good idea.' Stephanie indicated Hanna's plate. 'Finish your food first...'

'Oh, I've had enough,' Hanna said.

As she sailed through the door, she heard her mother say, 'Hanna needs some younger company, Paddy,' and Paddy made a joke about being an old fogey and a stick-in-the-mud. She heard them laugh as she stepped outside.

The air was still warm and balmy as Hanna rushed over towards the cottage, Roy at her side, looking up, his eyes inquisitive.

'We're going to see Oliver,' Hanna said and the dog barked happily.

She knocked on the door and waited, listening eagerly for the sound of footsteps, or for the door to open. She knocked again, thumping harder. There was no response. She looked around. The blue Peugeot hadn't moved. Hanna cupped her hands to stare through the window, peering at a white bookcase, a television, a wooden table, a Persian rug. On one wall there was a framed picture of a horse galloping. There were several potted plants, an array of green leaves. A heavy jumper had been left on the back of a pale sofa. But there was no sign of Oliver.

Hanna knocked again – this would be the last time, then she'd give up.

The door was flung open and a young man with fair hair stood in the gap, wrapped in a bath towel, water dripping onto his face. He stared at Hanna. 'I was in the shower for goodness' sake—'

The towel was slipping from his waist and Hanna covered her face with her fingers so he wouldn't see her smile. 'I'm so sorry. I'm Hanna – I wanted to invite you to dinner?'

Oliver Palmer was confused. 'Who? What? I've just come back from working all day – I was up at five.'

'I'm Stephanie's daughter, Hanna.' She was laughing now. 'Sorry – is this a bad time?'

'It is, but...' Oliver wrapped the towel tightly round him and stuck out a hand, brightening. He could see the funny side. 'I'm Ollie – and yes, that would be great. Pleased to meet you.' He shivered. 'Dinner when?'

'Pardon?'

'When should I come round for dinner?'

'Wednesday night.' Hanna had an idea and was suddenly excited. 'I was planning to cook Chinese for the whole family. And it'll be plant-based.'

'Then I'll be there.' Ollie wriggled awkwardly. 'What time? Is seven okay?'

'Seven's perfect.' Hanna took in his uncomfortable expression. 'You'd better get back in the shower – it's a bit cold out here.'

'You're right.' The towel fell again and Ollie hugged it to him desperately. 'Nice to meet you. I'll look forward to Wednesday then.' He shivered and closed the door with a clunk.

Hanna couldn't stop smiling. 'That was Ollie,' she told Roy. 'I'm going to need the kitchen to myself on Wednesday afternoon. We're cooking for the whole family – I'll do jasmine rice, fried tofu, the taste of Guangzhou. I'll have to go into King's Lynn tomorrow to buy all the ingredients.' She gave a little skip and Roy barked excitedly. 'Oh, this will be such fun.'

14

Brea finished the last morsel from her bowl of porridge before starting the master's breakfast. There was a bustle in the kitchen this morning: the slaves were running late, chattering as their hands worked furiously.

'Mistress Aurelia's brother likes his bread dipped in oil.' Galyna panted as she rushed around collecting piled dishes and laying them on a tray. 'He's very partial to cheese. I can't stand the smell of it – it makes my stomach turn.'

'He's very handsome, the lady's brother – he's called Lucius Aurelius.' Chloe was pouring water. 'It's a shame he'll be leaving soon for the north.'

'He won't go until after the big wedding.' Daphne was making more garum. 'And master Marcellus will go off to the wars too not long after. But I dare say he'll have time to make sure his new wife has a baby growing in her belly.' She gave a throaty laugh.

Brea picked up a tray and the jug of water.

Chloe frowned. 'Where are you going with those?'

'Aurelia likes breakfast in her room.' Brea thought sadly that the new bride-to-be needed something to cheer her mood.

'I don't see why you were picked to be her slave and not me,' Chloe grumbled. 'I'd have loved that job. I adore her clothes – all the latest fashions from Rome. And have you seen her jewellery? The gold ring the master gave her, beautifully engraved. And the necklace! Oh, I'd die if someone gave me that necklace. Imagine wearing that.'

'Don't be silly – no one will ever give you anything other than a good hiding,' Galyna said impatiently. 'I remember the master Marcellus's first wife Claudia wearing the same necklace. It's a present given in marriage; it belongs to the family.' She pressed her lips together cynically. 'I expect there will be a third woman wearing it before the next year is out.'

'Why do you say that?' Daphne asked.

'Marcellus is a tall man, muscular. Aurelia is slight, just like Claudia was. A baby will never pass through her loins,' Galyna grunted. 'Marcellus needs a proper lusty woman with broad hips.'

'Like you?' Chloe laughed and Galyna lifted a hand, slapping her hard. Chloe cried out in pain and rushed back to making flatbread. Then her face took on a dreamy look. 'I'd love to try it on, though – just to see how it looked. Such a necklace would make any woman look beautiful.'

Brea took her tray up the stone steps towards the *cubiculum* where Aurelia hid away for most of the day. She found her at the window, dressed in her night robe, staring out at the drizzling rain.

Aurelia sighed. 'In Rome, the weather is pleasant. Here it seems to be cold and wet all the time.'

Brea had never known anything else; she was tempted to explain that this was summertime and things would get much worse as the year passed. Instead, she said, 'I've brought you breakfast.'

Aurelia went over to the bed and stretched out languidly. 'I have no appetite.'

'You must eat.' Brea placed the food in front of her. 'You must stay strong. Your wedding will be soon.'

Aurelia sighed, about to say something, then she looked away.

Brea tried again. 'Would you not enjoy taking your food into the *triclinium*? The master will be there, and Marcellus, and your brother. They may cheer you.'

Aurelia met her eyes. 'When does my brother join his legion in the north? I forget when he'll go.'

'After your wedding.'

'And what will become of me then? Lucius is all I have.'

Brea offered the dish again. 'You may do as you wish. You'll be a noble wife. You may go into Camulodunum where you will be entertained, enjoy fine company.'

'Everyone expects me to spend time with Julia.' Aurelia groaned. 'She goes to see the gladiators in combat and cheers at chariot races. I would rather be home, listening to poetry, or spinning thread, alone with my thoughts.' She shuddered. 'Julia wants me to be a sister, to behave like her, but, in truth, I think her loud and lewd. I know Marcellus would be disappointed to hear me speak so.'

'I believe she has an unhappy marriage,' Brea said quietly.

'And I shall too, I'm sure, marrying a man I don't know.'

'As every woman does. But in time you may grow to love him. He's well favoured and kind...' Brea stopped herself.

'Do you really think so? No woman loves her husband – marriage is a duty.' Aurelia leaned forward and held out a hand, plucking a date, nibbling like a small mouse. 'I'm just so afraid. My mother told me about what would be expected of me on my wedding night.'

Brea did not know what to say. She poured a goblet of water and held it out. 'Mistress.'

'I shouldn't talk about this to a slave,' Aurelia said sadly, sipping from the cup. 'But who else do I have?' She gazed around the room. 'Can you dress me now? I'd better put on my robe and his necklace and the bracelets and go to the *triclinium*. Lucius is there and he brings me good cheer.'

'Of course.' Brea removed the tray and lifted a light robe. 'Will you wear this one today?'

Aurelia slid from the bed. 'I suppose so. It matters not.'

* * *

An hour later, Aurelia joined the group in the *triclinium*, sitting next to Lucius, taking his arm in hers. Brea hovered nearby, waiting to be dismissed.

Publius Julius was talking to Marcellus animatedly. 'He's but twenty years old, yet they say he is tyrannical and cruel.'

Marcellus glanced at his wife-to-be, his expression concerned. 'I don't listen to rumours, Father, but I've heard it said.'

'Indeed. He's an angry, wilful young man. And he's not a good emperor. Apparently, he leaves most of the decision-making to the Stoic philosopher Seneca and the prefect Burrus.'

'Nero's young – he needs their guidance,' Marcellus said.

'I'm an old man – but people do not ask me for guidance. The young do as they wish. I've heard people say, "Oh, Alba Barba, he does nothing now but sit in the baths, talking with other old soldiers, and they will all die soon."'

'Father, your reputation will live on forever. You were a wonderful soldier, a great leader of men. Everyone in Camulodunum respects you.' Marcellus glanced at Aurelia again, who leaned her head against Lucius's shoulder as he whispered gentle words of encouragement.

'No good will come of this Nero,' Publius Julius continued. 'Emperor Claudius was a better man – he expanded Rome into Britannia and beyond. He was an accomplished leader who brought forth improvements to the judicial system. What has Nero done but develop a reputation for being obstinate? I heard that last year he tried to drown his own mother by having lead piled on her ship. Imagine – an emperor who would kill his own mother.'

'Sir.' Lucius stood and bowed slightly. 'Publius Julius, my sister would like to walk in the garden if the rain has stopped. I ask your permission to accompany her.'

Publius Julius lifted a hand. 'It might be better if Marcellus went with her.'

Brea took the moment as a cue to collect the dishes from breakfast.

Aurelia clung to her brother's arm nervously. Tears appeared in her eyes.

Marcellus said, 'Father, she should walk with her brother. I'm sure they have much to talk about. They must miss their father and their mother, and they can share fond memories of home. I'd be glad if you would allow it.'

'Very well.' Publius Julius swiped a hand as if annoyed by a fly. He watched for a moment as Lucius bowed, then offered an arm gallantly to Aurelia and escorted her towards the stairs.

Brea heard her voice, hushed with emotion, telling him that she had no idea what she would do once he joined his legion in the north.

Publius Julius had become impatient. 'I wish to go to my *balneum*. My bones need the comfort of the waters.' He called loudly, 'Petre, Linus. Come.'

Two tall, shaven-headed slaves in loincloths appeared instantly, bowing low.

Publius Julius lifted his arms helplessly. 'I'll go to my bath – it's the best place for a tired old man. Here – what keeps you? I wish to go now, not when it's past noon.'

Brea kept her head low, collecting dishes, as the master was helped from his chair and down the stairs by the two strong slaves. She piled wasted food on a tray and turned to go. She had taken two steps when she heard Marcellus call her name. 'Brea.'

She turned, the dishes in her arms. 'Master?'

Marcellus shook his head. 'My wife-to-be is filled with melancholy. Do you know what ails her?'

'Nothing more than a long journey and the strangeness of a new life, I imagine. She finds change difficult, and it will take her time to become accustomed to this place.' Brea did not want to speak out of turn.

'I haven't seen her smile yet,' Marcellus said.

'She may, in time.' Brea had no more words of comfort.

'I think perhaps not.' Marcellus had not moved. 'Truly, I'm sorry for her.'

Brea had nothing else to say, so she waited to be dismissed, but Marcellus seemed to want to talk.

'Today I am going into Camulodunum to try a new horse, a stallion.' He watched Brea carefully. 'Do you think Aurelia may wish to accompany me?'

'You must ask her yourself, Master.' Brea was conscious that she was still holding the pile of dishes. They were unstable and she feared she would drop them.

'You're a woman – perhaps you understand how she feels,' Marcellus said and Brea almost laughed at his statement. 'What would you do, if you were invited to view a new stallion?'

'That's easy,' Brea replied. 'I love horses. I rode as a child, until I was brought to this place. My tribe had many strong stallions.'

'You'd wish to see my new horse?' Marcellus repeated. 'You could tell me if I'd bought a fine stallion or a weak one?'

'I could.' Brea shifted her stack of dishes and Marcellus was at her side.

'Forgive me.' He took the dishes from her, placing them on a low table. 'I am keeping you from your work. But I love hearing how you feel about horses. I too have enjoyed riding since I was a boy.'

'What is the name of the horse you are going to try out today?'

'He's a black stallion by the name of Venator, which means hunter. If I choose him, I'd ride him everywhere.' Marcellus was suddenly staring at her. 'I may not have seen Aurelia smile, but your smile is as bright as the breaking of a new dawn.'

Brea lowered her gaze. 'Master, I have much to do.' She snatched up the dishes. 'If I'm late, Galyna will be displeased.'

'I'm sorry – I have been keeping you selfishly.' Marcellus's tone held a sadness. 'Please – do go about your work.'

'Master,' Brea muttered and hurried to the steps, the dishes in her arms. She was imagining his horse Venator, a muscled black stallion rearing boldly. Marcellus was sitting astride the horse and she was in front of him; they were galloping through a forest, the sunshine glinting through branches, dappling the grass.

Brea rushed towards the kitchen clutching the dishes, pushing the thoughts away. But they came back more vividly, and this time, she and Marcellus had dismounted and were standing beneath a shady tree, and she was in his arms, his lips against hers. She caught her breath, furious with herself for being weak.

Brea closed her eyes, but the image was still there, imprinted behind them. And for a moment, she believed it was real.

15

The kitchen was filled with the aroma of cooking. Three faces watched Hanna, their eyes round with expectation, as she placed an assortment of plates on the table in front of them. Roy settled at Paddy's feet, looking hopefully for scraps.

Paddy was astonished as he poked a cube of tofu with his fork. 'So, you'd better tell me – what's all this funny ole food we've got to eat here?'

'We have' – Hanna flourished an arm – 'deep-fried golden tofu, stir-fried asparagus with garlic, bean shoots, aubergine in black bean sauce, Pak choi and broccoli in ginger, garlic and soy, and fragrant jasmine rice.' She met Paddy's eyes. 'Enjoy.'

'I certainly will.' Ollie was already digging in. 'What a feast!'

Stephanie smiled proudly. 'Hanna made all this. She wouldn't let me help. And it's all plant-based – but not a beetroot sausage in sight.'

Paddy placed a spoonful of aubergine on his plate, making a face as if he was sampling poison. 'Well, I'm going in. Wish me luck.'

Hanna poured wine into four glasses. 'It's what I ate all the time while I was in Guangzhou.'

'You look all right on it.' Paddy piled asparagus on top of rice and chewed contentedly. 'Well, I'm getting it down me and I'm not dead yet.'

'It's delicious,' Stephanie insisted.

'It beats what I cook in the cottage – it's the best food I've had in ages,' Ollie agreed, reaching for his glass, lifting it high. 'To Hanna, the super cook.'

'And good luck, Hanna – she starts her new job tomorrow at the café in Little Rymer,' Stephanie added. 'Three days a week, is it, love?'

'Yes – the days Serenity's most busy. I'm glad she'll be there – I've no idea what I'm doing, but it shouldn't be too hard to learn. And, Mum, just so you don't worry – I've already told her I can't work on the second of September. So...' Hanna raised her glass in a toast. 'Cheers, everyone. To weddings and families.'

They all held up their glass and chorused, 'Cheers.'

Then there was no sound except munching, Ollie making low groans of appreciation as he sampled each new dish. Then, Paddy announced, 'Well, I have to say, it's not bad at all. I thought I was going to hate it, but it's tasty nosh.'

'Better for the environment than meat every night of the week.' Ollie took his chance. 'So, Dad – I need to sit down and talk through some plans for the farm. I picked up loads of tips in Cambridge last weekend. Sustainable farming – replacing old vehicles and equipment with new electric ones, using solar or wind power and switching feed providers for a more local, eco-friendly brand. We could eventually use wind turbines and more ecological herbicides...'

'Hang on, Oliver. I'm not saying I'm not prepared to listen but...' Paddy held his hands up, alarmed. 'How much will this cost me?'

'I'm going to put it on a spreadsheet, with the relevant costs – make a five-year plan.'

'I'll be dead and gone by then, what with the worry of all this new machinery and expense.' Paddy was incredulous.

'Oh, I do hope not,' Stephanie said anxiously.

'Hear me out,' Ollie protested.

'I just think things are all right as they are. We're doing well, keeping afloat. Why change everything just because it's trendy?' Paddy waved his fork.

Hanna leaned forward, listening. There was an honesty between father and son as they shared their views across the table. And despite their disagreement, there was warmth, mutual respect. She decided she liked them both. And Ollie's words made sense – he would become an ally. It felt good to be among a normal family. It was something she'd never experienced before and she found that she was smiling.

'It's more than that. We need to develop sustainable farming methods, Dad. The focus on environmentally-friendly organic produce isn't new.'

'What does that mean?' Paddy laughed. 'Sounds like new-fangled poppycock.'

'Perhaps we should just enjoy the food, boys?' Stephanie was a little alarmed.

'Hanna agrees with me,' Ollie almost shouted. 'Don't you, Hanna?'

Hanna wasn't aware she'd agreed with anyone, but she could see his point. She reached for the bottle, topping up everyone's glass. 'I think there's a discussion to be had.'

'The tofu is delicious, isn't it, Paddy?' Stephanie insisted.

'Mmm. Where was I? Ah. This farm has been run the same way since my father and his before him.' Paddy spooned tofu and rice onto his plate. 'Why do we need to change what works?'

'Because, by the year 2030, the global demand for food will rise around 35 per cent. Consumers will expect farmers to meet this growing demand – we'll have to consider factors like water shortages and harmful chemicals.'

'Welcome to family meals at Bramble Wood Farm,' Stephanie said. She'd assumed the role of peacemaker, lightening the tone. 'At least the food has almost all gone.'

'It was delicious.' Ollie wiped his mouth. 'Can we do this again?'

'I love it, us all being round the table.' Hanna seized the opportunity. 'How about I cook something plant-based once a week and we'll all sit down together?'

'As long as we don't argue about farming,' Stephanie suggested. 'I'm exhausted.'

'But it's interesting, learning about the new methods. And talking about it makes me think, well, Oliver might have a point. As long as it works.' Paddy was coming round to the idea. 'And it's good to sit down and discuss things as a family, now we're going to be married, Steph.'

'Is there any pudding?' Ollie wanted to know.

Hanna grinned. 'Not this week. I'll make coffee and I think there's a box of chocolate mints.'

Paddy rubbed his belly. 'Sounds good – but there's still some of these nice squashy things left.'

'Fried tofu, Dad,' Ollie began.

Roy sat up high, his paws raised, begging.

Paddy laughed. 'Sorry, Roy, are we leaving you out? Here – try a piece of tofu.' He held one out and Roy snaffled it eagerly, diving back onto the tiled floor, smacking his lips. Paddy was impressed. 'Even Roy likes Hanna's food. Do you mind if I finish it all off, Hanna?'

'Not at all.' Hanna was delighted. 'Shall I put the coffee on?'

'I'd better go and sort out the horses – they need bringing in from the fields for the night.' Ollie shifted in his seat.

'I'll make the coffee – you two go and see to Nutmeg and Hunter,' Stephanie suggested.

Hanna glanced at Ollie. 'I'd love to meet them.'

'Right, come on.' Ollie stood up. 'We won't be long – just as long as it takes for the coffee to percolate and the mints to arrive at the table.'

* * *

Hanna and Ollie stepped outside from the boot room in wellingtons and jackets, leaving the light of the house behind them. They walked towards the cottage, where a single porch lamp gleamed, and they continued beyond to the stables.

Hanna pushed her hands into deep pockets. 'It's dark here – I mean, really dark. In China, I lived in a big city and got used to it being hazy all the time.'

'Light pollution,' Ollie murmured. 'I love living in the countryside, the darkness, the solitude. The land has its own smell, a dampness to the earth, the low-hanging mist.'

'I'd forgotten all about it while I was away,' Hanna agreed.

'Norfolk is in my blood – I couldn't live anywhere else,' Ollie murmured.

'It's good to travel, but it's nice to come home,' Hanna said.

'So, what are you going to do here?' Ollie asked. They were level with the stables, walking beyond to a field where two horses were grazing in the dark.

'Besides work in the café? I'm not sure.' Hanna faced him. 'Did you go to school in King's Lynn? I was at the Academy.'

'I went to King Edward VII, then Easton College in Norwich. That's where Dad said I got all the new-fangled ideas. I think he's coming round to the modern way of thinking, though.' Ollie paused by the gate. 'I'm thirty-two, so I was a couple of years ahead of you at school. I don't think our paths crossed.' He gave a low whistle and the two horses trotted over. He held up a fist and the bay nuzzled it affectionately. 'This is Hunter.'

'Nice name – it suits him.' Hanna stroked the fur of Hunter's nose and he snorted.

'Yes, I named him when he was born. Dad asked me what to call him and it just popped into my head.' Ollie laughed, reaching towards the chestnut mare. 'This is Nutmeg. She's Hunter's mother. She has a lovely temperament.' He tugged open the gate and led the two horses towards the stable. 'I always bring them in at night. It can get muddy and the wind is bitter.'

'I can imagine.' Hanna stared into the darkness.

'We'll give them some hay and I'll come back tomorrow before work, muck out the stables and turn them out to graze.' Ollie had a sudden thought. 'Do you ride?'

'Years ago,' Hanna said by way of explanation.

'How about I pick you up after you've finished work at the café on Saturday? We can go for a ride if you like. You can take Nutmeg.'

'Right, you're on.' Hanna felt confident that she'd be safe enough on Nutmeg; Ollie's smile reassured her, as if Hanna clambering on a horse after twenty years was the easiest thing in the world.

They had reached the stables and the horses ambled inside. Hanna helped Ollie fill hay nets, hanging them on each stable before placing a rug over each horse.

He grinned optimistically. 'It must be time for coffee?'

'Mmm, yes.'

They turned to walk back to the farmhouse.

'I really enjoyed this evening,' Ollie remarked.

'I enjoyed it too,' Hanna agreed. 'It's so nice to be part of a family, just sitting round the table, discussing, sharing food.'

'It's good to have an ally. Dad's happier now he's met Stephanie, but I struggle to bring him into the twenty-first century. He thinks I'm crazy, driving an electric car, eating plant-based food. And I have so many plans for the farm, but I don't want to upset him.'

'I like Paddy,' Hanna admitted. 'It's nice to see him and Mum together. They are sweet.'

'It was tough when my mum died.' Ollie was quiet for a moment. 'Dad and I had a hard time of it. And it was hard for Abby too – she'd just moved to Australia. I'm glad he's met your mother. She's brought lightness to his life.'

'It can't have been easy for any of you,' Hanna said gently.

'It wasn't. But we do all right now, me and Dad.' Ollie grinned. They had almost reached the farmhouse. 'And we have a wedding to celebrate. I hear you and I are going to be witnesses. I may have to make a speech at the reception – you too.'

'Really?' Hanna was surprised. 'Oh, I'd have no idea what to say.'

Ollie winked. 'We'll work on it together. Maybe we can plan something when we're out riding on Saturday.'

'I'll look forward to it.' Hanna paused. A thought had occurred to her. 'Ollie, can I ask you something?'

'Of course.'

'You've lived here all your life, haven't you?'

'Man and boy.' He grinned. 'Why?'

'Would you say...?' Hanna thought for a moment how to phrase her next words. 'Would you say this place has an eeriness to it?'

'Oh, most definitely.' Ollie didn't look at all concerned. 'You grew up in Little Rymer.'

'I did, but the village was different. It's here, outside the village, out in the fens, that feels creepy.'

'I know,' Ollie agreed.

'The thing is – as soon as I arrived here, I—oh, it's ridiculous. I thought I saw something. I don't expect anyone to believe me, but...'

'But?'

'I was in the pig field with Roy and he lay down and whined, then I thought I saw someone moving in the mist.'

'It's an atmospheric place.' Ollie looked around, staring into the darkness. 'There are all sorts of tales about what people have seen around here – the locals will tell you all about this place after a pint or two in The Dribbling Duck.'

'Oh?'

He met her eyes. 'It's an old landscape, the farmland, the fens – it goes back to the times of the Romans, to a time before they came, when the Celtic tribes set up their villages. When I was a kid, I found an old Roman coin in one of our fields – it had Claudius's face on it. The archaeologists went mad for it. It's in a museum now.' He took a breath. 'But I can tell you about a few weird experiences I've heard of around here, that's for sure.'

Hanna shivered without meaning to. She put a hand to her head. An image cleared in front of her eyes and an image from her dream swirled back. A man she knew from somewhere looked at her, his gaze blistering as he placed a necklace around her throat.

'Hanna?' Ollie's voice came from a distance. 'Are you all right?'

Hanna blinked hard, took a breath and said quietly, 'I'm fine – thanks, Ollie.' She turned shakily, meeting his eyes. 'Since I've arrived back here, though, there's definitely been a strong sense of the past all around, and...' She paused: there was plenty of time to tell him about the necklace. 'Oh, it's probably my imagination. It's easy to imagine things in the fens...'

16

Several days passed and the rain eventually stopped. That evening, Publius Julius was invited to a feast at Caius Fabius and Julia's house, returning in the early hours in a fine mood. Many of his old soldier friends were there drinking the best wine, and the discussion had been about politics and Rome, which he'd enjoyed immensely. Marcellus, his young wife-to-be and her brother also attended as honoured guests of Caius Fabius. The evening, however, had dampened Aurelia's mood and she complained of a headache as soon as she reached the villa. Brea prepared her for sleep, combing her hair and soothing her with kind words before retiring to the slave quarters to fall into her own hard bed.

She woke before dawn the next morning; Daphne and Chloe were already in the *culina* with Galyna, preparing the morning meal. Brea met Addedomaros outside the atrium carrying a box of fruit, which he thrust into her hands. 'Brea, good morning to you. I've picked these for your mistress's breakfast. They are fresh from the dew-damp trees. I wish her a good appetite.'

Brea was grateful. Everyone had heard of Aurelia's melancholy; she had often been seen walking in the garden with Lucius, her face wet with tears. 'Thanks, Adde. How goes the work?'

'We're kept busy all the time. Yesterday, many of us worked until after the sun set. The vegetables grow more quickly than we can pick them. And the wedding is soon, so we'll need to gather fresh fruit.'

'I believe some food will be brought in for the wedding feast – there's a ship coming from Rome with all sorts of new fruits. Figs are coming from Africa, and the master has ordered special garum from there too.' She laughed. 'I have no idea where Africa is, Adde, but it must be a long way away.'

'I hear it's so hot there that the ground is covered with a yellow dust that swirls in the wind,' Addedomaros said. 'And there are creatures with stripes and spots on their bodies, and animals with long noses to the ground, the like that no one has seen.'

'Who can imagine such things?' Brea mused.

'Have you seen the master's new horse in the stables?' Addedomaros raised an eyebrow in appreciation. 'A beautiful stallion. He rides it all the time, and rarely sees his new bride-to-be. She doesn't like horses.'

'I haven't seen it yet, but I would like to.' Brea smiled. She imagined Marcellus astride a tall horse. She hadn't seen him for a few days and she missed his company and their conversations. He had shared his feelings with her and she was becoming accustomed to listening, to offering her thoughts. It surprised her how much she was looking forward to seeing him again.

'It's a very tall and majestic battle horse. He's called Venator,' Addedomaros said. 'May he keep the master safe.'

'Praise the gods, he will.' Brea muttered a secret prayer to Andred, the warrior goddess, that she would keep locked in her heart. 'I must go back to the kitchens. I'm already waited for.'

'Take care, Brea – it brightens my day to see you.' Addedomaros waved a hand and was gone.

Brea carried the box of fruit, wondering if the mistress would eat some with honey and bread, perhaps a little wine.

When she arrived at the *culina*, she heard voices shouting. Galyna turned to her wildly. 'Brea, we are all sent for. The master has called us to the *triclinium* without delay.'

Brea was puzzled. 'Are we to carry trays of breakfast there?'

'No, not yet. White Beard wants to talk to us. I fear there's something wrong.'

'Perhaps the mistress has died in the night?' Daphne said cynically as she reached for Brea's hand. 'Perhaps she's taken her own life rather than marry the master's son?'

'That is ridiculous.' Galyna slapped at her, just missing her face. 'We'll have no such talk.'

Chloe was anxious, fidgeting with her robe, rearranging the neckline. 'Why has he summoned us then? It can only be trouble.'

'Come – we're late,' Galyna said quickly. 'Brea has kept us waiting.'

The four slave women adjusted their clothes to look as tidy as possible, then they clambered the stairs to the *triclinium*. Already, a group of slaves had assembled, Publius Julius's personal slaves, some from the garden, including Addedomaros, who glanced nervously towards Brea. There were many slaves from Gaul who cleaned the villa and those who tended the furnace, people whom Brea rarely saw, all standing in a row, their heads bowed respectfully.

Brea took her place and Daphne grabbed her hand again for comfort. She whispered, 'Look at old White Beard's face – he's angry. And he has Aurelia with him and her brother. What can be amiss?'

Tension filled the room like ice. The slaves were silent. Lucius placed a protective arm around his sister. Publius Julius was reclining on his couch, his face arranged in an expression of discontent.

Chloe took her place on the other side of Brea, clutching her arm, shivering as she whispered, 'Are we in trouble? Old White Beard looks angry – do you think I should go back to the kitchen? I have so much to do.'

Galyna shot her a withering look.

Publius Julius raised a finger, a signal that he was about to speak.

'I bring you here today because of a serious matter.' He stood up slowly, painfully. 'This morning I offered a prayer to Jupiter. A terrible thing has occurred and there will be justice.'

Brea's heart leaped. She wondered if Marcellus's horse had thrown him, if he was injured. She squeezed Daphne's hand and felt the pressure returned.

'You all know my son is to marry the lady Aurelia from Rome.' Publius

Julius's voice thundered despite his age. 'And to mark their intention to wed, he has given her jewellery. The band of gold he placed on her finger will never be removed. But one of the fine pieces belonged to my wife – a gold and carnelian necklace fashioned by a master craftsman in Rome. It is a valuable heirloom, and it has been taken from her room.'

The room was silent. Aurelia swayed a little and her brother put out an arm in support.

Publius Julius stared at the slaves, his face furious. 'Which of you stole it from her *cubiculum* while she slept?'

There was no movement. All slaves' eyes were centred on the mosaic tiled floor, fearful of being accused.

'I ask you again. Which of you took it? I intend to deal with the thief in the most severe way.'

Brea waited. On her left, Daphne's clammy hand was in hers. She felt it quiver. To the right, Chloe let go of her tight grip for a moment, then something cold and hard was pressed into Brea's palm. She knew what it was right away. She touched the smoothness of the gold, the rounded stones. She turned to Chloe and mouthed, 'What is this?'

Chloe mouthed, 'Help me...' and shook her head quickly. Brea knew that Chloe wanted her to act decisively on her behalf, to hide the necklace she had stolen. Brea could feel Chloe tremble as they huddled closely together.

The silence was unbearable. Publius Julius broke it with a command to two of his slaves. 'Search them.'

Brea had no idea what to do. She couldn't return the necklace to Chloe; she couldn't hide it.

The master's slaves were moving among the huddled group, examining hands, lifting robes.

Galyna muttered, 'If a man touches me beneath my robe, I will certainly faint from fear.'

The two slaves were approaching quickly and efficiently. Brea glanced at Chloe, who had tears on her face, terrified that Brea would report her.

Then Brea's voice broke the silence. 'I'm sorry – I have it here, Master.'

Every face turned to stare as Brea held up the necklace.

Galyna hissed, 'Thief.'

Brea felt the necklace tugged from her grasp, then she was seized by the wrists, hauled to the front of the group and pushed to her knees.

Publius Julius said, 'You were entrusted with the lady Aurelia's care and you have proved yourself to be wicked. You will be flogged.'

Brea glanced up to see Aurelia looking at her in disbelief. Brea met her eyes and with an imperceptible movement of her mouth denied that she had taken it.

Aurelia's hands flew to her lips. 'Please,' she gasped. 'I think I may have lost it somewhere. The slave must have picked it up for me.'

'Jupiter has answered my prayers. The slave will be beaten. Take her to the garden.' Julius waved a hand as if that was the last of it.

The two slaves grasped Brea's arms and hurried her towards the steps, lifting her feet from the ground. Her hair came loose from its tie and tumbled across her face. She felt the material of her tunic tear at the back.

Then a clear voice called, 'It was not her fault. I stole it. She's hiding it because I made her do it.'

The two slaves gripped her firmly, twisting around as Addedomaros spoke again.

'Do not blame her. I made her hide it for me. I stole it from the mistress's room last night.'

Brea felt herself flung to the ground. The slaves ran towards Addedomaros, twisting his arms until he was on his knees. Brea called out, 'He didn't do it.'

But no one paid any attention to her.

Publius Julius waved a flat palm in the air; he had reached a decision. '*Sceleris plenissime!* You are a criminal.' He stood up, his face grave. 'Take the slave outside and thrash him. Then take him to the *ludus*, sell him to Marcus Rubrius for as much money as you can get. I will not keep a thief in my home.'

The slaves watched as Addedomaros was hauled out.

Publius Julius clapped his hands. 'What are you all doing, watching in idleness when you should be at your work? Return to your duties now or I will have you all whipped.'

The slaves scurried away.

Brea picked herself up from the floor as Chloe rushed past, a look of apology on her face. She watched the slaves disappear as she stood dishevelled, her hands to her face, shaking. Addedomaros had just saved her skin.

Publius Julius shouted, 'Where is my food and wine? I have not broken my fast yet.'

Brea looked up to see Aurelia holding out a hand to her.

Aurelia spoke kindly. 'Will you accompany me to my room? I need a rest.'

Brea followed her dutifully.

Once inside the *cubiculum*, Aurelia sat on the bed and sighed. 'I know you didn't take it, Brea. What happened?'

Brea took a breath. 'I don't know who stole it, Mistress.' She disliked lying, but she was determined to protect Chloe. It was the Iceni way, to protect weaker ones, to be loyal. 'It was passed around from slave to slave as we stood before the master, and it found its way into my hand.'

'Then why did you say you had it?'

Brea lifted her chin. 'Someone would have been punished and I couldn't find it in my heart to pass it to someone else.'

'I would not have been so brave,' Aurelia said. 'And the young slave who spoke up for you, who said he had given it to you?'

'He was trying to protect me.' Brea felt a tear trickle down her cheek. Addedomaros would be outside in the garden now. It was too late to save him from a flogging.

'He loves you, this slave?' Aurelia looked sad.

Brea had never considered that Addedomaros might love her, but he clearly cared enough to take her place. She felt fiercely loyal and desperately sad; his life had changed forever, and she would do her best to help him. She lifted her chin. 'He's a warrior from a tribe not unlike mine. We understand each other.'

'I wish Marcellus had been here.' Aurelia was thoughtful. 'He would have known what to do. But he's with the horse he has recently bought, the black stallion he thinks so highly of. It gives him comfort to ride it. He thinks constantly of leaving to go to battle. I believe he will be happier there.'

Brea had never heard her speak so many words. 'I think not. I'm sure he cares for you.'

'It's true,' Aurelia said. 'He seeks to do his duty, as I must.' She shook her head. 'Such is our lot that we must suffer. And you too, Brea, your life is hard. But I'm very glad you didn't take a beating today. You'll be my only comfort here, especially when Lucius has departed. I would be lost without you.'

Brea saw her chance. 'Then please... when my lord Marcellus returns, please tell him what came to pass today with Addedomaros. It's bad enough that he has been scourged, but if he is sent to the gladiator school, his life will be even harder. Please, you must beg him to intervene.'

'I can't do that.' Aurelia shook her head. 'It's not my place.'

'Then I'll ask him myself,' Brea muttered under her breath.

Aurelia had not heard. 'I must lie down, just for a moment, and rest my eyes.'

'Come, my lady.' Brea stood tall. 'Allow me to put the necklace on you, in its rightful place. Then you can relax while I go to the *culina* and fetch some fruit. You must enjoy a hearty breakfast, because the slave who fetched it for you has paid dearly.'

Brea took the necklace from Aurelia's slender fingers where the engraved band of gold hung heavy, and clasped it around her neck, then she fled for the kitchen. She hoped there would be news of Addedomaros, that he had survived the beating, that he had not yet been taken to the gladiator school. She was determined that as soon as she saw Marcellus, she'd tell him what had happened and plead for her friend's safe return. She believed that Marcellus would listen.

17

Hanna leaned on the counter, her head in her hands, resting. She'd slept badly for the last two nights. Her dreams were tangled images of clashing swords, two men in an arena facing each other, the noise of a baying crowd. At one point, a young man was dragged into an orchard of fruit trees and whipped until his flesh bled. She had woken abruptly, her skin damp, her mind troubled. She was glad of the distraction of working in the café but she still felt exhausted.

Thursday and Friday had been busy days at Serenity's. Hanna was just getting the hang of the coffee machine. She'd learned how to froth milk, make ice-cream shakes and smoothies, a range of teas. Serenity was good company, but from eight o'clock in the morning they'd been busy until after the lunchtime rush, then things calmed a little until they closed the café at five.

Serenity pressed a mug into her hands. 'Chai latte. Take a break. You look exhausted.'

Hanna glanced up at the clock. 'It's not yet two.'

'Go on – grab a sandwich. I'm all right by myself for a while – we're not too busy.'

'It's been frantic all day.' Hanna sipped her drink gratefully.

'So,' Serenity grinned, 'will you be back next Thursday or have I put you off working here?'

'It's been great,' Hanna admitted. 'It's nice to have a change of scenery from the farmhouse.'

'You must be a bit limited there – it's so isolated.'

'Maybe, but it's in an idyllic position...' Hanna cupped her hands around the mug.

'I'm going to King's Lynn later,' Serenity said. 'My mum works in the South Gate Arms, and I usually catch up with her on a Friday or Saturday night for a bite to eat, then I meet up with friends and go clubbing. You could come along if you like.'

'Thanks.' Hanna felt far too tired. 'I promised Ollie we'd go out on the horses later. But some other time, definitely.'

'Ollie sounds nice.' Serenity gazed towards the door where a new customer had come in, a young woman with a suitcase. 'I don't know him really, but we've bumped into each other once in The Dribbling Duck. I know he was engaged and then they broke it off.'

'Oh?' Hanna wondered how she'd ask him about his past. Perhaps it was better to hear it from Serenity.

'I only know what I heard. She lived over Swaffham way, a farmer's daughter. They met at agricultural college in Norfolk and were together for years. Then, all of a sudden, they split up.' Serenity turned her attention to the customer. 'Hello, the usual, is it? Espresso coming up – and a chocolate brownie. I made them freshly this morning.'

Hanna marvelled that Serenity, who must have got up before six o'clock to make cakes and biscuits, was still full of energy. She gazed into her mug and felt a wave of tiredness sweep over her. Her stomach made a low growl. 'I haven't eaten since breakfast. If it's okay, I will grab a sandwich and sit out the back.'

'Take as long as you like,' Serenity called over her shoulder.

Hanna picked up a wrapped roll and pushed open the door that led to the little rest room where coats and bags were kept. There was a small window, a table and two chairs, the dishwasher, a slim washing machine and several cookery books. Hanna sat down, stretching her aching legs and put her hands to her head.

Immediately, she was standing in the mist, wearing the necklace. The gold shone in the hazy sunlight, the carnelian stones like drops of blood between her fingers. Hanna blinked. The person was her, yet not her – she was someone else, a woman with a mass of long hair, a green dress that hung below her calves. People were surrounding her, moving shadows. She felt afraid.

Hanna shook herself, reaching for the roll, unwrapping it. Cheese and pickle. She took a bite, feeling the sharpness of the breaking crust against her mouth, the tang of pickle. She tried to concentrate on normal things, chewing, drinking. Later, Ollie would give her a lift home and they'd take the horses across the fields. Then she'd eat a family meal and have an early night. Tomorrow was Sunday – she'd sleep until lunchtime.

Hanna wondered about her dreams. She'd never spoken about them to anyone. Perhaps she should, but they had always felt like her secret, one she shared only with the woman in the dream. Since falling from the trampoline all those years ago, she'd said nothing about her experiences. To this day, she still had no recollection of lying on the gym floor, speaking in a strange language. Her mother had told her about it – it had given everyone quite a scare. Hanna remembered feeling very confused when she came round, somehow different. She wondered what a psychoanalyst would make of it all.

The dreams may have subsided in China, but they were more vivid than ever since she'd come home to Little Rymer. Yue's enigmatic words came back to her: 'She has long been gone, but she is not at rest. And you are not able to rest, until it is finally resolved.'

Hanna shivered: it was true, she certainly couldn't rest. She wondered what needed to be resolved, and how she could do it. It occurred to her that she might talk to Ollie. He seemed rational: when they had spoken outside the farm on Wednesday night, he'd been warm and sympathetic. And he had a clear understanding of the local history, the myths of the fens. It might be a good thing to confide in him.

Hanna finished the last mouthful of her latte, left the roll half eaten and stretched her arms. She pushed open the door – and met his eyes. Instantly, the power of his gaze sent a shockwave through her body, jolting her heart. Hanna didn't move. The dark-haired man stared at her for a moment

longer and she couldn't tug her eyes away. Then he smiled briefly at Serenity, paying for two cups of coffee, and turned to go. Hanna watched him, the
smart black jacket, the faded jeans, as he walked over to a table in the
corner, sitting opposite a woman in a short skirt who was staring at her
phone. She wasn't smiling; neither she nor the man looked happy as they
spoke quietly, their coffees untouched.

Hanna busied herself arranging a shelf of crisps that didn't need tidying, then she picked up an empty cup that had been left on the counter.

Serenity placed a hand on her shoulder. 'Are you all right now?'

'Yes – fine, thanks.' Hanna wasn't sure if Serenity was referring to the
short break she'd just had or her stunned reaction to the man. Hanna
frowned; her heart was still thudding. It didn't make sense: she'd never
spoken to him, yet he'd been in her dreams, or someone very like him – she
felt she knew him already.

Hanna pushed the thought away; he probably thought her behaviour
odd, staring pointedly at a complete stranger. Or perhaps he recognised
her; she had almost cannoned into him on the bicycle outside his house.
She felt suddenly embarrassed.

'I'm glad you had something to eat. You looked a bit wobbly,' Serenity
said.

'I've been all over the place since I came back from China. I forgot to eat
lunch.' Hanna grinned. She glanced over to the table where the man was
speaking in a low voice as the woman turned away abruptly, as if
disagreeing.

'Do you know him?' Serenity asked, indicating the couple in the corner.

'No.' Hanna heard her own voice rise awkwardly. 'I've never spoken to
him before.'

'He comes in here sometimes with his girlfriend. He lives in Little
Rymer and I think she still lives in London. The two-forty-five to King's
Cross is due here soon, so I expect she's catching that.'

Hanna wondered whether to mention that the man had moved into the
three-bedroomed terraced house in Mawkin Close. She recalled the incident where she had almost bowled him over. It was best to say nothing.

Serenity leaned on the counter. 'He's been living here for a few months.
I expect she'll move here too.' She gazed towards the couple. 'It must be

difficult, living in a quiet place like this after somewhere like London. I wonder what he does for a living – he looks like a journalist or a solicitor.' She grinned. 'You'll have to ask him, Hanna.'

'Me?' Hanna felt her cheeks tingle.

'The way he looked at you, I was sure you knew each other.'

Hanna glanced down at the cup in her hand, feeling suddenly awkward. 'I'll just wash this.'

There was a sudden scraping of a chair and the woman rose abruptly, flinging her handbag across her shoulder. She muttered brief words of anger and reached for her case. The man stood up as if to calm her or to apologise. She waved a hand dismissively and Hanna heard her say, 'Don't bother.'

He leaned towards her, speaking quietly, then he sat down again as she rushed towards the door, pushing it open, her case rattling across the tiles. She was clearly furious. He didn't watch her go.

Serenity hadn't noticed the argument. A tall woman with a child had come in and she was chatting happily to them, frothing a milkshake, reaching for a bag of crisps.

The man brought the coffee cup to his lips and Hanna watched his face for a reaction. His girlfriend had rushed out without so much as a goodbye. Hanna thought that he seemed resigned as he sat alone thinking. Then he collected the half-full cups, bringing them back to the counter, placing them in front of Hanna.

'Thank you.' His eyes held hers. They were filled with sadness.

For a moment, she was standing in a wide field and he was there too, holding out the gold necklace. He was wearing a red cloak pinned at the shoulder and her heart was beating hard, just as it was now. She saw herself take the necklace from him, their fingers touching, and he gazed at her with an emotion so powerful it might break her heart.

Hanna blinked and she was back in the café. She nodded to the man in exaggerated agreement. Then she picked up the cups and rushed towards the sink as if she'd been scalded. She rinsed them under the tap, but Serenity said, 'We have a dishwasher out the back – there's no need to do that.'

Hanna whirled round, but the man had gone.

The swing doors opened to let in several more customers; the train to King's Cross had just arrived and there was a bustle on the platform, a porter slamming doors. Two teenage girls approached Hanna, wearing identical blue hoodies with a white logo, members of a sports team.

'Can we get two flat whites please,' one of them said and Hanna picked up clean cups and turned to the coffee machine. She was glad of something to do, to settle the buzzing in her veins, the knot of thoughts clashing in her head.

18

It was the warmest time of the day, the sun high overhead. Addedomaros had gone. Brea stood in the orchard watching the slaves work, but there was no sign of him. She had expected to see – she wasn't sure what – a discarded whip, blood on the grass. But there was nothing. It was as if he'd never been there. She watched the slaves picking fruit. None of them met her eyes; no one would talk to her about Addedomaros. As far as they were concerned, he was in the past.

Brea returned sadly to the kitchen, where work was already underway for the evening meal. The other slaves needed help – they were often behind with their work now Brea spent so much time tending to Aurelia.

Chloe turned as she came in, her eyes round with apology, and went back to making the milk puddings flavoured with honey, pepper and a little garum.

Galyna was gutting a fish. 'Who'd have imagined that one of our slaves would steal the mistress's necklace? How foolish. He must have known there was nowhere he could keep it. Did he intend to sell it and buy his freedom?'

Chloe muttered, 'Can we stop talking about it? I'm sure it was just a moment's madness and he... he regrets it now.'

'They gave him a good thrashing, I heard,' Galyna continued. 'Then he was sent straight off to the *ludus*. The trainer there is a nasty piece of work. The slave will wish he'd kept his hands to himself. It's a hard life, being a gladiator.'

Daphne shivered. 'Poor Addedomaros. And he was so handsome.'

Brea tried to distract herself by making some wheaten flatbread, but Galyna was still keen to discuss the morning's activities. 'And you had a near miss, Brea. I thought you'd be hauled out for a whipping until the slave admitted it was him. He saved your skin, that's for sure. What did Aurelia say to you when you were in her room?'

'Nothing. She wanted to rest.' Brea was unwilling to join in the conversation.

'It's a good thing that Julia wasn't here.' Daphne rolled her eyes dramatically. 'She'd probably have taken the whip and beaten Addedomaros herself.'

Chloe cringed.

Galyna lashed out with her hand, slapping Daphne's cheek. 'Let's have some respect from you. The lady Julia is our master's daughter.'

'She always gives the male slaves a good looking over – haven't you noticed?' Daphne sulked. 'She's married to that old man with the wet eyes. I don't blame her.'

'You were his friend, Brea,' Galyna said. 'Aren't you surprised Addedomaros is a thief?'

'He isn't a thief.' Brea couldn't help herself. 'Adde is a good man. He took someone else's place.'

Chloe froze where she was, shivering. She had said too much.

'Whose place? Yours?' Daphne gasped.

'I'm no thief, nor is Adde.' Brea took a breath. 'The necklace was pressed in my hand as we stood in a huddle listening to the master speak. I have no idea who gave it to me – someone pushed past me and there it was.'

'Well, imagine.' Galyna patted her chest nervously. 'What if the necklace had been passed to me? I'd have fainted there and then.'

'I would too,' Daphne agreed.

'And I.' Chloe looked as if she'd keel over where she stood. She leaned against the table for support.

Brea briefly rested a hand against Chloe's back, her voice low with sympathy. 'How Adde was treated was harsh and cruel. We need to find a way to get him back.'

'Oh, the master will never allow him to return,' Galyna said. 'And I doubt he will thrive in the *ludus*.'

'Then we need to do something,' Brea insisted.

'What can we do?' Daphne moaned. 'We're just slaves – and women slaves, at that.'

Brea clenched her teeth as she shaped the loaves. 'There will be a way.'

'Can someone help me with this hare? It needs skinning.' Daphne was flustered. 'And there are fish to prepare.'

'I'll do it.' Chloe pushed herself forward, glad to have something to concentrate on. Brea pressed her arm gently, a complicit sign that she'd say nothing. Chloe met her eyes and mouthed, 'I didn't mean to keep it – I don't know what came over me.'

Then a slave rushed into the room and spoke to Galyna. 'The master Marcellus is in the atrium. He has just come in from riding his horse and he is asking for wine.'

Galyna rushed over to pick up a jug. 'I'll fetch it.'

'The master has asked for the slave named Brea to bring it.'

Galyna thrust the jug into Brea's hands, suddenly interested. 'Why would he ask for you specially?'

'He expects me to take a message to Aurelia,' Brea said quickly. 'That will be the reason.' She was secretly surprised that Marcellus had asked for her personally, and the thought made her breathing quicken.

She clutched the jug and a goblet and made her way up the steps where Marcellus was waiting in the atrium. He watched Brea pour wine, took the cup and drank thirstily. Eventually, he spoke. 'Brea, can you tell me what happened this morning with Aurelia's jewellery? I've just heard about it from my father.'

'Yes, I can tell you.' Brea met his eyes. 'My friend Addedomaros was wrongly accused and beaten. He has been sold to the slave trainer in the *ludus gladiatorius*. It's not right what has happened.'

'My father said that you were accused first. Is this true?'

Brea took a deep breath. She'd have to lie for the sake of others. 'The necklace was thrust into my hand. I don't know who put it there – we were all huddled in the *triclinium*. But Addedomaros said he'd stolen it to save me from a beating. He was wrongly punished.'

Marcellus frowned. 'Are you saying that my father has made a mistake?'

'Master, I am,' Brea said boldly.

'It would be the right thing to buy the slave back and bring him here, but I can't go against my father's command.' Marcellus was thoughtful. 'Perhaps I should have bought him as a slave for my sister – he could tend to her in her *domus*.'

'I think that may not be a good idea.' Brea imagined Julia's eager reaction to finding Addedomaros in her home.

'Then I've no idea how I can help…'

'Life is hard in the *ludus*, Master – the slave trainer is a harsh man.'

'Brea, I have seen many men die.' Marcellus gulped from his cup, finishing the wine. 'I've killed many, ordered the deaths of many more, women and children too. It sits heavily with me. But what can I do to save the life of one wronged slave?'

'There is much you can do – you're a kind man, powerful. I believe despite everything, there's good in your heart.'

His eyes met hers and the moment stretched. Brea couldn't look away. She was astonished by her own words: how could there be good in him after everything he had done? Marcellus murmured, 'My father has decided the fate of this slave, even if he's innocent. I cannot disobey him.'

'You could free Addedomaros,' Brea said quickly. 'You could buy him and let him go.'

'You ask me to do that?' Marcellus was astonished by her request.

'I know it's bold of me, but Adde is a good man. He doesn't deserve to be punished and,' she caught her breath, 'I trust you…'

Marcellus took in her words, nodding slowly. 'I can't go to the *ludus*. If I were seen buying that particular slave for myself, my father would hear of it. Camulodunum is full of retired generals and legionaries and they are all his friends, he feasts with them regularly. News of my actions would displease him greatly.'

'Then send me. Give me some coins and I'll buy Addedomaros in the name of an unknown master.'

'Can you do it?'

'I believe I can.'

'And you aren't afraid?'

'No. Marcus Rubrius likes the company of women, but I'm not afraid of him. The last time I met him, I kicked his shins, but he won't remember a woman's face. And I believe I can drive a bargain.'

Marcellus said gently, 'Is this slave a man you love, Brea?'

'No, but he is a friend. We understand each other.'

Marcellus's face was full of admiration. 'If you'd do this for a friend, how loyal and brave would you be for a man you loved?'

Brea looked directly into his eyes. 'I am Iceni. It is our way.'

'Then I'll trust you with silver coins. You may go to the *ludus* and see if you can buy your friend's freedom.'

Brea's eyes shone with hope. 'I won't let you down, Master.'

Marcellus smiled and his eyes were gentle. 'No, Brea, I know it.'

* * *

Brea wrapped herself in a woollen cloak against the wind that stirred up dust in the streets. She scurried past the waterworks, drawing level with the Temple of the Divine Claudius. As she always did, she paused to stare at the tall white pillars, imagining her father labouring hard, lifting stones. She could see the expression on his face, a warrior waiting for the chance to be free, to find his family.

There was no one at the temple and Brea hurried on, past the small theatre down towards the river Colne. She paused outside the *ludus gladiatorius* to listen. The training was in session; Brea could hear the lash of the whip, the groan of men fighting, the clash of swords against shields. She held her breath. The silver coins made her hand moist. Then Marcus Rubrius appeared at the door, the usual leer on his face as he clutched his small statue of Minerva.

He pawed Brea eagerly. 'Have I seen you before?' He rubbed his hands together. 'Well, I have to say, you are prettier than the usual *meretrices* they send me. The last one was a pock-faced worn-out whore, a *puella defututa* – she stank of garum and her teeth were all rotten. I was sure she'd come straight from another man's bed.' He pawed her again. 'Yes, you'll do nicely.'

Brea stood tall. 'I speak for my mistress, a woman of much importance, who wishes to buy a slave. I have money.'

Marcus Rubrius frowned. 'Who'd trust a slave with money? They'd steal it and run...'

'I mean to make a purchase for my mistress,' she reiterated.

'Let's take the money instead, and go off to the public baths together for the afternoon and have some fun. We can buy the best wine and good food, then come back here and—'

'Can you show me the slaves?' Brea insisted. 'I'll choose the one my mistress wants. She doesn't like being kept waiting.'

'Oh, you're proper snooty,' Marcus Rubrius said. 'Show me your money.'

'Only when you show me the slaves.'

Marcus Rubrius heaved a huge sigh as if he was doing Brea a favour. 'Follow me. But this is no place for a girl. My men fight hard.'

'I'm here to buy, not to have a lesson in how to wield the *gladius*,' Brea replied.

Marcus Rubrius led the way to an outdoor arena and Brea caught her breath as she gazed around. Men in loincloths were lifting heavy weights, performing push-ups, sit-ups and lunges, perspiration gleaming on their bodies. Not far away, younger men were fighting with wooden swords, while two huge older men were practising with short *gladius* swords and shields. The arena smelled acrid, of sweat and blood.

Marcus Rubrius lifted his statue of Minerva. 'I'm a lucky man. All these men belong to me. Now show me your money.'

Brea gazed around again. 'I can't see the one that I want...'

'Then pick another.'

'My mistress wants one slave in particular. He came in just this morning. He is called Addedomaros, a Trinovantes.'

'The one that Publius Julius sold to me earlier on after he'd had a whipping. I know the one.'

'So where is he?' Brea felt herself tremble. She couldn't be found out.

'Oh, you can't have him. He's inside, getting his cuts seen to.'

Brea was insistent. 'My mistress wants him. She'll pay good money.'

'Well, she'll have to ask his new owner. He was bought just an hour ago.'

'By whom?'

Marcus Rubrius's face was cunning. 'That would be saying.'

'Who bought him?'

'The lady Julia, the daughter of the old, retired general who sold him to me.' Marcus Rubrius sniffed, wiping his nose on his sleeve. 'I thought it was a lot of a fuss about nothing really – he could have just given the slave to her. Still, I got a good price for him.'

'So he's sold? He's to be a slave to Julia at her *domus*?'

'Not a slave – she wants him as a champion.'

Brea hesitated. 'A champion?'

'Yes, she's paid me to patch him up and train him, so she can send him out into the arena to fight. She picked him out specially. He'll be her champion, fighting against another gladiator just for her.'

Brea could hardly move. 'What can be done to stop it?'

Marcus Rubrius laughed. 'If you've heard of the lady Julia, you'll know, once she makes her mind up, no one will change it. She likes her own way, that one.'

'Then what will I do?' Brea felt her heart sink.

'You could choose another slave – I have plenty. Villains, thieves, men condemned to death. This place is their best chance – they get square meals and at least five fights a year. The discipline's tough here, but my men know the score – they don't have much choice. Pick another one.'

Brea looked around, despondent. 'No, I must go.' She pulled herself together. 'My mistress will be waiting.'

Marcus Rubrius gave a mock bow. 'Come back again soon with your mistress's money. I have plenty more slaves.' He guided her to the door.

It was then Brea saw him, in the far corner of the arena. He was fighting another man with a wooden sword; his leg was shackled, his hair and beard were unkempt and he was much thinner, but the thump of her heart told her immediately that it was him. She was still staring as Marcus Rubrius ushered her outside and closed the door.

Brea shuddered, feeling sudden anguish seize her heart so furiously that she wanted to cry out in more pain than she had felt for thirteen years. She had just seen her father.

19

Brea stood outside the *ludus gladiatorius*, breathing hard. She was sure it was her father: she knew him by every small movement of his body, by the expression on his face, the way her heart sang at the sight of him. She had to speak to him, to find out what had happened to her mother.

Brea was overcome with a familiar sadness; she'd never been hopeful about finding her mother – she knew what Romans did to women, how little respect they had for them. If she could only speak to her father, she'd know for sure.

Then, somehow, she'd free him.

Brea's brain pounded, thoughts rushing through her mind, one after the other. She could steal the mistress's necklace – Aurelia trusted her – and Chloe had already proved how easy it would be to prise it from her. The gold and carnelian would surely pay for her father's freedom – they could run away together, head towards the Iceni tribes in the north-east. The plan didn't sit easily with Brea – she was no thief and she was sure that Marcus Rubrius would simply take the necklace and laugh in her face. She'd need a better idea. Even if she offered him her body – and Brea would kill Marcus Rubrius with his own sword before she'd allow him to touch her – there was no guarantee that he'd release her father. The trouble was, she had no power, no value, not against this uncouth Roman man.

Brea turned back towards the villa. She'd need to be clever to find a way. More than anything, she needed an ally, and there was only one person who would help her.

She felt the silver coins in her hand, that had been intended to buy Addedomaros. She could offer the money for her father instead. But that was not what she'd agreed with Marcellus. She'd go to him honestly, ask for his support.

Her head ached, pounding with each step as she broke into a run. Her intention had been to help Adde – there had to be something she could do for him. And her father – he'd looked weak, tired. She had to find a way to help him, to help them both. Brea hoped that she could speak to Marcellus in secret. She intended to beg him to free her father.

She hurried through the gardens into the atrium, but there was no sign of Marcellus.

She was met by Daphne, who pushed a tray of bread, fruit and olives into her hand. 'Where have you been? You're summoned to take supper.'

'I was sent on an errand,' Brea began.

'Your mistress is in the *triclinium* with her brother and Julia. They've asked you to bring refreshments. Go – I'll follow with the wine and water. Julia's here to speak to the mistress and she's in a merry mood. Let's keep it that way.'

Brea took the tray and rushed towards the *triclinium*, where Aurelia was reclining on a couch, Lucius next to her, patting her hand. Julia was stretched languidly on the other couch, her *ornatrix* Balbina standing behind her silently. When she saw Brea, Julia said 'Ah, the refreshments are here at last. Put them down on the table where we can reach them, *ancilla*.'

Brea glanced at Julia, her face scornful. Addedomaros had been bought, a plaything for Julia's entertainment, and it took a great effort for her to hide her disdain. She bowed her head and did as she was told, then she stood back, waiting to be dismissed. Daphne was by her side, pouring wine into three goblets, handing them round. Brea noticed how Julia drank thirstily, as did Lucius, while Aurelia just cradled the cup in her lap.

Julia bit into an olive. 'So it's agreed. You'll accompany me to the theatre tomorrow and to the arena in three days' time.' She clapped her hands. 'We'll have a good time.'

'I'm fond of the theatre,' Lucius said. 'My sister and I would often go in Rome – my favourites were the old comedies of Terence.'

'I love a good comedy.' Julia's eyes sparkled. 'We shall have such fun. My favourite character is the *adulescens*, the unmarried man in his twenties. He is usually unspeakably handsome, and he always pursues the love of a prostitute or slave girl, which would be completely ridiculous if she wasn't later revealed to be a free-born woman, and therefore eligible for marriage.' Julia laughed. 'I always see myself playing that role.' She turned to Aurelia. 'Which character do you most favour?'

Aurelia gazed into her goblet, then fidgeted with the heavy gold band on her finger. 'I always feel sorry for the *virgo*, the young unmarried woman who is often spoken of, but remains offstage. Of course, she loves the *adulescens*, but she herself isn't important.'

'The *miles gloriosus*, the soldier, is my favourite. I've liked him best since I was a child because he is so funny.' Lucius gulped wine, speaking quickly, his eyes darting towards Julia. 'I aspire to be a great soldier. I believe a man can have no greater wish than to be brave and to fight for Rome. That's why I am so honoured that my sister will marry Marcellus.'

Brea peered at his face, the flush of pride, the gentle expression, and wondered what kind of soldier he would make.

Julia crossed her legs with a swish, revealing a thigh. 'I aways think the best thing a man can aspire to be is a great lover. In the bedroom, only he and his lady know the truth of his manhood.' She raised an eyebrow. 'Might you aspire to that, Lucius?'

Lucius's cheeks deepened in colour. 'In truth, I have little knowledge of such matters.'

'Then perhaps you need a woman who is gifted in these things to be your teacher.' Julia leaned forward. 'But more of that later. We were talking of the theatre, and the arena. I've purchased a fine slave to be my champion. I paid well for him too – the vile man who works at the *ludus gladiatorius* is just like the *leno* character in the comedy we will see – a pimp, a slave dealer. I think I've chosen well.' She smiled sweetly at Aurelia. 'You and I will watch him fight in my name and it will be a glorious sight. Of course, I'll tell Caius Fabius that it won't interest him and he can stay home. I intend to be the first to congratulate my young champion as he leaves the arena, sweat gleaming on his muscles, fresh blood on his sword.'

Aurelia shuddered. 'Perhaps just a visit to the theatre would suffice – I've more need of an uplifting comedy than a bloody contest.'

'Not at all – I won't hear of it. We're to be sisters,' Julia protested. 'You need to be tutored in the ways of a good Roman wife.' She laughed at her own joke. 'By the way, where's Marcellus? I think he's fallen in love with his new horse. It wouldn't surprise me – he shows little interest in anything else.'

Aurelia muttered, 'I believe he's in the *tablinum* with his father, discussing business matters.'

'Then we'll ask him to come here.' Julia rubbed her hands. 'I want him to come to the comedy with us tomorrow night.' Julia gestured towards Brea. 'Go and find him – what are you waiting for?'

Brea took to her heels – she was glad to have the opportunity to speak with Marcellus. She wanted to return his money, to tell him how she'd failed to free Addedomaros. And she was sure he could help her to find her father. This was her chance and she intended to seize it.

* * *

It was early evening at Bramble Wood Farm and Hanna was glad of the chance to be outdoors after working in the café all day. Nutmeg plodded along the bridle path gently, Hunter by her side, as Ollie guided them towards the woods. Hanna was wearing an old jacket of Abby's, her riding hat and boots that fitted quite well, but she still felt the cold from the stiff wind that blew the wheat in the field so that it bowed.

Ollie was impressed. 'I thought you hadn't ridden a horse in years. You're doing well.'

'Nutmeg's looking after me,' Hanna said with a smile. 'My body's like a sack of potatoes – I'm so out of practice. I didn't know there were so many bones in my bum that could ache.'

'So how was work? Are you enjoying life at the café?'

'Yes, it's great fun.' Hanna wondered for a moment how to explain the strange recurring experience with the man who'd come in today. She decided to say nothing – she thought she'd sound like a stalker or a woman obsessed. Instead, she said, 'Do you know Serenity?'

'Not well. I encountered her in The Dribbling Duck on New Year's Eve several years ago. She was totally out of it, drunk as a skunk, and she grabbed me at midnight and snogged me.' Ollie grinned. 'I quite enjoyed it, but I don't think she remembers. She's hardly spoken to me since.'

Hanna laughed. 'I can imagine her doing that.'

'Oh, she's a live wire, a party animal, I think.'

'She's great fun, Ollie. I ought to find out more about her. I just don't want to launch in with too many questions – I might seem a bit nosey.'

'I think she had a long-term partner, but they split up a while ago.'

'She said the same about you,' Hanna blurted without thinking. She placed a hand over her mouth. 'Oh, I'm sorry.'

He shrugged as if it wasn't important. 'I'm surprised Dad hasn't told you the whole gory story of me and Amber. We were engaged for six years.'

'That's a long time,' Hanna said.

'Amber thought so too. I think she lost patience with me. She dumped me for a bloke who runs a scaffolding business. She's married with a baby on the way now.'

'Her loss.' Hanna offered a warm smile.

'It probably wouldn't have worked.' Ollie pulled a face. 'She liked the idea of life on the farm, the horses, the landscape, but, in reality, I was a bit too obsessive-compulsive for her.'

'You're great as you are.' Hanna held tightly to Nutmeg's reins as Ollie leaped down from Hunter to open a gate to the woodlands.

Ollie clambered back in the saddle. 'How about you? Your mum said there was a boyfriend in China, then there wasn't.'

'She was right. I don't find it easy to settle.'

'I can understand that.' Ollie manoeuvred Hunter onto a path where trees hung low. He dipped his head beneath the branches.

'The thing is, I've never really told anyone this but...' Hanna couldn't believe that she was about to confide in him. 'I had an accident when I was thirteen – I fell from a trampoline. Since then, I've had strange dreams...'

Ollie gave her his full attention. 'What sort of dreams?'

'Dreams where I'm me, but not me, in another time, centuries ago. Me as another woman – I don't look like me, but I feel exactly what she feels. There's a man I meet, and he seems… important. There are lots of soldiers, battles and slaves building a temple. I have a necklace…'

'That's incredible,' Ollie said.

'But the really amazing thing is – I found a necklace in the pig field the other day, and it's the same as the one in my dreams. Well, Roy found it. He dug it up.'

'Where is it now?'

'In my room, in a drawer.'

'Is it valuable?'

'I don't know. It's gold with red stones. Very old, I think.'

'Can I see it?'

'Yes, of course.' Hanna felt relieved to be able to confide in Ollie. 'Look, I haven't mentioned any of this, not even to my mum. Can we keep it to ourselves for now?'

'Of course – I'm flattered that you trust me enough to tell me.' Ollie led the way into more open ground. There were trees to either side, a cluster of holly bushes.

Hanna watched Nutmeg follow Hunter calmly. 'The horses know the way.'

'It's a trek I often do,' Ollie said. 'It skirts around the farm, so I get to check the wheatfield and the pigs and a few fallow fields as I ride. It gives me time to do a lot of thinking.'

Hanna gazed up at the sky. The sunlight was glaring and bright but a cold wind was picking up, stirring the grasses. 'It's a beautiful place – I feel strangely calm here.'

'The horses like it,' Ollie agreed. 'There are one or two places they are less keen on. The pig field spooks them a bit, and Bramble Woods beyond. They don't like it there much.'

'Why?'

'I've no idea. Horses pick up things we don't, they are instinctive creatures. Maybe there's something in the air.'

'You mean like vibrations, a sense of the past?'

'Or wasps or midges?' Ollie grinned. 'How about we turn and head for home? I'm making pizza for supper. You're welcome to join me.'

'Oh, that would be nice.'

'In fact, you can help me cook it,' Ollie said hopefully. 'Then afterwards – maybe you could show me this necklace.'

'I ought to,' Hanna admitted. 'I found it on Paddy's land. Strictly speaking, it belongs to him and you.'

Ollie winked. 'It may be real treasure.' They had reached a turn in the bridle path that led through another field and he leaned forward. 'Right, Hanna, Nutmeg's been a good girl and given you an easy ride so far. How about we live a little dangerously and try a trot all the way home?'

He dug his heels in lightly and Hunter sprangled forward. Nutmeg copied the stallion's movements exactly and Hanna clung to the reins for dear life, bouncing up and down in the saddle, following Ollie with a broad smile on her face as he sped away towards home.

20

Three hours later, Hanna and Ollie stretched out on the Persian rug in his living room, a bottle of wine between them, Roy snoozing happily at Hanna's feet. On the rug, the necklace gleamed from the tissue paper it had been wrapped in.

Hanna met Ollie's eyes. 'What do you think? Is it a slice of history?'

Ollie poked it tentatively with a finger. 'It's certainly old. I'm a bit scared to touch it.'

'I think it's gold,' Hanna suggested. 'It looks like it could be.'

'We need an expert's opinion.' Ollie was thoughtful. 'Shall we try Google?'

'Good idea,' Hanna said, watching Ollie reach for his laptop. They stared at the screen together. 'What shall we start with?'

Ollie frowned. 'I told you I found a Roman coin years ago? Perhaps the necklace is Roman? It might be Iceni, though – there were a lot of tribes around here, Boudicca and her lot.'

'Let's try Iceni jewellery first then,' Hanna said, as Ollie's fingers moved on the keyboard. Images came up, chunky gold and silver torcs, brooches, bracelets and coins. She pointed at an ornate torc, a large rigid choker. 'None of these look similar – our necklace is delicate. Give Roman jewellery a go.'

Ollie's fingers tapped again and another image appeared. There were coloured gemstones, gold and silver jewellery fashioned in intricate designs. As Ollie scrolled down, they both stared at a wide banded gold ring with an elaborate engraving, then a carnelian necklace with a huge gold pendant, a stone in its centre.

'That's just like it,' Hanna gasped. 'What do you think?'

Ollie glanced at the necklace and back at the screen. 'It looks like it could be.' He was thoughtful. 'What shall we do now?'

'Find someone we can talk to about it.'

'Where would we start?' Ollie frowned. 'I was about ten when I found the coin – I can't remember who we told about it, but I think it was probably the *King's Lynn News*.'

Hanna raised an eyebrow. 'Can I try?'

'Of course.' Ollie slid the laptop towards her and watched as Hanna typed in *Cambridge University – archaeology*.

A website came up immediately, and Hanna scrolled through names, clicking on one then another. Then she said, 'He's our man. Dr Roland Keys, Professor of Archaeology. Look.'

They both stared at a photograph of a white-haired man standing in a museum, a gleeful smile on his face as he clutched an Iceni torc necklace proudly.

Hanna was delighted. 'I bet he'll be able to tell us all about it. Let's see if we can email him. I think if we try his name plus @arch.cam.ac.uk, it will get to him.'

'Hanna, you're a genius,' Oliver said. 'I'll take a photo of the necklace, shall I, and attach it. That should whet his whistle.'

'Great idea.'

Twenty minutes later, the email was sent, complete with a perfect photograph of the necklace.

Ollie reached out to pour more wine into their glasses and Hanna rubbed Roy's ears. He stirred, his tail wagging twice, then he settled back down to sleep. Ollie stretched his arms. 'That pizza we made was scrumptious. I'd never have thought of putting wilted spinach on there.'

'Successful night all around then.' Hanna grinned. 'And your dad and my mum think we're here talking about their wedding.'

'Perhaps we ought to,' Ollie suggested. 'It's only two weeks away.'

'I need to get organised.' Hanna yawned. 'I haven't found a dress Mum approves of yet...'

'Dad's got me trussed up in a penguin suit.' Ollie pulled a face. 'And we have speeches to write. Or,' Ollie had an idea, 'I have some soya ice cream in the freezer – salted caramel. We could finish it off.'

'Pure decadence,' Hanna exclaimed. 'Why not? Who said that Saturday nights in Little Rymer were dull?'

* * *

Brea stood outside the *tablinum* for a long time, waiting to be summoned. Publius Julius and Marcellus were talking. Brea looked down at her feet on the mosaic tiles: it was quite usual for the Roman masters and mistresses to talk freely, whether slaves were listening or not. It didn't matter – slaves were not deemed important enough to understand and, if they did, there would be no one else to talk to about it. There would be a beating at any sign of disrespect or disobedience.

Brea listened carefully; she believed that everything the Romans spoke about created a picture of the lives they led, and she might find the information useful.

Publius Julius sounded excited. 'Suetonius speaks highly of you. He says in his letter that he is pleased you'll be joining him on the Island of Mona. You've developed a reputation as a strong leader, Marcellus.'

There was a pause, then Marcellus said, 'Thank you, Father. I could only ever be half the man you are.'

Publius Julius chuckled with pleasure; he enjoyed flattery. 'Well, the sooner we have you married and away to battle, the better.' His voice changed, a tone of complicity. 'So, this new bride we've got for you. What do you think of her?'

'I like her well enough,' Marcellus answered humbly.

'She's very quiet, but dutiful. I think she'll improve over time, as she settles to life here. She needs a few babies to keep her busy. She is a little thinner than I'd hoped – she has no appetite. She'd do well to eat properly.

Now, a woman like Julia, she's built for childbearing...' He scratched his sparse hair. 'How come she has no sons yet? I can't understand it.'

'Who knows?' Marcellus said cryptically. 'Julia does just as she wishes – I dare say she'll have children when she wants them.'

'So.' Publius Julius waved the paper in his hand. 'Back to my message from Gaius Suetonius Paulinus. He's very impressed by the way you handled the incident with the Iceni tribe. Firm and direct. He writes that he's delighted that you're joining him after your wedding to deal with the wretched Druids. They practise human sacrifice, you know, and our gods don't approve, so Jupiter will be with you in battle. Our great Emperor Claudius declared Druidic practices illegal six years ago, and these defiant barbarians need to be destroyed. Suetonius says he'll be glad of your leadership alongside him. So much so that he will arrive here two weeks after your wedding to feast with us. It is a good opportunity for you, for your career, to receive him here to be entertained. We will have boar, venison, wild goat, mutton, lamb. Then we'll finish the meal with cakes filled with honey and enough wine to swim in. We'll do all we can to impress him, and Aurelia must be a good hostess. After the meal, he'll stay overnight and you'll leave with him for Mona the following morning.' Publius Julius sounded pleased. 'What do you think of that?'

'It will be a great honour to welcome him to our *domus*.'

'Julia will be there of course, and Caius Fabius.'

'Aurelia will be mistress – it'll be her first duty.' Marcellus sighed, as if it might prove difficult. 'Of course, our slaves are efficient workers. All will be well.'

The mention of slaves reminded Publius Julius that Brea had been waiting for a long time. He turned to her sharply. 'What do you want, *ancilla*?'

'My lady Julia would like to talk to the master Marcellus in the *triclinium*. I have been sent to bid him to come.'

Publius Julius wasn't listening. 'Just remember what I've said to you, my son. Suetonius is a great leader and he thinks highly of you. We must do all we can to keep in his favours. But now my slaves are waiting for me in the *balneum* so I'll take my leave.'

His toga rustling, Publius Julius swept away and Brea found herself face to face with Marcellus.

She held out her hand, offering him the two silver coins. 'Here's your money, Master. I didn't spend it.'

Marcellus lowered his voice. 'Could you not buy the slave?'

Brea shook her head sadly. 'Your sister has already sponsored him. He'll be her champion in the arena.'

'Then I don't know what I can do.' Marcellus paused. 'That's a hard life for a young man. It's a great shame.'

'Master...' Brea paused. She wasn't sure how to say the next words.

'What worries you, Brea?'

'I think I saw my father there.'

Marcellus was puzzled. 'You saw your father at the *ludus*? He's a fighter?'

'I haven't seen him in thirteen years.' Brea swallowed hard. 'But I saw him today, I recognised his face. He didn't see me. But I know it's him, just as I know my own hands.'

'What are you asking me to do?'

Brea wondered if she should fall to her knees, grasp the hem of his toga and beg. 'My father will be approaching fifty years. He shouldn't be in the arena, a laughing stock for people to heckle while he fights with men half his age. He's a proud warrior, Master, just as you are.'

'I suppose I could offer to buy him as one of my slaves.'

'My people are not meant for slavery,' Brea replied quickly.

Marcellus shook his head sadly. 'I need to think about it.'

'What do you need to think about, Master? You're rich and powerful – you do as you wish and you have a life of privilege and luxury. In your place, I would've already...' Brea covered her mouth. Her tongue had run away with her. She examined his face for signs of anger or impatience, but he was smiling.

'You're indeed a very special young woman.' He touched her shoulder warmly. 'I understand you're troubled by what you saw at the *ludus*. But we need to be sure that your father is there and if he is, then we must find a way to help him. I've also not forgotten the slave, your friend, who was sold unjustly because he spoke up for you. I respect loyalty. I wasn't suggesting that I wasn't moved by your story. I am. I was merely explaining that I need time to think, to find the most practical way to bring these men to safety.'

'I'm sorry for my hot-headedness,' Brea began.

'No, you speak from passion, from the heart,' Marcellus said. 'I admire it more than I can say.'

Brea met his eyes, her own fierce with determination. 'Then you'll help me?'

'I'll do my best.' Marcellus thought for a moment. 'Do you know how many days it is until the next spectacle in the arena?'

'Three days, I believe – your sister's arranging a visit for you and my mistress and her brother.'

'Then we have time. I'll work out the best way to discover if your father is there and what I can do to free him.'

'Master, thank you from my heart.'

'Brea...' Marcellus's eyes were dark with thought. 'Tomorrow, when you have dressed Aurelia and brought the meal to the *triclinium*, I'd like you to go to the orchard and find flowers for her room. I'll be back from my ride by then and I'll meet you in the atrium and take them from you, so that I can give them to her myself. There, I'll be able to tell you what we can do for your father.' He shook his head. 'I know the trainer from the *ludus*. He's an avaricious man, and a lewd one.'

'I know it too,' Brea agreed.

'We'll have to be careful. No one must know we're doing this, other slaves or your mistress Aurelia. No one.'

'Of course.' Brea had no intention of breathing a word. 'Thank you, Master.'

Marcellus nodded once. 'I must go to my sister now. I've kept her waiting long enough.'

Brea watched him go and her heart leaped. He'd agreed to help her: she couldn't believe her good fortune. Brea whispered a little prayer to Andred, asking that her master Marcellus would be safe in the wars he would fight throughout his life, that he'd return home a hero. She was beginning to admire him more than she could express.

21

Hanna's dream was more vivid than ever, and it shook her to the core. She was standing in a wide field, mist rising from the damp earth. The sound of combat was a dull thrum all around, as if her mind had blocked it out. She was wearing the gold necklace, facing someone who was threatening her, speaking boldly, her lips moving soundlessly. A voice in her ears was mocking. *'You are no Roman woman.'*

In her dream, Hanna threw down her sword. She was determined not to fight; the stakes were somehow too high: she would lose. She wondered how to escape. She was surrounded by shadows moving in the haze, and she felt desperately sad.

Holding her head high, she said, 'I'll return to my people, and that will be an end to it.' Then she was running for her life, darting one way, dodging soldier's swords, changing direction. She reached a clearing. There were a few trees in front of her. If she could get to the forest, she might be safe.

In her dream, Hanna felt the lurch of her heartbeat. The necklace dug into her palms, she was holding it so tightly. She stopped to look at it, and the garnet stones had become drops of blood embedded deep in her hands, the gold chain made round holes in her skin.

The necklace was snatched into the air by unseen hands and she ran for the woods as fast as she could, her feet sinking into marshy ground, wet mud spattering her dress. There was a noise, a loud whoosh through the air like a sigh. Then her face was against the damp earth and she couldn't breathe. Her mouth was crammed with dirt, her nostrils full of it, and she thought that she might die. There was a loud drumming noise behind her, an urgent sound of running feet.

Hanna opened her eyes quickly and gasped to fill her lungs. She was suddenly wide awake. There it was, the noise, tap, tap, tap, filling the room, breaking the silence. She sat up in bed and looked around into the darkness.

It came again, a low patter against the window, as if a branch was being buffeted against the pane once, then once more.

Hanna listened, her ears straining. Nothing for a few moments, then again, a low rhythmic bang of something light against glass. She froze. There weren't any trees outside the window.

The sound was louder, more insistent. Hanna slid out of bed and moved slowly towards the curtains. She needed to convince herself that there was nothing to worry about.

There was another rattle, then silence. Hanna stood listening, waiting. She held both curtains in her fists and took a breath, then drew them back quickly. But there was no branch outside the window, no bird pecking the pane. Nothing.

She stared into the field below, not able to make out the boundaries of fence and hedge in the absolute darkness. Everything was in shadow. Then she saw a movement, a thin trail of gauze. She stared harder. It was there again, a waft of mist, a lightness against the dark, a moving shape crossing the field. It shifted quickly, as if in a hurry, then the transparent slice of light seemed to pause. Hanna thought she could make out an arm, a body that turned on the air and looked towards her for a moment. It was her – the woman she'd seen so many times. The spirit lifted a hand towards her as if beckoning. Then she was gone.

Hanna's skin was ice cold. She rushed back into bed and snuggled into the warmth of the duvet, but she was shivering. She closed her eyes tightly and hoped that sleep would come and that, when it did, the dreams would leave her alone. She was exhausted.

* * *

The following morning, Hanna woke feeling surprisingly energised. Paddy was in a jovial mood at breakfast, offering to take everyone to lunch. A family walk through the woodlands ended up in The Dribbling Duck in Little Rymer. Ollie chose a nut roast, while Paddy selected the roast beef and Stephanie fretted about whether her wedding dress would fit if she had a pudding. Hanna was surrounded by her new family, enjoying the perfect Sunday together, and she was consumed by happiness. For a while, all thoughts of her dreams were forgotten.

The next day, Hanna stayed indoors, perpetual rain falling outside the windows. In the evening at supper, Stephanie served up a hearty stew for the three of them, claiming that it felt like winter so she was going to cook winter food.

Paddy helped himself to a huge plateful as Roy tucked himself dutifully beneath the table in case any scraps fell. 'I've been a bit worried about two of the piglets today.'

'Why?' Stephanie sat down, her face anxious. 'They can't be more than a few weeks old.'

'Suckling,' Paddy said. 'I'll have to keep an eye on them.'

'What's wrong with them?' Hanna asked.

'I wouldn't be surprised if it isn't coccidiosis. I'm not sure – early signs, perhaps.'

'That sounds serious,' Stephanie said.

'It's an annoying protozoal disease that affects the small intestine and causes scour in suckling piglets,' Paddy explained. 'I'll know if it is. They get watery diarrhoea that smells so foul you can hardly go near it.'

'Paddy!' Stephanie was shocked. 'It's mealtime.'

Paddy tucked into the stew, unbothered. 'It might be worth getting someone to give me another opinion. I've had it before with piglets, it's not uncommon – it's easily remedied with medication.'

'Oh, that's good.' Stephanie sighed.

'Of course, the worst stuff for a bad stink in pigs' droppings is swine flu. I went to a farm once where the pigs had it years ago, and the smell was the most awful stench—'

'Paddy!' Stephanie had heard enough. 'We're eating. Please.'

Hanna was laughing, wondering how her mild mother was going to transform herself into a hardy farmer's wife. Then an idea came to her. 'Mum, how about we go to Norwich tomorrow and look for a dress for me to wear to your wedding?'

Stephanie flapped a hand in front of her face, as if to get rid of the memory of the pigs. 'Oh, yes please, Hanna – let's discuss the wedding. Anything rather than talk about animal poo at the table.'

'I only said that pigs can sometimes smell a bit—'

'Paddy!' Stephanie gave him a warning glance that changed quickly to one of affection. 'I don't want anything to change about you. I love you dearly. I'm marrying a fabulous farmer and that's a wonderful thing – but no pigs at the dinner table, dear.'

'Very well, Steph.' Paddy grinned. 'Have we got anything for pudding? That'll shut me up for a while.'

'I have some apple crumble.'

'Nice.' Paddy finished the plate of stew. 'I'll have a drop of cream with mine. Lovely.'

* * *

Hanna slept well on Monday evening; she pushed the dreams to the back of her mind and tried to forget about the tapping fingers against the windowpane and the misty shape she'd seen in the field below. She was determined to concentrate on her mother's wedding, which was only twelve days away.

On Tuesday, they went to Norwich and Hanna bought a dress in the first shop they visited. They both saw the cream-coloured silk maxi dress with bright flowers around the border. It immediately satisfied Stephanie's desire for something that would complement her own dress and Hanna's craving for something a little more individual. Stephanie insisted on buying it straight away and they made for the nearest coffee shop to celebrate.

They bought cappuccinos in a busy café with wooden tables and chairs and a huge window. Stephanie took her tray to an armchair and low table, where she could watch the shoppers pass by in the sunshine. She sighed happily. 'Ah, this is the life.'

'It is,' Hanna agreed as she joined her, taking a huge mouthful of coffee, wiping a milky moustache from her lip.

'And I'm just so excited about the wedding, Hanna. I can hardly sleep.' Stephanie smiled at the thought. 'I suppose that's silly at my age.'

'Not at all,' Hanna said. 'You'll be a lovely bride.'

'I should have asked you before but...' Stephanie leaned forward, her face suddenly anxious. 'You do like Paddy, don't you?'

'I think he's a star – he's warm and funny and he loves you, Mum. And he makes me smile.'

Stephanie was unconvinced. 'You've never really had a proper father figure. I mean, not that you need one at your age but – well – Paddy will be a sort of stepfather, I suppose.'

'He will – and I'm delighted. I love being at the farm. And there's Ollie, he's a star too.'

Stephanie glanced up as she sipped her drink. 'You do like him, Hanna?'

'I think he's great.'

'You've been getting on well. You had dinner round his house.'

'I did.' Hanna suddenly became aware of where the conversation was leading. 'He's just like a brother, Mum.'

Stephanie seemed disappointed. 'A brother – nothing more?'

Hanna waved the idea away. 'What can be better than a brother? I never had one.'

'What about a boyfriend?'

'Ollie? I don't think so – to be honest, Mum, I've never really thought of it – although I have seen him practically naked.'

'You have?' Stephanie spluttered into her cappuccino.

'When I went round last week to invite him to supper, he'd just got out of the shower. He came to the door in a towel and he had no idea who I was.'

Stephanie smothered a laugh. 'I'd like to have seen that.' She tried again. 'I mean, I wouldn't – he's practically my stepson – I just meant that it must have been hilarious.'

'It was.' Hanna reached over and pressed her mother's hand affectionately. 'It's so nice to be home.'

Stephanie looked alarmed. 'Does that mean you're thinking of going off again already? You've just arrived...'

'I've no plans to go anywhere,' Hanna soothed.

'It's just – I was saying to Paddy – and he agrees with me...' Stephanie's eyes were misty with emotion. 'It's so good to have you back with us. I did miss you when you were in China. I'd love it if you met someone special and stayed in Norfolk. Do you think you might?'

'Stay?'

'No.' Stephanie shook her head. 'Do you think you might meet *the one*?'

Hanna exhaled patiently. 'When I do, you'll be the first to know.'

'Oh, that would be my dream. Another wedding, maybe next year, but at the church in Little Rymer, not the registry office in King's Lynn like me and Paddy. I can imagine you in a white dress, just like Kate Middleton wore, with a long train...'

'Mum.' Hanna laughed. 'You're getting a bit ahead of yourself.'

Her phone pinged and Hanna picked it up, reading the email quickly. It was from someone called Roly Keys, and it took Hanna a few seconds to work out who he was. He said he was very excited about her find, that he wanted to come over from Cambridge and meet her at the earliest opportunity and look at the necklace – he believed it might be quite special.

Hanna was thoughtful for a moment. It could be awkward: she hadn't told her mother or Paddy about the necklace, nor had she mentioned that she and Ollie had contacted Dr Keys and that he was an archaeologist. She wondered how to bring them together, then an idea came to her. She'd create the perfect opportunity for the whole family to be a part of the discussion about the necklace.

Stephanie stood up, smoothing her skirt. 'I'm just popping to the ladies.'

'Right, Mum.' Hanna watched her go and smiled. She took the opportunity to reply.

Dr Keys – can you come round tomorrow? The necklace was found on my step-father's land and I'd like to include the whole family in our discussion. We could sit down for lunch and look at it together?

An answer came back almost immediately.

The train from Cambridge takes less than an hour. I'll be at the station at 11.45 tomorrow. Can someone meet me to drive me to your house?

Hanna replied.

I'll be there – looking forward to it.

Seconds later, the phone pinged again.

Splendid. I'm sure the necklace will give us a lot to talk about.

Stephanie returned to her seat, sipping the last of her drink. 'Well, what shall we do now? Do you want to do more shopping or shall we go and sit in Waterloo Park and enjoy the glorious summer sunshine?'

'I need to shop for ingredients for lunch, Mum.' Hanna gave a mock-guilty smirk. She ought to have said something to her mother before now. 'There's something Ollie and I need to tell you and Paddy and it's really exciting.'

'You've changed your mind – you've fallen in love?' Stephanie teased.

'No, it's better than that. You're both going to be really intrigued, but you'll have to wait until tomorrow. Oh, I can't wait to tell Ollie.'

Stephanie stood up, picking up her handbag. 'The suspense is already killing me – you'll have to give me a clue.'

'Well.' Hanna wrapped an arm around her mother. 'We have a gentleman coming from Cambridge tomorrow for lunch. He's an archaeologist. And I'm picking him up from the station in Little Rymer to show him something exciting I found in the pig field. But that's all I'm telling you for now – you'll have to wait to find out more.'

22

The *culina* was filled with the smell of cooking even before dawn broke. Daphne and Chloe were stirring huge pots of porridge, which the slaves would eat with flatbread and fruit before beginning their labours. Galyna was making wheat bread and Brea busied herself with fresh biscuits for the master's breakfast. Brea hummed as she worked; already, she was imagining her father free, riding back to his tribe. Then, one day, she'd join him. She was sure of it.

'You've no time for singing, Brea – there's too much to do.' Galyna was irritable this morning.

'You can give me a hand with the porridge if you've finished.' Daphne panted. 'It's hot work.'

'I won't be a minute – let me just finish the biscuits.' Brea smiled.

'Old White Beard has been talking about all the things he's ordered for the wedding,' Galyna grumbled. 'They are bringing food on a boat from Rome and from Africa too, and other places I can't remember the names of. No expense is being spared. There will be many guests and we are to wear clean robes and serve food. Chloe, you are to stand by with bowls of water, so the guests may wash their hands after each morsel. And there will be so much food from sellers in Camulodunum – oysters, eggs, sardines. The master wants seven dishes of fish, meat and poultry, vegetables and he's asked for sauces – extra fishy *liquamen* and juicy *frutum*. We'll have to prepare the bread and the cake here in the *culina*.'

'We'll be so busy, we'll be worn out.' Chloe fanned her face. 'But at least we'll get to see the bride in her beautiful wedding robe. And all the jewellery.' She met Brea's eyes and blushed, remembering the necklace. Chloe tried again. 'It must be wonderful to be marrying a man like master Marcellus.'

Daphne snorted. 'They don't seem to be making any effort to get to know each other. Everyone says the master spends all his time with his new horse, and Aurelia just lies on her bed and stares at the ceiling. I think it would be good if they could come to like each other.'

'They don't need to like each other,' Galyna said. 'She must do her duty as a wife and he must fight the Druids and take over this *domus* when old White Beard dies.' She glanced towards Brea. 'What are you tempting him with this morning? He has no appetite half the time. And the young mistress eats like a bird, pecking this, nibbling that and leaving the rest.'

Chloe indicated the pot of porridge. 'I'm going to have some of this before the garden slaves get to it. They always have more than their fair share and I'm starving.'

'We're hungry because we work hard. All Aurelia does is lie on her back all day.' Daphne gave a raucous laugh. 'Mind you, she'll do that a lot more once she's married – perhaps that will give her an appetite.'

A slap came from nowhere and Daphne put a hand to her sore cheek. Galyna snapped, 'Hold your tongue – don't dare to speak that way about your betters.'

Daphne sulked, turning to the huge pot of porridge, helping herself to a bowl.

Galyna shaped the wheat dough into loaves. 'You spend time with the mistress, Brea. Tell us – is she sick with love for the master Marcellus? Does she lie on her bed and sigh for him, or is it her home and family in Rome that she is sick for? I have heard many say that she will fade away once her brother leaves for war.'

'*You're* gossiping now,' Daphne grumbled, scuttling away sharply as Galyna raised a hard hand.

'My mistress is a good woman. I think it must be difficult for her to adjust to life in Camulodunum.' Brea's mind was elsewhere. 'In my tribe, a man and a woman share everything equally – work, making decisions, food, family, war, love. It is an honourable life. Here, a woman is no more than a slave to a man. She wears his fine clothes and jewellery, she's his possession. I don't envy her such a life. It is better to be a slave. At least there's honesty in work.'

'But to marry someone like the master Marcellus?' Daphne was staring. 'I would gladly be possessed by such a man.'

'No man will ever want to possess you.' Chloe laughed. 'You stink of fishy garum.'

'Nor you,' Daphne retorted. 'Who'd want a woman who smells of clammy porridge?'

'It's the same for us all,' Galyna agreed. 'We'll be working flat out here until the day we drop.'

Brea lifted her tray of fruit and honey. 'I'm off to wake Aurelia.' She was looking forward to her meeting with Marcellus. 'Then I'm heading to the gardens – I've been asked to fill her room with flowers.'

'I'll take the tray to the *triclinium*, then.' Galyna busied herself with placing pancakes on a dish. She turned to Chloe and Daphne with a smirk. 'It's your job to feed the slaves with the porridge. Good luck with the starving hordes,' she grunted. 'Here we go, another long, hard day to struggle through until I can rest my poor aching feet.'

Brea clambered up the stairs towards Aurelia's *cubiculum* to find her lying on her bed, staring at the heavy gold ring on her finger. As Brea brought in her tray, she heard a loud sigh.

'Good morning, Mistress.' Brea placed the tray on a low table. 'Shall I dress you, then you can eat?'

Aurelia didn't move. 'I'm not sure I want to rise this morning. Marcellus has told me that he wishes to take me out, but I would prefer to stay here.'

Brea frowned. She wondered where Marcellus intended to take his bride-to-be, and if he would help Brea to find her father first. 'So – where is he planning to take you? Perhaps to the lady Julia's villa on the other side of Camulodunum?'

Aurelia rolled over languidly. 'Julia wishes me to be her friend, her sister, but in truth I'm nothing like her. Spending time with Lucius is my only joy, but soon he'll be away with the Ninth Legion.' She eased herself to a sitting position. 'Do you think me foolish, Brea? I live here in a beautiful house but I long to go home.'

Brea met her eyes. 'I long for home too, Mistress. And I believe that one day, I'll return to my tribe. Maybe you will too.'

Aurelia was surprised. 'Do you think we will? It's what my heart yearns for.'

'Mine too. And yes, I think it's good to wish to go back to the place we came from. It's where we belong.'

'Then we are the same, you and I.' Aurelia had tears in her eyes. 'I pray that you're right.'

'I pray for it every day.' Brea helped Aurelia to stand and held up a grey robe. 'Until then, we must be strong.'

'We must,' Aurelia said and Brea saw something in her mistress's expression that she'd never noticed, the beginnings of an inner determination, the will to survive.

Brea smiled. 'Perhaps you and I are on the same path, Mistress. We must wait for our time. It will come.'

'I believe it will. Yes, your words have encouraged me, Brea.'

'Our hands must be busy while our hearts are filled with hope.'

'That's true. I must learn to be a wife, and then a mother. Who knows – one day I may find a reason to take my children to Rome to visit my parents and to teach them about where they came from. I could show them the baths, the temples, the aqueducts and basilicas.' Aurelia's face had taken on a new sheen. 'When that day comes, I'll take them with me across the seas and never return to Camulodunum.'

'And I'll return to my own people and live as an equal,' Brea said determinedly.

Aurelia seemed taller than she had been before. She tilted her chin. 'Come – I'll wear my pale blue robe today, not this drab grey one. It brings out the colour of my eyes and the blush of my cheeks. I wish to look my best for my new husband-to-be...'

* * *

Three hours later, Brea rushed back to the kitchen with the empty tray. Aurelia had eaten everything, then she'd asked Brea to accompany her to the *balneum*, where she was oiled, washed and emerged from the water feeling cheered. She was now in the *triclinium*, talking to Lucius about how much she was looking forward to their trip with Marcellus later in the afternoon. Brea smiled to herself; Aurelia had turned a corner, perhaps she'd grow into the role of lady of the *domus* after all.

It felt strange to be in the garden without Addedomaros to talk to. Brea realised how much she missed him as she waited for the slave Kastor, whose expression was always blank, to bring her the flowers that had been ordered for Aurelia's room. Brea thanked him briefly as he filled her arms with sweetly fragrant blooms, but Kastor left without a word. She could tell by his empty eyes that he worked without hope, each day the routine existence of a slave. And now Addedomaros had been sold to the *ludus gladiatorius*, the others knew they were one mistake away from following him. Brea's heartbeat quickened; she was different. She believed that Marcellus would help her. She'd never lose hope.

Her feet pounded on the stone steps that led to the atrium. Marcellus wasn't there, but Chloe was approaching, an empty tray in her hands. Brea looked around for Marcellus; she couldn't wait for long: she'd be seen and questioned. She hesitated, fussing with the flowers – if anyone asked, she was rearranging the bouquet for her mistress's room.

Chloe paused. 'Those flowers are so beautiful.' She sniffed the petals. 'The mistress's room must smell like Mount Olympus.'

'I'm ordered to fetch fresh blooms – they cheer her,' Brea said.

'I just saw the lady with master Lucius Aurelius in the *triclinium*. I'm to bring them more water and fruit. She seemed in good spirits, laughing and talking – do you know, she actually looked happy,' Chloe whispered.

'I'm pleased she is growing stronger. The air in Camulodunum must agree with her,' Brea said quickly, wishing Chloe would be on her way.

'I was hoping they'd leave some scraps from their tray for me to eat. The porridge barely filled me this morning and we didn't have enough flatbread to go round. Galyna slapped me because she said I didn't make enough.'

'I'll find you some leftovers after supper,' Brea said quickly.

There were footsteps behind her – Marcellus was coming in from the garden. Her eyes searched his for news as he drew level with her.

'You have brought the flowers for my lady's room, *ancilla*? Then I'll take them to her myself.' He took the blooms and turned to Chloe, his expression impatient. 'Have you no work to do?'

Chloe scurried away.

Marcellus glanced towards Brea and murmured, 'This afternoon, Aurelia will summon you to go with her into Camulodunum. I have persuaded her and Lucius to visit the *ludus* with me and Julia to inspect the slave she sponsors as her champion. It will give me the chance to see how your friend Addedomaros fares. And you must find a chance to slip away and find your father. If he is there, tell him to be hopeful. I'll find a way of freeing him if I can.'

'Master, I'm grateful...' Brea began, the words coming from her heart.

'Say no more.' Marcellus's voice was hushed. 'We mustn't be overheard. Now I'll take the flowers to my lady's room and she can arrange them there. She'll send for you soon to inform you that you'll go with her. Say nothing of this until then.'

'Master,' Brea muttered as Marcellus strode away and was gone. She took a deep breath.

It was going to happen. After so many years of hoping and praying, she was going to see her father.

23

It was late, almost twelve o'clock. Hanna sat on the edge of her bed in pyjamas, deep in thought. She loved the pretty bedroom, the bright yellow wallpaper and the soft down duvet. By day, it was a cheerful sun-filled room to relax in and read. But at night-time, a new feeling of dread came over her as soon as she opened the door. The dreams would come; she'd fall into the midst of them as soon as she closed her eyes and experience the fears of the other person whose skin she filled. But there was something else – a new terror had found its way into her emotions and stayed there. The rapping that she'd heard against the window had unsettled her more than she realised. She recalled the faint outline of moving mist below that had assumed a human shape. Hanna shivered, visualising the woman at the station when she'd first arrived. She was sure it was the same person she'd seen watching her in the field as she picked up the necklace.

She hadn't forgotten Yue's words: 'Someone else is searching, just as you search. She is not at rest.'

Hanna was suddenly cold. Instinctively, she moved to the window and pulled back the curtains, staring into the shadowy field below. She half expected a solitary figure to be standing in the mist, waiting. There was no one there. She reminded herself that tomorrow was going to be an exciting day. The archaeologist was coming to lunch. She'd show her mother and

Paddy the necklace and ask Dr Roly Keys what his opinion was. Hanna snuggled into bed and promised herself a good night's sleep. Once she discovered the story behind the necklace, she hoped the dreams would stop.

The face of the man in the café popped into her mind, she recalled the moment their eyes met, the intensity of their mutual gaze. Hanna wondered about the connection, if it was nothing more than attraction: but he was the same man who appeared in her dreams. Perhaps she subconsciously superimposed his face there after she'd seen him? He certainly wasn't interested in her – he had a girlfriend. No, Hanna could explain her giddy behaviour easily: it had been a while since her last romantic entanglement – she was simply out of practice. It was nothing more than that, a chance meeting with a handsome man who was unavailable. She'd forget him.

She rolled over and closed her eyes; she was cosy and warm, and sleep lifted her gently.

* * *

Hanna woke next morning, the sun filtering a narrow strip through a gap in the curtains, brightening the pillow. She stretched languidly – she'd slept deeply and was refreshed. It was early, just six, but she leaped from her bed, dressed quickly and rushed downstairs, her hair tousled.

Paddy was sitting at the table, tucking into eggs as Stephanie stood at the Aga pouring coffee. She was surprised to see Hanna. 'You're up early.'

'I've got a lot to do.' Hanna grabbed a mug and filled it with coffee, taking a deep sip. 'I'm preparing lunch, then I'm going to pick up Dr Keys.'

Paddy waved a dismissive hand. 'Oliver was going on about this yesterday – apparently, our visitor's an archaeologist and he's very interested because you found some ole relic in the pig field. Is that right?'

'Exactly.' Hanna sat down. 'I want to show it to you at lunchtime and ask Dr Keys his opinion. I might as well tell you – it's a necklace and it looks like it's made of gold.'

'Real gold?' Stephanie was interested. 'Can we see it now?'

'I've got it wrapped in tissue in a drawer,' Hanna said.

'Gold, though. You might become rich, Paddy,' Stephanie joked. 'Who knows what else is in the pig field? Perhaps there are matching earrings in the mud too.'

Paddy didn't laugh. 'There are rules about these things, once you find old treasure. I went through it all when Oliver found the coin as a youngster. It has to be reported to a coroner if it's of cultural or historical interest. The museums want to know about it too.' He scratched his head. 'It might have been better if you'd left it in the ground.'

Hanna was surprised. 'But wait till you see it, Paddy. It's really old and so beautiful. I'd love to know who it belonged to. And Dr Keys is fascinated by the photo I sent.'

'As long as nobody disturbs my pigs, I'm happy enough to go along with people digging around,' Paddy grunted. 'Right, well I'll be off, Steph. I'll be back at one o'clock for lunch, mind. I'm not missing some good grub and I want to get to the bottom of all this fuss and nonsense about a necklace. I wouldn't be surprised if it isn't some piece of tacky old rubbish from Woolworths.'

'Woolworths, remember that place?' Stephanie exclaimed. 'That takes me back. I was a Saturday girl at Woollies in King's Lynn when I was a teenager.'

'I do. I used to love the pick and mix,' Paddy grunted. 'Oliver and I will be working in the field across from the pigs, if you need us. What's for lunch, Hanna? Are we having tofu again?'

'I'm playing it safe and doing a buffet.'

'What, a couple of vol-au-vents and a wilting salad?' Paddy laughed. 'Your archaeologist will still be starving hungry by the end of it.'

'Not at all.' Hanna grinned. 'We're having chaat masala potatoes, quiche, cauliflower wings, pâté, hummus, bread, tabbouleh – and I have some salmon.'

'I don't know what half of that is – but I'll get it down me.' Paddy shook his head as he struggled into his jacket. 'Well, I look forward to the lunch and to meeting your Cambridge doctor. It should be very interesting to hear what he has to say.'

'Maybe it is treasure, and we'll be on TV.' Stephanie kissed Paddy's cheek. 'So, Hanna, let's have some breakfast, then we'll get started on lunch.' She offered a warm smile. 'I'm guessing you'll need a hand with all those dishes.'

'Thanks, Mum. So – you made the bread yesterday, and I did the potatoes last night, and the pâté and quiche are bought, but yes, please.'

Hanna finished her coffee and stood up quickly. She paused. For a moment, she leaned against the table and closed her eyes. The image of the woman in the mist came back to her and she shook her head to clear her vision.

Hanna turned to her mother and instinctively lowered her voice. 'I have a strange feeling about the necklace, Mum. There's something special about it. I'm desperate to find out what it is.'

* * *

At eleven forty, Hanna parked the Range Rover at the station and rushed across the bridge to the platform. She paused at Serenity's café to wave through the open door; Serenity grinned and waved in reply, turning her attention to the coffee machine and a line of customers.

Hanna gazed along the platform where groups of passengers huddled against the draught that funnelled from the tracks, waiting for the train. She was cold; despite the late August sunshine, the air hung like ice on the platform.

A tinny voice in the speakers announced that the eleven forty-five from Cambridge would arrive shortly. Several passengers shuffled forwards and Hanna stared into the distance, waiting for a glimpse of the train. She had to admit she felt excited, her heart jumpy. Meeting an archaeologist was going to be interesting, but what really thrilled her was that she could be so close to finding out about the origin of the necklace. At times, just holding it between her fingers took her straight back to the moment she clutched it in the dream.

A gust of wind buffeted along the rails, picking up a stray piece of newspaper, tossing it in the air. It dropped between the tracks and flapped. Hanna watched it flutter, pushing her hands deep into jacket pockets – she should have worn something warmer. She'd soon be back at the farmhouse. Lunch was ready, her mother would be fussing over the food. Hanna smiled fondly as she thought of Stephanie engrossed in her work, so excited about the lunch guest, gabbling nervously that she hoped Paddy would behave himself and not say anything out of turn. She wouldn't put it past him – he was adorable, but he could be a bit blunt in company.

The clatter of thunder on the tracks made Hanna look up. The train was lurching, slowing to a stop. She stood back, watching passengers clamber off, others tugging cases up the steps to get on. She examined each passenger, hoping she'd recognise Dr Keys. Then there he was – she knew it had to be him from the photo online. A stocky man wearing a brown leather safari hat over unruly white hair, a khaki corduroy safari jacket and heavy boots trudged towards her, a case in his hand.

She turned to greet him. 'Dr Keys?'

'Yes, you must be Hanna.' He held out a hand, his smile wide. 'It occurred to me on the train that I had no idea what you looked like. I didn't know if you were young or old, tall or short.'

His handshake was warm, enthusiastic. 'It's good to meet you, Dr Keys,' Hanna said.

'It's kind of you to invite me, and please call me Roly. Everyone does, if they're being nice to me.' Roly's eyes crinkled at his own joke. 'When I saw the photo of the necklace, I had to make space in my schedule to come and see it. This part of the country is quite special, you know, in terms of its history. That's why I chose to live here.'

Hanna couldn't detect an accent. 'Where are you from originally?'

'The north-east, Sunderland – but that was long ago. I've been in Cambridge for thirty-five years.'

Hanna studied his face. It was kind, intelligent; his brown eyes warm with mischief. She decided he must be very experienced – he'd have so much knowledge to share. She was dying to ask. 'So why do you think this part of the country is so special?'

'It's rich in ancient history.' He paused, engrossed, oblivious of the woman with a large case who almost bumped into him. 'The Romans came to Colchester – it was their first capital, they called it Camulodunum. And the tribes of ancient Britain lived all over East Anglia. The Iceni tribe was a Britannic tribe during the Iron Age and early Roman era. Their territory included present-day Norfolk and parts of Suffolk and Cambridgeshire, and bordered the area of the Corieltauvi to the west, and the Catuvellauni and Trinovantes to the south.'

Hanna was puzzled by his words. 'I remember doing it at primary school. We were taught about Boudicca and the Iceni and we went to Thetford on a school trip.'

'The Iceni came from all over these parts. Prasutagus and Boudicca lived not far from here.' Roly still hadn't moved. There was a gleam in his eyes. 'They've been at the heart of my work for years – I've found one or two ancient relics, but not enough to tell us what we need to know. I led a dig that found an Iceni torc not far from Swaffham.'

Hanna remembered the picture on the university website of Roly clutching the torc, a huge grin on his face. 'That must have been exciting.'

'The Iceni have left only a few clues about their lives.' He waved an arm enthusiastically. 'Where we stand now on this station platform, there would probably have been an Iceni village almost two thousand years ago.'

Hanna looked around. 'That's incredible.'

'So, you see,' he raised his eyebrows, 'the necklace could be an important find. I'm looking forward to examining it.'

'Absolutely. Right – we should get off home.'

'Yes, we should.' Roly was suddenly impatient.

Hanna led the way to the car park and they clambered into the Range Rover. She started the engine, Roly hunched beside her, and began the drive home.

'And so, the Iceni...' He was still chatting about history, his eyes shining. Hanna assumed he was consumed with it every day. 'They were fascinating people. They had villages here, they grew crops and lived alongside their animals. Their relationship with the Romans was never good. Cultural differences, of course. There was little economic exchange between them. The Romans saw the Iceni as a threat. The Roman governor, Publius Ostorius Scapula, decided to disarm the tribes in AD 47.'

Hanna was driving along the familiar stretch of road where the hare had stood stone-like, refusing to move. She shivered. 'Do you think history is still around us, Roly?'

'I'm sure it is,' Roly muttered. 'In my work, we're always unearthing the past, treading carefully, trying not to damage relics. These things are our heritage – they are part of who we are now.' He raised an eyebrow inquisitively. 'Why do you ask?'

'I'm being silly...' Hanna gave a light laugh. 'But I was driving home once and a hare sat in the road. I mean, it was only a hare, but there was something strange about how it looked at me.'

'Hares are fascinating animals, always have been,' Roly exclaimed.

'Why?'

'They were sacred to Andraste, or Andred, the Iceni goddess of war, and they were used in rites of divination. When Boudicca faced the Roman Army in battle, she released a hare, hoping it would lead her army to victory.'

'Oh.' Hanna shuddered again. They had almost reached the farm. She decided to change the subject. 'I hope you're hungry. I've made a buffet lunch, so you can choose what you like.'

'I'm always hungry.' Roly rubbed his hands together. 'Thank you so much for inviting me.'

Hanna turned the car into the farm drive to see three figures waiting for her by the door, standing in a line. Ollie's face was glowing, full of anticipation, Stephanie smiled a kindly welcome and Paddy grinned, his arms folded.

Roly opened the car door and Paddy hurried forward, grabbing his hand and pumping his arm. 'Hello, Dr Keys. Welcome to Bramble Wood Farm.'

'You must be the owner.' Roly was delighted.

'I am – Patrick Palmer – and this is my son Oliver and my wife-to-be, Stephanie. You're very welcome.' Paddy beamed. 'Now, if you don't mind, I'm bloody starving. Let's get ourselves inside and have a spot of lunch, then we can have a look at this necklace and work out if it came from the Romans or from Woolworths.'

24

The small party meandered slowly through the streets of Camulodunum, Marcellus talking quietly, Julia laughing from time to time. Next to Marcellus, Aurelia lingered, her arm through Lucius's as she gazed at the unfamiliar surroundings. Several paces behind, Brea and Balbina walked together, their eyes cast down. Brea was listening to the conversations, although her heartbeat was quickening now, wondering how she would free herself from the group to speak to her father in the *ludus* and what she would say to him.

Julia's laughter tinkled. 'I can't wait for you to inspect my champion, sister. He's a fine specimen. While we are there, Marcellus should sponsor one for you too. We could watch them compete together while the men are away.'

'Oh, no. I fear it may upset me,' Aurelia said quietly. 'I am beginning to settle a little in this cold country now. But I prefer to spend my time in reflection in the *domus*.'

'Nonsense,' Julia insisted. 'You and I will be such friends. We'll attend the theatre tonight and enjoy the delights of a fine comedy. Then, in two days' time, we'll all go to the arena and share the thrill of the combat between two chosen adversaries.'

Marcellus held Aurelia by the elbow, as if to support her. 'You may enjoy the sport more than you expect.'

'I think not,' Aurelia replied stiffly. 'I prefer to be in the warm at home, to listen to poetry.'

'That will change once you are married.' Julia chuckled. 'Being a wife means making the most of a difficult situation. When I married Caius Fabius, I was an innocent, like you. On my wedding day, my hair was parted into six strands using a bent iron spearhead that had been used to kill a gladiator. Gladiators are our symbols of virility and the spearhead ensures a fertile union.' She let out a peal of laughter as if the idea was ridiculous. 'Of course, in Caius Fabius's case, it wouldn't matter what symbols were used. He'd still be half the man he was. But I...' She glanced at Lucius and took a breath. 'I'm still young. I love to see a battle, the fresh rush of spilled blood on the ground, the gleaming sweat of a champion.' She smiled sweetly, lowering her voice as she murmured to Aurelia, 'Marcellus will often be away. I believe you may change your mind in time, sister. Many wives here do.'

They had drawn level with the Temple of the Divine Claudius. Aurelia paused to gaze at the pale building, luminous in the sunlight. She pointed a finger. 'What a beautiful sanctuary; it's so calm. It must be a place of great contemplation. Marcellus, I'd like to go there one day soon and pray to the gods for my family in Rome.'

'It will be arranged, of course,' Marcellus replied kindly.

'The temple looks to be very newly constructed, of fine material – look how the light catches the stone and makes it shine, as if it shows the beauty of Claudius, who is truly a god now in Mount Olympus,' Lucius observed. 'Such a building must please the gods. Great care has been taken in the construction.'

'It was built from a rare polished golden marble, *marmor aureum* from Tunisia, and stone,' Marcellus explained. 'It took many men to build it.'

'Many slaves, many lives lost,' Brea muttered under her breath and she noticed Balbina glance towards her. She lowered her eyes again.

'What an incredible homage to the divine Emperor Claudius, our god,' Lucius said. 'The temple will stand strong for many years.'

'I'm sure it will. It's as fine as any in Rome,' Julia agreed, offering Lucius a compelling smile. She turned to Aurelia. 'Finer, perhaps.'

Brea recalled Luna's words, as she'd sat on the steps, indicating the magnificent temple – *it is of no consequence. It will not be here long.* She wondered what the beggar woman meant by it. The temple was tall and spectacular, made of the sturdiest stone – it would surely be standing when the inhabitants of Camulodunum had long gone.

They continued their walk through the town and Brea knew they would arrive at the *ludus gladiatorius* soon. She felt her pulse quicken. She trusted Marcellus to help her to find her father. She wondered what he would do, and how he would hide his intentions from the others.

They paused at the door to the *ludus*, and Aurelia turned to Brea. 'Will you stand next to me when we are in this place? I fear the air will not be pure, that it will smell foul, of many poor men who toil here in combat. I may falter.'

'I will.' Brea took her place close to Aurelia. She glanced at Marcellus, suddenly anxious about how she might speak to her father.

'Please don't concern yourself, Aurelia. I'll be close to you at all times.' Marcellus placed a reassuring hand against Aurelia's back. 'We won't be here for long.'

'You may walk around the *ludus* with me, Aurelia,' Julia promised. 'You too, Lucius. I want to know what you think of the gladiators. Does a tall slim man make a better fighter or should he be shorter, stocky and well-muscled? Or maybe he should have thick arms to wield a sword.'

The door was tugged open and Marcus Rubrius was there, clutching his whip and the small statue of Minerva. He bowed briefly to Marcellus, casting his eyes down slyly, his voice obsequious. 'Master, welcome. May the gods watch over you.' Then he saw Julia and he was immediately fawning. 'Mistress, you are lovelier than ever today. You are here to view your champion. He makes good progress now, he learns quickly.' Marcus Rubrius lifted the whip eagerly as if to prove a point. 'I run a strict regime here, and it's all about training. They eat well and fight hard, my boys. Come inside, and I will tell you more.' Marcus Rubrius led the way into the *ludus*, standing back to let his visitors in. 'I feed them up and keep them fit,' he announced proudly.

Brea gazed around. The wide-open area was filled with men, training with weights, stretching and doing exercises, pairs of gladiators practising moves with wooden swords and shields. Her father was nowhere to be seen.

Marcus Rubrius clapped his hands and Addedomaros, wearing a loin-cloth, his head freshly shaved, was led in by a hefty man. His ankles were shackled by chains, but he stood tall, his chin raised. Brea noticed that he had a livid slice across the bicep of his left arm, a puckering wound. He avoided her eyes, understanding that it was best for both of them that they showed no signs of recognition.

Julia approached him, running a finger along the taut muscle of his arm, pausing to rest on the deep open scar. 'So – my champion is doing well. I look forward to seeing him fight.' She met Marcus Rubrius's eyes. 'I demand that he faces a gladiator worthy of him. It must be a battle that tests his courage and his skills.'

'Oh, it will be, I promise you. I have an experienced fighter in mind, one who seldom loses a contest.' Marcus Rubrius smiled slyly. Addedomaros didn't move.

'How many times a year do your men fight?' Marcellus demanded.

'Five times.' Marcus Rubrius grinned. 'If they can win all five contests and their wounds don't kill them, they live for another year, praise Minerva.'

'Then after five more contests, are they released?'

'Oh no, Master.' Marcus Rubrius's eyes widened. 'Most of these men are criminals and prisoners of war. This is their only real chance for honour and recognition. They do not expect to be set free. They expect to win, to be glorious.'

Marcellus was thoughtful. 'I am a legate of the Roman army, second only to the Governor General Suetonius. It pleases me to see men fight, but it also pleases me to see them rewarded for their valour.' He met Marcus Rubrius's eyes fiercely and Brea noticed the slave trainer squirm. 'My sister has found herself a champion, and I expect him to please her with his contests. But your rules offer no incentive, Marcus Rubrius. The gladiator must be freed after winning a number of contests, surely. How else will he have a reason to fight hard? Something important must be at stake.'

Julia laid a hand on Marcellus's arm. 'Oh, what a great idea, brother. We'll make him fight for his liberty. It increases the drama – if he wins for me several times, then we show great grace and allow him to go, then I'll select another gladiator.'

Marcus Rubrius was unhappy. 'It's possible – but it's not cheap. He's strong and he'll look good in the arena. He'll make a lot of money for me.'

Marcellus put up a hand to stop him speaking. 'I go to quell the Druids soon. I'd like to see him fight before I leave. We should give him a chance to prove his bravery. If he wins two contests for my sister, I will pay you for him to walk free.'

'That is too kind, Master,' Marcus Rubrius muttered submissively.

'Oh, how exciting. Marcellus, you're so clever.' Julia was delighted.

Addedomaros tried to keep his face composed, but his eyes gleamed. The prospect of a new life was now a possibility. Brea felt her heart expand with gratitude to Marcellus, and she was aware of another feeling she couldn't describe. She admired him more than she had believed possible.

Aurelia gazed at Marcellus, her eyes tender. 'I'm glad you feel sorry for these poor men. They shouldn't be made to fight until they die. There has to be some point where they are released.' Her expression was filled with compassion. 'Look at some of them – they are old, battle-scarred and weary. It makes me sad to think they will end their lives being humiliated and slaughtered like animals for public entertainment.'

Marcellus took her hand. 'Aurelia has spoken from the heart. I'll buy a champion for her too, and he'll be released after his next fight.'

'Two fights,' Marcus Rubrius interrupted. 'Just like my lady's champion.' He indicated Addedomaros, who stood still as a statue.

'Oh, but how could I choose one?' Aurelia faltered.

'I wouldn't ask it of you, my dear. You are far too gentle. *Ancilla*.' Marcellus waved a hand towards Brea, not looking at her. '*Ancilla*, you will walk around and choose a champion for my new wife.'

'This is most irregular,' Marcus Rubrius began.

'But you wouldn't refuse the future wife of Nero's legate?' Marcellus faced him sternly.

'No, Master, of course not.'

'Go, *ancilla*,' Marcellus whispered. 'Find someone for your mistress, and quickly.'

'Master,' Brea muttered, conscious of her thumping heart, and her feet were propelling her forward, her eyes searching every corner. She heard Julia's laughter tinkle.

'Marcellus, you're the best of brothers. You've entertained me today. I can't imagine how brutally these slaves will fight for their freedom. Their contests will be the most exhilarating.'

Lucius agreed. 'It is good to see men compete when their hearts are full of courage. I hope too to be fierce in battle when I join the Ninth Legion.'

'But I'll worry with you so distant,' Aurelia murmured, then Brea was too far away to hear. She was pretending to inspect gladiators exercising. She gazed around nervously: none of them was her father.

Beyond, a man sat on the floor, his leg chained. He was bent over, drinking water from a bowl. He glanced up and Brea gasped, holding her breath. Then she was level with him, looking into his eyes. The years fell away.

'Father?'

Esico looked up at her, his expression filled with doubt. 'Brea – is it you?'

Brea's voice was quiet, but the urgency was unmistakable. 'Father, listen. I don't have long to speak...'

Esico stood and Brea noticed a scar across his cheek, from his eye to his top lip. She caught her breath.

'How long have you been in this place?'

'One year – I've endured five contests in the arena. Before that, I was a slave, forced to build the temple.'

Brea wished she could fling her arms around him, cling to him. Instead, she forced her voice to be calm. 'And my mother?'

'I don't wish to speak of it to you, Brea. The Romans do terrible things to women. She is dead now... she'll suffer no more.'

Brea took a deep breath, holding back tears. She hadn't much time. 'I'm a slave at a *domus* in Camulodunum. My master is a good man. He's promised to help you leave here and return to our tribe.'

'How? That's not possible. The slave trainer wouldn't allow it.' Her father's face hardened.

'You mustn't show that you know me, Father. But I promise – he'll help.'

Marcellus had drawn level with her. She saw the concern in his eyes. Then his voice was firm. 'Is this the man you've chosen as my new wife's champion, *ancilla*?'

Brea cast her eyes down. 'Yes, Master. He's scarred and old, but I believe him to be strong and brave. He'll fight his way to freedom, I swear it.'

Marcus Rubrius had joined them. He raised his whip. 'This old scoundrel?' He laughed. 'Your slave can't pick a champion.' He raised the whip to slash at Esico and Aurelia called out.

'No, don't beat him. How dare you!'

'The lady orders you,' Marcellus snapped.

Marcus Rubrius cowered back. 'Master, it's as you wish.'

Aurelia gazed at Esico, her eyes kind. She spoke gently. 'How old are you?'

Esico shrugged. 'Almost fifty summers...'

'Then it's time for you to end your time as a fighter, old man,' Aurelia said quietly. 'Thank you, Marcellus. This man is to be my champion. Brea chose well.'

'You'll fight just two more contests in the arena,' Marcellus spoke to Esico as he pressed coins into Marcus Rubrius's hand. 'Then you'll win your liberty.'

Esico bowed his head, scowling.

Brea looked from Marcellus to her father, almost afraid to believe that she'd found him and he might soon be free. She badly wanted to thank the master. Instead, she lowered her gaze.

Lucius grasped his sister's hand. 'Now I hope you'll enjoy the contest. You have a champion, and he'll fight in your honour. And although he's old, there's something about his eyes that shows he's still a warrior.'

'He is Iceni. They are a tribe of fighters,' Marcus Rubrius muttered. He turned to Julia. 'And my lady's champion is from the Trinovantes tribe. They'll both battle hard. But I'll find them worthy opponents for their contest.' He opened his hand greedily and Marcellus pressed another coin into his palm.

'We must go.' Marcellus turned to Aurelia. 'My lady, you need to rest. Let us return home.' He met Marcus Rubrius's eyes briefly. 'Treat our champions well, feed them good food. I wish them both to fight to the best of their abilities. Do you understand me?'

Marcus Rubrius nodded. He stretched out his palm wide again, his eyes moist with entreaty, but Marcellus ignored him, shepherding Aurelia towards the exit. Lucius followed; Brea could hear him talking excitedly about swords and shields, and how a champion should be hot blooded and ready for the fray. Julia was still inspecting Addedomaros, running a finger across his cheek. He didn't flinch. Balbina stood quietly, watching.

Julia tilted Addedomaros's chin, forcing him to look at her. 'I look forward to seeing you in the ring, my handsome champion.' Her voice was low. 'Don't fail me – I expect a hard battle and I want you to win well for me.'

Addedomaros's eyes moved imperceptibly.

Then Julia was on her way, her robe skimming the dusty earth as she spoke warmly to Lucius, Balbina scuttling behind. Her voice trilled. 'It will be such an exciting contest. And tonight, we'll have a wonderful supper and then we'll all go to the theatre. I adore comedy.'

Marcus Rubrius was gazing at the coins in his hand. Brea followed quickly behind her master, turning once to look back at her father. He was still watching her, his eyes level. In that moment, she knew he was determined to win.

25

Lunch passed quickly in a flurry of excited conversation. Paddy's plate was piled high as he told everyone how much he loved chaat masala potatoes smothered with hummus. He buttonholed Roly for most of the meal. 'What do you reckon to this tabbouleh stuff then? It looks like pigeon feed, but it's very tasty.'

'I was in Lebanon many years ago, examining Paleolithic sites associated with Neanderthals, and we ate the best tabbouleh there.' Roly lifted his plate in Hanna's direction. 'Apart from this one. It's delicious.'

'And what about these spicy crunchy things? They've got cauliflower in them. Can you believe that?' Paddy looked down at Roy, who had assumed the begging position at his feet, ready to dive for scraps.

Roly smiled. 'They're very popular in the wine bars in Cambridge.'

Stephanie's face shone with pride. 'Since Hanna's been home, we've eaten so many incredible things.'

Paddy refilled his plate. 'I can't get enough of these spicy spuds.' He grinned amiably. 'So, you think we've got treasure here, Roly?'

Ollie overheard. 'I can't wait for you to see what Hanna and Roy found. We'll fetch it in a minute. You'll be really impressed.'

'It will take something to impress me more than this buffet has.' Paddy smiled happily. 'Hanna, why don't you get the necklace now? Steph and I will make a bit of space on the table – I'll just refill my plate with the last of the spuds and the hummus.'

'Right.' Hanna raced upstairs and realised Ollie was hot on her heels. He followed her into the sun-filled bedroom, watching as she fumbled in the drawer for the necklace.

'Well, you played a blinder, Hanna. Everyone loved the food and now they can't wait to see the treasure.' He took a breath. 'Dad was fretting all morning. He's already concerned about a few of the piglets – we've got the vet coming on Friday because they've got suspected coccidiosis.'

'That's curable, right?' Hanna remembered Paddy had mentioned it before.

'Oh, yes. But Dad's a worrier. I know he looks all roughty-toughty and blasé, but he's quite fretful beneath the surface. He's had to do everything by himself for so long. He was really troubled at first by the idea of Roly coming here.'

'Oh?' Hanna held the tissue in her hands.

'He was terrified we'll be swamped with hordes of archaeologists with metal detectors wanting to dig up his land for bits of old tiles and jugs and Roman coins. But, as usual, he's come round.' Ollie took a step forward as Hanna lifted the tissue from the necklace. 'Oh, my goodness. I'd forgotten how perfect it is. It has to be gold and – what do you think the stones are – rubies or garnets?'

Hanna took a breath. 'Come on, Ollie. Let's find out what we really have here. Treasure or trash.'

Moments later, they all stood around the table gazing at the necklace wrapped in tissue. The gold was dull and tarnished, the stones still encrusted with soil.

Stephanie said, 'It's extremely beautiful. But it looks very old. How did you say you found it, Hanna?'

'I was walking with Roy in the pig field. He dug it up.'

Roy barked and came to sit next to Hanna's legs. She ruffled his ears as he gazed up with round eyes.

Hanna held her breath as Roly stared at the necklace, touching it lightly with a fingertip. Then he made a low grunting sound, which might have signified interest, and picked up his case, rummaging inside for a pack of dental picks and a brush. He delved in his pocket and brought out a pair of half-moon glasses and put them on with steady hands. Then he bent over the necklace, removing some of the soil with the dental pick, carefully sweeping away debris.

Paddy said, 'Don't keep us all in suspenders. What have we got?'

'Mmm,' Roly mumbled again, and continued picking away soil, brushing it gently onto the tissue.

'Is it old?' Stephanie asked.

Roly lifted the round pendant with his fingers, applying the dental pick and the brush again. 'Gold. And the stones are carnelian. I reckon I'd date this at around AD 60. And it's definitely Roman.' He took out his phone and began taking photos.

'So the Romans were here in Little Rymer all those years ago?' Paddy scratched his head. 'That's a rum ole thought.'

Ollie was excited. 'I found a Roman coin in one of the fields when I was a kid – you remember, Dad. So maybe the same people dropped the necklace. Or someone died wearing it.'

'Mmm,' Roly said again. 'It's a bit of a puzzle, this – I have to admit, I'm mystified. I have a few theories though.'

'What theories?' Hanna's voice was hushed. She was both moved and fascinated by the ancient relic.

'Well, we know the Romans disarmed the Iceni in AD 47. It could have been very close to here, where they attacked the tribe. Then they came back after King Prasutagus died in AD 60 to steal Iceni land. Roman law only allowed inheritance through the male line, so they annexed the kingdom by force.'

'Oh, that's awful,' Stephanie said as her hands flew to her mouth.

'Maybe some battle or another took place here. Boudicca herself and her tribe might have lived and fought on these very farmlands. But that doesn't explain the presence of the Roman necklace.' Roly scratched his head. 'You've given us quite a difficult dilemma, Hanna.'

'Why?' Hanna edged closer. The necklace gleamed now; she could glimpse the sheen of old gold.

'Well.' Roly took off his glasses and rubbed his eyes. 'I'm sure that it's Roman. It's typical of their style and it shows the high-quality work of their artisans. Romans were highly conscious of how they presented themselves in public and this necklace would have belonged to a lady of high status who might have worn it to show that her husband was wealthy.'

'So, what's it doing here?' Ollie asked.

'Exactly.' Roly's eyebrows came together. 'Why would an important Roman lady be here with the army, wearing a necklace? She wouldn't. Roman women, unlike their Iceni counterparts who knew how to use swords, were genteel and almost always under the jurisdiction of a male, either a paterfamilias or a husband.'

'You mean they had no rights,' Hanna suggested.

'Exactly.' Roly was still captivated by the necklace. 'The owner of this piece of jewellery had a husband of high status. You'd expect a wife who wore this to have lived in a Roman settlement – London or Colchester, St Albans even – but why would she be out here?'

'Perhaps her husband had it in his pocket as a gift?' Paddy suggested.

'Or the Iceni stole it?' Ollie wondered. 'Perhaps it was looted in battle.'

'Or used in payment for something?' Hanna offered.

'It could be any of those reasons,' Roly replied. 'I suppose we'll never know. But it's Roman, I'm sure.'

Hanna took a deep breath. The pale outline of a woman in the mist came back to her. Hanna remembered the cascading hair, a colourless face, melancholy eyes. She wondered whether to mention it, but it was the wrong place and time – everyone was chattering excitedly, and the apparition in the fields felt like a confused memory. Hanna assumed that Paddy would think she'd imagined things, although she knew the road to Bramble Woods had unnerved him. And any talk of a ghost might make her mother edgy. She'd ask Ollie's opinion – they'd planned to go to for a ride across the farmlands on Nutmeg and Hunter after she finished work on Friday. She was looking forward to it, and it would be a perfect chance to discuss the pale figure she thought she'd seen.

'So, what happens now?' Paddy folded his arms. 'I suppose we'll have to report it to the coroner and say we found treasure on our land?'

'You will.' Roly's eyebrows descended again. 'But I'm very glad you invited me here to see this. It's a most important discovery. And it raises so many questions about the people who lived in this area and what they were up to.' He met Hanna's eyes. 'You've given me a puzzle here, young lady, and I'm intrigued. A Roman woman on Iceni land? Or at least her jewellery. I'd love to know how it got here.'

'Perhaps she was a prisoner?' Ollie suggested.

'Or maybe she married an Iceni man?' Stephanie was thinking about her own imminent wedding.

'How would we find out?' Hanna asked. 'Are there records, Roly?'

'Some – but other than their final battle, the Iceni left no trail. They didn't write things down. That's why no one knows exactly how Boudicca spelled her name.' Roly chuckled as he began to pack away his equipment. 'This necklace is important, though – I'm sure of it. Mmm.' He was thoughtful. 'I'll talk to a colleague of mine back in Cambridge, see what she thinks.'

'Meanwhile,' Paddy scooped up the necklace in the tissue, 'I'll put this somewhere safe and make a few phone calls. No doubt they'll send someone to take it away and get it looked at.'

'It will find its way back to me, hopefully.' Roly reached for his jacket. 'Well, lunch was wonderful and seeing the necklace was a privilege. Sadly, it's time to go.' He glanced at Hanna. 'Can you give me a lift to the station?'

'Of course.' Hanna turned to her mother. 'You're not to do a thing until I'm back, Mum. We'll sort the dishes out later.'

* * *

Roly spent most of the journey to the station thanking Hanna profusely for inviting him to see the necklace. He was clearly delighted with the find.

Hanna brought the Range Rover to a stop in the car park. 'So, what happens now?'

'You mean with the necklace?' Roly asked. 'I'd love to get my hands on it again – it opens up a minefield of questions. Why it was there, who put it there and – most excitingly – what else might be there too?'

'In the pig field?' Hanna asked.

'Or the adjoining land. Oliver found a coin. So – there's history buried beneath the soil. I wonder what else is there.'

'What time's your train?' Hanna wondered if she had time to take Roly for a coffee in Serenity's café and pick his brains.

Roly checked the old-fashioned watch on his wrist. 'At twenty to four. In ten minutes.' He gave a short sigh. 'Well, it was lovely to meet you, Hanna. You've got the cogs in my brain whirring.'

'Me too,' Hanna said. 'It's quite a strange place, the land around the farm. It feels like there's something... unexplained out there.'

Roly was suddenly interested. 'In what way?'

'It's hard to say.' Hanna wriggled in her seat. She hadn't intended to mention the sighting of the figure in the mist. 'The fenlands are spooky sometimes. The mist comes down and there's a sense of...' She paused. 'I know, I'm being silly.'

Roly was watching her. 'There are some who might agree with you, though.'

'How do you mean?'

'I've spent most of my life digging in the soil or rocks or dust, looking for the past. When I find something, it always feels like I've been given a gift. I'm a down-to-earth archaeologist. Yet there's no doubt that rooting about in history sometimes brings a strange feeling with it. You know, a kind of residual sense that something has happened long ago that left its fingerprint on time.'

Hanna shuddered. 'I know what you mean.'

'So it doesn't surprise me at all that you say the place has a strange atmosphere. Would you describe it as a bit creepy?'

Hanna nodded. 'Yes, I suppose so.'

'Mmm,' Roly said. 'Not really my sphere. I just dig things up and analyse them. But a good friend of mine is very much of the belief that the past remains with us, or at least, some shred of it stays behind. She'd certainly be interested to talk to you about ghostly atmospheres...' He glanced at his watch. There was so much more she wanted to ask.

'Roly – please do come back soon. I'm sure I can persuade Paddy and Ollie to let you look in the area around the pig field. Maybe after Mum's wedding...'

'Of course – I have your email address. Let's sort out a convenient time after the big day.' He clambered out of the car and shook her hand warmly. 'Perhaps you'd like to come over to Cambridge and meet the team sometime.' He was on his way towards the bridge. 'Nice to meet you, Hanna. We'll catch up again soon.'

Hanna watched him stride away, the safari hat pushed over his wiry hair, the khaki jacket becoming smaller as he crossed the bridge towards the platform. She slid down in her seat, touching the keys to the engine, thinking. The necklace would be taken away to be examined, but the mystery remained behind it, hanging in the air.

26

Brea was finding it difficult to concentrate. Her father filled her thoughts: their conversation had left so much unsaid. They'd had little chance to say what was in their hearts or exchange information, apart from the news about her mother: although Brea had feared that Cartimandua was long dead, there had always been a shred of hope. Now it had gone. But her father was living and training in the *ludus*, fighting in the arena, and her hand shook with fear for his safety. She almost tipped the fruit on the tray over as she placed it on the low table in the *triclinium*. And as she filled Publius Julius's cup with wine, she was momentarily back at the *ludus* again and the wine reached the top of the goblet before she had chance to notice. Publius Julius drank deeply, then he reached for a piece of honey cake.

'I am looking forward to the theatre tonight. A comedy will cheer us all.' He leaned pointedly towards Lucius, who lay on a couch next to Aurelia. 'So, you'll leave for the Ninth Legion straight after the marriage?'

'I intend to leave after a few days.' Lucius glanced at his sister. 'I know Aurelia will miss me, but I'm keen to prove myself as great a soldier as you, sir, and as Marcellus.'

Marcellus stretched his legs, reclining alone on the third couch. 'You'll be a fine tribune. But the life of a soldier has its hardships, Lucius. You have much to learn.'

Aurelia spoke up. 'I'll pray to Minerva and Vesta to bring you safely home.' She smiled at Marcellus. 'And you too, my lord. Will you stay here long after our wedding?'

Publius Julius reached over and patted Marcellus's thigh. 'Long enough to father a son, I hope.'

Brea saw the blood rush to Aurelia's face. She moved closer to her mistress, refilling her cup.

Marcellus smiled. 'I'll stay for two more weeks. Our general, the governor of Britannia, Suetonius, will dine with us then, and I'll return to the island of Mona with him.' He glanced towards Aurelia. 'It will be pleasant to spend time with you here.'

Aurelia inclined her head politely. 'I look forward to it.'

Lucius coughed lightly. 'And Julia will be at the theatre this evening.' He was momentarily awkward. 'She wants to sit next to me and share her thoughts about the comedy. She promised that I would enjoy it even more than the plays we've seen in Rome.'

'The *cavea* in Camulodunum is far too small. There is no luxury in the place,' Publius Julius grunted. 'It needs knocking down and a bigger one constructing. Where are all the slaves that were used to build the Temple of the Divine Claudius? They must be idle now. Perhaps they could build a wonderful theatre.'

Brea was at his side, filling his cup again. She thought briefly of spilling wine onto his toga, but it would end in a beating. She moved back to Aurelia who stood up, stretching her limbs.

'I need to change my clothes before we leave for the theatre.' She turned to Brea. 'Will you help me with a new robe? And I'll need my jewellery.'

'You will.' Publius Julius chortled. 'You're about to become the wife of an important man. A first public appearance can be daunting, Aurelia.'

Marcellus leaned forward. 'I'll be by your side.'

'Thank you, Marcellus. I look forward to a pleasant evening in your company.' Aurelia smiled. 'Come, Brea.'

Brea hurried after her as she left the room.

In the *cubiculum*, Aurelia turned anxious eyes towards her. 'Do you think I'm learning to be a dutiful wife?'

'I'm sure you are.' Brea frowned. Their ideas of duty were very different.

'I am determined to succeed, for my family's sake.' Aurelia sat on the edge of her bed. 'My mother spoke to me for many hours about being the wife of a great legate. I will do my best to please Marcellus. It's an honour to be married.'

Brea held up a robe. 'The pale green one this evening? And a warm cloak against the night air.'

'Yes.' Aurelia stood languorously, lost in thought. 'I believe I can run the house efficiently, and I will love our children and school them well. And I pray to the goddess Diana that I will have sons and that they will be great soldiers.'

Brea was helping Aurelia on with her robe. 'I wish it may happen.'

'The thing that worries me is...' Aurelia shuddered. 'I know what will be expected of me on my wedding night. A woman must bend to a man's desires. But I fear it will not be easy to bear.'

'It may not be as difficult as you think.' Brea smiled. She remembered many years ago that each day her parents would smile at each other, kissing each other's lips tenderly. She understood the natural warmth and affection they shared. 'If you love the master Marcellus and he loves you—'

Aurelia's brow puckered. 'I don't expect love, Brea. I wonder how it feels to be married, what changes will happen to me? I understand duty and respect, but I've never felt love except for my mother and father, and my brother.'

'It may come in time, as you get to know the master.'

'I think not,' Aurelia said sadly. 'Perhaps I'm too cold-blooded. I don't think I'm capable.'

'Everyone is capable of love, I'm sure of it.' Brea held up the gold and carnelian necklace, placing it around Aurelia's neck. 'In your place, I'd be looking forward to being married. Imagine, holding such a man in your arms, pressing warm lips against his, knowing how much he must love and desire you, and feeling the same way...' She paused, putting a hand to her mouth. 'I mean that – I pray it may happen for you.'

'You've spoken passionately, from your heart, Brea.' Aurelia turned round, her face filled with surprise. 'Is there a man you love?'

'No, not ever.' Brea took a step back – her own words had shocked her and she wished she'd said nothing. 'I meant simply that the master is a kind man and in time you may grow fond of each other. My own tribe marries for love.'

Aurelia put a hand to her hair, smoothing it. 'Do you think Marcellus respects me?'

Brea smiled encouragingly. 'Of course he must respect you. He'll be your husband.'

Aurelia's face was sad. 'It will be what it will be. Come, Brea – we must go.'

'We?' Brea hesitated. 'I have much to do in the kitchens. I know the others there find it difficult without me. I need to wash the dishes and prepare for tomorrow.'

'I can't go to the theatre alone,' Aurelia gasped. 'I may need you next to me to carry my cloak and adjust my hair if it comes loose. A woman must be seen with her slave – how else will she look like the wife-to-be of a great legate?'

'If I must go.' Brea lowered her eyes. 'Very well.'

'How do I look?' Aurelia swirled her robe. Her jewellery glittered and her clothes suited her well, but there was something weary about her demeanour. She knew already that she wouldn't enjoy the evening.

'You look like the betrothed of a great soldier.' Brea told her what she wanted to hear.

'Then all is well.' Aurelia clapped her hands. 'Come – we mustn't be late. I wouldn't be surprised if Julia isn't there already with Caius Fabius. And I don't want to keep Marcellus waiting.'

She swept from the *cubiculum*, her head held high, already on the way to the atrium. Brea followed her, but she felt troubled. She had spoken her thoughts about love without keeping them in check, about the passion she might feel in Aurelia's place. Aurelia hadn't noticed how her cheeks had tingled, how her heart had begun to thump. Brea was angry with herself for not holding her tongue – in the future she'd be more careful. The problem was, as she'd counselled her mistress on how easy it would be to care for Marcellus, Brea had imagined herself in Aurelia's place. It was a thought she could never allow again.

* * *

Brea stood a few paces behind Aurelia in the theatre, holding her cloak, watching the play unfold, listening to the various types of Roman laughter in the audience. Publius Julius had a loud bark, Caius Fabius a wheezy giggle, Julia a high shriek and Aurelia a discreet tinkle. Marcellus had a low, throaty chuckle and Lucius always looked around before he laughed, as if asking for permission. Brea wasn't sure why they were laughing – she didn't find the play at all amusing. All the actors wore masks, so it was impossible to see their faces. Brea thought it was difficult to believe in them.

The comedy didn't entertain her – it was simple, contrived. The characters were easily identified by their elaborate costumes. A purple costume signified a rich man. Boys wore striped togas, soldiers wore short cloaks, red costumes indicated a poor man. A yellow robe meant the character was a woman. She was sure the actor beneath the mask was a man. The woman was referred to often, but seldom came on stage. She was unimportant, an invisible prize, a possession. And Ancilla, the maid, was no more than a messenger. Brea didn't understand it at all.

The slaves wore short tunics, to show that they were poor. The mischievous slave, Servus Callidus, made the Romans howl with laughter, but Brea thought the character foolish. No slave would be allowed to humiliate his master's father. And as for Adulescens, the young lover, he was so empty-headed that no sensible woman would give him a second thought. A yellow tassel meant the character was a god, although it was played by a man who spoke in an exaggeratedly deep voice. And Matrona, the mother figure, was absurd – she was temperamental and intolerant of her husband. The play was ridiculous. Brea couldn't work out why it entertained the Roman audience so much.

Brea's eyes strayed to Marcellus, sitting between his father and Aurelia, and wondered what his feelings were. She found her thoughts drifting to Aurelia's wedding night and there she was again, in her mistress's place, her arms tangled around her new husband.

As if in answer, Marcellus looked over his shoulder and met her eyes. A smile flickered across his lips and Brea looked down at her feet, determined to avoid his gaze and calm her thumping heart. She wasn't sure what was happening to her, but she knew that it had to stop.

Brea glanced towards Julia, who rested a palm against Lucius's knee. Caius Fabius had not noticed, but Lucius shifted uncomfortably in his seat as Julia slid her fingers towards his thigh. Brea caught Balbina's sly smile – Julia's maid was standing nearby in attendance, just as she was. Brea looked away – it was not her place to judge.

The play ended quickly and Julia kissed Lucius's cheek, whispering good night, lowering her lashes, then she and Caius Fabius departed to their *domus*, followed by Balbina and Caius Fabius's slaves.

Marcellus led the way home, his head close to Aurelia's. Brea heard them talking about the play, Aurelia saying how confused she was by the character of Meretrix, the courtesan. Brea heard their conversation clearly.

'I don't understand why Adulescens falls in love with her, though, Marcellus. He has bought her – he can do as he wishes with her. She's a slave.'

'He only *thinks* she's a slave,' Marcellus explained gently. 'In truth, she's free-born.'

Aurelia gave a light laugh. 'Of course, she must be free-born or the play would make no sense. Adulescens wouldn't have married her at the end. He's a rich man.'

'I suppose he loves her. She's beautiful and virtuous,' Marcellus said.

'Nonsense – no slave can be either of those.' Publius Julius had overheard. 'The purpose of a slave is to serve. I know some men use their slave women as whores. But that's really the point – they are just there to oblige their master's whims.'

Brea lagged behind awkwardly, not wishing to hear any more.

'I enjoyed the play immensely.' Lucius spoke loudly. 'But I was fascinated by Meretrix. She is not what she seems – she's no slut, she's beautiful and free to marry.' He sighed. 'I'm sure many a man has his heart stolen by a woman who belongs to another. But we cannot help who we love.'

'Nonsense, it is a man's duty to love a proper woman with social standing,' Aurelia insisted. 'What do you think, Marcellus?'

'I am a soldier. I don't give much thought to these things. After all, it was just a comedy. No one really cares about slaves and their lives.' Marcellus shrugged. Brea could see the movement of his shoulders beneath the toga. Tears pricked her eyes; his dismissive words had bewildered and hurt her.

'I agree.' Publius Julius laughed. 'A few moments of pleasure, that is all a play is. The same could be said about a brief encounter with a slave woman.' He shook his head. 'Nowadays, little pleases me as it once did – food, the company of women. But conversation and fine wine, they keep my spirit alive.'

They had reached the *domus*.

Publius Julius said, 'Well, I am for my bed now. I bid you all good night.'

'I doubt I shall sleep well.' Lucius put a hand to his head as if it ached. 'My thoughts buzz like flies. I will go to the *lararium* and say some prayers to Venus, that she may help me rest.'

Marcellus took Aurelia's hand gallantly and said, 'I wish you sweet dreams, my lady. *Ancilla* – go with my lady Aurelia and prepare her for rest, please.'

Aurelia waved her away. 'There is no need, Brea. I need time alone. Go and finish your work in the kitchen. And then sleep – I'm sure your day has been long and busy, as mine has.'

Marcellus met Brea's eyes meaningfully. 'May you sleep well.'

'Thank you,' Brea murmured and hurried away, passing Lucius, who had positioned himself at an altar, kneeling with his head bowed to pray. She hurtled down the steps towards the servants' quarters, intending to go to the kitchen and help Galyna and the other slaves, but suddenly she swerved towards the gardens, making her way towards the orchard. There was no one around and she needed a few moments to herself, to calm her racing thoughts.

Brea sank down under a fruit tree on the grass, ignoring the dampness seeping into the material of her tunic, covering her face and stifling a sob. She realised that all day she'd been holding a heavy feeling of sorrow inside, afraid to let go.

Seeing her father, noticing the livid incision that scarred his face, the weariness etched around his glittering eyes had been hard. He was sinewy, strong, but worn thin. She'd wanted to fling her arms around him, to cling to him, but instead she had to pretend that they were strangers.

Another sob escaped from somewhere deep in her chest: her mother was gone forever, and so was the small hope she'd had of seeing her again. And her father would risk his life, fighting to gratify the frivolous entertainment of idle men and women. It was so unfair. She gulped back hot tears of anger.

Brea's thoughts shifted to Marcellus. He'd helped her today, he'd shown kindness, but he was rich and privileged. He had no idea how wrong it was that her father, a noble warrior of a great tribe, should be shackled by the leg and made to fight for his liberty.

A tear slid down her cheek and Brea wiped it away quickly. She was determined to be strong. Marcellus was a soldier. Life was cheap to him. It had meant nothing to attack her tribe, to humiliate the Iceni queen and her daughters. She ought to hate him, to be filled with vengeful thoughts. Brea was furious, yet, at the same time, it was impossible to shake away a weakness that came from her core, that was deeply disturbing and troubled her even now.

She'd heard Marcellus talking about his opinion of slaves on the way back from the theatre. His voice had been dismissive as he'd said, 'No one really cares about slaves and their lives.' Brea had heard him say those exact words to Aurelia. As she'd walked dutifully behind him, he'd clearly forgotten that she was there. Marcellus had only helped her to find her father because he was essentially a kind man. But Brea was no more to him than an *ancilla*, a servant of the lowest order. She had been foolish to think that he considered her special.

Her tears came fast now. Brea couldn't stop them. They came as sobs, torn from somewhere deep, and she wrapped her arms around her knees and cried out loud. This wasn't how she normally behaved. She was Iceni through and through, and she was ashamed of her tears. But she wept for her shackled father, for her lost mother, for her lonely life as a slave, for the misery of her existence. She wept because Addedomaros had been flogged and sold, and because he and her father would have to scrap for their lives in an arena while a crowd heckled and cheered and booed.

But most of all she cried because she was filled with sorrow for herself, for the feelings that were tearing her apart. Her heart was so filled with love, she feared it might break.

27

Hanna served a young woman with a flat white coffee to go, then she leaned against the counter. Serenity bustled around, collecting cups and plates: it would soon be closing time. There were half a dozen people seated at tables, some talking in groups, some reading newspapers, gazing at phones. She glanced at the wall clock – almost five o'clock on a Friday afternoon. He probably wouldn't come in now.

In truth, she'd spent the past two days in the café either looking out for the mystery man or telling herself she was being silly. She leaned towards the second point of view. It really didn't matter to her if she saw him or not. She was just looking out for him simply for the thrill of catching his glance. It was a pointless game. He was good-looking, yes, but that was as far as it could ever go.

There was a train due from King's Cross. Hanna wondered if he was standing on the platform, waiting to meet his girlfriend from London. Perhaps he hadn't time to come into the café for a coffee; perhaps they'd come in after the train left. Hanna glanced towards the large window, just in case she could glimpse him. But he wasn't among the groups of passengers huddled in groups or seated on benches.

Serenity placed her tray of dirty cups on the counter and grinned. 'So, what are you up to tonight?'

Hanna shrugged. 'I'm going out horse riding as soon as I get home. Ollie and I are going to take Nutmeg and Hunter along the bridle path.'

'It's a lovely day for it. The sunshine's glorious.' Serenity grinned. 'You could get off a bit early if you like? We're not busy – I'll put the dishes in the machine and lock up.'

'Thanks, Serenity.' Hanna watched the King's Cross train shunt in. There was no sign of the mystery man or his girlfriend. She was annoyed that she felt a pang of disappointment. 'That's great. I will.' She dragged her thoughts back to reality. 'What are you up to?'

'I'm going into King's Lynn when I've finished. I'm popping in the South Gate Arms to see my mum. She says they are doing a good pie selection there tonight, gravy, chips, the works.' Serenity suddenly had a thought. 'Your mum's wedding is a week tomorrow, isn't it?'

'It is.'

'Where's she getting married?'

'The registry office in King's Lynn. Then there's a sit-down meal at The Sprowston Manor Hotel, followed by a disco.' Hanna beamed. 'You could come and join us for the disco, after seven.'

'I'm always up for dancing,' Serenity admitted. 'So, what's your mother doing for her hen party?'

'She's not having one.' Hanna hadn't even considered the idea.

'Well, she should. I'll talk to my mum about it – we could have a hen night at her pub. Why don't we all go to King's Lynn and have a meal at the South Gate Arms one evening next week?'

'It would mark the occasion, wouldn't it? I mean, what's a wedding without a hen party?' Hanna smiled slowly. 'I'll ask her.'

'Great, talk to her when you get back home.' Serenity lifted the tray. 'We'll finalise details tomorrow then.'

Hanna grabbed her bag and jacket. 'Fab. See you tomorrow.'

As she drove back to Bramble Wood Farm, the idea of a small hen party started to appeal to her a great deal. A nice meal in a friendly pub was just what Stephanie would need to calm her pre-wedding nerves.

The open countryside flashed past the window as she drove along the road. The expanse of fenland stretched for miles, wild grassland, a deep irrigation ditch, then an open sky filled with low-hanging clouds. It was a beautiful evening.

As Hanna passed a field of barley buffeted by the gusty wind, she shivered. This expanse of open road always made her feel edgy. She'd be glad to get back to the warmth of the farmhouse, get changed and go to the stables, nuzzle Nutmeg's nose. There was no traffic, and Hanna was uncomfortable with the feeling of isolation that sat with her in the car. In the fens, the past was never far away. Hanna constantly looked around, as if at any moment she might glimpse a lonely figure in the distance.

* * *

An hour later, she'd forgotten about feeling jittery on the journey home. She and Ollie were on horseback, chattering as they trundled down the bridle path across an open fallow field. Nutmeg was pleased to see Hanna, accepting the treats she'd offered as she clambered onto her back. Hunter was lively, wanting to trot, and Ollie reined him in with a grin. 'We'll pick up speed on the way home, Hunter. Be patient, boy.'

'I'm happy plodding,' Hanna said. 'My muscles have just got back to normal.'

'You're a natural,' Ollie said kindly. 'Well, it's been an interesting week. I've been thinking...'

'That's dangerous,' Hanna teased.

'We found a coin, a necklace. Don't you think there must be a whole lot of stuff in the fields, just waiting to be excavated?'

'It had occurred to me, and Roly thinks so,' Hanna admitted. 'He said there must have been Iceni people living on your land. He even suggested Boudicca might have been here.'

Ollie laughed. 'Maybe this is where she fought her big battle?'

'Maybe,' Hanna said. 'This place certainly has a strange vibe.'

'Do you think so?' Ollie asked. 'I've worked on the farm since I was a kid. I'm out here from dawn to night-time...'

'And?' Hanna asked. 'Have you ever seen anything strange?'

'Such as?'

Hanna wondered how to say it. 'The past is all around us. I wondered if you'd seen anything ghostly.'

'Not me,' Ollie joked, then his face was suddenly serious. 'Dad claims to have felt something odd in the car one night, a presence or something weird. And that's Dad we're talking about here – I mean, he's the most down-to-earth person I know. So if he felt something, then maybe there's some truth in the rumours.'

'What rumours?'

'Oh, just local stuff.' Ollie shrugged. 'I've heard one or two tales in the pub about this stretch of road near the farm. There's one bloke in The Dribbling Duck who's sure he saw a figure standing in the mist one night.'

'Really?' Hanna met his eyes.

'Most people think he'd had too much to drink, but he swears that he was sober, and he would have been, driving his car. I don't know what I believe – I think there may be something in it because of how the animals react sometimes.' Ollie tugged the reins, turning Hunter to the right, heading down the bridle path that ran parallel to the pig field. Nutmeg followed.

'How do the animals react?' Hanna was curious.

'They are very switched on to – how would you say it? – the atmosphere of places. The horses don't seem to like the pig field or Bramble Woods beyond. And I've seen Roy behave strangely around here once or twice.'

'How strangely?'

'In the pig field, he's cowered down a couple of times and his fur stood up. Roy's very obedient normally, but he didn't respond when I called him – he was just gazing into the distance, his ears flat.'

Hanna nodded. She'd seen Roy do that herself.

Ollie grinned. 'I'm not scaring you, am I? I mean, I'm not the type to see ghosts.'

'Not at all...' Hanna took a breath. She'd seen the figure three times now.

Then Ollie pointed. 'Oh, look – there's Dad.' He waved an arm. 'We won't go into the pig field, Hanna – Nutmeg really doesn't like it there. But we'll just ride down to the hedge here and say hi.'

Hanna glanced towards the pigs, rooting in the mud, rows of pig arks behind them. Two figures were standing next to a sow and several piglets, bending down. Paddy waved as Ollie guided Hunter over to the hedge, Hanna at his shoulder. Then the other man stood up, meeting Hanna's eyes, and she felt a sudden jolt of recognition. He stared straight at her; he was wearing a wax jacket and wellingtons. The wind blew his hair across his face.

'We're just looking at the piglets,' Paddy said by way of explanation. 'It seems they do have a touch of coccidiosis, but our new vet's given me something for it.' He turned to his companion. 'You remember my son, Oliver? And this is Hanna, Stephanie's daughter.'

Hanna wondered if the mystery man would mention that she'd served him coffee and almost mown him down on her bicycle, but he simply nodded and said, 'Hello.'

'Lucas is our new vet – he works out of Kingdom Farm Vets in King's Lynn, but he lives in Little Rymer. He bought Steph's old house, would you believe?' Paddy nodded. 'It'll be useful to have him living just down the road.'

'I'm sure.' Hanna thought she ought to say something. She was still staring.

'Lucas, can you take a look at Nutmeg's wolf teeth while you're here?' Ollie asked. 'I'm worried they might be making her mouth sore.'

'Of course, we'll be back at the farmhouse in about half an hour,' Lucas said. 'Will that be okay?'

'Great, thanks – it'll give us time to finish our ride,' Ollie agreed. 'Come on, Hanna, let's go home through the woodlands.'

Ollie turned Hunter, taking off at speed, and Nutmeg followed eagerly. Hanna wasn't expecting a sudden jerking movement and she lurched backwards inelegantly, gaining her composure as quickly as she could. She caught up with Ollie.

'As Dad said, that was Lucas Wright, our new vet,' Ollie remarked. 'The one who used to come round before, David Heron, has retired. He wasn't half as sweet with the animals. Lucas talks to them as if they are people. He's got a lovely way with them.'

'That's good.' Hanna wasn't sure what else to say. Her thoughts were speeding forward to when they'd arrive back at the farm and the new vet would be there to look at Nutmeg's teeth. She'd be standing just a few feet away from him. She promised herself she'd be sensible and calm. The last thing she wanted to do was to babble and make a fool of herself. She told herself crossly that she was behaving like an adolescent.

They rode through a small gate into Bramble Woods. The air was chilly, and Hanna was reminded that the summer was coming to an end. It was late August and already she thought she could smell a dampness that signalled the change of the seasons. The thought cheered her – she was a Norfolk girl through and through, in touch with nature.

The horses ambled along the path steadily, their hooves silent on the moist ground of mud and leaves. Blackberries clung to bushes in little ripe clusters, and Hanna thought about making jam at the weekend with her mother. Light filtered through the trees, dappling the earth.

'Shall we trot home?' Ollie called, urging Hunter ahead, and Nutmeg followed dutifully, Hanna bouncing on the saddle. She leaned forward, a smile on her face, forcing her thighs against Nutmeg's belly. She was getting the hang of riding again.

Paddy was waiting at the stables with Lucas Wright when Hanna and Ollie arrived. Hanna climbed off Nutmeg and Ollie clambered down from Hunter and took the reins.

He stroked Nutmeg's damp neck. 'Thanks for taking a look at her, Lucas. I just want to be sure she's not in any discomfort.'

Lucas moved close to Nutmeg and Hanna took a step back.

'You'll be all right by yourselves – I'm off indoors out of this cold wind,' Paddy grunted. 'I'll ask Steph to get the kettle on.'

'Right, Nutmeg,' Lucas said kindly, stroking the horse's neck. 'Can you let me have a look?'

Hanna watched as he gripped the horse's mouth firmly, lifting the soft flesh, pulling the lower lip down and stretching the upper one to expose large yellow teeth. Nutmeg stood placidly.

'So, I wonder – is this wolf tooth giving you any pain or can we leave it as it is?' Lucas's hands were gentle against the whiskery mouth as he scrutinised a huge long tooth, touching it with careful fingers. He was thoughtful for a while, then he said, 'So, this is a big wolf tooth sitting immediately in front of the first upper cheek teeth. It's large, but I think it's all right for the time being.' Lucas let the skin go, rubbing the horse's nose affectionately. 'We'll keep an eye on that tusk, shall we, Nutmeg?'

'It doesn't need to come out then?' Ollie asked, relieved.

'That would be quite traumatic for her – I leave them alone if I can,' Lucas said, and Hanna noticed the same sadness in his face. 'Only 20 per cent of mares have wolf teeth. They are quite rare – she's a special girl.' He patted her neck again. 'I can do a bit of dental floating – file the sharp edges down – if it becomes troublesome, but she's fine as she is for the time being.' Lucas gazed from Ollie to Hanna. 'I'll check again when I'm next here.'

'Right,' Ollie said, and Hanna was conscious she was standing around with no purpose, saying nothing.

She forced herself to speak. 'Thanks.'

'No problem.' Lucas's eyes met hers and again she felt the shock. She'd expected it to subside, but no such luck.

'Do you want to come to the house and have a cup of tea?' Ollie asked.

'Thanks, but no, I'm running late – I've another call to make.' Lucas glanced again at Hanna. 'Next time, perhaps.'

'Great. Thanks for your help, Lucas,' Ollie said. 'Shall I see you to your car?'

'I'll sort out the horses,' Hanna blurted, grabbing Hunter's reins.

'I'll be back in a moment to give you a hand,' Ollie called over his shoulder as he walked away with the vet.

Hanna leaned her head against Nutmeg's face and breathed out, relieved that Lucas had gone. Being in his company had been awkward – she'd felt jittery the whole time. It was silly, she told herself – she was behaving like a teenager. But she couldn't deny the powerful attraction and she wondered if he was aware of it too.

28

Brea shivered; it was cold in the orchard. The wind tugged her hair free from its pins. She ignored the fallen strands, wiping tears from her face with the back of her hand. Another sob shuddered in her chest, but she wouldn't cry again, she wouldn't feel sorry for herself. She promised herself she'd focus on her father – he came first.

There was a shadow, a figure hovering above. She looked up into the eyes of Marcellus and was immediately apologetic. 'Oh – I'm sorry, Master – I was just—'

He sat down next to her. 'You're trembling. Brea, what is it?'

'It's nothing.' Her eyes flashed. 'I was just taking a moment to compose myself before I went back to the kitchen to finish the chores. I-I hope that's all right, Master.'

'Brea.' Marcellus said her name in a whisper, his voice tender. 'I was concerned – I came to find you. It must have been a difficult day, seeing your father for the first time in so long.'

'I'm just grateful for your help.' Brea took a deep breath. 'You have been most kind, finding a way to help my father earn his freedom.'

Marcellus frowned. 'It wasn't what I wanted. I was hoping to buy him outright.' He paused, noticing Brea flinch at the word *buy*. He tried again.

'I'd intended to find a way for your father and the Trinovantes slave to be freed at the same time without the need for them to step into the arena.'

'As I said, I'm grateful.' Brea breathed. 'You've been very kind. I realise that the hardships of a slave are not your concern.'

'You're wrong,' Marcellus protested, resting a hand on Brea's arm. He sighed. 'I'll do my best to help your father, you too.'

'Thank you, Master.' Brea made to move away, alarmed by the power of his touch. 'I must go now – I have chores to attend to...'

'Wait a while?'

'If you command it, I will wait.'

'No.' Marcellus shook his head. 'I'm not commanding – I'm asking you. I'd like to talk with you.'

'I'd be content to listen,' Brea said hesitantly.

'The thing is,' Marcellus removed his huge hand from her shoulder, 'you know I must marry, then I leave for the Island of Mona.'

'Everyone knows it,' Brea said simply.

'And I wonder...' Marcellus seemed unsure how to frame the question. 'Does the lady Aurelia talk about me often?'

'It's not for me to repeat her words,' Brea replied.

'Does she speak of our marriage?'

'I cannot say.' Brea met his eyes, her own defiant. 'You must ask her yourself.'

'I fear she does not want to marry, in truth,' Marcellus said sadly. 'Her father and my father arranged the wedding for both our sakes. Aurelia would be happier in Rome. And I'd be happier if she were there too.'

'You shouldn't tell me this, Master.'

'Why not?' A sigh shuddered through his large frame. 'Who else should I tell? I can't speak to the lady herself – we are so polite, it is as if we're both afraid of the truth. And I can't speak to my father of anything but duty.'

'Then you must marry her without telling anyone your feelings,' Brea told him. 'Life is not easy, and we often can't choose what we'd like.'

'But what if you could choose, Brea? What would you choose for yourself?'

'It's easy – I'd choose for my father to be free.'

'And what else?'

'He and I would return to our own tribe.'

Marcellus sighed again. 'Would that make you happy?'

'Yes,' Brea replied honestly. 'I could live a good life there.'

'But what about love?' Marcellus's eyes glowed.

Brea looked away; his stare made her feel uncomfortable. 'I don't think about love.'

'Why not?'

'I'm a slave. I came here when I was thirteen years old. I've never been given choices. I don't expect them.' She was momentarily impatient. 'You're fortunate, with your wedding to come and the prospect of a family and the freedom to do as you wish.'

'But if you could choose,' Marcellus repeated, his hand was on her arm again. 'If you could find someone whom you cared for, who cared for you too...'

Brea felt a tremor go through her body. She didn't want to talk to Marcellus of such things – she couldn't admit the growing strength of her feelings, even to herself. She glanced away into the trees. The sky was dark velvet overhead, tiny diamond stars. A hush hung over the orchard, the wind stirring the leaves.

'Brea.' He lifted her chin with his fingers. 'I don't wish to marry Aurelia. I have already given my heart to someone else.'

'Have you spoken to the lady?' Brea replied. She felt a sinking disappointment: she had not considered that Marcellus might desire someone else. 'Is she married to another? Is it one of lady Julia's friends?'

'It is someone closer to me,' Marcellus whispered. He wrapped an arm around her, pulling her closer, nuzzling her ear. 'You must know it.'

'I know nothing,' Brea said as Marcellus covered her lips with his.

Brea closed her eyes, and the kiss and his arms lifted her. For a moment, she felt in a dream, held there by a sweetness she'd never known. The breath was taken from her lungs as she kissed him back, leaning into his embrace. They tumbled on the ground and Marcellus kissed her neck and she felt her own blood beating in her ears. She gasped, tugging herself away, tugging back. 'Master.'

'If I am your master, then I'm also your slave,' Marcellus murmured. 'Brea, I swear to you...'

'No, you mustn't...' Brea wriggled away from him. 'You think I'm a fool.'

'I care only for you. I've known it for a while – I can't help it,' Marcellus said.

'And in several days' time, you'll marry the lady Aurelia.'

'That's my duty – that's not love—'

'Think of the words you're saying – you're toying with me, and it's unfair.' Brea was suddenly angry. 'I heard what your father said, that some men use their slave women as whores. Those were his exact words.'

'That's true.' Marcellus shook his head. 'But you're different to other women, slave or free. I've never met a woman like you. It comforts me to think of how strong you are, how brave, and it's you I want.'

'As a *meretrix*? Once you are married to the lady Aurelia, you think I'll warm your bed?' Brea's eyes flashed. 'I am worth more than that.'

'You are.' Marcellus's face was sad. 'I want to tell you that my feelings are honest. I want to help your father to be free.'

'So that I'll fall into your bed in gratitude?' Brea scrambled to her feet. Marcellus was still seated on the ground and she was conscious that it was wrong to look down on her master, but she hadn't finished speaking her mind. 'I heard what you said to the lady Aurelia when we were leaving the theatre. You forgot I was there. Then you said, "No one really cares about slaves and their lives." You can't deny it. I heard you say it.'

'I did.'

'Then don't try to fool me with kindness and soft words. I am no man's *puella defututa* and I won't be treated as one.'

'I meant nothing bad by what I said,' Marcellus protested. 'What I meant was that people don't care enough about slaves and I believe they should – I care for you more than you know.'

'Is this all just pretty talk to make me fall for you?' Brea was breathing hard. 'I confess, I believe you're a good man and I'm grateful to you for what you've done for my father. But I won't pay for it with the only thing I have left that is mine to give...'

'I don't ask that of you, Brea.'

'Then I'll take my leave while I may. Good night to you, Master.'

'Brea—'

Brea was running through the damp grass towards the kitchens, her hair tumbling below her shoulders as she looked back briefly. Marcellus stood beneath a tree, watching her go. She hurried onwards, her feet almost slipping on the damp grass, until she reached the warmth of the kitchens.

Galyna was there alone, preparing oats for porridge. She gave Brea a disapproving look. 'Where have you been? You're late – I have much to do before I can retire.'

'I'm sorry.' Brea was breathing quickly, tidying her hair. 'I hurried from my mistress's chamber. I had to stay with her while she went to the theatre, then later, to help her undress.'

Galyna's mouth twisted in a snarl. 'It's all right for some, going to the theatre with their betters, spending time with them while they unwind. Now you're a lady's maid, all the extra work falls to me.'

'And I'm here to help. Let me prepare the porridge for tomorrow while you retire to bed.'

'Why would you do that?' Galyna was suspicious.

'I know how busy you are.' Brea smiled. In truth, she'd be happy to have some time alone, to compose her thoughts. She was terrified that Marcellus might sweep into the slave kitchens, grab her by the wrist and insist she hear him out again.

'Well, if you're sure,' Galyna said, her face doubtful.

'Of course.' Brea offered a sweet expression. 'It won't take me long.'

She watched Galyna slink tiredly away to the small bedroom, then she turned her attention to stirring the oats. Her mind flickered back to Marcellus, and the emotions she'd denied in the orchard flooded back so quickly she put a hand to her head to steady herself. It was almost like a dream, the declaration of love, the kiss. Brea forced herself to breathe calmly. She needed to think things through.

Marcellus had strong feelings for her, she believed that much was true. She'd felt it in the kiss; her own response was to kiss him back and not stop. She'd wanted nothing more than to hold him in her arms, to be swept from her feet. But she was a slave, she was wise and she knew what might have happened if she'd allowed her emotions to rule her head. Most likely, she'd be lying alone on the damp grass now while her master returned to the warmth of his room. Marcellus wasn't a bad man – she wanted to believe he loved her and probably, while he was protesting his feelings, he truly did –

but she wouldn't allow herself to become his mistress. She couldn't let it happen.

The rush of weak feelings came back, the moment he'd kissed her, and Brea was enveloped in powerful desire again. It would be so easy to bend, to be swept away on the moment's tide.

But there was something more important to fill her thoughts. Her father was alive; he was two fights away from freedom. She held her breath – if Marcellus truly loved her as he'd protested, perhaps he'd set her free too. Then she and her father could leave Camulodunum forever. If that happened, she'd never look back. Another thought followed quickly. She'd craved nothing more than her freedom since the day she was taken as a slave, and to be with her tribe. Now, it would be hard to leave Marcellus – she'd never be able to forget him.

She wiped her hands; the porridge was done, ready to be warmed the next morning. On silent feet, she made her way back to the servants' quarters, telling herself she was calm now, she was focused on the one thing that mattered, setting her father free. In the shadows, she saw the vague outline of three figures lying on tiny beds, breathing regularly in slumber. There was a low sigh; Daphne was dreaming.

Brea slipped off her tunic and clambered beneath the thick blanket, closing her eyes. She'd wash her face before dawn tomorrow, brush her hair, clean her teeth with a chewed, frayed stick. Now, she was tired and all she wanted was to fall asleep.

It was cold beneath the blanket and she shuddered. Brea thought about the long difficult day, the emotions that had tossed and troubled her. She thought again about how she'd sobbed in the orchard, the turbulence of knowing she'd lost her mother, but finding her father at last.

She wrapped her arms around herself to keep warm and, suddenly, she was in Marcellus's strong embrace again, and the wave of passion that lifted her made her dizzy.

But she was no concubine, no plaything. Brea promised herself she'd never allow herself to be so close to her master again. From now onwards, she'd keep him at arm's length.

It was the only way she'd be safe from her swirling emotions.

29

Hanna sat on the edge of her mother's bed and watched Stephanie, whose emotions were wavering between excitable and hysterical as she flung clothes from the wardrobe, trying to decide on her outfit for the hen evening in King's Lynn.

'I can't wear this dress, Hanna – it makes me look frumpy.'

'Wear jeans, Mum.'

'Will Serenity's mother be wearing jeans?'

'She might – I don't know. She's probably serving at the table – she works in the pub.' Hanna smiled fondly. 'It's just a meal...'

'It's more than just a meal. I'll only ever have one hen night.' Stephanie was anxious again. 'Oh, perhaps I can just go in casual clothes. It's not as if I haven't been married before. I have a thirty-year-old daughter, for goodness' sake.'

'I'll be thirty in November.' Hanna rolled her eyes affectionately. 'You're putting years on me.'

'Oh, I don't know why I agreed to this.'

'You deserve some fun. And it's just a quiet meal in the South Gate Arms.' Hanna's voice was calm. 'We'll have a nice time, and you can have a couple of drinks – I'm driving.'

'You're right, you're right.' Stephanie flapped a hand in front of her face.

'Oh, look how nervous I am and this is only the hen night. The wedding is in three days' time and I'm a wreck.'

'You'll have the time of your life.' Hanna smiled. 'It'll be a gorgeous wedding and a lovely reception.'

'And Paddy keeps inviting more and more people to the disco in the evening – the place will be jam-packed.'

'Ah – I invited Serenity. Is that okay?'

Stephanie breathed deeply. 'It will have to be. Oh, I mean – of course it will. What time do we have to be in King's Lynn? Oh, goodness – it's almost seven – we'll be late.'

'We won't. Put your jeans on, Mum, and a sparkly top. You're the bride – you can do whatever you want. Make the most of it.'

'You're right.' Stephanie pulled open a drawer and began riffling through layers of denim. 'Which jeans should I wear? Faded ones, black ones? Oh, I'm not sure these faded ones fit me any more.'

'Wear the black ones, and the silver sparkly top.'

'Yes, right, I will.' Stephanie took another deep breath, pulling on her clothes hurriedly. 'We haven't even got a honeymoon planned. I mean, what sort of wedding will it be, with no proper honeymoon?'

'I thought you were going somewhere in November.'

'Paddy hates to leave the farm – either he's ploughing or harvesting or it's the pigs... but he's promised we'll book somewhere soon.' Stephanie shook her head. 'Oh, do I really want to be a farmer's wife?'

'Of course you do,' Hanna soothed. 'Come on, Mum. Right, are we ready to go?'

'I'm ready.' Stephanie paused, thinking. 'Do you know, we're getting married on Saturday afternoon and this morning, Paddy said he'd just have time to start on the muck spreading before we left for the registry office.' She placed her hands on her hips. 'I said, "Really, Paddy?" We're getting married at two thirty and he's seriously going to stand next to me as a bridegroom, having just spread twenty-five acres of manure?'

Hanna wrapped an arm around her. 'Time to let your hair down, Mum.'

'Oh, I nearly forgot – the hairdresser is coming round on Saturday morning at half nine, and I've asked her just to have a quick look at yours too – is that all right?'

Hanna pushed a hand through her pixie cut. 'It'll all be fine, Mum. Come on, we've a hen party to celebrate.'

* * *

Hanna and Serenity were sitting opposite Stephanie, who was drinking champagne courtesy of Serenity's mother, Patsy, who sat next to the bride-to-be, filling their glasses.

Patsy raised her drink. 'To Steph and Paddy.' It was the third toast she'd made in the last half an hour. 'Right, we've finished the starter. How was the prawn cocktail, Steph?'

'Lovely.' Stephanie put a finger to her nose; the champagne bubbles tickled.

'It was clever of you to get the night off, Mum.' Serenity had hardly touched her starter.

'I wouldn't miss a hen party,' Patsy admitted. 'And I really wanted to push the boat out for you, Steph. It's so important to make memories. So – what was I saying, Serenity, oh, I remember – my ex-husband Bob, he was a real stick-in-the-mud. He wanted to call her Christine after his mother. I mean – can you imagine my Serenity being called Christine? And I was a mad flower-power hippy, long hair, short skirts. It was either going to be Serenity or Indigo...'

'Christine's a great name,' Serenity countered. 'At least I wouldn't have been teased at school.'

'Your father wanted to call you Marguerite, Hanna,' Stephanie said.

'I didn't know that...' Hanna began.

'Oh, there's a lot you don't know about your father,' Stephanie spluttered into her champagne. 'Simon could be a real stickler. He was rarely home, but when he was, he cast such a cold shadow over the house.'

'Good riddance to them both, I say, your Simon and my Bob.' Patsy swigged from her glass and looked around. 'Oh, good, here's the food. Thanks, Gina, love.' She grinned in the direction of the small waitress who carried a heavy tray. 'So, the rare steak is mine – it has to be only just dead, you know – and the well-cooked one belongs to our bride-to-be here and our two girls are having the risotto.' She winked towards Serenity. 'We're saving room for puddings.'

The waitress placed a huge plate of seared meat and piles of chips in front of Stephanie, who stared at it unbelievingly. 'I won't fit into my wedding dress.'

'You only live once, Steph – get it down you.' Patsy filled everyone's glasses again.

Hanna placed a hand over the top of her sparkling water just in case Patsy poured champagne in it. She smiled at the waitress. 'Thanks – this looks lovely.'

'The food here's great,' Serenity said. 'Are you sure you're okay with doing the driving while we're all drinking like fish, Hanna?'

'Absolutely – this is Mum's special night.'

'I'll be totally useless tomorrow morning.' Serenity hadn't touched her food, but she'd almost finished a glass of champagne. 'I'm glad you'll be in the café. Mind you, Thursdays aren't usually too bad.'

Patsy wrapped an affectionate arm around her daughter. 'Serenity's a chip off the old block, just like her mum. A proper party girl.'

Stephanie sipped champagne. 'I'm sure Hanna's had her share of parties.'

'Did you party much when you were in China?' Patsy asked, munching. 'I bet it was all work and no play...'

'It was an international language school – I made loads of friends, and we all tended to go out as a big group. It was fun.' Hanna smiled, remembering.

'You didn't meet the man of your dreams there, though?' Patsy asked.

'I still live in hope.' Stephanie drained her glass. 'It seems strange being the bride first before my daughter – I can't wait until Hanna finds Mr Right.'

'Same,' Patsy wailed, refilling glasses. 'I liked Serenity's last boyfriend.'

'He wasn't even nearly the one, Mum.' Serenity pushed her plate away and reached for her glass. 'It will take someone special.'

'Exactly,' Hanna agreed with a complicit grin.

'Shall we get puddings afterwards?' Patsy wasn't listening. 'They do great chocolate brownies – with whipped cream.'

'Oh, I'm so full already,' Stephanie protested, staring in disbelief at her heaped plate.

'It's a special occasion.' Patsy laughed. 'Then afterwards, we can go to The Sphynx and let our hair down. It's ladies' night – free entry.'

'Oh, what a great idea,' Serenity said. 'We'll be able to dance until midnight.'

'Mum?' Hanna glanced at her mother nervously.

'Why not?' Stephanie drained her glass and Patsy promptly filled it. 'It's my hen night and I haven't been clubbing in ages.'

* * *

It was past twelve as Hanna emerged from The Sphynx, her arms around Stephanie and Serenity. She was holding her mother up. Stephanie was laughing. 'I danced non-stop, thanks to all that champagne. A young man I've never met in my life propositioned me and he couldn't have been over thirty-five.'

'I saw it, Mum.' Hanna recalled prising her mother from the arms of a short man who wore a pink shirt and matching tie. Stephanie and Patsy had been prancing around on the dance floor for an hour, waving their arms like gladiators in an arena. Then the man in pink had tried to kiss her.

'He told me he thought we were sisters, you and me, Hanna. He thought I was a model.' Stephanie almost fell over the kerb. 'I said I was getting married and he said it was such a waste.' She burst out laughing.

Hanna smiled to herself. 'Let's get you home.'

'Mum will be all right,' Serenity said. 'She found a few of her friends. She'll be going back to someone's house.'

'She has some constitution,' Hanna admitted.

'More than I do,' Stephanie wailed.

'But have you had a lovely time?' Hanna asked.

'Wonderful, I felt like the star of the show with you looking after me.' Stephanie waved an arm loosely and it landed around Hanna's neck. 'It's been a great hen night. I'll pay for it in the morning.'

'You can sleep in,' Hanna suggested kindly.

'Whereas you and I will be in the café.' Serenity sighed.

They had reached the car park, and Hanna carefully strapped her mother into the back seat of the Range Rover, then she and Serenity clambered into the front.

Stephanie yawned. 'I might just fall asleep.'

'We'll drop you home first, Mum,' Hanna suggested.

Stephanie yawned. 'Yes – Paddy will be back. He and Ollie went for a quiet drink in The Dribbling Duck. He'll help me to bed.'

'I'm sure he'll be delighted.' Serenity grinned. 'I'm on my own so I'll have to crawl upstairs.'

Hanna drove the car through King's Lynn, where a few people still loitered in the streets, and then she took the road through the countryside. She turned on the radio to a channel playing pop music and sneaked a peek through the driver's mirror. Her mum lolled sideways, her eyes closed.

The car idled at Bramble Wood Farm as Paddy rushed outside, scooping Stephanie in his arms as she rested her head on his shoulder. He glanced towards Hanna. 'Did she have a good time?'

'We went clubbing,' Hanna admitted. 'Mum was dancing all night. She's exhausted, but she enjoyed herself.'

'She was the best dancer there,' Serenity gushed, although she'd owned the dance floor herself for most of the evening.

Hanna wound down the window. 'What about you, Paddy? Did you have fun in the pub?'

'Everyone kept buying me drinks.' Paddy laughed. 'I must've invited most people in the bar to the disco at The Sprowston. I'm a bit worse for wear.' He kissed the top of Stephanie's head. 'Come on, love – let's get ourselves inside.'

'Make yourselves strong coffee.' Hanna watched fondly as they shuffled towards the front door. She called, 'I'll be back as soon as I've dropped Serenity off.'

Hanna drove along the dark road towards Little Rymer. Serenity was wide awake, chatting constantly. 'I wish my mum would stop banging on about me finding a boyfriend.' She made a face. 'She said she liked the last one, but she was always telling me I was too good for him.' Serenity paused, remembering. 'She was right.'

'My mum's the same,' Hanna admitted. 'I'm such a disappointment. She wants grandchildren.'

'I'm happy as I am. I'm in no rush,' Serenity said.

'Exactly.'

Hanna glanced towards the deserted platforms as they passed the station. They left the Little Rymer sign behind them, then Hanna swung the Range Rover into the main street and stopped at a three-storey house that was divided into flats. Serenity had her front door keys ready.

'Thanks for a great evening. I really enjoyed it.'

'Me too,' Hanna agreed.

Serenity slid out of the car. 'If you want to roll in at half nine, that's fine. I'll open up,' Serenity called, then she was at her front door, waving.

'Oh, I won't be late.'

Hanna pulled away, turning the radio up for company, leaving the village behind. The road was empty and she drove slowly, the headlights bright in the centre of the road, the edges in shadow. Trees hung overhead, a dark latticed canopy, then she was out in the fenlands, surrounded by an expanse of fields and waving grasses and the mist drifting in from the lowlands. Clumps of straggly haze hovered in front of the car, then it thickened to a hanging fog that shone eerily in the lamps. Hanna pressed the brake lightly as the road beyond was enveloped in a shifting vapour. Suddenly, she could see very little beyond the car bonnet.

The radio began to whine, as if the station had become distant. Hanna reached out, her fingers pressing the buttons, but the interference continued, a distorted whimper. She turned the radio off and the car was filled with eerie silence.

The mist was thick now as Hanna edged forwards. Then the clumps parted and the road was visible again. A silver-grey figure stood in the centre, her head down. Hanna's automatic reaction was to brake suddenly and the car stalled with a shudder. The woman stood in the beam, shrouded in mist, raising her head to look straight at Hanna. Her face was filled with sadness. She opened her mouth as if to cry out, then the fog swept across the road like a veil and the wraith swirled away.

Hanna started the engine furiously and leaped as the Range Rover was filled with sudden roaring. She pressed the accelerator, lurching forward.

The car was enveloped in cold air as the fog parted like the threads of chiffon and the road ahead was clear, luminous in the yellow headlights.

Hanna felt as if someone had placed an ice cube against her skin, cold water melting down her back as she drove towards the farm. Then something moved behind her. She could hardly breathe – she was not alone in the car. Hanna was sure the figure she had seen in the mist was inches away now, in the back seat, touching her neck with delicate cold fingers.

She shivered and headed towards home as fast as she could, too terrified to glance in the driver's mirror. From behind, she could hear the sound of light breathing.

30

For the next few days, Brea was busier than ever. When she wasn't comforting Aurelia, who was suffering from wedding nerves or panicking about what to wear for the gladiator tournament, she was rushing around the *domus* with other slaves, preparing for the marriage. Canipectus had arrived with several servants, carrying newly fired pots, fine dishes and jugs of various shapes and sizes for the feast. Galyna was weary, attempting to organise where the food should be kept and the pottery should be stored. Chloe, doing two tasks at once, stumbled and broke a smooth brown beaker and was promptly slapped for her mistake, Galyna threatening that if she broke any more, she'd have her whipped.

Brea managed to avoid Marcellus, although he was in her thoughts all the time, no matter how hard she tried to push them away. She knew that he spent a lot of time riding Venator and when he wasn't out in the forests outside Camulodunum, he was in the baths, talking to his father and other soldiers, so she stayed in the kitchen or with Aurelia. She wouldn't venture into the orchard.

Aurelia sought out her company regularly, although mostly Brea was asked to sit and listen to her reminiscing about her family in Rome.

It was the day of the gladiators' combat in the arena, three days until the wedding. Brea woke early and took a honeyed pancake to the *triclinium*, where she found Publius Julius sprawled on a couch. He waved her over. 'I hope you've brought wine, *ancilla*. I have a thirst on me this morning.'

'It's here, Master,' Brea said. She knew Publius Julius would always drink wine even if his appetite wasn't good. She handed him a cup and he took a deep draught.

'Where's my son? And Lucius isn't here yet – I haven't seen much of that young man for several days...'

Brea pretended not to know. She'd heard the gossip from some of the servants, Daphne particularly, that the young soldier made his way to Julia's house most evenings and didn't return until the following morning. Brea thought it was none of her business, but she wondered how Julia managed to keep her nightly affairs secret from her husband. She wondered if Caius Fabius no longer cared what his wife did. She muttered, 'Master,' and glanced at her feet.

Publius Julius pushed a morsel of food into his mouth with his fingers, licking sticky honey. 'I can only eat the breakfasts you make, *ancilla*.'

'Master.' Brea acknowledged the compliment.

He leaned forward. 'It's the gladiator games later.' He smacked his lips. 'I believe my daughter has a champion and it'll be a good contest to watch. I intend to be there and I've invited my friend Caius Fabius, although he's not keen to watch the games nowadays. He tires easily,' Publius Julius grunted as he drank from his cup. 'I have had enough now, *ancilla*. I'll rest awhile and then my slaves will take me to my baths. You may go.'

'Master.' Brea picked up the tray of food and wine and rushed back to the kitchen. Galyna was complaining that more wedding food would arrive today and Daphne was busy preparing a fish.

Chloe thrust a tray of bread and fruit into Brea's hands. 'There you are – your mistress's breakfast.'

Brea smiled. 'She'll need it. She's a nervous bride.'

Daphne didn't turn round. 'In her place, I'd be ravenous – and not just for breakfast.'

'Master Marcellus has become more handsome than ever,' Chloe agreed. 'He's back from riding his horse, rugged and tousled.'

Brea said nothing and made to leave, the tray in her hands.

'If I were Aurelia, I'd have already sampled the goods.' Daphne laughed and Galyna swiped a hand, clipping her ear.

Brea made her escape, hurrying up the marble steps towards Aurelia's room. She found her sitting on the edge of her bed quietly. Brea placed the tray on a low table. 'How are you feeling?'

'I might spend some time at the loom today.' Aurelia stretched her limbs. 'Weaving calms me. And I have much need of being calm.'

'Are you still listless?' Brea chose a blue robe, hinting that she was ready to help Aurelia into it.

'I am. I have seen little of Marcellus, but we'll go to the arena together later. I'm not looking forward to seeing the contest. Brea...' An idea had occurred to Aurelia. 'You'll come with me and we'll turn our backs and you can arrange my hair, so I don't need to watch my champion. I wish Julia and Marcellus hadn't persuaded me to take one.'

'I'll stay close to you.' Brea felt nervous; she wanted to watch her father fight, but the thought of him battling against a strong gladiator half his age worried her. She intended him to know that she was there at the arena, that she believed he could win. She was sure that he would. He'd always been valiant and fearless. She wouldn't allow herself to think otherwise.

Aurelia extended an arm, so that Brea could dress her. 'Yes, I'll wear the blue one, and my jewellery, of course.' She sighed. 'I'm to be married in three days, then Lucius will leave to join his legion. I've seen so little of him recently.'

Brea gazed at her feet. 'Mistress.'

'I long to see him, Brea. He's the only person who makes me feel happy. I'm trying hard to be a good wife, but Marcellus is often busy.'

'Perhaps he's giving you time to prepare for the wedding, to contemplate?' Brea said awkwardly. She was unsure how to talk to Aurelia about her husband-to-be now. She felt ashamed and disloyal after what had happened in the orchard. From now onwards, she would try her hardest to support her mistress.

'I know my duties. I won't shirk them. I'll run the household, be a good hostess to guests, be dignified and treat my husband with respect.' Aurelia sighed. 'When I'm alone, I think constantly of my mother and wish I was in Rome.'

'Perhaps the gladiator contest will give you some cheer,' Brea tried hopefully. 'All eyes will be on you as the bride-to-be.'

'I'll be glad when it's all over and Marcellus goes off to battle. At least then I can weave during the day, or bathe in the waters. Heaven forbid that I should spend much time with Julia – all she talks about is her lovers.'

Brea wondered if Aurelia suspected her brother was spending time at Julia's house. She said nothing as she lifted the gold and carnelian necklace and draped it around Aurelia's neck, sliding the snake bracelet on her arm.

Aurelia smiled. 'Do I look well?'

'Indeed.'

'And I'll look very much the bride in the beautiful robe they have prepared for me.' Aurelia sounded bored. 'I'll eat some of this fruit and then I'll spend time at the loom. You may go about your duties, Brea, but come to me again before the gladiators' contest. I'll need your company.'

'Very well,' Brea said, scuttling from the *cubiculum* towards the kitchen as quickly as she could.

She bumped into Marcellus approaching from the other direction, striding from the orchard. She met his eyes, aware of the dark brooding gaze, and she looked away. She was almost past him when she heard him call, 'Brea?'

It troubled her that he used her name instead of the usual *ancilla*. It was acceptable for Aurelia to call her by her name – she was her personal maid – but when Marcellus said 'Brea', it was suddenly intimate. She hoped no one had heard.

'Master.' She stared at the tiled mosaic floor. He needed to remember that she was a slave – she was afraid that other slaves might see them talking together.

'I've just come from riding Venator. We went into the forests outside Camulodunum. It's most pleasant there.' Marcellus clearly wanted to make conversation.

'Master,' Brea said again quickly.

'How is Aurelia?'

'She's well.'

'And does she talk of me, of our marriage?'

'You must ask her yourself.' Brea refused to be drawn into conversation. She heard him exhale.

'Brea.' Marcellus's voice was thick with emotion. 'I wanted to talk to you, about what happened in the orchard, to explain how I feel.'

'You explained well enough,' Brea muttered, forcing her eyes upwards to meet his. She wanted to examine his expression. His eyes gleamed with warmth.

'Brea, we can go to the orchard to talk now. You can bring me wine, as if I have ordered it.'

'I'd rather not.' The words were out before she could help them. 'It's not fair, Master. You'll be married soon. I won't be used as many slave women are.'

'That's not what I want. I...' He took a breath as another thought came to him. 'This afternoon, we'll go to see your father fight. I pray that he'll win, that we'll free him soon.'

'I pray for it too,' Brea said quietly. 'I thank you for all you've done. And I'll repay you in any way I can – but one.'

Marcellus's voice was so low it was a whisper. 'Do you care for me, Brea?'

'May I return to my duties?' Brea murmured. She needed to be away from Marcellus. Every moment she spent in his company made it likely that she would betray her feelings.

'Tell me,' Marcellus persisted. 'Do you feel, as I feel for you?'

'You know it,' Brea said quickly, then she glanced up and saw Daphne coming towards her with an empty platter. She assumed Lucius had returned and had finished breakfast. She called out eagerly, 'Daphne, could you bring the master some wine?'

'Of course.' Daphne's face flushed with anticipation.

'Thank you, *ancilla*,' Marcellus said swiftly, and was on his way.

Brea smiled in Daphne's direction and rushed off to the kitchen, her heart thudding.

* * *

Later in the afternoon, Brea's heart was still beating too fast as she stood behind Aurelia in the arena, among the many spectators who had flocked to watch the fighting. Caius Fabius and Publius Julius sat together, their heads close, talking, not watching. Julia clutched Lucius's bicep as she viewed the sport below, Balbina hovering. Addedomaros was competing furiously against a tall, muscular man in a loincloth, their swords clashing fiercely. The sound of cheering and heckling rang loud in Brea's ears as she glanced at Aurelia, pale and tired. Marcellus sat on the other side of his wife-to-be, his eyes on the contest.

Brea watched, hardly breathing. Addedomaros fought well; he moved easily, forward and back as if in a dance, then he thrust his sword and caught his opponent in the thigh. Blood oozed from the wound. Julia clapped her hands eagerly, cheering, her face flushed with excitement as Lucius watched her, rapt. As Addedomaros moved closer and raised his sword, his opponent made a swift stabbing movement and sliced his lower arm. Brea watched as Addedomaros's face changed from triumph to sudden pain, then he brought his sword down hard and his victim fell on his knees in the sand, defeated. Addedomaros raised his hands in triumph towards his sponsor and Julia cheered.

'My champion won. Oh, I chose well, didn't I?' She turned to Lucius, breathing lightly. 'You and I will leave now – I have something of great importance to share with you at our villa.' She tugged at his wrist and he hurried after her like a skittery pony. They were halfway down the steps, then Julia glanced over her shoulder and waved a hand towards Balbina. 'Lose yourself, *ornatrix*. I won't need your services for an hour or two.' Then she turned a corner and disappeared, and Balbina scampered away obediently.

The arena was empty. Brea watched intently as a man entered the ring wearing a loincloth, a face mask covering his expression. He waved a sword high and lifted a bright shield.

Publius Julius smiled, mildly amused. 'Look who it is – Buteo the bold. How many times have I seen the rogue emerge victorious here?'

'Many.' Caius Fabius leaned forward. 'This should be interesting.'

'One thing's for sure, his opponents rarely last long.' Publius Julius laughed.

Brea knew before her father entered the ring that it would be him. Esico walked calmly into the arena, standing at a distance, his sword in one hand, a shield raised. A ripple of laughter came from the spectators, then loud jeering. A scrawny old man wouldn't be likely to offer a real fight.

Brea felt Marcellus move behind Aurelia, placing a hand on her back as if for support. He leaned towards Brea, murmuring in her ear. 'I have faith in our champion.'

'I don't wish to watch,' Aurelia said, covering her face with trembling hands. 'Brea – come and stand with me, tend to my hair. We will look away.'

Brea followed her mistress as she moved behind the spectators. The sound of the crowd cheering and yelling grew louder and Brea was grateful not to watch and yet she longed to know what was happening.

Aurelia met her eyes. 'I see you enjoy the contest as little as I do. The blood has left your cheeks.'

'I'm sorry for it, Mistress,' Brea mumbled as she adjusted pins in Aurelia's hair with shaky fingers. 'I'm not afraid, though. If you wish it, I can go to see how your champion fares.'

'He will lose.' Aurelia looked sad. 'I have chosen badly. It seems to be the way with me, I always make wrong choices.'

'Perhaps not,' Brea replied. The spectators were shouting, waving fists excitedly, their cheering at fever pitch. 'Perhaps your champion makes a good fight of it.'

'I pray that it's soon over.' Aurelia shook her head sadly.

Brea glanced towards Marcellus, who turned to meet her eyes at that moment. He nodded, an imperceptible indication that Esico was competing strongly. Brea's smile of gratitude was undetectable to anyone but Marcellus.

The crowd made a sound that suggested something dramatic had happened. Brea knew a gladiator had fallen; the contest hung in the balance; a judgement was imminent. There was a moment's silence, then the crowd roared and began to cheer. Brea's heart thudded in her ears; she wondered if her father was still alive. She was almost too afraid to ask. But whatever had happened, it was done, the fight was over.

Then Marcellus was at her side. 'He has won.' He was speaking to Aurelia. 'Your champion has prevailed, my dear. Come, you must acknowledge him. It's expected.'

He shepherded Aurelia to the front of the group of spectators, bringing Brea with him. Esico stood humbly in the arena, a sword in his hand, Buteo the bold kneeling defeated on the sand. Brea scrutinised her father for signs of a wound and found none. Esico stared up towards Aurelia, and she inclined her head graciously in congratulations. Esico's eyes blazed, and he bowed lightly, then he looked up again and smiled.

Brea held her breath. Her father's smile had not been for Aurelia, a polite gesture of thanks for the woman who had sponsored him as her champion. It had been for his daughter, a gesture of his love. Brea smiled back, pressing her fingers against her lips.

Her father would be free soon – he was halfway there.

31

For three nights, Hanna suffered the same turbulent dream. She was the woman who stood in the road, motionless in front of the stalled car. She couldn't move, she opened her mouth, but she couldn't cry out for help. She was completely powerless. Then she was whisked up in the air to a different place, in some sort of arena, forced to watch from a height as men battled below, a macabre dance. Emotions she couldn't understand tossed her as if on stormy water. The men who fought in the sand were taking part in a contest. It troubled her; she was afraid for their safety. It was as if she wanted to watch, but coils of dense mist drifted in front of her eyes and for a moment her vision was blurred. She tried to call out, to scream, but something stopped her mouth. The mist filled it, it choked her, and she fell as if something had hit her from behind. Her lungs wouldn't work. She couldn't breathe. Then a man was beside her, holding out a hand. His gleaming eyes burned into hers, as if imploring. It was Lucas Wright. Then it wasn't: it was someone else, a soldier, a man with a fierce horse, armour, a sword. Her heart began to pound and she was falling again.

Hanna woke in a sweat. The figure she'd seen in the mist on the night of her mother's hen party was still with her, the cold of her fingers, the rasp of her breath; she couldn't shake the image from her mind. She glanced at her phone on the bedside table. It was early, just past two, Saturday morning.

Her alarm was set for eight – it was her mother's wedding day; she'd need to be rested and ready, but she felt tired, worn out by her imagination.

Hanna rolled over, in a desperate attempt to sleep again. Her heart was still pounding; part of her stuck in the dream, held fast there. She shuddered beneath the covers and remembered that Roly had told her about a good friend who believed the past was somehow still present. Hanna wanted to meet this person.

Her phone was still in her hand and she searched for Roly Keys. She didn't hesitate to think as she thumbed a message.

Hi Roly, Can you come back and look for more treasure next week. By the way, I'd love to meet your friend and talk about a strange experience I had near the farm. Might it shed some light on the jewellery? Hanna.

She sent it before she had time to reconsider, then she read it back and wondered what Roly would think of it. But she needed help and had no idea who else to turn to. It wasn't something she could mention to her mother or Paddy, and certainly not now – the wedding was later today. She'd tell Oliver afterwards. But she wanted to confide in someone, as she lay in bed, still terrified. She trusted Roly – part of him lived in the past. He'd understand – she knew he would.

She tossed over again and closed her eyes. Hanna breathed in deeply, out again to calm her mind. Behind her eyes, she saw the wraith in the mist, standing in the centre of the road in the fenlands. The pounding of her heartbeat became the thundering of feet on the ground, people charging into battle, running hard. It became the thumping and clapping of hands, spectators in an arena, jeering and yelling. Then it changed again – it was hushed but still insistent, a gentle tap-tapping sound of fingers against glass. Hanna opened her eyes. It was there again, fingers rapping lightly against the windowpane.

Hanna listened, staring into darkness, silence filling the room. There it was, she was sure of it, fingers brushing glass, a light scratching.

She sat up straight in the bed and listened again. For a few moments, there was nothing, and she wondered if the sound had been part of a dream. Then it came again, more insistently, and Hanna's heart thudded in her throat. Just outside the window, there was a rattle of fingers behind the glass. Hanna knew the figure was out there again in the field below, a shadow between the boundaries of fence and hedge in the absolute darkness. But she had to be sure.

Hanna slid out of bed, asking herself what she was doing. She should be resting, thinking about her mother's wedding, trying to sleep. But she approached the curtains, her feet silent against the floorboards, and took a deep shaky breath. Again there it was, an imperceptible tapping, like a bird's beak against the pane. She hoped that's what it was, a tiny creature hovering outside.

Her fingers gripped the curtains and she pushed them back.

A face glimmered from behind the glass, a pale woman with loose hair, shining eyes, her mouth wide as if crying out.

Hanna closed her eyes, feeling her heart pound. When she opened them, her reflection was gazing back. She stared through the pane into the darkness below at murky blackness, fields and hedgerows. Her brain was overactive, she was feverish and tired. She must have imagined it.

* * *

Brea opened her eyes and reached for her clean underwear, wrapping a *strophium* around her chest, tugging on the underslip, her tunic over the top, tying it roughly. She brushed her teeth and combed and pinned up her hair. It was her mistress's wedding day. She'd need to wake her with some food, a light meal of fruit and wine or water, then she would dress her. Brea had decided to concentrate hard on the tasks in hand, to make her mistress look beautiful. She wouldn't think of anything else.

She rushed through the *domus* that had been decorated with garlands and wreaths to announce a special event was taking place. Ribbons were hung from every corner, bright colours waving in the early-morning breeze. Brea arrived in the *cubiculum* with a tray piled with fruit. Aurelia was still in bed, but her eyes were open. She murmured, 'Is it time already?'

'Today is a blessed day,' Brea said encouragingly.

Aurelia groaned and sat up. 'Then today I shall be a bride,' she said. 'I must look my best.'

Brea busied herself for the next two hours, dressing Aurelia in a golden robe. She paid special attention to her hair, separating it carefully into six locks, tying each in place with ribbons that formed a cone shape. Brea placed a wreath of flowers and a saffron veil over her head, adorned her with jewellery and she was ready.

Brea scrutinised Aurelia's face. 'How do you feel?'

'I feel the same as I do each day. Am I supposed to feel excited?'

Brea felt sorry for her mistress; she knew exactly how she'd feel in her place.

Aurelia was thoughtful. 'Perhaps if my parents were here, I'd feel better. I should enter my husband's house having smeared the doorways with sheep's wool covered in oil and fat, so the gods will protect me now that I live here. Last night I prayed to Juno, Venus and Hymen that I would have many sons.' She was quiet for a moment. 'Do you think Marcellus is handsome?'

Brea looked away. 'It's not my place to think such thoughts.'

'But you're a woman,' Aurelia persisted. 'In my place, wouldn't you think yourself fortunate to marry such a man?'

Brea chose her words carefully. 'It matters only what you think.'

'He's kind, handsome, strong, rich. I could have been given a husband who is less pleasant. But it matters not to me.'

Brea tried to change the subject. 'I think there has been a sacrifice of a pig as dawn broke. I could smell it from the atrium. The rituals have started...'

'I've known for years that I'd marry Marcellus. After his first wife died, I was chosen by his father and mine to be next. I knew then that Marcellus didn't want to marry again. I was nineteen years old then. Marcellus must be thirty years of age now.'

'I don't know how old he is,' Brea said.

'Neither of us wishes to be married. We are courteous to each other – we know what is expected.' Aurelia wanted to talk, needed to confide in someone. 'My mother told me I was blessed to be betrothed to such a man. But I cried every night when I found out I'd have to come to this cold country and leave my family. Lucius offered to accompany me. He wants so much to prove himself. He isn't yet twenty-three.'

'He loves you dearly,' Brea began.

'And he'll leave soon. Then what will I do?' Aurelia's face clouded. 'I know what I'll do. I'll be strong. I know my duty.' She stood up slowly. 'And tonight, when my new husband takes me to his chamber and I am carried over the threshold, I'll be made a wife.'

'There is a wedding to be celebrated before then,' Brea said, in an attempt to cheer Aurelia, whose face was forlorn. 'I'm sure the feast is prepared and the guests will be gathering in the atrium. It's time for us to go.'

'It's time.' Aurelia stood up. 'My life will change forever. But I do my father's bidding.'

Brea watched her walk towards the doorway, her head held high, her robe sweeping across the tiled floor. She followed, feeling just as sad as her mistress.

* * *

Hanna sat across the table in pyjamas, munching toast, her eyes bleary, as Stephanie continued to fret. Her hair had been done beautifully and she looked lovely in a shimmering ivory tube dress. But she was nervous. 'Hanna, I ought to text him at least. What if Paddy's still asleep? Should you go over to Ollie's cottage to check?'

'It's gone eleven, Mum.' Hanna smiled. 'Besides, I smelled bacon frying, coming from Ollie's kitchen, when I put the rubbish in the bins an hour ago. That can't be Ollie, can it?'

'Do you think we're being silly, not seeing each other until we get to the registry office?'

Hanna shook her head, reaching for coffee. 'Tradition is important to you, Mum. Every wedding is different and you like these rituals. You can have just what you want – it's your day.'

Stephanie glanced at the wall clock. 'It's almost half past eleven and I'm not yet ready. I haven't put my jewellery on. I want to wear the gold pendant Paddy gave me for my birthday. It'll bring luck.'

'Is it in your room – shall I fetch it?' Hanna offered.

'No, I'll go. You need to get dressed, Hanna. And why wouldn't you let Sheila do your hair when she came? She's very good.'

'Oh, she is, you look gorgeous,' Hanna agreed. 'But mine's such a simple style. I'll just have a quick shower, throw the dress on and I'll be ready.'

Stephanie was aghast. 'Will you be like this at your own wedding, so laid-back?'

'I'd probably go to St Kitts and jump over a broomstick,' Hanna joked, then she saw the horror on her mother's face. 'You'd be the first to know, don't worry.'

'But I do worry, Hanna.' Stephanie paused, her expression suddenly nervous. 'When I come back tonight, I'll be Mrs Palmer, a proper farmer's wife. I hope I'll be good at supporting him.'

'You'll be brilliant – you're wonderful at everything, Mum.' Hanna leaned over and kissed her mother's cheek. 'Now don't worry so much. Just enjoy your day. The weather couldn't be better, you look a billion dollars and you're marrying a man who adores you...'

'You look tired out, love.' Stephanie touched Hanna's cheek. 'Have you been sleeping badly?'

Hanna opened her mouth; she was almost ready to tell the whole story, about her dreams, her sleepless nights, the figure in the mist. But that would be selfish and unfair: it was her mother's special day. She stretched her arms above her head. 'I'll be fine after a hot shower. I'm off to get changed. You get your jewellery on and I'll be with you in ten minutes.'

'Ten minutes?' Stephanie was horrified.

But Hanna was already on her way upstairs, her feet padding lightly as she ran.

32

Brea held a jug of water so that visitors could wash their hands whenever they pleased. The other slaves vied for good positions, all wishing to glimpse the bride in her beautiful golden robe and the groom in his vermillion toga. But she was happier to watch from a distance. She felt sad for Marcellus, for Aurelia and for herself. It was a wedding no one involved really wanted. Julia seemed bored as the *pronuba*, the bridesmaid, leading her new sister-in-law to the altar before the couple joined right hands. Aurelia spoke her vows clearly for all to hear. '*Ibi tu Marcellus, ergo ibi.*' 'Wherever you go, Marcellus, I go too.' Then they signed the marriage contract, Publius Julius clapping his hands in pleasure.

Sweet notes rang out from flutes and the celebrations began. Torchbearers filled the atrium and there was dancing and feasting. Marcellus and Aurelia sat side by side on a couch while they were served with a variety of dishes. Brea watched as Galyna tried to tempt Aurelia with honeyed almonds. Aurelia, demure throughout the celebrations, had little appetite, although she smiled briefly as Marcellus broke the ritual wheat cake over her head and she nibbled a piece hesitantly, knowing it was expected of her.

Brea watched as Julia, with her husband on the other side happily talking to Publius Julius, whispered into Lucius's ear, pressing a hand against his thigh. Then Daphne was next to her, whispering, 'Everyone knows that the bride's brother is Julia's plaything. Everyone except her husband.'

Brea nodded. 'It is best to say nothing.'

'It's wonderful to behold her antics, and how embarrassed he is. Look – his ears burn red.' Daphne's eyes danced. 'Caius Fabius is a bad commander, as they say in Rome – he can't keep his wife in check, although I believe he was once a great soldier.'

Brea was about to move away. 'Our guests need to wash their fingers...'

'But if he's caught with Julia, master Lucius will have slaves' urine poured over him. Or worse. I hear they castrate men who sleep with a rich man's wife.'

'I don't think about it,' Brea said honestly.

'A rich man may do as he pleases, though. Do you think the master Marcellus will have another woman as his concubine?'

Brea shook her head. 'I don't know.'

'A famous Roman once said, "You visit your wife out of duty, but a brothel for pleasure."' Daphne laughed. 'I wouldn't refuse him.'

Brea looked down at her water jug. Then Marcellus caught her eye, a smile on his lips.

Daphne grasped her wrist. 'Did the master just smile at you, Brea? Are you one of his favourites, even on his wedding day?'

Brea made a muffled sound, as if Daphne was talking nonsense. 'He merely wants me to bring water so the mistress can wash her hands.' She moved away quickly.

The sky was growing darker outside and much of the food had been eaten or wasted. Wine had been spilled on the tiled floor; there would be plenty of cleaning to be done. Brea glanced across to where Aurelia was talking quietly to Marcellus, inclining her head to listen to him, and she looked nervous. The feast was drawing to an end and it would soon be time for the bride and groom to leave together. Brea took a deep breath and approached her mistress, ready to offer her services.

* * *

Hanna had never seen her mother look so happy. From the moment she signed the wedding register with shaky hands, Stephanie hadn't stopped smiling. She grinned broadly as photographs were taken of her and Paddy beneath a whirl of confetti, and her smile was still wide now as she glanced at Ollie over the three-tier cake as he made a best son speech.

Hanna had to admit that Ollie was very entertaining and the guests loved his humour too. He read an emotional text from Abby in Australia, wishing she could be there, sending love from her and from Holden, promising to visit next year. Then he took a deep breath.

'Well, it's been an emotional day, even the cake is in tiers.' He rode the laughter and went on to joke, 'All those among you who know Stephanie well will know that she is a wonderful, caring person. She deserves a good husband. Thank God my dad married her before she found one.' But then he grew more serious and Hanna's eyes filled as he said how much he missed his mum who'd died years ago and how lonely his father had been, but how he embraced Stephanie as his mother now and how she was exactly right for his beloved, eccentric father.

The applause resounded and Hanna realised it was her turn to speak. She'd deliberately decided to keep it short, which was just as well – Ollie's speech had gone on for twenty minutes.

She stood calmly and smiled. 'Hi, I'm Hanna, Stephanie's daughter and... Paddy's stepdaughter and... Ollie's stepsister.' She grinned and was rewarded with warm laughter. She carried on, without a speech in her hands. 'I'd just like to say congratulations to my lovely mum and to Paddy. They deserve the greatest of happiness. So, Mum, Paddy – my wish is that your marriage will be a thing of beauty and joy forever, always as beautiful as you both are today. And may the loveliness of your marriage increase with each year. So, please, if you'd all raise your glasses. To Mum and to Paddy, my new dad. Here's to a sweetheart, a bottle and a friend. The first is beautiful, the second is full and the last is ever faithful.'

Glasses were raised and there was applause and a few tears. Stephanie's cheeks were damp and even Ollie's eyes glistened. Paddy raised his glass towards Hanna, his face filled with warmth and admiration.

Ollie leaned over and patted her hand. 'That was awesome, Hanna – you blew everyone away.'

'You too.' She grinned. 'I suppose I ought to call you bro now?'

'It's a pleasure to be related to you, sis.' Ollie smiled. 'Bags I get the first dance at the disco. They're setting it up now and it's going to be heaving in here in an hour or so.'

'The more, the merrier,' Hanna said happily as she gazed across at her mother and Paddy, whose lips were locked in a kiss.

* * *

Marcellus and Aurelia were about to leave the feast and move towards the *cubiculum* for their wedding night, according to tradition. Julia was tipsy, her arms wrapped around Lucius's neck, openly ignoring custom and the surprised stares of other guests. Publius Julius and Caius Fabius had left for the baths. Most of the other guests were hovering, having feasted and drunk wine for hours.

One man, a retired general in the army who knew Publius Julius well, leaned over to give some paternal advice. 'I hear you're going away into battle soon, Marcellus? Let me remind you, the marriage contract states that the only real reason for any marriage is to unite and have children.' He patted Marcellus's arm, both to convey his wit and to help him stand: he was very drunk. 'So, before you depart for the Island of Mona, make sure you leave her with a good serpent sting.' He laughed at his own joke.

Aurelia leaned against Marcellus as if she might faint.

Marcellus looked around for Brea and waved a hand. 'Can you attend upon your mistress a while? She has need of your support.'

Brea followed quietly as Marcellus escorted his new wife to one of the *cubicula* and he stood back in the doorway to let her through. She glanced into the room and hesitated: she didn't want to witness any of what might follow. A huge *lectus* had been prepared for the wedding night, a long couch strewn with flowers.

Aurelia stood nervously, trembling beneath her robe. She put her fingers to her mouth and murmured, 'I am yours to command, Marcellus.'

Marcellus took her hand and kissed it tenderly. 'Aurelia, I have no desire to bend to tradition, to pretend to kidnap the bride while you feign being unwilling and coy. I respect you too much for that.'

'I thank you.' Aurelia seemed baffled.

'It's been a long day and you must be weary,' Marcellus said politely. 'And my first duty as a husband is to treat my new wife with reverence and gentleness.'

'Thank you for your kindness, husband.' Aurelia shivered as he placed a hand on her robe; she believed he was about to untie it and slip it from her shoulder. Brea looked away and hoped she would be dismissed soon.

Marcellus stood back and bowed slightly. 'Then I wish you good rest. May Somnus allow you blissful sleep.'

'Marcellus?' Aurelia was mystified.

'Brea, can you attend your mistress?' Marcellus turned to her and his eyes blazed, a moment's understanding passed between them. Then he spoke to his wife, his voice hushed. 'I hope to see you tomorrow in the *triclinium* for breakfast, Aurelia. May your sleep be untroubled.' Then he turned on his heel and walked away.

Aurelia placed her fingers against her temples as if a pain had lodged there. 'He's left me alone. I didn't think for that to happen.'

Brea was by her side. 'He respects you, Mistress. He knows you're tired.'

'But...' Aurelia indicated the couch and was lost for words. She sank down on it, not able to talk.

'Why don't you do as he says, and sleep?' Brea soothed.

'Have I failed already in my duty as a wife?' There was a tremor in Aurelia's voice.

'Not at all,' Brea whispered. 'He's being thoughtful.'

'Guests may have seen him leave me – people will think that I'm unattractive, or that I've sent him away.'

'They'll think nothing of the sort,' Brea said encouragingly. 'They're all too busy drinking and feasting. I believe most of them have left already.'

Aurelia shook her head. 'What kind of wife am I that my husband turns his back on me on our wedding night?'

'You have your whole life in front of you. There's plenty of time.' Brea was doing her best to calm Aurelia, whose face was streaked with tears.

'Do you think so?'

'I do,' Brea coaxed. 'You have a husband who respects you enough to wait until you are ready to embrace him. What could be greater?' Her words echoed and hung in the air. Brea knew well why Marcellus had walked away from his wedding bed and left his wife confused. She also knew why he'd made sure she was there to witness it. Marcellus was reminding her that, however much he respected her, he wasn't in love with his wife. Brea suddenly felt ashamed. 'How can I help you now, Mistress?'

'You've assisted me more than you know, Brea. I was filled with the disgrace of a wife who believed she was a failure. But now I'm happy again. Marcellus respects me and we will share our wedding night when I'm ready. Now please, if you would – will you loosen my gown and remove my jewellery. Marcellus was right, I am weary and ready for sleep.'

'Of course,' Brea said quietly. 'Let me comb your hair for you and when you're rested, I'll go to the atrium and help the others to clear away the food and drink. It has been a day of great celebration, but we must make the *domus* clean by tomorrow, or the master will be unhappy.'

'My father-in-law?' Aurelia sighed, closing her eyes as Brea smoothed her hair. 'Everyone calls him Alba Barba, old White Beard – even his own daughter uses that name.'

'I have heard it...' Brea said quietly.

'And it seems that Lucius is now entangled with Julia. Brea, I was the last one to suspect it, then I saw her with her arms around him today. I must talk to him – it isn't proper for him to behave so, and my father would be shamed by it.'

Brea took a breath. 'Your brother leaves for the Ninth Legion soon. Perhaps it may be better to say nothing.'

'And then Marcellus will leave me to ride with the great Governor General Suetonius, and I'll be here alone. Do you think...' Aurelia twisted her head to look at Brea. 'Do you think I may be with child by then?'

'If the gods will it,' Brea replied simply.

'My husband will be away when the next gladiator contest takes place in the arena, when my champion fights again. I'll have to go there alone...'

'The master's father will be here, and the lady Julia.' Brea began to remove Aurelia's jewellery.

'And you will be there with me too.' Aurelia turned anxious eyes on Brea. 'It seems you're the only one who understands me, the only one who can help.'

'I'm a slave.' Brea lowered her eyes to hide her feelings. Aurelia was turning to her as a friend, and that could never be possible for so many reasons. Brea was filled with an aching guilt: Aurelia trusted her and Marcellus loved her. It made her feel regretful and sad. Whichever way the future unfolded, Brea could only find herself torn. She offered an arm as Aurelia lay down, covering her lightly with a blanket. 'Sleep well, Mistress.'

Aurelia's eyes were already closing. 'Thank you, Brea. You've lifted my spirits and filled me with hope.'

'May it always be so,' Brea said quietly and she meant every word.

She slipped quietly from the *cubiculum*, passing through the atrium towards the kitchens. Brea hurried forward; there was so much to do.

Then a man stepped in front of her, barring her way. His vermillion toga fluttered in the breeze and he uttered her name like a prayer. 'Brea.'

'Master?'

'I wish to talk to you, in the orchard.'

'I have work.'

'It's important,' Marcellus said quickly.

Brea stood in front of him, meeting his eyes boldly. She didn't trust herself to be alone with him again. The last time she'd run away, but she wasn't sure she'd be able to pull herself from his embrace a second time.

Marcellus took a breath, his gaze locked on hers. 'I have given a lot of thought to the matter I must discuss with you. I'm sorry for the pain I've caused, for being unfair to both you and to Aurelia. But I have a solution that will benefit us all. Please, accompany me to the orchard and hear me out. What I have to say concerns us both, and it has to be said tonight. Brea, please come with me. It won't wait.'

33

The function room of The Sprowston Manor Hotel was filled with music that vibrated from each wall. Hanna was really enjoying herself. She'd been dancing with Ollie for half an hour, copying his moves, he copying hers, laughing as they developed their own choreography. Ollie favoured a lot of hip swinging and finger clicking, but he quickly picked up Hanna's innate sense of rhythm, took her in his arms and invented his own ridiculous style of dirty dancing, which made them both laugh. Steph and Paddy had been in each other's arms since their first dance to 'Can't Take My Eyes Off You'. Hanna wondered if it was time to remind them to cut the cake.

Then the opening notes to 'Y.M.C.A.' boomed through the speakers and the bride and groom moved away while everyone else launched into the famous dance moves. Hanna turned to see Serenity standing behind her, in denim shorts and braces and an oversized hat. Hanna beamed in greeting and she, Ollie and Serenity threw themselves into the dance together.

Hanna wiped her forehead as the music ended. 'Does anyone want a drink?'

'I'm fine, thanks,' Ollie said and Serenity shook her head.

Hanna moved to the bar, leaving them dancing to 'Macarena', raising palms, bumping buttocks in perfect synchronisation. She watched the barman approach in a white shirt and dicky bow, and recognised him. He'd been to the same secondary school, although she hadn't seen him for years. 'Hi, Scott. Can I have a sparkling water.'

'Nothing alcoholic?' Scott asked. 'It is your mum's wedding.'

'I've had enough champagne.' Hanna grinned. 'How's life? I haven't seen you since sixth form.'

'I've worked here since I was eighteen. I'm a manager now. Two kids. I married Lauren, then we divorced.' Scott shrugged. 'It's all very amicable though. You?'

'Still footloose.' Hanna grinned as he placed a glass in front of her.

'Ice?'

'Lots,' Hanna began, then she was conscious of someone standing next to her.

'Same for me, please,' a voice said and Hanna turned to look into dark eyes. She felt the jolt immediately. Then Lucas Wright smiled. 'I'll get these.'

Hanna watched as he swiped his card, then she said, 'I suppose Paddy invited you.' She offered an apologetic smile – she hadn't meant to sound dismissive. She said, 'He's invited the whole village,' and was immediately worried she'd made things worse. She wondered why her heart was thumping and reminded herself to get a grip.

'I bought him a drink on his stag night,' Lucas said. 'He was inviting everyone in the pub.' He glanced around. 'It certainly looks like they all turned up.'

'Just for the disco and cake.' Hanna drank eagerly from the glass. 'It's thirsty work, all this dancing.'

'I noticed.' Lucas leaned against the bar. He looked handsome in a crisp white shirt and black jeans. Hanna wondered if he'd brought his girlfriend, if she'd appear from the ladies' at any moment and wrap her arms around him. Or perhaps she was in London. 'How's Nutmeg?' he asked.

'Oh, the wolf teeth? Yes, there's been no problem.' Hanna raised her voice over the music. 'Nutmeg's fine. I love her to pieces. I'm learning to ride again.'

'Paddy said you just came back from China?'

'Yes, from Guangzhou. I worked there in a language school.'

'Sounds fascinating. Can you speak Chinese?'

'I picked up some Mandarin while I was there.' Hanna decided she'd impress him. 'I speak French, German, Spanish, Latin, quite a bit of Italian and I can order food in Russian.' She grinned. 'Although I've never been to Russia.'

'That's a lot of languages,' Lucas agreed.

'But I can't file a horse's teeth,' Hanna joked.

'Oh, that's easy compared to some of the things I have to do.' Lucas raised an eyebrow. 'I'm not a great fan of cuterebra.'

'What on earth is that?'

'Cuterebra are large flies whose larvae infest the skin of dogs and cats. But this is a wedding – I'll change the subject.'

'How long have you been a vet?' Hanna asked. She was aware she was asking banal questions again, but there was something about Lucas that unsettled her, made her behave like a schoolgirl. She reached for her glass of water and took a sip, hoping to calm her jangling nerves.

'Let's see. Eight years training, five more working in London, then I came to live in Little Rymer.'

'What made you want to come to Norfolk?'

'I used to come here on holiday with my parents when I was a child.' Lucas sipped his water and the ice clinked in his glass. 'We stayed at Brancaster beach and I fell in love with the area. This is where I want to live and work.'

Hanna was struck again that a sadness clung to him. There was something else that drew her – it was almost as if she knew him already.

She offered her warmest smile and felt a little calmer. 'It's a special place. I've been in China for a while, but it's so good to come home.'

'I know what you mean,' Lucas agreed. 'I was born in London, but I really feel at home here.'

'So you bought our old house in Mawkin Close. I was riding past there on my bike – I think I nearly knocked you over.' Hanna laughed.

'I remember.' Lucas grinned. 'I knew it was a welcoming place as soon as I stepped through the door.' He met her eyes. 'There's an atmosphere to these parts that you can't ignore.'

'What do you mean?' Hanna was fascinated by his words.

'Tradition, history, I suppose. A warmth, a sense of belonging.' Lucas drained his glass. 'I love working here – the rugged fens, the flatlands, the animals. The pace in London is so fast and furious. When I was at Paddy's farm the other day in the pig field, it felt as if time stood still. Does that sound strange?'

'Not at all.' Hanna was staring at him. 'Did you hear about the necklace I found there when I was walking with Roy?'

Lucas shook his head. 'Paddy didn't mention it.'

'Looks like it's really old, Roman in fact. It fits in with what you were saying about the fens being steeped in history.'

Hanna gazed around the hall; her mother and Paddy were sitting at the table now, sharing champagne; Ollie and Serenity were still dancing in the middle of the pulsing throng, enjoying the wild moves of Michael Jackson's 'Thriller'. Everyone was occupied. She turned back to Lucas: he clearly understood how she felt about the fenlands; it was so easy to share her thoughts with him. Now she was desperate to tell him more. She made her move.

'Lucas – I hope I'm not being forward but – can we pop to the pub for a coffee and talk about all this? It's noisy in here and—'

'You can come round to your old house and I'll make us a coffee there,' Lucas offered. He smiled and the sadness she'd seen in his eyes seemed to disappear. 'I hope I'm not being too forward either.'

'Not at all,' Hanna said lightly, although her heart was thudding. 'It was what you were saying about the area being connected to the past. I want to tell you about how I found the necklace and – lots of other things about living in the fens. I'd be keen to get your reaction.'

'I'm all ears,' Lucas said.

Hanna grabbed her jacket and followed Lucas as they stepped outside into the cold air, leaving the boom of the music behind them. The night skies were filled with tiny stars, and a crescent moon hung like a low hook. She fell in time with his step as they walked through the quiet streets, past the church, the heavy scent of night stock drifting from the grassy borders. They were making small talk, Lucas asking about the wedding, Hanna replying with far too much enthusiasm. She was conscious that her heart was beating fast; she couldn't wait to tell Lucas more about herself, to confide in him about her dreams, and about the figure she'd seen in the mist. She asked herself if that was the real reason she was going with him to his home...

She wondered where their conversation would go, and what it might lead to. She gave Lucas a sidelong glance and he smiled at her. Hanna was taken aback at that moment by how incredibly good-looking he was – she felt the powerful tug of magnetism.

She'd got herself an invitation to his house because she wanted to share her recent experiences. But there was more to it than that. There was an empathy between them that was tangible, and something else, an unescapable, predetermined attraction that made her skin tingle.

Whatever happened next, Hanna was sure it was meant to be.

* * *

Brea followed Marcellus towards the orchard, her head down. Various slaves passed on their way to the atrium, busily tidying and cleaning the wedding debris away, their eyes moving towards her inquisitively. She hoped they'd think she was running an errand for Marcellus or his new wife. She prayed they wouldn't gossip. But Marcellus strode on ahead and she scuttled dutifully behind him, wondering what was so important. His words had intrigued her: *What I have to say concerns us both, and it has to be said tonight. It won't wait.* She wondered if it had anything to do with her father.

The orchard was all shadows, the grass sweet-smelling and damp. Brea felt the dew against her legs. They reached a tall tree with a thick trunk and a canopy of overhanging branches. In the darkness, it looked like a waiting giant.

Marcellus turned to her abruptly, his face severe. 'Brea, I'll try to be brief.'

'Master.'

'We came here to Britannia when I was twelve years old, my brother and my father, who was a legate in Claudius's army. My mother died when I was born. My brother was killed in battle when I was fifteen. Being the only son has given me a strong sense of duty to my father.' He took a breath. 'I was betrothed to my first wife at seventeen. You'd just arrived here at the *domus*, a little slave girl with fierce eyes who couldn't speak our tongue. I was aware of you; I heard that you were wild and had to be schooled in our ways. Then my father sent me away in the army, fighting for Emperor Claudius, learning to be a better soldier. I came home and was married. Claudia was a good woman, full of wifely virtues – and we were young and starry-eyed. We fell in love, but we spent many months of our time apart.'

Brea wasn't sure why he was telling her all this, especially since he said he'd be brief. She pressed her lips together in a secret smile. She was suddenly filled with affection for this honest, lonely man.

'I noticed you often. You were different from other slaves.'

'Because I am Iceni?'

'Because I was drawn to you. Not just your beauty and your strength. You have something else – integrity, honour. I'm a soldier – I value these things.'

Brea's voice was just audible. 'And as a soldier, you've killed my people. You were responsible for what happened to our queen and her daughters.'

Marcellus didn't flinch. 'I was.'

'And were you also there when my village was attacked and I was taken from my people and brought here? Were you part of that army?'

'I was a young soldier, but yes, I witnessed it,' Marcellus admitted with a heavy sigh. 'My father sent me along with a sword in my hand, to please him, to learn from observing others. It was I who chose you to be brought here.'

'Then how can I truly respect you, Master?'

'I can't answer that.' He took a step towards her. 'I believe you love me though.'

Brea edged backwards. 'I can't help how my heart is. You are a good man, you helped me be reunited with my father.'

'But do you love me?'

'I love who you are but not what you do,' Brea answered honestly. 'But today you married my mistress and we shouldn't be here talking of these things. You know it's wrong.'

'It is,' Marcellus said. 'That's why I've decided that, when I come back from battle, I'll set you free.'

Brea thought she had misheard. 'Free?' She was staring at him. 'You mean you'll stop your feelings for me and give all your attention to your wife?'

'No, I mean that, although it will pain me beyond words, I'll persuade my father to give you your freedom and you'll leave Camulodunum and return to your tribe. Your father will be free too and you'll go together.'

Brea marvelled at his words. She couldn't yet believe it. 'But why?'

'I ask you only to care for my wife while I am away fighting the Druids. If I don't return, I'll leave word for you to be freed in one year. But if I return sooner, you'll be free to leave immediately.'

'You would do that for me?'

'I've promised it. Because I love you most in the world, Brea. And although it pains me to let you go, it's the best way that I can show how much I care. Then I'll try to be a good husband to Aurelia. Perhaps in time we will learn to live together well. Earlier...' Marcellus closed his eyes for a moment, remembering. When he opened them again, he said, 'I should have behaved like a husband. But you saw it, Brea – I walked away. I couldn't stay with her. My lady thought I offered her a kindness. But I was thinking only of myself and of you. She deserves better than my indifference. So – you'll get your freedom.'

'Master.' Brea looked up, her eyes meeting his. 'I'm grateful, really I am.'

Marcellus gazed at her without speaking for a while. Then he said, 'I'm doing my best to make up for the many things I've done wrong, to be a good person. That's all.'

Brea saw the kindness in his eyes and she was filled with thankfulness. She placed a palm against his face. 'Master, you're the best of men.'

Marcellus seized her hand, bringing it to his lips. Brea heard him murmur her name and she closed her eyes: the thought flitted into her mind that if only she were free to love this man, she'd be truly happy. Then she was in his arms, their faces close.

Brea whispered, 'It would be easy to allow my feelings to control me, but I won't...'

'You're right,' Marcellus murmured, but he held her fast. 'May I ask one thing of you?'

At that moment, Brea would have agreed to anything. 'Ask.'

'I want to show you Venator, take you for a ride on him, just once. I love the way your eyes light up when you talk of horses.'

'I can't refuse you that,' Brea replied.

'Then tomorrow...' Marcellus thought briefly of a plan. 'Tomorrow your mistress will send you into Camulodunum with a message for a free woman who weaves wool. I will buy her a cloak and she'll send you with the instructions. Then, once you've delivered them, I'll be waiting with the stallion and we'll ride into the woods.'

'Very well.' Brea hesitated and Marcellus understood. She was still in his arms and he spoke into her hair.

'You can trust me to treat you well, to respect your honour.'

'I trust you.' Brea pulled away, feeling the sudden chill of the night air. His arms had kept her warm. More than anything she wanted to linger, but she said, 'I must go to help with the cleaning.'

'You must.' Marcellus didn't move. 'Until tomorrow then?'

'Tomorrow,' Brea replied, breaking into a run towards the atrium. There was so much work to do, but she didn't mind. Her heart was singing. Her master would set her free. To return with her father to her people was all she'd ever wanted in the world.

As she reached the atrium and began collecting empty cups and dishes, Brea was aware of another feeling that stirred behind the exhilaration. She knew what it was: it disturbed her, held her back from true happiness.

However much she longed to be free, leaving Marcellus would not be easy.

34

Hanna snuggled into plush cushions, cupped her hands around a mug and stretched her legs, feeling far too formal in the silk dress. She gazed around the room that had once been her home. It looked completely different now; the carpets had been taken up and floorboards varnished. The old leather three-piece suite had been changed for two cream sofas, there was a smaller modern TV and white bookshelves filled two walls, holding volumes of books of various sizes. The old wood burner still nestled in the hearth. Hanna searched the photos on the mantelpiece for signs of the girl-friend. Instead, she found animals, a horse, a fluffy dog.

Lucas sat opposite, sipping coffee, reading her thoughts. 'I guess this place has changed quite a bit?'

'Mum didn't do much to the house over the years. It looks fresher.'

'It's home,' Lucas said. 'A comfortable place to come back to after a long day.'

'It's very nice. So...' Hanna decided to ask the question that was buzzing in her head. 'Do you live by yourself?'

'Yes, it's perfect for me.' Lucas hesitated. 'My ex-girlfriend was going to move in, but it didn't work out.'

'Oh?' Hanna was interested; she couldn't help herself. 'Was she the woman you were with in Serenity's café?'

'Beth, yes,' Lucas explained. 'I used to meet her from the train at week-ends. But she didn't really like it here – she said the place was too quiet and I wanted to leave the bustle of London. She couldn't settle, we couldn't agree, then we split up.'

'I'm sorry,' Hanna began, her expression hiding a relief that she imme-diately felt guilty about.

'No,' Lucas said with a slight shrug. 'It was meant to be that way. In the end, it was less about love and more about location.'

'So, you were a vet in London?'

'Yes – it was a very different life working there.'

'Oh?' Hanna leaned forward.

'Not so many long days on farms, looking after sheep and pigs, up to my knees in muck, or delivering foals.'

'Do you prefer it here?'

'I do, definitely – and I'm determined to make it work.'

'How do you mean?' Hanna asked.

A sadness crossed Lucas's brow. 'Beth said I'd be back in London before the end of the summer. She was angry – she said I wouldn't be able to take the long hours, coming home to a cold house in the dark.'

'It does sound tough.'

'It makes me happy. It's a vocation,' Lucas said. He paused before asking the question. 'How about you – is there a boyfriend back in China?'

'I'm free and single,' Hanna enthused and wondered if she was coming across as too available, so she said, 'I'm not looking.' She decided that she shouldn't have said that either: she sounded as if she wasn't interested.

'So will you stay at the farm for a while, or are there other projects coming up?'

'I don't know yet,' Hanna said honestly. 'It's been strange coming back. What I was saying to you before – about feeling connected to the past...'

'Tell me.' He met her eyes and Hanna was suddenly ready to tell him everything. She took a breath.

'It started when I was a teenager. I used to do gymnastics and I had an accident and fell. Since then, I've had really vivid dreams. They went away for a bit when I was in Guangzhou, but since I've been back, they've been really intrusive.'

Lucas urged her to go on, curious and sympathetic. 'What kind of dreams?'

'They're flashbacks to the past, but in my dreams I'm someone else, a different woman, and there are battles going on or I'm being chased. It's terrifying...' Hanna paused. She'd expected to feel vulnerable, exposed, but Lucas gazed at her levelly and she felt immediately safe to confide in him.

'I can imagine.' Lucas frowned. 'Have you told anyone about it? A doctor or—'

'No – I just deal with them. But then I found a necklace in the pig field and that's been in my dreams too. I'm often wearing it or holding it.'

'What's it like?'

'I invited an archaeologist to look at it. It's Roman, gold, set with carnelian stones.'

Lucas was thoughtful. 'So what do your instincts tell you? Do you feel that you're revisiting a past life, or are your dreams based on things that affect you in the present?'

Lucas's question took her breath away for a moment. He believed her absolutely: he understood. 'I've no idea,' Hanna said. 'What do you think?'

He shrugged. 'I've little experience of these things. Animals have a very simple view of the world. Although an animal will react to something we can't see. It can be quite unnerving.'

Hanna agreed. 'The horses certainly don't like being near the pig field. And Roy cowered there when I thought I saw the figure in the mist.'

'Exactly,' Lucas said. 'It's as if they have a sixth sense.'

'Thanks for listening.' Hanna suddenly felt a burst of gratitude; she was somehow lighter for being able to speak about it aloud and be believed. 'It's been with me so long, I never feel comfortable talking about this to most people.'

'I'm really fascinated,' Lucas said. 'The question is, what will you do about it?'

'I've contacted Roly, the archaeologist, to ask him about, you know, the ghostly side, and what his views are, since he spends so much time dabbling in the past. He has a friend he recommended I talk to. After that, I'm not sure.'

Lucas was concerned. 'How do you cope with the exhaustion all these dreams must bring?'

'I'm often quite troubled by it,' Hanna admitted. 'I sometimes go to bed feeling anxious, like I'm a slave to my dreams. But I'm curious too. It's been with me since I was a teenager, the sense of someone linked to me. I want to find out for myself. I don't want to go through a psychiatrist, experience regression, that kind of stuff...'

'I can understand that.' Lucas glanced at the wall clock. It was past midnight. 'Can I get you another coffee? Anything else?'

'A coffee would be nice,' Hanna said, watching him as he took her mug and left for the kitchen.

She eased herself back on the sofa and closed her eyes. It was exhilarating to be in Lucas's company – time flew by. She wasn't ready to go home yet – there was so much more to talk about. He was captivating, charismatic and completely empathic: she was sure an undeniable closeness was developing. She wondered if she should tell Lucas that she'd felt she'd seen him before, that his gaze was the gaze of the man who haunted her dreams. She decided that was probably a step too far tonight. But she liked him a lot – she'd known it for some time. He was sympathetic; he'd understood about her dreams. And he was drawn to the local area, so much so that he and his girlfriend had ended their relationship over it.

Hanna hoped he was interested in her romantically. It was too early to be absolutely sure – what if it was merely friendship? She wouldn't rush anything, although her instincts cried out that they had a deep connection. But the sadness that surrounded him suggested that his last relationship had been difficult. He needed space to heal and move on, but he was certainly good company. And very handsome.

Hanna curled her legs beneath the silk dress and hugged a cushion, closing her eyes. She exhaled slowly; it felt good to have told Lucas about her dreams. She felt her body relax into the sofa and her breathing deepened. The image of the soldier standing in a field, woodlands stretching behind, filled her mind. He looked at her with Lucas's level gaze and as he opened his arms, she walked into the embrace, put her face against his chest and breathed out. She felt warm and safe. He kissed her hair and muttered something sweet and Hanna sighed with contentment. She was conscious that someone was covering her with a blanket. Then she looked into the dark gaze of the soldier and was utterly calm. His arms tightened around her and Hanna sighed again, a smile on her lips. She was sound asleep.

* * *

Brea walked quickly to the weaver's house at the edge of Camulodunum and knocked at an old door. It was opened by a small woman in a pale tunic, her hair pinned up tightly. Her face was shrivelled like a walnut. She pointed a finger. 'You have come to ask me to make a cloak for your mistress?'

'How do you know?' Brea was surprised.

'I heard there had been a wedding just yesterday. And the weather is about to change – it grows colder. Your mistress will want a warm cloak. What colour?'

'My master says it must be indigo blue, dyed with woad.'

'Tell him I'll have it ready for collection in ten days' time.'

'I will.'

The woman closed the door abruptly and Brea turned away. She heard the echo of horse's hooves on the ground and Marcellus was there, wearing a vermillion cloak, sitting high on a black stallion. Brea immediately put her hand out and the huge beast snuffled her fist, allowing her to stroke his neck.

'He likes you,' Marcellus said. 'He's an intelligent beast.'

He reached down and pulled her up onto the saddle in front of him. Brea leaned over to pat the horse's neck.

'We can't be away for long,' Marcellus whispered in her ear. 'But I wanted you to meet Venator, to experience how fast he can gallop.'

He turned the horse and they thundered towards the woods outside Camulodunum. Brea caught her breath; it had been too long since she'd felt the exhilaration of riding at speed. She called out, 'I like him very much.'

Venator plunged forward into shady woodlands, hooves crunching against bracken and twigs, and Brea clung on, not able to stop smiling,

Marcellus behind her, his arms around her, holding the reins. The horse slowed in a leafy glade, trotting towards a river that meandered beside a grassy bank. Marcellus dismounted and held out a hand.

Brea slithered down.

'What do you think of it here?' Marcellus placed his cloak on the bank and sat down quietly.

Brea joined him. 'It's pleasant and quiet.'

'Here in the woods, there is no master and slave, only Marcellus and Brea.'

Brea's eyes met his. 'It's only a moment in time where we may be at peace. Then we'll return to our lives again.' Her face was serious. 'In a month, less perhaps, my father will fight at the arena again. He'll win and then he'll be free.'

'And I've promised you the same, once I return,' Marcellus said quietly. 'In two weeks, I'll be travelling west along Watling Street to fight a new battle.'

'I'll pray for you,' Brea said quickly – she was suddenly afraid for his safety and the new emotion surprised her.

'To Mars and Bellona?'

'To Andred.' Brea watched the ripples spread across stones and she dangled her fingers in, feeling the delicious iciness of it. She brought them to her lips and tasted pure water. The glade was quiet except for birdsong; Brea was filled with a new sense of freedom, being alone with Marcellus, away from the *domus*. She could speak what was in her heart. 'I'll miss you.'

'If the world was different, Brea, you'd be my wife and I'd take you in my arms now and swear to you that I'd think of you every moment that I'm away.'

'We can't change how we feel,' Brea said. It was important to be honest with him now. She took his hand and held it in both of hers, afraid of the new images of him that formed in her mind, battling fiercely on horseback, sword raised. 'If I were your wife, being here with you would be all I'd wish for. And I promise you, while you're away, my dreams will be filled with you. But not a word of it will pass my lips, ever. And when I'm free...' She gave him a look of pure tenderness. 'You'll be locked in my heart, not only as the one who loved me enough to let me go, but the one I gave my heart to before I left.' She murmured, 'You've brought me here so we can talk secretly about what we truly feel. But we can never act on it.'

'You're right. But if...' Marcellus put out a hand and touched Brea's cheek. 'If one day, when you are back with your tribe, if things change, I will find you.'

'It won't change. We're different.' Brea felt sad at the truth of her words.

'But we're the same,' Marcellus insisted. 'Flesh, blood, bone. We're bound together. You know it.'

'I do.' Brea put a finger to his lips and his eyes held hers, soft with passion. She took a breath, wanting to pull him to her, to kiss his lips, to seize the chance to forget about the world beyond the woodlands. In a single moment she could have lost herself to him completely. But she stood up. 'We must think of my mistress. She's a good person. We should go back now – we've stayed away too long.'

'You're right.' Marcellus closed his eyes, forcing the same thoughts away. He whisked up his cloak and pulled himself on the horse, tugging Brea in front. 'We'll head back. But we'll come again. When are you collecting the cloak?'

'In ten days.'

'We'll meet then. It may be the last time we'll spend together.'

Marcellus urged Venator forward and the horse was off at a canter, heading back towards Camulodunum. Brea leaned back against Marcellus, thinking of his last words. It disturbed her that he was going to fight, that he'd be in constant danger. She knew well what a soldier's life was. She was surprised to find a cold tear on her cheek as she imagined him saying a final goodbye.

Marcellus dropped her where he had picked her up and headed off without a word. She watched him cantering into the distance as she hurried towards the *domus* and felt suddenly alone. A stiff breeze blew through the town as she passed the Temple of the Divine Claudius and, as she always did, she looked towards the steps for Luna, the beggar woman, but she was not there. A few leaves stirred at her feet and dust blew from the road. Brea sniffed the air; the weather was changing; it was becoming colder. Soon the rains would come.

She arrived at the *domus* and immediately the sound of a woman sobbing met her ears. Marcellus had arrived already; she could hear his soothing tones. She rushed into the atrium, where the family were gathered horrified as Aurelia tugged Lucius's arm. Her face was twisted, tear-stained; she clung to him desperately. 'You mustn't go. I can't let you. You mustn't leave me.'

Lucius jerked away, but his face was full of regret. 'I am a tribune. I must go to my legion.'

Brea watched as Marcellus tried to calm his wife, as Publius Julius looked on astonished, Julia at his shoulder, her face without emotion.

Aurelia's body shook with sobs. 'Stay, Lucius – I can't manage without you.'

'Anyone might think she was losing a lover,' Julia quipped.

Marcellus put an arm around Aurelia. 'He will be back home soon. We'll welcome him with a feast.'

'Sister, I have to leave now – my horse waits...' Lucius freed himself for the final time. He hesitated, glancing wildly from Julia to Aurelia, then he muttered, 'May the gods watch over you,' and rushed away, out of sight.

Aurelia's wails increased as Marcellus hopelessly tried to comfort her. Then she held out her arms, her face desperate. 'Brea, what must I do?'

'She asks this of a slave?' Julia pulled a face.

Brea rushed over, taking Aurelia's hand. 'All will be well, Mistress. But you must let him go...'

Aurelia turned to Brea and hugged her, burying her face on her shoulder. Her sobs were muffled as she cried, 'What will become of me now?'

Julia's face was scornful. 'I think I'll take my wine in the *triclinium*. Caius Fabius will arrive soon. Would you believe he's dyed his hair brown with the green hulls of walnuts?' Her laughter tinkled. 'He means to look younger, I fear. Come, Father, let's go together.'

Brea watched them go. Marcellus met her eyes and Brea knew he felt hopeless; he couldn't help his bride. He strode away and Brea was left in the atrium trying to calm her distraught mistress who was still sobbing.

'My life will never be the same. Oh, Brea, what am I going to do?'

35

On Sunday morning, Hanna huddled at the breakfast table, still wearing the silk dress. Stephanie handed her a mug of coffee.

'You're a dirty stop-out,' she joked. 'So, did Lucas give you a lift home?'

Hanna smiled into her cup. 'Yes, he dropped me outside. He had an emergency visit in King's Lynn.'

'And you spent the night on his couch?' Stephanie asked.

Hanna hadn't slept so well in a long while; the dreams had stayed away and the first thing she'd known was when Lucas woke her at seven with a cup of tea.

Paddy leaned down and ruffled Roy's ears. 'Maybe Hanna doesn't want to say exactly where she slept, Steph.'

'You said the vet texted you last night to tell you that she'd fallen asleep on his couch,' Stephanie repeated.

Paddy grunted. 'I don't know what all the fuss is about. Lucas told me Hanna was at his house so you wouldn't worry. I thought it was very decent of him.'

'You don't get it, love,' Stephanie said excitedly. 'So, Hanna, is romance in the air?'

'We just had a coffee and a chat, Mum.' Hanna grinned.

'Is that what they call it nowadays?' Paddy chuckled.

'Are you going out with him again?' Stephanie tried. 'On a date?'

'We swapped numbers, Mum. That's all. Now I'm off for a shower.'

'Let me make you some breakfast. It's past nine,' Stephanie protested.

Paddy looked up from his newspaper. 'I thought we were going to research booking a holiday today.'

'A *honeymoon*, Paddy.'

'Right, Steph,' Paddy grunted. 'You said that a wedding isn't a wedding without a honeymoon. So I promised we'd look at a few places for November.'

'Let me make Hanna some breakfast first.' Stephanie stood at the Aga stubbornly. 'I want to hear all about Lucas.'

Paddy guffawed. 'The kids are grown up now – they do as they like. I heard Oliver's car drive in at two this morning. That was a rum 'un – I wonder where he was off gallivanting. Maybe he slept on someone's couch after coffee and a chat.' He scratched his head. 'Is that the same thing as Netflix and a chill?'

Hanna spluttered a laugh.

'So, this young man, this vet...' Stephanie began.

'Lucas.' Hanna shook her head, exasperated. Then the phone vibrated on the table and she picked it up. 'I'd better take this – it's Roly.' His voice rattled in the speaker. 'Hi, Roly, thanks for getting back.' She listened for a moment. 'Oh, that's so kind of you. I don't know – hang on, I'll ask...' She gestured to Paddy. 'Roly wants to come over next week with his team and the metal detectors and have a look in the pig field... he thinks the necklace is part of a set and there might be more.'

'I don't mind him looking. I invited him back but...' Paddy stood up, putting his hands in his pockets. 'I don't want my pigs disturbed.'

Hanna listened again, then she said, 'Roly says the pigs won't be troubled – they'll do half the field while the pigs are in the other half, then swap.'

'Oh, well, that's good. Yes, I can move them up, rope them off – it's a big enough field. Tell Roly I'm pleased as punch. When's he coming?'

Hanna paused, listening. 'Oh, definitely – ah, that sounds good, right... Tuesday would be perfect. Thanks, Roly. And I'll look forward to meeting her very much. Yes, bye.' She glanced at Paddy. 'So, Roly says thanks, he'll come on Friday morning when the weather forecast is good, and he'll bring a small team. And he's also popping up on Tuesday to introduce me to a friend who wants to talk to me about the... local history. That'll be really interesting.'

'Will we have to make a lunch again? I had a shopping trip planned to King's Lynn on Tuesday,' Stephanie said anxiously.

'Roly's treating me to lunch in the pub – he did say to bring you all.'

'I'll be busy on the farm, and so will Ollie. We've got ploughing and the last of the harvesting.' Paddy sighed. 'No time for lunches or honeymoons.'

'We'll book a honeymoon for the winter, somewhere warm,' Stephanie soothed. 'You go to lunch on Tuesday with Roly by yourself, love.' Then she had a thought. 'Unless Lucas is free?'

'We'll see.' Hanna grinned as her mother passed a piece of toast. She buttered it, already deep in thought. She was delighted that Roly was visiting, and he was bringing a woman who apparently had a great interest in – what did Roly call it? – the spiritual side of archaeology. She was very keen to talk to Hanna.

Hanna munched her toast thoughtfully. Tuesday couldn't come fast enough.

* * *

A sharp wind blew across the fens on Tuesday, but it was a sunny September day. Hanna sat in The Dribbling Duck with Roly and an elegant silver-haired woman wearing a long velvet dress, who introduced herself as Cynthia Chandra. She had intelligent brown eyes that gleamed behind gold-framed glasses.

Roly took off his safari hat and placed it on the table. 'Cynthia's an old friend of mine – we go back years. She's done a lot of research into psychic archaeology, Hanna. I told her about you as we drove up here.'

Cynthia cradled a glass of lemonade. 'Have you actually seen a spirit?'

Hanna nodded. 'A woman. I've seen her several times, between the station and the pig field, and on the fens.'

'And what feelings do you get about her?'

'I think she's troubled – she's running from something or searching for something. I don't know.' Hanna put a hand to her head. 'I have dreams as if I'm her – as if I know who she is. If she speaks, I understand her, even though it's in another language. And there's a man with her, a Roman soldier, I think...'

'Your dreams sound exhausting.' Cynthia's voice was calm. 'And I assume they started when something traumatic happened?'

'I was a teenager. I fell in the gym. Oh...' Hanna suddenly remembered. 'I spoke to a woman on the aeroplane from China. She said some strange things, that the ghost is searching, just as I search, that we were connected.'

'She's right,' Cynthia said. 'What are you searching for, Hanna?'

'I don't know. Direction, what to do with myself...' Hanna laughed, a little embarrassed.

'This woman who spoke to you, what was her name?' Cynthia asked.

'Yue.' Hanna paused. 'It means moon, in Mandarin.'

A waiter had arrived, placing plates in front of them. Roly was already tucking into his risotto.

'My name also means moon,' Cynthia said thoughtfully. 'You shouldn't let these dreams worry you, but clearly, you're strongly linked to a spirit that can't rest. You both started from here, you're both of the fens.'

'You're not suggesting reincarnation?'

'Not at all.' Cynthia frowned. 'Things are not always simply one thing or the other. There is a spectrum. Some people will never see a spirit as long as they live. Others have some intuition. Some, like you, are gifted with a great deal of it, and therefore you are receptive – think of yourself as a channel of communication.'

'The Iceni believed in reincarnation,' Roly said between mouthfuls. 'The Romans thought that the deceased had a shade that lived on in the Underworld. They didn't really believe in the afterlife as such – they believed in honour in death.'

Hanna shivered. 'So, what should I do?'

'Eat lunch. Enjoy pleasant conversation and good company. Live your life. The rest will come to pass.' Cynthia lifted her fork.

'I don't understand,' Hanna said.

Cynthia smiled. 'I have my little yellow car parked outside. I know the way here now. Do you have any plans for Sunday?'

'No.'

'Then why don't I pay you a visit in the afternoon? You can show me some of these places where you've seen the ghost and I'll tell you what I think.'

'Oh, Cynthia will know.' Roly smiled.

'Know what?' Hanna was beginning to feel nervous.

'I'll just know.' Cynthia gave an enigmatic smile.

'Meanwhile,' Roly had almost cleared his plate, 'I can't wait for my team to start on the pig field on Friday. I'm darned if we won't find something. Did I tell you, Hanna, the necklace is part of a set that a rich Roman would give to his wife before their wedding day? I expect to find at least one other piece.'

'That would be exciting.' Hanna leaned forward. 'Maybe you could take Roy with you. He found the necklace.'

'Great idea. Come on, ladies.' Roly glanced at the two full plates. 'Eat up. I see they have a good list of puddings here. I want to treat us all to apple pie and custard.'

* * *

Brea was happy in her work, singing to herself in the kitchen as she counted down each passing day. Tomorrow couldn't come quickly enough. She'd go into Camulodunum to collect the indigo cloak from the weaver woman and Marcellus would be waiting for her on Venator; they'd ride into the woods. It would be their last time to be together before he left for battle and she had rehearsed what she wanted to say to him.

Two things were on her mind. First of all, she wanted to thank him for his kindness. Her father would fight in the arena for the last time soon, then he'd be free; her own liberty would follow. She loved Marcellus with all her heart for his selfless generosity. Secondly, she wanted to tell him honestly how strong her feelings were for him – it would be her last chance. He was leaving soon and she knew the war against the Druids would be dangerous; he might not return. Brea wanted to pour out her heart to him before he left. If she never saw him again, he'd know that she'd truly loved him. It comforted her a little, but the fear of him not returning from battle still haunted her.

Each day she would pass him in the atrium, sometimes in the orchard, and he would glance her way just as she met his eyes. The power of his gaze took her breath away; she knew the intensity of his feelings for her in that moment. It filled each day with hope.

'You're daydreaming again.' Chloe pushed a tray into her hands. 'This is for your mistress. She'll be awake by now, although I don't know why we take food to her. She never eats it.'

'She misses her brother.'

'I'd have expected her to be too busy with her husband.' Chloe chuckled.

Brea nodded briefly and hurried towards the marble steps: Aurelia seemed not to mind each night as Brea prepared her for bed that Marcellus stayed away. She was constantly anxious for Lucius, of whom there had been no news. Brea reminded her that Lucius had only been gone for just over a week. News would not come from Lindum Colonia, a city further to the north-east, for many days. He'd probably be busy there, subduing the Brigantes tribe.

As Brea approached Aurelia's *cubiculum*, she heard voices, a light tinkling laugh. She found Aurelia dressed in a woollen indigo cloak, her hair being combed by Balbina under the scrutiny of Julia. Brea put the tray down on a low table, puzzled, and waited for instructions.

Julia ignored her. 'You look well in the cloak, sister. My brother has chosen the colour well for you.'

'It was kind of you to have your *ornatrix* fetch it early,' Aurelia said.

'The same weaving woman made one for me dyed in oak galls. It gives a subtle shade of the sand in the arena – it reminds me of my champion.' Julia poked Balbina with her finger. 'I want you to make Aurelia's hair stunning. Make sure you perfume it properly. Marcellus must find you irresistible tonight.'

Brea glanced at her fingers nervously; the cloak she was to fetch tomorrow was around Aurelia's shoulders. It would be impossible to meet Marcellus now, to share the secrets of her heart with him. She assumed

Julia knew her brother hadn't visited his wife's bed. She was taking control of their marriage.

Julia raised her voice, yelling at Brea, 'What are you waiting for, *ancilla*? Go back to the kitchens. You're not needed here.'

Brea turned to go.

Aurelia raised a hand. 'Brea?'

'Mistress?'

'Could you inform everyone in the kitchen,' Aurelia raised her voice, determined to be the mistress of the house, 'there will be a feast. We expect a visitor. Governor General Gaius Suetonius Paulinus will dine with us tonight.'

Brea bent her head in acknowledgement. She couldn't help her next words. 'I thought he wasn't coming for four days?'

'How dare you speak, *ancilla*? Julia was outraged. 'Sister, you can't allow her to—'

'It's well, Julia,' Aurelia said calmly. 'Brea, the general has need of my husband now. He's brought him a fine battle horse to ride west. So tonight, we dine and offer good cheer. Tomorrow, Marcellus departs for the Island of Mona.'

36

The *cena* was a grand affair, with dishes of duck, goose, fish, fruit and extra garum for Publius Julius, who declared he could eat nothing now without the sauce. Brea took jugs of *conditum*, a mixture of wine, honey and spices, which the family drank in large amounts. Brea was constantly on edge; the celebration was too joyous, overly enthusiastic, as if everyone was thinking that Marcellus might not return but no one dare speak the words.

Wine flowed all evening in copious amounts. Aurelia had drunk far too much; Julia constantly refilled her cup, smiling, secretly amused to observe her brother and his wife together. Marcellus treated Aurelia with courtesy and kindness, passing her morsels to eat; she looked vulnerable, decked in a fine robe and jewellery, her ornate hair too severe for her gentle features. She laughed too loudly, desperate for Marcellus's attention, placing a hand on his thigh, leaning too close to him, finding it difficult to sit upright. Julia was enjoying her sister-in-law's clumsy attempt at seduction. Publius Julius seemed not to notice, as he was talking with Caius Fabius whose hair had been dyed an unnatural shade of chestnut.

Brea watched the Governor General Suetonius, a haughty, confident man, in deep conversation with Marcellus. His face was calm, but his eyes were hard and narrowed, as if he was constantly thinking about battle strategy. He seemed uninterested in anything but war; he talked of how he had suppressed a revolt in Mauretania, how he'd been the first Roman commander to lead troops across the Atlas Mountains. Marcellus listened, replying easily, but Brea sensed that her master was assessing his new general who clapped him heartily on the shoulder, drank wine in thirsty gulps and insisted that the only way of subduing the Druids was by merciless aggression.

At the end of the meal, Julia left the *triclinium* in a merry mood to go home, and Caius Fabius scuttled after her. A slave conducted Suetonius to his *cubiculum*, and Publius Julius was helped to bed, complaining of gripping stomach pains. Aurelia staggered to her feet and Marcellus caught her about the waist before she fell. She wrapped an arm around his neck.

'Husband, you know well how to catch a wife...'

She giggled at her own joke as she slumped forwards and Marcellus swept her in his arms.

Brea met his eyes briefly as he carried her towards her room; she knew immediately what he wanted her to do. She collected several dishes and rushed off towards the kitchen, Chloe and Daphne in pursuit carrying plates heaped with the remains of supper.

On her way back to the atrium, she paused in the orchard. Marcellus was waiting for her beneath the tree that stretched its branches like a shadowy giant. She checked that no one was watching, then she rushed to meet him. He gathered her into an embrace and kissed her. Brea felt herself lifted into his arms. He murmured in her ear, 'I must leave tomorrow.'

'I know.' Brea caught her breath. 'You will come back safely.'

'I will.'

'Where is the mistress?' Brea was suddenly anxious. 'Is she well?'

'I put her to bed – she's asleep now,' Marcellus said sadly.

'You could have stayed with her.'

'How can I hold her in my arms when all I can think of is you?' Marcellus's grip tightened around her. 'Tomorrow I'll be gone early. I will have no time for goodbyes.'

'Then I wish Andred will be with you.' Brea kissed him again quickly. 'I must go – I'll be missed.'

Marcellus held on to her hand. 'One thing.'

'I'll look after your wife – you know that in my heart I'm truly sorry for it all...'

'As I am, although, by law, Aurelia and I aren't married until I've lain with her...'

'So, what do you wish me to do?' Brea whispered.

'I'm to be given a new horse – can you take care of Venator, visit him?'

'I will.' Brea turned to go. 'How can you send word that you're well? I'll be waiting...'

'I'll find a way.' Marcellus let her fingers go and Brea ran back to the atrium to collect dishes. A sob escaped from her lips and she pressed them together.

She wouldn't cry.

* * *

On Tuesday and Wednesday night, Hanna slept deeply and the dreams stayed away. But on Thursday, she was transported to a dark orchard. The hem of her robe was damp, her feet too. She was alone, holding back tears. In her dream, her breathing was constricted as if a great weight was pressing against her, the heaviness of anxiety. She was worried about someone, a man she loved, who was about to leave for an island far away. She knew she would miss him badly and she was troubled about a battle he was to fight. Then she was standing in the centre of an old town. People were rushing about, terrified. Some were running, their belongings in bundles. Hanna heard loud footsteps approaching, thousands of feet marching, and she felt the menace in the air. Suddenly, a building was ablaze, the sky red with fire. In her dream, she could smell smoke, see the curling grey billows of it, the leap of flames. She cried out and sat up in her bed, wide awake, her skin cold. She could smell toast from the kitchen below. It was Friday, breakfast time.

Hanna reached for her phone and checked for texts. She'd expected to hear from Lucas, but there had been no word. It had been almost a week since she'd slept on the couch at his house. She could only assume he wasn't interested in seeing her again. She felt a sinking feeling, disappointment, sadness even. In a moment of sheer folly, without waiting to think it through, she thumbed him a message.

The archaeologists are coming today to dig in the pig field.

She pressed send and immediately felt silly. She could have asked him how he was, thanked him for the pleasant evening they'd spent together, even told him that Nutmeg's teeth were fine. But, instead, she'd sent a clumsy text that sounded like a code from an old-fashioned spy film. She laughed out loud to dispel her feelings of foolishness; she'd probably ruined any chance she had of a date now. Next time she saw him, she'd make a joke of it.

Hanna padded downstairs in pyjamas and helped herself to coffee and toast. Paddy was finishing a plate of eggs, Roy sprawled patiently at his feet. Ollie was drinking coffee. Stephanie had just sat down to breakfast. It was early, seven thirty.

Paddy grunted. 'They've been out there since half six. Apparently, it's going to rain later and they need to make the most of the morning.'

'The archaeologists?' Hanna asked, munching.

'Roly Keys just came to the door – Steph offered his team breakfast, but he was keen to get stuck in,' Ollie said. 'I'm going out there now to help him move the pigs. They've started in the corner, by the stile that leads to Bramble Woods.'

'They won't find anything – it's all nettles.' Paddy sniffed.

'I invited them to come for coffee at eleven,' Stephanie said. 'Just so they can have a break.'

'How many people are there?' Hanna asked.

Paddy put up four fingers. 'Roly, two lads with metal detectors and some woman in a velvet dress, wellies and glasses.'

'Cynthia, she's called,' Stephanie added, pointing to a bunch of dahlias in a vase. 'She's very nice – she brought me some flowers.'

'I'm going out to see how they're getting on.' Ollie stood up to go.

'I'll come. Give me a minute to get dressed.' Hanna slurped coffee. 'I can give them a hand. I'm working in the café later, but it'll be nice to see what they find.' She met Roy's eager eyes. 'Are you coming too?'

Roy barked once and was on his feet. Hanna scooted upstairs.

Twenty minutes later, Hanna stood in the pig field watching Ollie and Roy round up the pigs, moving them to the far corner. Paddy was dressed in a thick jacket, cap and wellies, busy rolling out wire as a temporary fence. She wandered over towards the corner of the field near the woods, where Roly stood with Cynthia, watching two men wearing khaki jackets, jeans tucked into wellingtons, as they trundled along methodically, metal detectors hovering over the soil.

Roly pulled his hat down over his hair. 'Nippy, this morning. There's a wind...'

'It's the fenlands,' Cynthia said quietly. 'There's always a wind.'

Hanna shivered. 'So what are you looking for?'

Roly was optimistic. 'There's more jewellery here. Cynthia's sure of it. We had a look at the necklace you found again and...'

'I held it in my hand,' Cynthia explained. 'I felt something at once. There's another piece – maybe two.'

'What makes you think that?' Hanna asked.

'Vibrations. We'll discuss it more when we meet on Sunday. I think we have a lot to talk about, when we're away from all this busy work,' Cynthia said. 'But I'm sure someone's searching for the other pieces.'

Hanna indicated the two men in khaki jackets. 'You mean someone in your team?'

'The spirit...' Cynthia said and stared into the distance. 'She isn't far away, even now.'

Hanna felt the breeze blow through her clothes and she shuddered. Then Ollie and Roy were by her side.

Ollie grinned. 'This is exciting. Have you found anything?'

'We will,' Roly said. 'Cynthia thinks so.'

Roy pressed himself against Hanna's legs and sat obediently beside her. She said, 'Is there anything we can do to help, Roly?'

'Ralf and Toby are doing all the hard work at the moment,' Roly said. 'They have a search pattern.' He indicated the two men who were bent over with metal detectors that made an intermittent low moan, and then were silent.

The wind ruffled Hanna's hair and she hauled up her collar, moving instinctively closer to Ollie. Clouds hung low in the broad sky overhead, grey ploughed furrows through silver. In the distance, a storm was brewing. Roly tugged his hat down again and Paddy walked over, his hands in his pockets, to join them. 'Rain's coming in early – rum weather.'

Ollie nodded. 'It wasn't due until this afternoon.'

'I reckon you should all go on inside,' Paddy suggested.

A large drop of rain fell, then another. Hanna raised her shoulders against the cold and felt the familiar ache lodged between them.

Then Roy was on his feet, bolting towards one of the men whose metal detector had started to whine. The sheepdog began to scrabble in the soil next to him, barking loudly. There was a high-pitched screech from the metal detector, a ghostly sound in the wind, and the man holding it shouted, 'There's something here.'

'We're coming.' Roly beamed at Hanna. 'Sounds like we've found treasure.'

Roly began to run, Hanna and Ollie at his side, Cynthia and Paddy just behind them. Roy was digging frantically, the two men beside him delving in the earth, pushing in a spade, then one of them lifted a piece of dirty metal. 'Look at this.'

'Well, I'm...' Paddy scratched his head beneath his cap.

'Would you believe it?' Roly had it in his hands, cradling it. 'It's a bracelet.'

Hanna peered over his shoulder at the dull gold circle fashioned in the shape of a snake, the head curled at the bottom next to the wiggly tail.

'It's definitely Roman,' Roly said as he passed it to Cynthia, who clasped it for a moment, saying nothing. Hanna held her breath.

'This, like its owner, has been long lost,' Cynthia spoke. 'And I believe there is one more piece, its companion...'

'Well done, Roy.' Ollie reached over and patted the dog's back. Roy woofed proudly.

It was raining now, fat drops splashing on the muddy ground. Paddy looked up at the skies. 'This will set in for a while. Nothing more to do here. Let's get back to the kitchen and warm up a bit. Steph will have some hot coffee and biscuits.'

'Great idea.' Ollie turned to Hanna. 'It's going to really chuck it down.

That's put paid to our horse ride this evening. I'd better go to the field and bring them in.'

The heavens opened as seven people and a dog broke into a run through the squelching mud towards the farmhouse as the skies opened. Hanna's face was damp, her hair drenched, and her jacket was soaked. She hurried along, her wellingtons heavy and water clogged. Just as she reached the farmhouse, she felt her phone buzz in her pocket and tugged it out, panting. There was a message; Hanna stood, water dripping down her face, and read it quickly, her eyes full of rainwater.

Great news. Dinner tomorrow at mine and you can tell me all about it?

For a second, it made no sense, then she caught the name of the sender and remembered the embarrassing text she'd sent earlier.

She was grinning with excitement, soaked to the skin, but the rain didn't matter. Tomorrow evening, she was having dinner with Lucas.

37

Brea hadn't seen Marcellus leave ten days before; no one saw him go. He and Suetonius had ridden away before dawn without a word. She made sure she visited his horse in the stables each morning and evening to give him an apple to munch. The slave who worked with Venator was not surprised to see her. He nodded once and allowed her to stroke the beast, to lean her cheek against his neck. Brea closed her eyes and thought of Marcellus and prayed for his safety – she missed him with all her heart.

But she wanted to do her best to comfort his wife; Brea was torn with mixed emotions – guilt, sadness. She spent a great deal of time with Aurelia in her room. Aurelia was listless; anxious about her brother. Brea had hoped that, once Marcellus had left, she'd grow into the role of mistress of the *domus* and throw herself into her duties. Aurelia did her best, but she moved around like a ghost.

One morning, Brea arrived in her mistress's *cubiculum* with a tray of fruit, to find Aurelia sitting on the end of the bed, lost in thought. Brea offered a smile. 'How are you today, Mistress?'

Aurelia sighed. 'I miss him every moment. There has been no word.'

'Of the master?' Brea asked anxiously.

'Of Lucius.' Aurelia looked up, troubled. 'Brea, I rarely think of Marcellus. I'm a bad wife. The truth is that I've failed to do my duty. So much is expected of me, but I can hardly move from my room. My thoughts are only for my brother.' She reached out and grasped Brea's hand. 'What should I do? How do you stay strong?'

'I'm always busy, Mistress. I have no time to think. But sometimes I pray.'

'Does that ease your heart?' Aurelia asked.

'It does.' Brea seized her chance. 'Why don't you go to the temple and pray there?'

'But I'd have to leave the *domus*.'

'I'll come with you. You can wear your warm cloak against the cold breeze.' Brea looked hopeful: a walk outside would do her mistress good.

'I think that is a good idea. Brea – yes, we'll go there now.'

Brea offered the tray and smiled. 'Perhaps a morsel of food first, to break your fast?'

'Perhaps.' Aurelia smiled back, reaching out for a plum.

* * *

An hour later, Aurelia, swathed in the indigo cloak, was standing on the steps of the Temple of the Divine Claudius, shivering. 'I will go inside and pour out my heart. When I come out again, I'll be strong and able to undertake my duties. Tell me that's how it will be...'

'It will be so.' Brea gazed up at the eight white stone pillars, the shadows of the priests moving inside, and was reminded sharply that the Romans had seized their land and the people who lived on it and used them now as a gift, an entitlement. She knew it made her people angry.

Aurelia's thoughts were elsewhere. 'I'll beg the gods to help me become a good wife. I'll pray for Lucius, that he returns safely. And Marcellus too. Will you wait?'

'I'll be here when you return. But...' Brea caught her breath. 'I wonder if I might go to the *ludus* and ask about your champion, if he is well, when the next contest will be.'

'Oh, of course – I forgot about him.' Aurelia handed her a coin. 'Ask the trainer to give him the best food.'

'Thank you, Mistress,' Brea said gratefully. 'May your prayers bring you peace.'

She watched Aurelia walk slowly up the last few steps and into the temple, her woollen cloak and hood disappearing through the dark entrance. Then Brea ran as fast as she could, desperate to see her father.

When she reached the *ludus*, she hammered on the door.

Marcus Rubrius opened it quickly, his whip raised. 'What do you want?' He didn't recognise her.

Brea didn't move. She showed him the coin, then snatched it from his eager grasp. 'My mistress sponsors one of your men as her champion. My master Marcellus Julius expects him to be well fed and cared for. Here's a coin so that he will eat the best food.'

Marcus Rubrius put out his hand and smiled slyly. 'Give me the coin and I will feed him.'

'I'll see him first.' Brea's eyes flashed. 'My master wants to be sure he grows stronger.'

'You'd better come inside.' Marcus Rubrius lifted the small statue of Minerva that he held constantly and opened the door wide. Brea could hear the clash of swords inside the arena, the shouts of men training. 'My men are at their labours. Don't trouble them.'

Brea rushed into the *ludus*, eyes constantly searching for her father. She saw Addedomaros exercising by himself, his legs shackled, and her eyes darted to meet his and away again. Then she saw her father in the distance, sitting alone, eating barley porridge from a bowl. She rushed across. 'Father.'

His face was scarred, lined, etched with hardship, but he smiled. 'Brea – it's good to see you.'

'I've brought money from my mistress – the trainer has been told to give you the best food.'

'The food is always the same, vegetables, wheat.' Her father shook his head. 'But perhaps I'll have more of it now. My next fight is in six days' time.'

'Six days?' Brea caught her breath. 'And then you'll be free?'

'I pray to Andred for it.'

'Father – my master has promised me that I'll be freed too. When he returns from the wars, he'll let me go.'

'He seems a good man. He may keep his word.' Her father frowned. 'But the word of a Roman means little. I'll hate them all until my last breath. Once I am away from this place, I'll do my best to drive them back to where they came from. I'll admit, your master has compassion in his face, but his people are our enemy and not to be trusted.'

'He's indeed the best of men.' Brea examined her father's expression. 'What will you do when you're free?'

'I'll fight. Our tribe is building an army – I hear rumours from the others here that numbers grow large, led by our wronged queen. And I'll never forget what the Romans did to your mother, how they took you into slavery, kept me from you.' His eyes glinted. 'There's no other way but to force them out of our land, Brea. We are many...'

Brea grasped his hand. 'You'll be free after one more contest, Father.'

'I'll win it,' her father said determinedly. 'For you, for my beloved Carti-mandua, for my tribe.'

'I must go. But in six days, you will be able to leave.' Brea glanced over her shoulder. Marcus Rubrius was striding towards her. She turned to face him. 'Here is your coin. My mistress instructs you to feed her champion well.'

'Oh, he'll fill his belly.' Marcus Rubrius hurried away and Brea followed him. 'He'll have much need of it.'

They were passing gladiators training with wooden swords and shields. The harsh noise echoed in Brea's ears. 'What do you mean, he'll have need of it?'

Marcus Rubrius stood by the door, throwing it wide. 'He fights in six days' time. He thinks he'll win his freedom, but I've selected my strongest opponent, one worthy of him. I'll lose them both anyway one way or another, so it makes good sense. We'll see a hard battle and your mistress won't be disappointed.'

He ushered Brea outside. She put out a hand to keep the door open. 'What do you mean, you'll lose them both? My mistress wishes to know – what are you planning to do?'

'Your mistress's sister has a champion too, a strong fighter, young. Both men stand to win their freedom. And both gladiators are Britons, from different tribes. The contest will be an interesting one, especially if I order them to fight to the death.' Marcus Rubrius's face held a crafty smile. 'It'll be good to see one pitched against the other in the arena – one a young stallion, one an old goat. I wonder who will triumph?'

'Wait,' Brea called out, but Marcus Rubrius had slammed the door. She stood outside panting, her heart knocking hard. Her father was going to fight, and his opponent would be Addedomaros – Julia's champion against Aurelia's. Only one of them could win.

* * *

'There's so much food.' Hanna offered Lucas her most winning smile as he ushered her to the little table in the dining room, covered in bread, cheese, salads, rice.

'I wasn't sure what you liked,' Lucas said. 'So, I made a Roman banquet, to go with the jewellery you were searching for.'

'Mmm. This looks amazing.' Hanna sat down as Lucas poured wine. She was delighted. 'It's so nice to have a glass of wine with a meal and not worry about driving home. Ollie's meeting friends at The Dribbling Duck, so he's offered to give me a lift.' She took a sip, then looked excitedly at the dishes of food on the table.

'I thought about the dig and I researched what the Romans might have eaten.' Lucas filled his own glass. 'Of course, I had to do my own version of it. They had herby cheese called *moretum*, so I replaced it with goat's cheese. And we won't eat dormice, although apparently the Romans loved them, but I roasted some little sausages in honey instead.'

'I'm impressed.' Hanna helped herself to salad, cheese and bread, then placed a mock dormouse on her plate. 'And I'm sure there will be pudding.'

'Of course.'

Hanna grinned. 'The Romans loved their puddings. They called them *mensa secunda*, which means second meal.'

'Well, we have cheesecake for our second meal.' Lucas's eyes gleamed and Hanna was aware of the tremor that passed between them again.

She glanced around quickly, taking in the white walls and glowing pendant lights. 'You've made Mum's house look lovely... Oh, I'm sorry, of course it's *your* house now!'

'Not at all, you're used to thinking of it that way. But I haven't done as much as I'd have liked. I'm always busy – and this week's been non-stop at work.'

Hanna heard a hint of sadness in his tone. 'Has it been tough?'

'I try not to complain. I went into it with my eyes open. My parents are both vets and I helped out in the practice where they worked from being a kid. I knew it wasn't all glamour and cute pets.' Lucas was thoughtful.

'The long hours must be tiring?' Hanna asked.

'The worst thing is knowing you can help an animal but a customer can't afford the treatment.' Lucas sighed. 'Or being asked to do something to an animal like declawing, which is prohibited thankfully. Euthanasia's very difficult. So is dealing with animal cruelty. And that's before we start on the paperwork.' He paused – Hanna's face was full of kindness. 'Beth said I took my work too seriously. She said I was too sentimental to cope with the demands of the job. She didn't exactly use the word sentimental.'

'What did she say?'

'That I wouldn't make it work.' Lucas gave a wry smile. 'She said vets needed to be tough and detached.'

Hanna frowned. 'Don't you need to be compassionate?'

'I think so. But the first time I had to euthanise an animal, I cried.'

Hanna wanted to take his hand. 'That's so sad.'

'And there's a fair amount of intimidation – one client who argued with the receptionist over a bill told me he'd be waiting outside my house with a crowbar.'

'In London?' Hanna asked.

'In King's Lynn. I'm fairly sure he doesn't know where I live.' He grinned. 'But I'm so determined to make this job work.'

Hanna thought about his ex-girlfriend saying that he'd fail, and she was momentarily overwhelmed with a feeling of loyalty. 'I'm sure you will.'

'There are so many pluses to living here. I can do home visits to sweet ladies with nervous cats. I get to ride horses again. I can't complain.' He glanced at her plate, almost empty. 'I hope the food's all right.'

'It's lovely.' Hanna was still thinking about what he'd said. 'I'd never imagined being a vet could be so stressful.'

'It's so incredibly fulfilling too. I love it when pets are put back into their owners' arms fit and well, and everyone's happy. Helping an animal to recover is what my job's about,' Lucas said. 'And what about you, Hanna? What can you see yourself doing next? You speak all those languages.'

'I don't know what I'll do.' Hanna reached for her glass. 'I'm fascinated by Roly's archaeology work though, and I met his colleague this week, Cynthia. They were so excited to find the bracelet.'

'I want to hear all about it,' Lucas said.

'The metal detectors helped us find it and we all stood in the rain and the mud and dug up a gold snake bracelet. It was a great feeling. We went back to the farmhouse and Roly cleaned it up and photographed it, then he made the calls to the coroner – you have to follow procedure if it's deemed to be treasure, but he says it will probably end up with him. They think there's even more jewellery in the field and they'll come back with their metal detectors when the weather improves.'

'And what about the dreams? Are you still having them? I mean, you look really well.' Lucas leaned forward. 'But I've been thinking a lot about the spirit you saw...'

'What about her?'

'Every time I drive home late from King's Lynn at night after work, I remember what you said. There's definitely an eeriness in the fens.'

'You've never seen anything?' Hanna asked.

'No, but...' Lucas shrugged. 'There's a feeling of something strange, in the fields or by the side of the road.'

'Or inside the car?' Hanna said. She remembered feeling icy fingers touching her neck after the Range Rover stalled. 'I spoke to Cynthia about it. She's a psychic archaeologist.'

'I didn't know there was such a thing.'

Hanna nibbled the mock dormouse. 'Apparently, she has lots of experience finding objects on archaeological sites and interpreting meaning from what she feels there. She's really interesting. I spoke to her about my dreams.'

'What did she say?'

'Exactly the same thing I was told before by a woman on the plane from Guangzhou. The spirit and I are linked in some way and I'm sort of in tune with her. She said that some people are more open to psychic or paranormal influences than others.'

'That makes sense – you must have more of a certain type of intuition than most people.' Lucas raised the wine bottle.

'Yes.' Hanna sipped from her refilled glass. 'Cynthia said something about intuition being on a spectrum. I wonder if that explains the way you're drawn to this area, that you've always felt you belong here.'

'I do,' Lucas said. 'Since I was a child, I've always had a powerful sense of belonging. Like an embrace I had to come back to.'

Hanna thought about his words: he'd chosen the embrace of Little Rymer to that of his girlfriend. It made sense now: the sadness she'd seen in his eyes when they'd first met; his resilience and determination to settle to his new life. Admiration filled her. She felt she had to ask again, to be completely sure. 'And wanting to live here came between you and your girlfriend?'

'It contributed to us splitting up,' Lucas explained. 'Beth had her own path. We never really talked about a future together, but she made assumptions. It made her angry that I wanted to be here. I suppose we were just people who found each other for a while and discovered that we weren't meant to be together, so we moved on.'

Hanna was relieved. Her eyes met Lucas's again and she felt the glow of connection. At that moment, she wanted to feel his arms around her. She wanted to tell him that the first time she'd seen him, she thought she knew him; he'd even appeared in her dreams, but she decided not to say anything. It was early days; it would be silly to spoil a lovely evening by saying something awkward. She'd have to be patient for now. Instead, she said, 'Is it time for pudding?' She glanced at her phone. It was almost nine. In two hours, Ollie would be knocking at the door to drive her back to the farmhouse. Time flew in Lucas's company.

'Cheesecake, then we can take coffee into the lounge.' Lucas stood up. 'I want to hear all about your time in China. And I can't wait to find out what happens next with Cynthia.'

'She's meeting me tomorrow, we're going to the places where I thought I saw the ghost so she can get a feel for it,' Hanna said, stretching her limbs, watching Lucas disappear into the kitchen.

'Keep me in the loop,' he called back.

'I will.' Hanna was smiling – she couldn't help it. Lucas was great company and the Roman banquet had been a really sweet thought. She hoped there would be another date soon. And then another. She liked him, certainly, but there was something more, something special.

They were destined to become closer – she knew it.

38

The days passed slowly, Brea thinking all the time about her father and the contest against Addedomaros. Aurelia dismissed her anxiety when Brea mentioned it, saying that a gladiator had to have an opponent and someone had to lose, but Brea was distraught. She couldn't tell her mistress that one of the gladiators was her friend and the other was her father, and that she was desperate to free them both. She wished that Marcellus had been there; he'd have offered to help.

The night before the contest, Publius Julius demanded a family *cena*, a lavish supper for Caius Fabius and Julia. Aurelia was hostess and she'd risen to the occasion, ordering a variety of food and sweet *conditum* wine, wearing a vibrant green robe, the weld colour overdyed with woad. She sat next to Julia, who was in fine form, Aurelia laughing politely at her remarks while Caius Fabius talked to Publius Julius about battles of the past, how much they'd enjoyed being part of Claudius's invasion seventeen years ago, how the Britons fell at their feet.

'We've brought so much to this country.' Caius Fabius had already drunk several cups of wine. 'It's rightfully ours, a part of Nero's great empire.'

'The Britons are unrefined people,' Publius Julius agreed. 'They are poor fighters and dull thinkers. Before we arrived, there was nothing worthwhile here. We established new towns, brought plants, animals, our religion and ways of reading and counting. Even the word "Briton" is ours.' He laughed. 'We've done them a huge favour.'

Brea tried not to listen. Thoughts jumped and jumbled in her head, about her father and Addedomaros, how she might help them both, and she tried to remain calm. She moved behind Caius Fabius to pour more wine into his cup.

'They are fit for nothing but slavery,' Julia agreed, raising a finger. Balbina stepped forward from her waiting position and adjusted Julia's hair. Julia waved her away. 'Though most of our slaves are Greek or Italian. They are a better class of slave. Balbina's from Naples, you know. She was abandoned as a baby and found in a *spurci lacus* – she was saved from a communal cesspit and I made her my *ornatrix*.' She laughed. 'You should get yourself a better slave, Aurelia, a Greek preferably.'

'Brea is very good,' Aurelia said without a glance. 'I'm happy with her.'

'As you wish.' Julia yawned. 'I lack stimulation. I'm looking forward to watching the gladiators fight tomorrow. The two Britons who are our champions will provide much amusement,' she continued. 'You'll be there tomorrow won't you, Father, when my handsome young gladiator slaughters Aurelia's old warrior?'

'I feel sorry for him, poor man,' Aurelia murmured, holding out her cup to be refilled. 'But my mind's elsewhere at the moment. I've heard no news of Lucius except that he's now with the Ninth.'

'I'm sure he's enjoying the fray,' Julia said, barely interested.

'And Marcellus has reached the island in the west. I hear he's battling with the Druids as we speak,' Publius Julius reminded her.

Brea's breathing was shallow. She imagined her father as Julia had described him, fallen in the arena, Addedomaros standing over him, his sword raised. She blinked and the picture was reversed, Addedomaros lying on the sand. Then it was Marcellus bleeding on the ground: the whoop of murderous Druids resounded in her ears. She knew the Druids were healers, soothsayers and teachers. But they were fighters too – they kept the severed heads of their most valiant enemies as battle trophies.

Brea thought again of Marcellus, of how so many people were against him, and she closed her eyes to stop the image. She recalled her father's words – once freed, Esico vowed he'd fight back. She understood that he had many reasons to hate the Romans and Brea tried to reconcile these thoughts with the admiration and love she felt for Marcellus, and her hand shook. She promised herself that once she was free, she'd leave Camulo-dunum and Marcellus forever. She'd never love anyone again, but Marcellus would have a chance to fulfil his life with Aurelia. Her heart ached to think of it.

'What are you doing? Stupid girl!' Julia snapped. Brea came to her senses; she'd overfilled Aurelia's cup, spilling wine onto her green dress. 'You should have her whipped.'

'It's just a splash.' Aurelia sat back as Brea grabbed a cloth. The dress was stained.

'If she were my slave, I'd get rid of her immediately,' Julia said viciously.

'I'm sorry,' Brea began.

Aurelia smiled kindly. 'Do excuse me, Julia. Brea, will you accompany me to my *cubiculum* and I'll change into another robe. Please – help yourselves to more wine and honey cake.'

'I have no appetite,' Publius Julius complained, stretching out his hand for a morsel.

'And I have nothing else but appetite.' Julia laughed, taking a hunk of cake as Aurelia stood up to leave. 'Make sure you beat her well, sister.'

Brea followed Aurelia to the small room and indicated a blue robe. 'Will you wear this one, Mistress?'

'It will serve.'

'I'm sorry for spilling the wine,' Brea began. 'I'll clean the robe tonight with chamber lye. I am sure I can remove the stain with urine.'

Aurelia frowned. 'I've never seen you this way, Brea. You aren't yourself. Something troubles you. You look as I do when I think of Lucius being so far away in the thick of the battle. Who do you yearn for?'

'Mistress.' Brea sighed. It was time to tell the truth, or at least some of it: Aurelia might be able to help. There was no one else now. 'The man who is your champion is my father; he's been a slave for these last thirteen years. I'm afraid that in a fight with my friend Addedomaros, one of them will die.'

Aurelia was shocked. 'Did my husband know that the slave is your father?'

Brea looked at her feet. 'He did.'

'And did he intend to free your father in order to reward you for your work here?'

Brea nodded. It was close to the truth.

'Marcellus thinks highly of you.' Aurelia pressed her hands together. 'He spoke to me more than once about freeing you, should he not return, that I should speak to Publius Julius. Of course, I agreed to his wishes.'

'Thank you,' Brea began, then she stiffened, listening hard. She could hear a noise outside the *domus*. In the street, there were shouts, crashing, the grate of iron-shod wagon wheels, the snorting of horses.

'What's amiss?' Aurelia was immediately anxious. 'I've never heard anything like it. Is it a storm?'

'I'll go and see.' Brea rushed outside through the atrium into the street and stared, unbelieving. Buildings were burning, throwing red light into the night skies. Brea could smell the stench as curling smoke wafted on the air. There were warriors everywhere, swords raised, their faces and bodies painted with woad, garish shapes and figures, animals. A fierce battle was already raging, horses charging, foot soldiers thrusting knives and swords.

Brea called out in her own language to a young man, his body glistening with sweat and blood. 'What is happening?'

He twisted to look at her, panting. 'You are Iceni?'

'I am.'

'Then grab a sword and join us. We are burning Camulodunum to the ground and all the Romans with it.'

'I don't understand,' Brea said.

'Boudicca leads us in battle; other tribes have joined us. The Romans have taken our land, humiliated our queen. It's time to fight back.'

Brea was already running towards the *ludus*. The fighting was fierce in the streets, Iceni against Romans. Brea dodged a man waving a sword, who immediately began to tussle with a Roman behind her. She almost fell over a body, sprawled on the ground. There was Marcus Rubrius lying twisted, his clothes bloodied, still clutching his statue of Minerva.

Inside the *ludus*, she hurried around frantically, weaving between men in combat. Then a hand grasped her shoulder and Addedomaros was next to her. 'Brea, we are free. Come with us. Your father's already killing Romans.'

He pointed to where Esico battled furiously, dispatching his enemy quickly before rushing to her side, breathing hard. Her father picked up the dead man's sword and put it into Brea's hand. 'Come – this is the chance we've been waiting for.'

Brea hesitated. 'I'll find my mistress first – I have to help her to escape.'

'Your mistress is Roman.' Her father's eyes blazed. 'They'll all die. We'll burn every trace of the Romans – there will be nothing left of them.'

'I'm going back to the *domus*,' Brea said quickly: she owed it to Marcellus to watch out for Aurelia's safety.

'Wait,' Addedomaros called after her. 'Where will we meet?'

'There are woodlands outside Camulodunum.' Brea turned round. 'I'll meet you by the river.'

She ran as fast as she could back to the *domus*. Everywhere she looked, buildings blazed, people were running, screaming. An old soldier staggered forwards, clutching a wound on his neck, falling to the ground. Several women tugging children scampered as fast as they could through the streets. A chariot drawn by two horses clattered past and Brea dodged the iron wheels. She rushed through the atrium and on to the *cubiculum*, where Aurelia was still holding the clean dress: she hadn't moved. Brea tugged it from her hands. 'You won't need that now. Grab your cloak and come – quickly.'

'What's happening?' Aurelia asked, but Brea had wrapped her in the cloak and was pulling her along through the orchard.

In the servants' quarters, she grabbed a clean tunic, a loaf of bread, and called to Daphne and Chloe who were still washing dishes. 'Run for your lives. Hide where you can.'

'I heard the racket. What's amiss out there?' Chloe gasped.

Galyna hurried into the kitchen, holding an empty tray. She was shaking. 'A wild man has just rushed into the atrium; his face was painted blue. He had a sword. I saw him attacking the master.'

Daphne wailed. 'Where shall we go?'

'Just run. As far from Camulodunum as you can,' Brea panted. 'The town's under attack.' Then she dragged a terrified Aurelia towards the stables, pushing her towards Marcellus's black stallion. Brea heaved a saddle on Venator, placing a calm hand on the horse's back. 'Climb on, Mistress.'

'I've never ridden a horse.'

'Climb on,' Brea commanded, hauling Aurelia into the saddle, clambering behind her, coaxing the horse forwards. Then they were out in the street, where fires blazed and fighters with woad on their faces jabbed swords and knives at any passer-by. Smoke was everywhere, choking their lungs, filling their eyes. Brea held up her sword. 'We'll have to ride through the town past the fighting, then on to the woodlands for safety. We'll meet our tribe there.'

'But I can't,' Aurelia gasped.

'You can't stay here. Just look.' Brea turned the horse, in time to see Julia rushing into the street, Caius Fabius behind her, toga billowing, attempting to catch up with her. Balbina was scuttling in the other direction.

Caius Fabius called after his wife, 'Where are you going?'

'To the Temple of the Divine Claudius. It'll be safe there.' Julia lifted her robe and ran ahead athletically, leaving her husband lagging behind. Brea saw a warrior lunge towards him. Caius Fabius fell easily and the Iceni whirled towards his next victim.

Brea urged the horse forwards, weaving past Iceni men and women, their hands wet with Roman blood, killing and trampling everyone in their wake. There were screams and clattering of running feet as the rebels set fire to buildings, swearing, looting, yelling fierce insults. A man turned to her, his face chalk white swirled with blue, his beard dyed with woad, and raised his sword towards the horse, screaming in her direction. Brea shouted something in Iceni and the man recognised his own language and turned away to slice another victim.

Brea encouraged Venator on, past the house where the weaver woman lived and into the night. She knew the way, although she'd only visited the woodlands once with Marcellus. Venator knew the road too, crashing forwards into shadows. Brea pulled at his reins and turned back to look at the burning town. Despite her cloak, Aurelia was shivering. Brea wrapped an arm around her, whispering in her ear, 'We'll find a place to stop before we meet up with my people. You'll need to change into my spare tunic, tousle your hair.'

'I don't understand,' Aurelia whispered.

Brea's voice was hushed. 'You can't speak Latin again. You're Iceni now.'

'But I don't know the language.'

'Then you must say nothing – we'll tell people you cannot speak.'

'What of my jewellery, Brea? I still have it on – Marcellus gave it to me, and it belongs to him.'

'We'll hide it beneath your clothes. Or we'll say we looted it.' Brea's heart thudded. 'It seems we left Camulodunum just in time.'

In the distance, the sky was burnt orange, the town now completely ablaze, plumes of silver smoke twisting upwards, flames swallowing every building. Brea could see Iceni warriors on horseback and foot, some in chariots, darting everywhere, looting, taking their revenge. They would not leave Camulodunum until the last Roman was killed and the final building burned to the ground.

Then she pointed. 'Look.'

A roaring sound came from the Temple of the Divine Claudius, the rush of flames leaping high, licking the white pillars as terrified screams filled the night air. Brea felt Aurelia shudder as the temple glowed and red stones crashed. She remembered the words of Luna, the beggar woman, as she sat on the steps. *A temple for a dead emperor who people think is a god? But it is of no consequence. It will not be here long.*

Brea closed her eyes against the blaze, but she could smell the sickening smell of scorched flesh; the screams of panic blocked her ears. There was nothing to be done now. She tugged the reins. Venator twisted away from Camulodunum, bursting forwards at speed, carrying Brea and Aurelia into the darkness.

39

Late on Sunday afternoon, Hanna cycled to the station, stopping next to the small yellow Beetle. She waved through the window. Cynthia Chandra waved back and pointed upwards, giving a cheery thumbs-up sign. It had rained almost constantly since they'd found the bracelet, but today the bad weather was holding off. Cynthia scrambled from her car, dressed in a shiny yellow raincoat that matched the Beetle perfectly. As Hanna joined her, she threw herself into a hug.

'Hanna, so nice to see you.' Cynthia smelled of a soapy, clean scent, like baby powder. 'I thought it would still be raining and we'd have to drive along your ghost route. I prefer to walk it.'

Hanna shivered a little at the mention of the ghost. There was a cold wind drifting from the fens, no evidence of sunshine in a washed-out sky hung with heavy clouds.

'I'm looking forward to finding out about our ghost.' Cynthia beamed. 'I thought we'd start here, at the station.' She noticed Hanna's confused expression. 'Isn't this where you saw her first?'

Hanna nodded. 'Yes, she was sitting on a bench. I was worried about her – I assumed she was local. But then she disappeared. Since then, I've seen her – or what I assume is her – in the road, near the fens and in the fields.'

Cynthia's gaze shone behind her glasses. 'And, instinctively, Hanna, what do you believe her to be?'

'Someone who's searching for something, and she has a heavy heart,' Hanna said honestly.

'And why do you think she appears to you?'

Hanna shrugged. 'Maybe she's trying to tell me something. Maybe we're connected.'

'In what way, do you think?' Cynthia asked again.

'I've no idea.' Hanna found the questions confusing. 'Maybe it had something to do with my fall from the trampoline?'

'But do you share something? Is there something you have in common?'

'I understand Latin in the dream,' Hanna tried. 'I understand the Iceni people, even though I don't know their language.'

'Go on.'

'In my first ever dream as a teenager, a man drew a sword and promised to protect me. I knew he was Iceni, that he was my father – I could tell from how I felt about him – and although I don't know the language, I knew what he was saying. From that point onwards, I was fascinated by languages,' Hanna explained. 'In another dream, an important Roman man sent me to buy pottery for a wedding. That was before I'd started to learn Latin, but I understood his orders. And I found languages easy after that.'

'It's time to see what we can find out about our ghost.' Cynthia was watching her closely.

'Okay – what do we do?'

Cynthia looked up at the sky. 'The rain's holding off. Let's go to the platform for a moment and see what happens.'

'Right,' Hanna agreed, securing her bicycle to a railing, wondering what to expect.

They huddled on a bench, and Hanna gazed down the track. There were no trains due and there was no one around apart from a man in a yellow high-visibility jacket who crossed the bridge to the car park. The café was closed. Serenity was spending today with a friend; Hanna recalled that she'd said they were going for a walk down the coastal path near Holkham beach. Hanna thought of Lucas as a boy, holidaying on the northern Norfolk beaches with his family. She'd assumed he was an only child who'd felt an affinity for the rushing tide, the shifting sand of the dunes. She recalled his determination, the way he cared so much about his work and how his ex-girlfriend had discouraged him, and she felt a powerful wave of affection. She hoped she'd see him soon.

She watched a lone pigeon pecking at the dust before it flew into the iron rafters of the station. The wind took her hair, ruffling it like straying fingers. Cynthia was staring ahead, and Hanna followed her gaze. Beyond the platform and the bridge was the car park, a crop of swaying trees behind, a dishwater sky overhead. The trees were already dropping leaves, russet colours swirling in the breeze.

Cynthia spoke quietly. 'The Iceni lived all over Norfolk, east of Thetford, extending to Cambridge.' She took a deep breath. 'There could have been a settlement here, but we know so little. They couldn't write – the only words of the Iceni language that we have are on coins. Roly believes that their language was Germanic. I'm interested that you understand their language in your dream. Can you remember any of it?'

Hanna shook her head. 'When I wake up, it's all gone. I'm just left feeling that there's so much unresolved.'

'I think that there's more jewellery in the field, another piece, the most important one. Roly's excited about it. He'll come back with the metal detectors as soon as the weather's a bit better.' Cynthia smiled. 'Although it will probably only get worse – it's autumn already.'

Hanna gazed around the empty platform. There was a feeling of loneliness and desolation in the silence. She murmured, 'There is a sadness here once all the people are gone.'

'You feel it too?' Cynthia asked. 'Sadness isn't something we associate with the Iceni. Anger, revenge, injustice, tragedy even, yes. Boudicca was a fighter. She burned Colchester completely to the ground.'

'She was a first-century feminist,' Hanna agreed. 'But you're right, there's no anger here.'

'Archaeologists have dug deep beneath the soil in Colchester, that was once called Camulodunum – they've found remains from Boudicca's revolt, including a blackened bed, charred dates, figs, wheat and peas, all of which had been turned to carbon by the intense heat of the fire.'

'After all this time?' Hanna was surprised. 'That's incredible.'

'So, as you say, Hanna, the intense feeling of loss I can sense as I'm sitting here doesn't seem to be related to Boudicca. Shall we move on somewhere else?'

'All right – where do you want to go?'

Cynthia smiled. 'Do you have wellingtons? I thought we'd stroll across the pig field together.'

'I'll cycle back to the farm and pick them up.' Hanna grinned. 'Pig field it is. Where Roly found the bracelet.'

* * *

Cynthia followed Hanna back to the farmhouse and parked her car. Ollie's Peugeot 208 was not outside the cottage, nor was the Range Rover. Paddy and Stephanie had gone out for afternoon tea in Holt.

Cynthia took Hanna's arm as they wandered towards the pig field in wellingtons. 'I thought if we went back to the place where two items of jewellery were discovered, our ghost might show herself. What do you think?'

Hanna gazed up at the sky. 'It won't get dark for a few hours... I've only ever seen her when it's been dark enough to doubt my own vision – or sanity.'

'I can understand that,' Cynthia agreed. They were crossing the field, heading towards Bramble Woods, wellingtons sinking in mud. Cynthia took a deep breath, then exhaled slowly. 'But I can feel she's not far away.'

Hanna was suddenly nervous. 'Really?'

'She can't stray far.' Cynthia was staring ahead again. 'This is the site where it happened.'

'Where what happened?' Hanna felt suddenly cold.

'That's what she wants us to know. Something tragic occurred here – can't you sense the touch of it on your skin?'

Hanna could feel the buffeting of the wind, her spine stiffening. 'I have the same emotion in my dreams.' She glanced around. The pigs were near their arks, grubbing in the soil. She and Cynthia walked on, reaching the stile that led to the woodlands.

'So, in these dreams,' Cynthia began, 'you mentioned a man, and you feel a strong attachment to him. Let's take that thought into the woods.'

Hanna shivered, her arm still tucked through Cynthia's as they walked along the narrow path, moss and cracking twigs beneath their feet.

Cynthia spoke quietly. 'Tell me about this man in the dream. Who is he?'

'There are two men – a man who might be my father. But there's another. He's a soldier, most of the time in uniform – a Roman.'

'Ah – the jewellery is Roman, so we have a clue there,' Cynthia observed. 'What does he wear?'

'Armour, a helmet, sometimes. A deep red cloak... I have the sense that he's an important soldier, a legate perhaps. A *legatus* had an elaborate helmet and body armour, a scarlet *paludamentum* and a waistband called a *cincticulus*.'

Cynthia remembered. 'You speak Latin as well as other languages. So, the legate, what is his relationship to our lost spirit?'

'She loves him,' Hanna said before she realised. 'When he looks at her, it's like a moment of electricity.'

'That's very interesting.' Cynthia turned to her. 'Is that an experience you've had yourself?'

'Yes,' Hanna admitted. 'Why?'

'Well, it's a powerful form of non-verbal communication that you're clearly receptive to. Eye contact triggers the release of oxytocin, the relationship-building hormone. It's a way of sharing empathy – a communication channel is opened. If you like, it's a special form of connection.' Cynthia offered Hanna a secretive smile. 'So that's something you and your ghost have in common – you're both in love.'

'I don't know,' Hanna said. 'There is someone, but it's a new relationship. I like him – there's chemistry.'

'A local young man?' Cynthia asked.

'No, but he... he's drawn to this place.'

'He's drawn to you, here – it's meant to be. That's how spiritual connections work.' Cynthia smiled.

'Oh, do you think so?' Hanna wanted to believe Cynthia: the strong bond with Lucas had gripped her from the beginning.

'I do. Something in his soul is looking for you. He's lost, troubled or unsettled. Am I right?'

'I think so – he needs a fresh start, but it's not been easy.'

'You have a symbiosis. You need his direction and to be grounded. He needs your ability to heal. You'll find it in each other.'

'That's interesting...' Hanna began, then her body froze in fear. A crashing noise from the forest made her jump and she clung to Cynthia without meaning to. It became louder, sticks snapping, as if someone was running fast from the thicket in her direction.

Hanna watched as a roe deer bounded from the shadows beyond the trees, pausing on the path for an instant before springing away.

'There are certainly very strong vibrations in Bramble Woods, and I know you feel it too. It's a powerful place filled with nature, birth, rebirth.' Cynthia looked around. 'Something very meaningful happened here. We're surrounded by it.' Her eyes swept up to the treetops and Hanna followed her gaze to the overhanging canopy. A squirrel scuttled along a high branch. A solitary bird chirped one note, making the eerie screech of a rusty gate. 'The forest has an unearthly feel to it. Unfinished business. There's a residual emotion of pain that has existed for a long time.' Cynthia offered a reassuring smile. 'We'll come back here, Hanna. We're close to discovering something important. I'll have to tell Roly. Perhaps he ought to bring his metal detectors into the woods.'

'Perhaps.' Hanna shivered. The deer had unnerved her. 'Cynthia, shall we go back to the farmhouse and get a hot drink? I'm freezing.'

'And my feet are numb,' Cynthia agreed. 'I've picked up quite a lot of vibrations from our ghost, and I must say, talking to you and being here has given me a great deal to think about.' She offered an enigmatic smile. 'A warm drink is just what we need.'

* * *

The night air was cold and Brea shivered as she brought Venator to a halt and clambered down, holding a hand out so that Aurelia could slither from the saddle. The horse's flesh steamed in the night air and he snorted softly before nibbling something from the grass. There was no one around; the forest was dark and it was impossible to see anything, although the bubbling river was not far away.

Aurelia's face was filled with tension. 'What do we do now?' She gazed at Brea's sword. 'Are you planning to kill me here?'

Brea bundled the tunic into her arms. 'Mistress, I'm trying to help us both survive. Put the tunic on. Dishevel your hair – you can't wear it in a Roman style.'

'But Roman women wear their hair dressed at all times. To wear it loose is uncivilised.'

'You're no longer Roman,' Brea said gently. 'We'll meet my father and the other soldiers here, we'll follow the army until we find an Iceni camp. Once we're safe, there'll be a way to help you. I don't know what it is yet. Perhaps we can get a message to your husband.'

'Or perhaps I can find a boat back to Rome?' Aurelia's eyes were wide with hope. 'Do you think I could?'

'It's possible. But you have to trust me, Mistress. No one must know you're Roman, and they certainly mustn't find out that you're Marcellus's wife. It's unthinkable.' Brea closed her eyes, visualising what might happen. 'So, for now, we'll follow the Iceni army, let them lead us to a safe place, then I'll help you.'

'Why would you do that?' Aurelia clutched the slave's tunic, her face frozen in fear.

'Because you've been kind to me, the master has been kind to me.' Brea wondered about Marcellus, imagining him miles away fighting the Druids. It would not take long for the news of the burning of Camulodunum to reach him: messengers on horseback passed news quickly. Then he'd return to fight the Iceni. He'd surely be killed. Brea's mind raced – she couldn't let that happen. She'd find a way.

'I'll do my best to get you to safety. I'm with my people, but they mustn't know who you are. I'll ask my father to say nothing of it. Now – quickly, get changed before anyone arrives.'

Brea watched Aurelia slip away behind a tree. She wondered how she'd manage to dress herself unaided, if she'd ever done it before. She'd have to learn so many things quickly.

Venator snorted; Brea saw the stallion's ears twitch. She walked over to him and stroked his mane, listening intently. Someone was approaching. She called, 'Father? Is that you?'

'It's me – Adde.' A hushed voice came from the gloom. 'Esico's still fighting in Camulodunum. He'll follow soon. I wanted to make sure you were here safely.'

'I am.' Brea was relieved to see Addedomaros step from the shadows. He was battle-weary, blood was smeared on his forehead and torso, but he was uninjured.

He glanced around. 'Where's the Roman woman?'

'Changing her clothes.'

'Why have you brought her, Brea? It makes no sense.'

'I promised her.' Brea sighed. 'I'll find a way to get her to safety.'

'Your father doesn't like it.'

'I know,' Brea agreed. 'But I couldn't leave her.'

'We're free now.' Addedomaros closed his eyes, as if in sudden realisation. 'I've longed for this moment for most of my life. And now we have the chance to get rid of every Roman in the country. The queen has sworn that it will happen. There are so many of us marching on Londinium and Verulamium. We'll burn both cities to the ground and all the Romans who live there.'

'I'm not afraid to fight,' Brea said. 'But my mistress will need me to stay close. She doesn't know how to use a weapon.'

'She'll learn quickly enough.' Addedomaros took a step forward, his voice confidential. 'There's news. The Ninth Legion has heard about our desire to destroy Camulodunum. We've been told that they're marching here as we speak. Spies tell us they have only five thousand men. We'll have a chance to show them what the Iceni and Trinovantes are made of. We'll wipe them all out in one bloody battle.'

'The Ninth? On their way here?' A small voice came from a distance. Aurelia emerged from behind a tree, her hair unkempt, wearing a slave's tunic, wrapping the indigo woollen cloak tightly around her. 'Did you say the Ninth Legion are coming here? To fight? But that can't be – my brother Lucius is with the Ninth...'

40

On Thursday morning, Serenity's café was busy, people bustling in for hot drinks and snacks. Trains rumbled out of the station, the platforms crowded with shivering travellers driven in by the perpetual grey rain and the harsh wind that chilled to the bone.

Hanna and Serenity hardly had a moment to speak once the doors opened. Serenity had brought in home-made crumpets that had sold out by lunchtime. Hot ginger tea and pumpkin-spiced bread were selling fast and Hanna had lost count of the number of times she'd been asked if they sold jacket potatoes.

Serenity said, 'So you think we should invest in a bigger urn for out back?'

'Why not?' Hanna grinned. 'Everyone's cold and starving today.'

'Right, I'll bring a vat of soup in tomorrow and see how it goes. There are so many pumpkins available right now.'

By four thirty, as a train of eight carriages shuddered away towards King's Cross, Serenity slumped across the counter exhausted and said, 'Time for a break. I want you to try my new hot chocolate recipe. I'm thinking of putting it on the menu.' She brought out a flask and poured steaming liquid into two mugs. 'Tell me what you think.'

Hanna was grateful for the chance to stop work. She took a huge gulp of the drink and sighed. It was creamy and comforting. 'Heaven. What is it?'

'Plant-based hot chocolate. I made it with coconut milk, cacao butter, maple syrup and spices. I thought I could serve it with some vegan whipped cream on top.'

'I'd buy it,' Hanna enthused. 'And I bet Ollie would love it.'

'He does.' Serenity pressed fingers over her grin. 'I made it specially, and took some with me when we went to the coast. I was thinking, a splash of bourbon would make it really delicious.'

Hanna straightened up, hands on hips. 'You went to Holkham beach with Ollie? Is there something you should've told me?'

Serenity nodded. 'We danced at your mum's wedding and he came round to my flat. We talked into the early hours. Then I saw him again in the pub on Saturday night. Sunday was our first proper date though.' She met Hanna's eyes. 'We went for a long walk, stopped on the beach for a hot drink and sandwiches that I made, talked about ourselves all day, then he gave me a lift home and we snogged each other's face off for half an hour...' Serenity watched a locomotive chug into the station. 'I like him.'

'Well, I never.' Hanna smiled. 'That's good news.'

Serenity drank from her mug. 'I hear you've hooked up with the local vet.'

'Early days,' Hanna said, by way of an excuse. She'd been hoping for a text: vets clearly didn't have much time to arrange dates.

'Ollie says you met him at your mum's wedding too – then he made you a meal at his house.'

Hanna laughed. 'Ollie's right.'

'When are you seeing him again?'

'I don't know,' Hanna said truthfully. 'I don't want to rush things. His job is stressful. And he's recently come out of a difficult relationship.'

'Oh? That'll be the girlfriend we saw him with.'

'I get the impression it ended badly.'

'We should double date,' Serenity suggested, a twinkle in her eye. 'We could all go clubbing in King's Lynn.'

Hanna rolled her eyes. She wasn't sure Lucas was the sort of person who'd enjoy clubbing. 'Or a long walk on Holkham beach...' He'd enjoy that so much more, she was sure of it.

Two women carrying small babies came in for a drink and one of them made a dreamy face as she pointed to Serenity's mug. 'What's in there? It smells gorgeous.'

'A new recipe. I'll put it on the menu tomorrow,' Serenity said quickly. 'Will chai lattes do for now?'

'With lots of spice,' the other woman enthused.

'I'll bring them over,' Serenity offered and bustled around the hot milk frother.

Hanna heard her phone ring and pulled it from her jeans pocket, her heart leaping. She hoped it would be Lucas. A familiar voice said, 'Ah, Hanna, good. Have you got a minute for a chat?'

'Roly. Of course.'

'I've just had a long conversation with Cynthia. We were discussing her visit. She said it was very useful, that Bramble Woods had a bit of an atmosphere, apparently. She thinks we should come out again and search around there. It's quite a large space though.'

'I'm sure Paddy wouldn't mind,' Hanna replied. 'You think there's another piece of jewellery there, don't you?'

'Well, Cynthia's sure of it. I'm very excited about recent developments.' Roly took a deep breath. 'I think this is just the beginning of some real in-depth research into the Iceni that I want to take further. I've got a few contacts to meet, to see if I can get some funding. I'd like to pursue the local tribes a bit more.' Hanna could almost hear the cogs whirring as he thought aloud. 'You've been really instrumental in our research. I'd like to show you around the university, point out some of the artefacts I've collected over the years. Then, afterwards, Cynthia and I and her husband and my wife would like to invite you to dinner in Cambridge. But I don't want you dragging yourself all the way to Cambridge by yourself. Cynthia says you have a boyfriend. You could bring him – you might ask Ollie and a plus-one too. He's been very helpful. What do you think?'

'It sounds lovely, Roly.' Hanna paused. Cynthia had referred to Lucas as her boyfriend: perhaps she had an insight into the future of their relation-ship. She imagined herself and Lucas as a proper couple and it felt right.

She wondered how to ask Lucas to come to Cambridge with her. It was a perfect opportunity.

'So, I'll send directions – how about Sunday afternoon? We could have a stroll around my collection of Iceni artefacts and then we could all go out for a meal?'

'That would be great. I'll look forward to it.'

'Talk to the others and text me with numbers.'

'I will.' Hanna put the phone back in her pocket and smiled. A day in Cambridge looking round the museum with Roly as a guide would be fascinating. It might spark vivid dreams, but Hanna was used to her sleep being interrupted. She wanted to find out as much as she could about the woman and her Roman soldier.

Serenity was busy, taking two mugs of latte to the women with the babies at the far table. Hanna took advantage of the moment. She tugged out her phone and thumbed a message to Lucas.

I've just had an invitation to Cambridge to have dinner with Roly on Sunday. Can you come? Hanna.

She deliberated over adding an x at the bottom and decided against it. She didn't want to seem too keen. She told herself that sending a text was forward enough, so she pressed *send* quickly before she could talk herself out of it.

Then Serenity was back. 'I'm sure if I made a big batch of hot chocolate, it would sell like mad. I might invest in an urn for soup and maybe do some fresh bread every day.'

'All made from scratch? You'd be even more busy.' Hanna was impressed.

'That's my motto, work hard, play hard, live life to the full.' Serenity laughed.

'And there's me dithering about my future. I still haven't decided what to do with myself yet.' Hanna mused: 'I envy Roly, who loves delving into the past, and Lucas, who's passionate about his work, and you're just incredible at what you do. Ollie is determined to improve things at the farm, to drag Paddy into the twenty-first century and make everything much more eco-friendly, and all I can do is tread water.'

Serenity patted her hand. 'Take your time. You'll know what's right for you when it comes along.'

'Maybe.' Hanna sighed. Her phone buzzed in her pocket and she tugged it out. There was a message from Lucas.

Just come out of theatre. Cruciate ligament repair on Billy the Staffy went well. Sunday sounds great. Will text later. L x

Hanna was smiling broadly. Lucas had replied promptly, he'd agreed to come to Cambridge with her on Sunday and he'd added an x at the end of the message. It was a great result all round for her and for Billy the Staffy.

Serenity noticed her grin and was immediately interested.

'So, what's made you so happy?' she asked inquisitively. 'Do you have a hot date tonight?'

Hanna shook her head. 'Not tonight. I just wondered – what are you and Ollie doing on Sunday? You know that double date you suggested? I may have the perfect place.'

* * *

The smoky smell of burning buildings was still in the air throughout the night and into the following day. The Iceni men and women crowded in the woodlands, resting, sleeping, sharing loot, bathing wounds and sharpening swords. Horses grazed near the river while warriors washed the blood of the dead from their skin in the water. Aurelia sat against a tree trunk brooding, her face miserable, refusing the pieces of bread Brea tried to tempt her with.

Esico's voice was low in Brea's ear. 'You shouldn't have brought her here.'

Brea sighed. 'I know how you feel and I'm sorry. But I couldn't leave her behind.'

'And what's going to happen when the fighting begins again?' her father asked. 'Brea, the Ninth Legion are on their way – they are hours from here.

The queen has just urged us to slaughter them all to the last man. What will we do with the Roman woman? She'll get in the way.'

'She's worried about her brother. He's a tribune in the Ninth.'

Esico sighed. 'Are you happy to take responsibility for her? Some of our men have already asked if she's wounded, why she won't speak when she's spoken to. This can only end badly.'

'I'll look after her, I promise.'

'I trust you, Brea. This is what I always dreamed of, you and me side by side, reclaiming our homeland.' Esico placed a gentle hand on her shoulder. 'But you have to promise, if she causes a problem, you'll deal with her swiftly. You know what I mean...'

'I won't let you down,' Brea said miserably. She had dreamed of freedom for so long, of being united with her father. And despite the joy of being with him, fighting shoulder to shoulder as she'd always known they would, their reunion had come at a great cost. Again, she uttered a silent prayer for Marcellus.

Her father's eyes were warm with affection. 'You remind me so much of your mother. She had a softer side too, but she was strong like you, and loyal.' His face was sad for a moment. 'But you need to prepare your weapons, make sure that fine stallion of yours is ready for battle. When the Ninth Legion come, it won't take us long to finish them off.'

Brea glanced over towards Aurelia, who watched Esico with a fearful expression. Although she didn't understand the Iceni language, she'd seen the glint in his eyes, heard the bitterness of his tone and noticed the involuntary raising and descending of his sword as he spoke. She dissolved into more tears and Esico shook his head before striding away. Brea sidled across to comfort her, placing an arm around her shoulders. Aurelia's wails increased and she covered her face.

Brea whispered that she should be brave, that the worst thing she imagined might not come to pass. In truth, Brea had no idea what to say.

* * *

The hours passed slowly; the day was almost over. There was a restlessness among the Iceni; they were rowdy and ready for battle. The victory at

Camulodunum, the fires smouldering in the distance, the stench of burning still filling the air had made them edgy and eager to fight again. There was a great deal of talk about marching on Londinium and Verulamium, reducing both towns to ashes. And afterwards, they were ready to meet Suetonius, the self-appointed governor general of Britain whom they despised, and they were sure they'd defeat him, the Fourteenth Legion and a detachment of the Twentieth Legion. They'd heard that Suetonius had been told of the Iceni triumph and the thought of his frustration excited them. He was the adversary they wanted to meet in the final battle of sweet revenge.

Brea listened to the talk as she brushed Venator, resting her cheek against his velvet face. Brea wondered where Marcellus was now. The thought filled her with a weakness she tried to push away, but the feeling stayed. And with it came anxiety; the Iceni were her people and they were baying for Roman blood.

Addedomaros was by her side. 'You're troubled. What's on your mind?'

'I'm waiting, as we all are,' Brea said quietly. 'The Romans will arrive soon.'

'I'm looking forward to it. The Ninth will fall easily. Then we can advance to Londinium.' Addedomaros's eyes shone; he was dreaming of conquest. He noticed Brea watching him. He indicated Aurelia, who was still sitting against the tree trunk, hugging her cloak. She had fallen asleep. 'You should have left her in Camulodunum.'

'Perhaps.' Brea thought for a moment about Daphne, Chloe and Galyna. They probably wouldn't have survived. Publius Julius had been attacked. And she'd seen Julia scurrying to the temple for safety. She would have met a horrible end there. Brea was imagining how she'd break the news to Marcellus. She intended to find him, that was the truth of it; she'd brought Venator and Aurelia, and she was determined to take them to Marcellus. That had been her plan from the beginning. He'd look after them both and then she'd leave with her own people. It would be difficult; it would break her heart, but she'd do what was right, then she'd walk away.

There was a stirring among the Iceni, people moving urgently, reaching for weapons, and Brea knew immediately what was happening.

Her father rushed over from where he'd been resting on the ground and pushed a sword into Brea's hand. 'The Ninth are approaching. Stay close.'

Brea glanced towards Aurelia. 'But what about my mistress?'

'Leave her there to sleep. It'll be over before she wakes. There are not many of them – two thousand, maybe a few more. We rebels outnumber them – it'll be an easy victory. They're crossing the field beyond. We'll attack them there.'

Brea was about to speak, but a huge cry went up and the Iceni began to rush forward, yelling and howling, swords in the air, painted faces twisted with fury. Brea glanced at Aurelia, who was still sleeping. She brandished her sword and followed her father.

The battle had already begun when she arrived in the field. Roman bodies and strewn armour littered the ground, fallen soldiers with swords still in their hands. Brea darted between the fighting mob, looking everywhere for Lucius. She hoped there might be a way to speak to him, to lead him to Aurelia. But the Iceni rebels were everywhere, slashing with swords and daggers, raising shields. Brea stood, looking around; the noise was deafening, clashing metal, wild shrieks of the victorious Iceni as the Roman soldiers clattered to the ground, one by one, cut down.

Then she saw Aurelia, running in an open space, her hair flying behind her as she searched the faces of the soldiers. She was shouting, her mouth was wide, but Brea couldn't hear the words. Her feet sank into the boggy ground; her tunic and cloak were spattered with mud and blood. She looked every inch an Iceni woman.

Brea watched helplessly as a Roman soldier lurched towards her, his sword raised. For a moment, the scene was in slow motion, the fear in Aurelia's eyes as she turned to run, the fury on the soldier's face, Aurelia falling to the ground, then Brea was next to her, sword lifted. She lunged and the Roman slumped forwards. Brea dragged Aurelia from the mud, shouting to her to stand. Aurelia stood shakily, clutching her thigh; a bloodstain was spreading through her tunic. Brea wrapped an arm around Aurelia, her sword in the other, and hauled her towards the shelter of the trees.

41

Brea bathed the wound in Aurelia's thigh with water from the river, bandaging it tightly with cloth she found among the items looted from Camulodunum. The gash was deep, the flesh badly torn. She hoped the bleeding would stop, but Aurelia's tunic was quickly dark with blood. Aurelia said little, wincing with pain, as Brea handed her fresh water to drink, saying, 'The wound will heal in time, but you must be still. Here – you'll be thirsty.'

Aurelia gulped gratefully. Then she murmured, 'Did you see Lucius? I searched every face–'

'I did the same, but I couldn't find him.'

'I pray he's alive.' Aurelia groaned as she tried to move. 'Is there news of the battle? Brea – can you go back and look for him? I can't help him now.' Her voice trailed away.

'Why did you come into the fray without a weapon?' Brea asked quickly. She hoped to distract Aurelia from any mention of her brother as long as she could. Her first concern was to deal with the huge slash in her leg.

'It was too heavy to carry,' Aurelia said weakly. 'Lucius is twenty-two years old. He's no fighter. As a boy, he was a gentle soul. He preferred writing and reading to wielding a sword. My father sent him here to

Britannia to make a man of him. I fear he has made him a dead man.' Aure-lia's lip trembled. 'Brea, I'm wounded – I feel frail. Will I die?'

'You need to rest and gain strength again. You mustn't move. Pray that your brother has managed to get away from the brawl.'

Brea glanced over her shoulder at a sudden noise. Iceni rebels had started to return, cheering, talking excitedly, moving to the river to wash. Lucius's survival was unlikely.

'The battle is over.'

Aurelia seemed to gather new strength. 'Can you find out if there were survivors – if there is news of Lucius?'

'Try to rest.' Brea stood up. There was blood on her tunic, Aurelia's, more Roman blood. She pushed her way through the battle-worn Iceni and found Venator tethered to a tree. She stroked his mane.

Her father appeared through the throngs of cheering men and women and smiled. 'I hoped to find you here. It was the best of battles for our tribe.'

'I'm glad you fought well, Father.'

'And your friend, Addedomaros. He is a great swordsman. Between us, we took many Romans; they fell easily.' Esico laughed. 'Every Roman is now feeding the worms in the field. The Ninth are no more, every last one gone. The warrior fighting next to me killed a tribune. His mother's milk was barely out of him. He fell to his knees and begged like a boy as his throat was cut.' He spat on the ground. 'We march on tomorrow. The queen will lead the way and we'll take Londinium, burn it to ash. We'll amass more rebels. We expect to be two hundred thousand strong, more. Then we'll meet the Roman general once and for all and take back what is ours.'

'All will be well, Father.' Brea smiled. But she was thinking of Aurelia, lying beneath the tree, a wound in her leg. She'd find it difficult to travel. When she knew that Lucius was dead, her will to survive would fail. And Brea was thinking of Marcellus. The Roman army would lose the battle against so many Iceni. She had to find him and warn him. She had no other choice.

* * *

Hanna, Lucas, Ollie and Serenity were discussing travel as they sat on the train to Cambridge on Sunday afternoon. Ollie had insisted on going by rail: he'd said, 'The greenhouse effect of gas emissions per kilometre on railway transport is 80 per cent less than cars,' at least three times on the journey. Serenity was delighted: it meant they could all have wine with their meal. They'd spend the whole day in Cambridge. Then, later, Stephanie had offered Hanna and Ollie a lift back to the farm.

Roly met them at the station, shaking everyone's hand, grinning. 'Pleased to meet you all. I have a lovely day planned. Shall we walk? It's only twenty minutes to the university.'

'On foot is always best,' Ollie piped as Serenity pushed an arm through his and snuggled close against the chilly wind that funnelled along Hills Road. They huddled behind Hanna, who fell in step next to Roly, Lucas at her side.

Roly walked quickly; he was eager to show off the collection of artefacts. He turned to Hanna. 'Cynthia hasn't stopped talking about her visit to the farm. She likes working with you.' He gave a single laugh. 'Apparently you're very psychically channelled.'

Lucas asked, 'How did it go on Sunday?' He moved closer to her. 'I've been dying to ask.'

'We didn't see anything ghostly.' Hanna smiled, making light of how nervous she had been. 'I was a bit jumpy when a roe deer crashed out of the woods.'

'Cynthia's tuned to mystical things, and she reminded me that deer are sacred to the Iceni,' Roly explained. 'She's usually right. She believes some areas of the country have more paranormal incidences than others – she says there are stronger vibrations left over from the past.'

'Which areas?' Lucas asked.

'Oh, she's been to sites in Kent, Lancashire, Wiltshire, a place near Bedford. She says Thetford has a special feel to it... there's a wonderful Iron Age fort there. Norfolk is high on her list, that's why she lives here.' Roly hurried on towards Norwich Street. 'So, what do you think to all this supernatural business, Lucas? Hanna says you're a vet. I don't suppose you get to see many ghosts.'

'That's true.' Lucas pushed his hands deep into jacket pockets. 'Some animals seem to have a sixth sense though.'

'I'd agree with you. Of course, my wife thinks it's all stuff and nonsense. She's a financial software developer, and she has no interest for things in the past.' Roly shrugged. 'You'll meet Prue later.'

'And Cynthia's having dinner with us too?' Hanna asked.

'Yes, she's bringing Manjeet – her husband's an engineer. Poor Cynthia's outnumbered tonight by people who don't understand what she calls her science. But I have faith in her. As I said, she's usually right.'

* * *

Roly led them around the Museum of Archaeology and Anthropology, talking proudly about all the exhibits as if he owned them. 'Do you know, there are two million years of human history and one million items under this one roof. The Classical Archaeology section houses one of the finest collections of plaster casts of classical sculpture in the world. And we have a preserved skeleton of a Roman woman, who inspired Sylvia Plath's poem, "All the Dead Dears".'

'I love the atmosphere in this place.' Hanna's voice was hushed. 'It's incredible, to be among all these special pieces of history.'

'It is...' Lucas was watching her, a smile on his lips.

The museum was quiet, their footsteps echoing on the flagstones. There were few visitors on a Sunday afternoon.

Roly led his group to a glass case behind which was an Iceni torc, several bluish and silver coins, and a few leaf-shaped arrow heads. He sighed. 'You see how little we have of the Iceni.'

'Is this all?' Hanna asked.

'I'm afraid so.' Roly nodded. 'The Iceni loved horses – we'll occasionally find bits of horse wear and coins, but precious little pottery. These coins were found in a drainage ditch in Norfolk. The torc was found near Wisbech – it's made of pure gold. The Iceni were cultivated people, very skilled. It's very similar to the one Boudicca would have worn.'

'It's lovely,' Serenity said. 'Does that mean Boudicca was a real person?'

'She was,' Roly replied. 'We know little about her except that she was a powerful queen and a strong leader. She was probably thirty-two when she died, according to the Romans who wrote her history. The Iceni left no records. The Roman historian Cassius Dio says that she was "very tall, the glance of her eye most fierce; her voice harsh. A great mass of the reddest hair fell down to her hips. Her appearance was terrifying." But I think he made that up. He was born a hundred years after she died.'

Hanna said, 'I suppose he wanted to make a woman warrior sound scary.'

'Quite,' Roly agreed. 'She and her daughters rode round in a chariot before battles, inspiring the Iceni to be brave. She was certainly a fierce leader.'

'Will our necklace and bracelet go in this museum?' Hanna asked.

'I hope so. And much more too, in the future.' Roly faced her, his eyes flashing. 'The Iceni need their story to be properly told, and I'm determined to tell it. Now, shall we continue our tour? I'd like to show you the stone sarcophagus, the skeleton of a Roman woman and the bones of the mouse and shrew that gnawed her ankle in her coffin.'

* * *

Several hours later, the friends were sitting in a Jordanian restaurant sharing a mezze platter, drinking red wine and limonana made with mint and lemons. Ollie was so enthusiastic about the food, he volunteered Hanna to cook another Middle Eastern meal for them all at the farmhouse.

'I'll help, of course,' he enthused. 'But Hanna's a great cook.' Serenity dug him gently in the ribs. 'Oh, and so's Serenity. We'd have a fantastic feast if we all cooked together, and my dad and Stephanie would love to see you all up at the farm again.'

'I'll hold you to that,' Roly said. 'We should have invited Paddy and Stephanie here today.'

'They've gone to a spa,' Ollie said between mouthfuls. 'Steph's still holding out for a honeymoon and she's dragged Dad off for a massage and a facial to soften him up.' He laughed. 'I can just see him, covered in mud, making comparisons to the manure in the pig field.'

'I do enjoy a spa,' Prue said. She was a slim woman with short slate hair and an intelligent face. 'Roly's not keen, of course. But I do like a hot stones massage.'

'I'm a reiki healer,' Cynthia added. 'Manjeet finds it very helpful after a difficult day at work.'

'I do.' Manjeet sipped limonana. He was an easy-going man with a ready smile. 'I don't quite know how it works, but it does.'

'Reiki works really well on animals,' Lucas agreed. 'We have a practitioner we recommend for stressed or nervous patients, or for their end-of-life care. Our reiki master does great work.'

'So, if we accept the power of healing but we can't see it,' Cynthia piped up, her face mischievous, 'why can't we accept the power of the supernatural world? Surely it's not such a stretch to think the past is always present?'

Serenity shuddered. 'I'm not sure what I believe.'

'I think it's a matter of people having a too-vivid imagination. The brain does the rest,' Prue said simply, sipping wine.

'Or,' Manjeet suggested, 'evil spirits or ghosts are psychological rather than an external entity. Their purpose is to frighten susceptible people.'

'Really, darling?' Cynthia's laughter tinkled. 'And how long have you known me? I'm rarely frightened by the supernatural. It's as I say, we all access the mystic world in different measures.' She turned to Hanna. 'Your dreams are a form of haunting. Do they scare you?'

'Sometimes they disturb me. But they inform me too,' Hanna began. She glanced at Serenity and Ollie to check they weren't uncomfortable with the conversation. Ollie gave her an encouraging grin.

'That's why it's so good to work alongside you, Hanna.' Roly lifted his glass. 'You're in tune with the past and archaeology fascinates you.'

'It does. The spirit near the farm unnerves me a bit though,' Hanna mumbled and Lucas reached out a hand and covered hers.

'There's no need to be afraid of her. She's communicating something important through you,' Cynthia replied.

'Or she's just a moving car headlight or moonlight in the mist?' Prue chuckled.

'Not at all,' Roly disagreed. 'I believe the past tries to speak to the present.'

'Through relics in the ground, surely, Roly,' Prue insisted.

'This talk of ghosts is worrying.' Ollie forced a laugh. 'We have to go home in the dark.'

'And Little Rymer station is creepy,' Serenity said.

Hanna shot her an inquisitive look. She had no idea Serenity felt that way: they'd never talked about the ghost she'd seen on the platform.

'Well, it's been a lovely meal.' Roly sighed. 'Shall I order baklava and coffee now? It's good to share food, to cement our working friendship. I hope we'll be able to come back to your farm soon, Ollie, and bring the metal detectors. I'm sure there's more treasure to be found in the fields.'

'There is,' Cynthia insisted.

Ollie had an idea. 'Why don't you come over tomorrow morning? The weather forecast is good. My dad will be pleased to see you all.'

'Thanks – I'll make it a priority if the weather's favourable. I'll call the boys tonight, get the team ready.'

'I'll rearrange my schedule so that I'm there. We need to go deep into Bramble Woods.' Cynthia gazed in Hanna's direction. 'That's where I feel we should start our search. I'm sure something of significance has happened there, and that it's linked in some way to Hanna's dream.' She raised an eyebrow. 'What do you think, Hanna?'

Hanna agreed. 'You could be right.'

She turned to Lucas and offered him a complicit smile. He smiled back and a moment of trust and understanding passed between them: he was a rock; she could depend on him. The glow of his eyes caught hers and she felt the familiar jolt. He was strong, thoughtful; he cared about her, and he understood exactly how she felt.

And in that moment, she was a woman standing in woodlands, her gaze held by that of a handsome Roman soldier who was whispering his feelings to her for the final time.

42

The army had left the woodlands, every last one of the Iceni rebels, the horses, carts and chariots had moved out two days ago. It was silent beneath the trees outside Camulodunum, except for the occasional twitter of birds. The twilight was falling. Brea was left behind with Venator, who grazed contentedly by the river, and Aurelia who leaned against a tree trunk, her eyes closed in pain. Brea whispered encouragement. 'We'll stay here for another day, two at the most, until you can stand on the leg. Then we'll follow Boudicca and my father.'

'What's the point?' Aurelia said weakly. 'I know my brother is dead. The Ninth were completely wiped out. And we're here, all alone, sheltering from bad weather and wild animals. Once it's dark, I'm sure we'll be attacked.'

'I have a sword, a knife, a shield. You do, too. We'll protect ourselves,' Brea replied, her eyes fierce. 'We have food, water, blankets. We'll stay until you're strong again. Then we must find a way to get to the Roman army. We still have your Roman dress, your jewellery. You can go to your husband wearing them – the soldiers will let you through. Then you can warn him of the attack.'

'Why would I do that?'

'Because he'll surely be killed in battle if you don't. Our tribe outnumber the Roman army tenfold.'

'I'd rather go back to Rome,' Aurelia moaned. 'It's only right that I tell my family about Lucius. I'll tell my father he died honourably, a hero, shouting the name of Mars in anger as he fell.'

'You're shivering.' Brea wrapped her arms around Aurelia, snuggling closer to warm her. The skin on her face was ice cold, but her brow was feverish. 'We can't stay here forever. Perhaps tomorrow you'll be well enough to travel. We ought to move on.'

'Perhaps tomorrow I won't wake up,' Aurelia said, her face miserable.

Brea examined her carefully. Aurelia's eyes were glassy; she was tired, she'd slept fitfully. Brea understood; her mistress was in constant pain and she was grieving. She tried again. 'Mistress, we'll survive. You'll get well and we'll find my people soon. Then you'll be reunited with your husband, I promise.'

'And what good will that bring?' A sigh shuddered through Aurelia that might have been a shiver. 'He does not love me, nor I him. You would be a better wife for Marcellus.'

'Me?' Brea was taken by surprise. 'I'm a slave.'

'No longer.' Aurelia closed her eyes. 'And he admires your courage, your spirit, I know he does. I've seen how he looks at you...'

Brea was quiet for a moment, thinking of Marcellus, of the moments they'd spent in the orchard and here, near the river. Her voice came in a whisper. 'He is your husband.'

'I admire you too.' Aurelia wasn't listening. 'How I wish I was like you. But that's not how we were brought up in Rome. We daughters knew we weren't valued. Our father's first wish was for a son, so we were greeted with disapproval from the moment we opened our eyes onto the world. Everything about us had to be controlled – our clothes, our hair, our manners. We were told from childhood that we must find a husband, do our duty, produce male heirs and then, eventually, after a life of obedience, we'd die quietly without disturbing anyone.' She groaned, shifting uncomfortably. 'My life is a waste.'

'It doesn't have to be,' Brea whispered. 'You've seen our Queen Boudicca, how she inspires us all to fight without fear. She is as fierce and brave as any man. My father and mother taught me that we are the same value – men, women – we stand side by side, we help each other.'

'I wish I'd had your life,' Aurelia whispered. 'You were a slave, but I was doubly a slave. Once as a Roman woman, and again as a wife. I have none of your skills. I can't fight, cook, I don't even know how to comb my own hair.'

'Then I'll teach you – your life can be wonderful,' Brea said quietly. 'Come, we'll sleep now and tomorrow we'll move on, not as mistress and slave, but as equals.'

'I recently lost a brother, and I never had a sister.' Aurelia's eyelids grew heavy. 'But if I had one, I would want one just as you are, a woman that I admire.'

'Then we're sisters,' Brea said kindly, but Aurelia was already falling asleep.

Brea would not rest yet. Her mind was alive with thoughts. Tomorrow she'd wake early and they'd start their journey to catch up with the Iceni. They wouldn't wait any longer. Her father and the Iceni would already be in Londinium, much of the city would be burned to the ground and the people slaughtered. She'd catch up with them in Verulamium or beyond, in Watling Street, the long road that led west towards the advancing Roman army. Then she'd find Marcellus.

Darkness fell and Brea reached for her sword. She would spend the night watching over Aurelia as she slept.

* * *

Hanna and Lucas sat side by side on the train. Beyond the windows, hedges flashed past in darkness, a small line of lights glowed for an instant as they slowed at a small station, then everything was indiscernible again, shadows beyond the glass. In the seat across the aisle, Ollie and Serenity were snuggled closely, their heads together. Serenity draped a leg across Ollie's knee and was whispering. Hanna was conscious of the space between her and Lucas; their shoulders were not quite touching. She wondered about their growing relationship; he was becoming important to her. She was sure he wanted to kiss her but, instinctively, she knew he wouldn't rush things.

Lucas noticed her watching him and offered a warm smile. 'Did you have a nice time today?'

'I did.' Hanna beamed. 'The meal was lovely and Roly's wife's a scream. I enjoyed the banter she had with Cynthia and Manjeet.'

'But you come down on Cynthia's side,' Lucas said.

'Oh, she understands me. She's explained my dreams.' Hanna sighed. 'I'm glad Roly and his team are coming over tomorrow. I feel I'm close to finding out something really important – as Cynthia said, you could sense it in Bramble Woods, something's still there...'

'I know that instinctive feeling,' Lucas said and Hanna met his eyes.

'What do you mean?'

'I always felt that Norfolk would be home.' He shrugged. 'Then when I saw you, it felt right to talk to you.'

'There's a connection between us.'

'Yes.'

'I feel it too,' Hanna said quietly.

Lucas thought for a moment. 'It's like we already know each other.'

Hanna smiled. 'It is.'

Lucas took her hand in his. 'I suppose it's easily explained – it's because you're nice and I knew that we'd get on.'

'Perhaps, but instinct is a really strong part of who we both are.' Hanna thought of the Roman soldier in her dreams who looked at her with Lucas's eyes. She glanced down at his hand that held hers, a dry hand that healed, that cared for animals, and she smiled.

'It's early days, I know,' Lucas said. 'And I've just come out of a long-term relationship. I wasn't looking to rush into anything, after Beth. She left me a bit... grazed.'

'Because she wasn't supportive?' Hanna's face was filled with sympathy. She understood the sadness now.

'She's quite angry. She sent me a few unpleasant texts. You know the sort of thing...'

Hanna didn't. 'Is she asking for stuff back that she left in the house?'

'No, she says that I deserve to be a lonely old man and she hopes I rot in hell.' Lucas forced a laugh.

Hanna was amazed. 'She sounds controlling.'

'At first, things seemed to work because I fitted in with what she want-ed,' Lucas said. 'But when I took the job here, it was just constant argu-ments. A bad relationship can be a lonely place.'

'That's awful, Lucas.'

'We weren't right for each other. I was relieved when all I had to contend with were some bitter texts. I felt much happier to get on with my life alone.'

'I bet.'

'Hanna – I don't want you to think I'm with you because I'm on the rebound. That's not the case. I'd intended to concentrate on nothing else but work, and then, amazingly, you came along. I've been trying to give you space so you don't feel pressurised.'

'Pressurised – to be with you?' Hanna almost laughed; she'd been desperate for him to phone or text.

'You're on the brink of making important decisions about your future.' Lucas spoke quietly. 'You might choose to move away, go back to China. I don't want to get in the way of whatever direction you decide to take.'

Hanna leaned her head against his shoulder. 'And do you think you'll ever go back to London?'

'Not on your life.' Lucas grinned. 'This is home now.'

'So, what do you think I should do?'

Lucas didn't pause. 'I love the way your face lights up when you look at all the artefacts. I saw how you came alive in the museum today. It was great to see you so enthusiastic.'

'You think I should work in a museum?' Hanna asked.

'No, I think you should do something that brings the same light and happiness to your face,' Lucas replied. 'I can see passion there, and the desire to discover things.'

Hanna thought about his words. Lucas was right; she'd been fascinated by the visit to Cambridge. But then, Lucas fascinated her too. He definitely made her feel alive. And happy. And safe. She squeezed his hand affection-ately. 'Thanks, Lucas.'

'What for?'

'For explaining that you don't want to rush things. For being honest. And for saying you feel a connection with me – I've felt it from the beginning.' She lifted his hand and wrapped it around her shoulder. 'Today was lovely.'

'It was special. I've never met anyone I've had such an immediate affinity with,' Lucas said. 'I have to call in at Bramble Wood Farm at some point this week to check Paddy's piglets over. I'll move the visit to tomorrow morning, if I can, so that I can see how Roly's search is going.'

'And I want to invite you to dinner at the farm. We country types like having the local vet to supper.' Hanna grinned, then she felt the train jolt and begin to slow down. They were pulling into the station at Little Rymer. She glanced over to where Ollie and Serenity were draped across each other, kissing frantically. 'I bet Mum's in the car park already, waiting to give me and Ollie a lift back home.'

'It's a ten-minute walk home into the village for me,' Lucas said. 'Five for Serenity. Unless you all want to come back for coffee? You could bring your mum.'

'I'd love to but... another time...' Hanna glanced at her phone. 'I'd better get back to the farm – it's past eleven and I know my mum will want to go to bed. It's a hard life being a farmer's wife.'

The train shuffled to a halt and Hanna stood up, followed by Lucas, as Ollie attempted to extract himself from Serenity's embrace. They left the warmth and brightness of the carriage behind them to step onto the cold platform, which was enveloped in gloom and mist, lit only by two glimmering lamps.

Hanna glanced across towards the car park. The Range Rover was there already, lights on.

Ollie and Serenity walked on ahead, their arms draped around each other. They'd almost reached the bridge when Lucas reached for Hanna's hand. The wind funnelled down the track and she shivered. She turned to face him. 'Thanks for a lovely day.'

Hanna wrapped her arms around him; she wanted to kiss him now, not in front of her mother. Their lips met – Lucas's were warm, and they stayed locked in a delicious embrace. Then Hanna moved away instinctively, glancing over his shoulder, and she caught her breath. Not far away down the platform, a young woman was watching. Mist swirled from the tracks behind her, spreading an eerie glow from the lamplight. Hanna blinked;

the woman was still there in the centre of the yellow haze, her hair tousled, a bedraggled green robe below her knees. Her eyes glowed.

'What is it?' Lucas felt the tension in Hanna's body. 'Hanna?'

He turned round, following her gaze. There was no one there.

Hanna was still staring. 'I'm sorry.'

'What did you see?' Lucas asked gently.

'I must have imagined it.' Hanna reached for his hand. 'The station's so creepy.'

The wind shuddered along the platform, lifting a stray piece of litter, tossing it along.

'It is,' Lucas agreed.

They crossed the bridge quickly, reaching the Range Rover behind Ollie and Serenity.

* * *

On the way home, Stephanie was full of questions. 'So, when are you going to bring Serenity round for dinner, Ollie. I like her – and I got on so well with Patsy, her mum. Oh, we could all get together at the farm for Sunday dinner one day. Hanna, you could invite Lucas.'

Hanna was snuggled into the back seat, relishing the warmth of the car, staring out of the window. She mumbled a reply. 'I've told him there's an imminent invitation...'

'And you must tell me all about Cambridge. Did you see any more Roman jewellery?' Stephanie asked.

'We had a lovely day,' Ollie said. 'We saw lots of artefacts at the museum – a real skeleton of a Roman woman. And a few bits of Iceni stuff. It was fascinating. Roly's coming over tomorrow, if that's okay with you and Dad – he's sure we'll find some more treasure.'

'Paddy will be excited. He thinks he might be famous if more relics are found on the land. He might be on TV,' Stephanie replied.

'He'd have enjoyed the food today,' Ollie said.

'Where did you go for a meal?' Stephanie wanted to know every detail.

'It was a Jordanian restaurant,' Ollie explained. 'We'll have to take you and Dad there. It's not far to Cambridge and the train ride's really comfortable.'

'Your dad would have preferred it to the spa,' Stephanie muttered. She turned on the windscreen wipers. A low mist had crept down and was hovering just above the ground level, drifting from the fens. 'He was unimpressed by being covered in mud and left for an hour to dry out...'

Ollie laughed. 'Did he make jokes about manure?'

'Of course he did.' Stephanie chuckled. 'And did you have a good time in Cambridge, Hanna?'

'It was really lovely.' Hanna was staring through the window. The mist was heavy now, enveloping the car.

'I like Lucas. He's a good guy. It was nice double dating,' Ollie continued. 'I promised him that he could borrow Hunter any time he likes, Hanna, and the pair of you can go for a long ride.'

'Thanks – I'd like that,' Hanna said. She pressed her face against the glass of the window. They were almost back at the farm now. The wind buffeted long grasses in the fields, the trees bending in strong gusts of wind that sighed and moaned, bumping the sides of the Range Rover.

Then the mist parted and Hanna saw her again, standing by the side of the road, watching, waiting. Hanna was sure it was her. She met Hanna's eyes as the car flashed by, her mouth open as if crying out.

Then she was gone.

43

The next morning, Brea washed herself in cold river water and woke Aurelia, who was confused, not able to recall where she was. Reality returned and she held back tears, remembering the Ninth had been wiped out and, with them, her beloved brother. Brea washed Aurelia's wound and bandaged it tightly. It was livid and swollen; a yellow crust had formed. Aurelia closed her eyes tightly against the pain, but said nothing. Brea helped her onto Venator and climbed behind, following the road the Iceni had taken towards Londinium. She would ask people in passing villages for directions and beg for food when their reserves ran out.

They travelled for days, stopping to rest when it became too much for Aurelia. She tired easily but received hospitality gratefully from the Iceni villages where they paused to accept warm soup and flatbread or porridge. Brea explained that Aurelia had fought bravely with the Iceni at Camulodunum and had lost her voice. Aurelia was astonished at the warmth and kindness she received at the hands of people who would kill her if they knew she was Roman. And each tribe was keen to explain which way the rebels had travelled; Boudicca had recruited more volunteers from every village she'd passed through.

They reached Londinium, which was still charred and smouldering, the stench of burning everywhere. The Iceni had slaughtered everyone they encountered. Statues were mutilated and gravestones smashed in anger. Verulamium too had been burned to the ground. An Iceni woman who had remained behind to nurse her injured son told Brea that most of the occupants had evacuated the city and taken everything they owned with them, but the Iceni killed everyone in their way and continued the journey along Watling Street. The rebels were excitable and ready to do battle with Suetonius. The news was that his armies, the Fourteenth and the Twentieth Legions, were advancing to meet them. Brea caught her breath; the Iceni had dreamed of this for so long. A victory would free Britain from Roman occupation once and for all.

As she and Aurelia travelled along on a weary Venator, Brea recalled the time Governor General Suetonius dined at the *domus*; she remembered his narrowed eyes as if he was constantly thinking about battle strategies while he was in conversation with Marcellus. Her heart leaped at the thought of seeing her master again. She tightened her grip on Aurelia who had fallen asleep.

They paused to rest on a riverbank beneath a shady tree and Brea unwrapped Aurelia's dressing to clean the wound. It wasn't healing well; liquid was oozing from it and it smelled foul. Brea was troubled as she wrapped it again; her mistress wasn't improving as quickly as she'd hoped.

Aurelia lay back against the tree trunk, her eyes closed.

Brea reached into her bundle and gave her a hunk of bread. 'You must eat.'

Aurelia held it in her hand. Her lips were dry, so Brea gave her water to drink. 'You need to get well, Mistress. We'll meet our people soon – everyone we've spoken to says we're close now. My father will be there – everyone is preparing for battle.'

'You should leave me here,' Aurelia said weakly.

'No, you have to speak to Marcellus and warn him. The army isn't far away now.'

'I can't go much farther...'

'We're nearly there,' Brea said encouragingly. 'Once we reach the Iceni, I'll find someone who'll know how to look after your wound better than I, and then, at night-time, you can get into the Roman camp.'

'The Roman camp?' Aurelia gave a high laugh, almost hysterical. 'I don't think of Marcellus at all. I just want to sleep.'

'Then let me wrap you in your woollen cloak.'

'I am too hot...' Aurelia waved her away.

'We'll move on. It's not far now.' Brea helped her to her feet. Aurelia's face was creased with pain as she struggled onto Venator, who had finished grazing. Her hands were cold, but her brow was feverish. Brea clambered up behind her, tied her bundle on the back of the saddle and urged the horse forward.

Venator plodded on obediently over stony ground and Aurelia groaned with each jolt. An hour passed, more, and the sun was setting, the sky blotched with crimson. Aurelia slumped forward in sleep as they turned a corner and Brea caught her breath. A field was filled with Iceni rebels, their faces painted with woad, their bodies decorated with moon shapes, or with spirit animals – horses, hares, deer.

Brea rode Venator between the men and women who were busy preparing for battle, the heavy gold and silver jewellery that adorned their flesh gleaming. Some men were completely naked, others wore loincloths, their hair spiked with lime. They clutched swords, shouted wildly, encouraging each other in preparation for battle. Brea's gaze swept across thousands of Iceni, all ready to fight. It would be impossible to find her father or Addedomaros, but they would be here. Then she stared into the distance; the Roman army were waiting, camped at the end of a narrow pass cut off by a forest at the back. Brea exhaled slowly; Marcellus would be with them.

Then she heard shouting and turned to see a tall woman standing in a chariot, her face painted with blue swirls. She was flanked by two younger women who could be no older than Brea had been when she was taken by the Romans. The woman wore a heavy gold torc around her neck and she raised a spear. The rebels cheered and waved their swords. There were children and elders, all brought within wagons, watching in silent admiration.

The woman's voice was filled with passion. 'Tomorrow morning, we'll attack them. We are many and they are few. And we are braver than they are.' There was loud cheering. 'I'm fighting because I lost my freedom. I'm fighting because they scourged my body, they assaulted my daughters. Andred will grant us revenge. I refuse to live as a slave. I'm an Iceni queen –

I fear no one. I urge you to have courage, to let it surge through your veins as it surges through mine. Tomorrow, we'll win this battle – I can promise you that.'

There was more whooping as she opened the folds of her dress and a hare leaped from her skirt. It bounded away and the woman addressed the crowd again.

'Look. It takes the auspicious path. We will win, praise Andred.'

There was more yelling and waving of fists and spears. Brea gazed across the field of blue and white faces, gleaming limbs raised in wild aggression, and beyond to where the Roman camp was silent, smoke curling from their fires. She slid from Venator and tried to help Aurelia descend. Her mistress was slumped awkwardly across the horse's neck. Brea reached up strong arms and eased her to the ground, where she lay dishevelled. She knelt beside her, examining the closed eyes, the calm expression, the limp body. Aurelia was dead.

Brea fought back tears: poor Aurelia's life had been short, and unfulfilled. She murmured a prayer. Aurelia had been a gentle person, a kind mistress, and, at the end, a friend. Her death had been a mistake, unfair, too early. Brea had tried her best to keep her alive, but she had let her down. Her mind worked quickly. She wanted to bury Aurelia in the bare earth, her head facing west – that was the respectful thing to do, a final gesture of love. But she glanced around; she hadn't time. The sky was growing dark. Men and women were cooking food over fires, settling down for the night.

Brea dragged Aurelia as carefully as she could to a hedge and removed her jewellery. She'd need it. A plan was forming quickly. Brea covered her mistress with a blanket, then she hurried back for Venator. She smoothed the soft hair on his neck, making calming sounds of affection, then she knelt by Aurelia, closing her eyes, muttering a quiet prayer.

'May the blessed sunlight shine on you like a great peat fire, so that strangers and friends may come and warm themselves at it.'

Brea opened her eyes, looking around. The rebels were busy talking excitedly, cooking and eating, sharpening swords. Some had already gone to sleep. No one would pay any attention to her. She patted Venator as he grazed, offered him water, then she reached for her bundle attached to his back. Inside was the Roman dress, the green one stained with wine, and

Aurelia's indigo cloak. She'd need them and her jewellery. She was going to visit the Roman camp in Aurelia's place.

Brea stood for a moment, intending to remember the place where Aurelia was, promising silently that she'd return to her when she could. Then she led Venator along the field, clucking to reassure him as they passed groups of noisy Iceni rebels seated around campfires, until she'd almost reached the edge of the field that led to the narrow pass where the Romans were camped. It was pitch dark now. Brea moved silently to the forest and whispered to Venator to be still. She took off her dirty tunic, struggling into the robe, wrapping herself in the cloak. She grasped locks of her own long hair, knotting them in a rough style, as Aurelia's and Julia's had been. It would have to suffice. She placed the gold and carnelian stone necklace around her neck, the snake bracelet on her arm and Aurelia's heavy gold ring on her finger. She pulled up the hood of her cloak and took a deep breath. Although her heart knocked loudly, she was ready.

She stepped out of the forest, leading Venator, her head held high. There were many Roman soldiers in iron armour, bronze helmets. She marched past blacksmiths who were busily shoeing horses, foot soldiers hunched around campfires drinking. Some soldiers were standing around clusters of small tents. Ahead was a tall leather tent with several horses outside. She hoped it might belong to Marcellus.

As she drew level with a group of soldiers, one laughed and pointed at her. 'Is that a *meretrix*, come to warm the legate's bed before tomorrow's battle?'

His remark caused great humour.

Brea swept past, leading Venator; ignoring such comments was wise.

Then a guard stepped in front of her, his hand on his sword. 'What are you doing here? It's no place for a woman.'

Brea gave him a level stare. He was a callous-faced man who looked as if he'd fought in many battles. She tried to keep her voice steady. 'I'm Aurelia, wife of the legate, Marcellus Julius Silvanus. I've ridden here from Camulodunum, which has been burned to the ground. I bring news of his family.'

'You can't come here, not now.' The guard looked her over. 'Go back where you came from.'

Brea took a breath. 'Marcellus will want to see me. Go to him, tell him I'm here.'

'Women aren't allowed.' The guard looked doubtful.

'I rode all this way on his horse,' Brea said determinedly. 'Give me a few moments with my husband so that I can tell him that his father has died, his sister too. Then I'll stay quietly somewhere until... until you have your glorious victory tomorrow.'

The guard sniffed. 'Wait.' Then he turned on his heel and marched towards the huge tent.

Brea glanced around. Many of the soldiers had decided to turn in for the night, huddled in tents in groups of eight. Someone sang a song, his voice low and full of sorrow. Brea thought of Aurelia and felt overcome with grief. She'd have to tell Marcellus how many people he had lost.

The guard returned. 'Follow me.' Brea tethered Venator and walked dutifully behind the soldier to the large leather tent, pausing outside while he rushed in and out again. 'Stay there. The legate will come to you shortly.' He walked away smartly, turning on his heel.

Brea moved towards the entrance of the tent. Two men were standing together inside, one of them talking in a clear, confident voice. It was Suetonius, discussing the battle plans with Marcellus. Brea edged closer.

'Our soldiers will be in full armour, in ranks, and we'll move forward in a wedge-shaped formation, slicing through the rebel lines in hand-to-hand combat, our cavalry on the wings. That way, they'll have nowhere to go and we'll cut them down, one after the other. Her superior numbers will be of no advantage in the narrow field. The Iceni will be wiped out.'

Brea felt her skin go cold. A shocking thought occurred to her: Suetonius had met Aurelia at the *domus*; if he remembered her, he'd know Brea wasn't Marcellus's wife. She felt her legs quake and held her breath. Then she heard Marcellus say, 'Your strategy is an excellent one, General. I have no doubt that victory will be ours. If you'd excuse me for a moment, the guard said that a visitor waits for me.'

'Of course,' Suetonius said curtly.

Brea stood back, concealing herself in shadows as Marcellus rushed out. Then she whispered, 'Master.'

Marcellus turned abruptly. 'Brea...' His face was full of surprise. 'How did you get here?'

'I have news.'

'I heard what happened in Camulodunum. I've been worried...' He held her at arm's length. 'Brea, I've thought of you each day. The guard told me that a woman had come to see me. And now here you are.'

'Master, I must tell you many things. I came here on Venator. He is tethered nearby.'

'Oh, there is much for us to talk of. But first, let me hold you in my arms.' Marcellus pulled her to him, kissing her, and she felt the warmth of his lips. He embraced her so tightly, she could hardly breathe as he murmured into her hair, 'My love.'

A sigh shuddered through her and Brea closed her eyes, holding onto the moment. She knew that it would pass soon, and she'd have to tell him the news of Aurelia and his family. But, for now, she was in his arms, kissing him as if her life depended on it, and she wished it could last forever.

44

It was almost midnight as Hanna sat on the edge of her bed, thinking about the enjoyable time she'd had in Cambridge, the visit to the museum, the fascinating artefacts she'd seen. She thought of Lucas, how close they were becoming, how they shared an understanding that went beyond attraction. Symbiosis, that's what Cynthia had called it. Hanna remembered her words: 'You need his direction and to be grounded. He needs your ability to heal. You'll find it in each other.' It was the beginning of something deep and special; it was the basis for love.

Then she remembered the sorrowful figure she'd seen at the station, and again in the mist as her mother had driven home. She wondered what her tragic story was. Tomorrow, Roly and his team would search the woodlands for treasure. Hanna decided she'd help them; she felt intuitively they'd find something interesting.

She snuggled beneath the duvet and thought of Lucas again. The dream started almost immediately. She was on the fenlands, gazing into Lucas's eyes, there was the familiar shock of connection, the strong swirling of desire. His arms were around her; they were lying together on the ground beneath a tree, warm and contented. He kissed her and murmured into her hair, 'My love.' Hanna knew in the dream that she had never been so happy, her heart was so full it might burst. Then he stood up and pulled her to her feet, and said, 'Now is the time.'

Then Lucas was no longer Lucas. He was taller, broader. His face was not Lucas's face, and she was no longer Hanna. Her hair was long, and she wore a green robe that had once been beautiful but was now dirty and spattered with mud. The gold necklace was around her throat, the snake bangle on her arm. The man kissed her again and she was swept away on a mixture of emotions – desire, fear, sadness, all at once. She gazed at him: he was a soldier, an important man, but he loved her with ferocity, the same passion that he showed as he fought battles, and, at the same time, with the same tenderness he'd feel for a fragile animal, as Lucas felt tenderness for the animals he treated. The dream confused Hanna and she turned away to see shadows of people facing her, enveloped in mist.

To Hanna's surprise, Serenity stepped forward from the vapour, dressed in an indigo cloak. Blood seeped through her tunic, down her leg. Then it was no longer Serenity, it was an auburn-haired woman for whom Hanna felt admiration and respect, for whom she was deeply sorry. Hanna didn't know her name in the dream. Ollie was there, too, mist churning behind him, and he stood next to the woman who had been Serenity, taking her hand. He was dressed in Roman uniform. Then he was no longer Ollie and he and the woman clasped their arms around each other, tears on their faces. The woman called him 'beloved brother' before the mist swallowed them both.

There was another man, much older, carrying a sword. He had a deep scar down one side of his face; he wore a loincloth and his skin was painted with blue woad, ancient symbols, a hare, a roe deer on his chest. Hanna recognised him but she didn't know his name. She found her voice and called out, 'Who are you?'

'I'm your father.' The man's face was tired, weariness etched around his glittering eyes. Then he was no longer the same man. He wore a naval uniform and she recognised her own father, whom she hadn't seen since she was a child. His voice was the voice she'd forgotten, but now she remembered it so well. 'I couldn't help you. I had to leave.' Then the mist drifted and he was gone too. Hanna shivered.

She felt strong arms around her, and she turned back to the Roman soldier as he pulled her to him and she was warm again. He held out an engraved gold ring and took her hand in his. He kissed her fingers, sliding the ring on, and murmured, 'You and I are one.'

She was lifted by a happiness beyond anything she'd ever felt. She threw her arms around the handsome man and he whispered in her ear.

The familiar smell of burning was everywhere, the drumming of heavy feet hammering on the ground, the clash of metal swords, and Hanna was afraid. She grasped the man's hand and saw soldiers in armour running towards her. One of them lifted a sword, swinging it high, and Hanna ran as fast as she could, across a muddy field, into the shady woodlands, then she fell. Soil and the crack of twigs were rough beneath her hands, dry dirt in her mouth – she dragged herself to her feet, crashing down a narrow track beneath a canopy of trees, looking around in fear as the ring fell from her finger. A roe deer ran across her path, pausing for a moment to gaze at her, and she screamed.

Hanna sat up in bed, wide awake. Her forehead was damp. Part of her was still stuck in the nightmare and she closed her eyes, breathing deeply, taking time to come back to reality. At first, she was confused, thinking about the figures she'd seen in the mist, Serenity, Ollie, her father. Like Lucas, they had turned into someone else, people of the past. She and the spirit woman of the fens were linked – even now she was trying to tell her something important. The people Hanna loved represented the people she had loved beyond measure: their lives were connected. Then a smile broke across Hanna's face. The dream was suddenly clear to her. She knew where to look and what to look for.

She reached for her phone. It was four in the morning, but she'd message Lucas and Ollie and then Roly. She'd tell them to meet her in the woodlands bright and early. They'd find the third piece of jewellery. She knew what it was now, and she knew exactly where to find it.

* * *

Brea watched Marcellus's expression change as she told him the story, that his father, then his sister was killed in Camulodunum, and finally that Aurelia was lying in a field among Iceni rebels, covered in a blanket. She'd never seen him look so miserable, his eyes filling with tears. A sigh shook him, then he said, 'Thank you for coming to tell me this.'

'What will we do?' Brea asked.

Marcellus's face was a mask of grief. 'Since I was a boy, all my father wanted for his sons was for them to be great soldiers, as he was.' He shook his head. 'What is it all for? My brother died in battle – he was just a young tribune.' Then he remembered. 'Lucius? Does he live?'

'The Ninth were all killed,' Brea murmured.

'It's a terrible waste, nothing more. I've just come back from fighting the Druids – I saw things there I can't repeat... it wasn't the honour we believed it would be.'

Brea watched him and her heart ached. 'Shall I go now, Master?'

'Where would you go?'

'Back to my tribe, in the field beyond.'

'What would you do there?'

'I'd fight with the rest of the rebels tomorrow,' Brea said sadly. 'I'd fight the Romans.'

'Then you'll be killed, all the Iceni people will be massacred. The queen and her army can't win. Suetonius is a great strategist – he's lured them into a trap and they have no idea that they'll be slaughtered, one after another by Roman swords and spears...' Marcellus took her arm. 'We must talk. Walk with me, we'll bring Venator. Do the guards believe you're my wife?'

'They do.'

'Then we'll go to the woods together.' They left the tent behind them, hurrying towards the tethered horse. He patted Venator's neck, raising his voice for others to hear. 'It does my heart good to see my horse again. And I am happy beyond words to see you.'

'And I too,' Brea murmured. He filled her gaze. She'd believed she'd never see him again. She took his arm, leaning against him, feeling the heat that came from his skin as it warmed hers. It lifted her spirits with a joy she had not felt since he'd left.

Marcellus and Brea strolled arm in arm to the forest, past the sleeping guards, their heads together, talking as any husband and wife. Venator followed behind, plodding contentedly. They reached a clearing and Brea sat on a dry log that had fallen from a tree.

Marcellus collapsed beside her and said, 'I can't be part of an army that will slaughter your people tomorrow. I can't do it, Brea – I've seen enough.' He wrapped an arm around her. 'I'm ashamed of my past, it's true. Since I spoke to you of it in the orchard, it has been always with me, that I had done so much wrong. I was a young soldier and stood by when you and your people were taken into slavery. I followed Suetonius's orders and ordered Boudicca to be whipped and I allowed her daughters to be...' Marcellus buried his face in his hands. 'I can't be part of it again.'

'Then what's to be done?' Brea put a hand on his shoulder. 'Can you persuade Suetonius to withdraw tomorrow?'

'No, it will be a bloody battle. Suetonius says the Romans will have an honourable victory.'

'My father is in the fields, preparing to fight, and Addedomaros too... they will not turn away from the battle,' Brea whispered. 'They believe they can win. They think because there are so many Iceni...'

'Perhaps they will survive. Who knows? Perhaps Suetonius's plan will fail. It is in the hands of the gods now,' Marcellus said. He was thoughtful. 'Brea, do you love me?'

'You know I do, Master. With all my heart.'

'Not master now, but Marcellus.'

Brea smiled as he touched her cheek. 'Marcellus.'

'And would you risk everything to be with me?'

'You know I would – I'm not afraid.'

Marcellus took a breath. 'Then we'll leave tonight, me and you. We'll ride somewhere far away, and be together.'

'Where will we go?'

'Somewhere we can start again and have a future together. We could go south, or west, to Aquae Sulis. I've heard it's very beautiful there.'

'You want me to be a Roman?' Brea asked.

'I want you to be my wife.' His fingers touched the necklace at her throat. 'I gave these to Aurelia.'

'I'm sorry for it – I had to wear them to pretend to be her, to gain access to you,' Brea said hurriedly.

'No – they suit you well.' Marcellus almost smiled, then his brow clouded. 'Poor Aurelia. It was hard for her, coming to Camulodunum. She never wished for it.'

'You were kind to her. You did the best you could.'

'It was always you I wanted. I saw how good you were to Aurelia. You surprised me with your strength and honesty. I want nothing more than to be with you for the rest of my life. We can go east. I'll live with the Iceni, learn their language.'

Brea shook her head. 'I don't think there's a place for a great Roman legate among the Iceni people.' She smiled slightly. 'We must be alone; we'll be running away forever. If you leave the Roman army, they'll send soldiers after us. They won't let you leave, I know it.'

'Then we'll go now. We'll make the most of nightfall,' Marcellus whispered. 'You take Venator, and I'll make an excuse that my horse is restless before the battle and I must ride him. Take the path that runs directly through the forest, and I'll catch up to you as soon as I can. I'll bring food, coins, water to sustain us for a few days.' He swept her in his arms, kissing her lips. 'Ride fast, Brea. The gods have given us this one chance and we must seize it.'

He kissed her again and stood up, walking quickly back towards the camp. Brea watched him. She was troubled for her father, for the battle that would come, but she could not help them. She closed her eyes and prayed to Andred that they'd survive, that Boudicca's large numbers would overcome the Romans. She was sure they could.

Then she felt a moment of hope, a new lightness in her heart. Perhaps, after so much sadness in their lives, she and Marcellus would find a way to be happy.

* * *

The darkness was a blanket that concealed them as Brea and Marcellus took the road east, Brea on Venator and Marcellus riding his grey war horse, Bellicus. Marcellus suggested that they head for Iceni country, then towards the coast. He wondered if they could take a boat and find their way to an island where they could live quietly for a while.

Brea couldn't think beyond the moment. 'It pains me to leave my father.

I didn't say goodbye to him – he won't know where I am and... I may not see him again.'

'I pray that many of your people will survive the battle tomorrow,' Marcellus muttered.

Brea sighed. 'Aurelia is still lying in the field.'

'I pray for her too, that flowers will grow where she has lain down.'

'I will never forget her,' Brea said. She gazed up at the sky. 'It's beautiful to be here at night, on the road heading back to the countryside I know so well. Look at the stars. Can you see how brightly they shine?'

'I've heard of people who claim to be able to read the signs and portents of the stars,' Marcellus said quietly. 'Who knows what the fates have in store?'

'I met a poor beggar woman on the steps of the Temple of the Divine Claudius who told me what would come to pass.' Brea was quiet for a moment. It seemed so long ago. 'She was called Luna. I stole food for her from the kitchens.'

Marcellus smiled. 'You are indeed a wonderful person.'

'She told me some terrible things – she warned me the temple would not last long. Then it was burned to the ground.' Brea shivered. 'She also said that the chance of love would come to me and I must seize it. She said I would give my heart away.'

'Then she spoke the truth.' Marcellus reached out a hand to touch her cheek. His eyes were filled with affection. 'This must be our chance, my love. We had no choice but to leave.'

'Luna said that love comes at a cost – that I'd be searching forever. I have to admit, I was troubled.'

'She was a beggar woman – she probably said the same to every young slave she met in the hope that they'd steal food for her.'

'I'm not sure,' Brea said.

'We'll be far away in several days' time.' Marcellus brought Bellicus to a pause, sliding to the ground. 'Come, let's make the most of the moonlight. We'll find the stream and rest awhile. Will you sleep in my arms while the horses graze?'

'I will,' Brea whispered. She allowed herself to be lifted down from Venator and leaned tiredly against Marcellus, resting her head against his chest. She was happy in his arms, warm and loved. But it worried her that her father would fight a battle tomorrow that the Iceni would lose. And she knew the Roman army wouldn't allow Marcellus to desert, to walk away from his responsibilities. He'd be hunted down. Maybe soldiers on horseback were following them at this very moment.

Suddenly, she felt very afraid.

45

They travelled for several days, staying away from Iceni villages for fear of hostility. On horseback, they were conspicuous, a solitary Roman soldier and his wife, so they searched for places where they could buy simple clean tunics and rustic cloaks with the coins Marcellus carried. Brea offered to venture into an Iceni village alone and barter for some new clothes, but Marcellus was worried that it was risky. He threw away his helmet and armour and rode on, dressed only in a tunic and cloak, but he kept his sword and knife close by his side. He was sure that, after one more day's ride, they'd reach the coast, where they'd take a boat to an island and begin a new life. Brea wondered if Druids still inhabited the islands, but many of the isles were very small, with only a few villages scattered there. She imagined living in a wild, beautiful village across the seas not far from the coast, where she'd rise every day to make breakfast in the smoky hut and gaze across the waves towards the land they had left. She hoped with all her heart that she and Marcellus could set up home, build a hut and keep a few animals. She knew how to cook; from the first days of her childhood, her mother showed her how to weave, to grow vegetables; she'd learned a little of pottery and metalwork from her father. She and Marcellus would develop their skills together and be happy.

But every time she thought of her father, Brea's heart ached. The battle

against Suetonius's army would be over now. She wished she knew what
had happened – she expected the worst. If Marcellus was right, and Brea
was afraid that he was, her father and Addedomaros would be dead in the
field, perhaps the queen too. Brea knew what dreadful fate would await her
if she was captured: Boudicca would never allow herself to be taken
prisoner.

As they rode along together, Brea delighted in Marcellus's company. He
was attentive, seeming to know when she was anxious and when she was
troubled by thoughts of her tribe, he cheered her. Marcellus, too, had
moments where he said little and was lost in thoughts that sat heavily on
his shoulders. They were both grieving. But at those moments, their eyes
would lock and they would give each other courage.

Brea looked forward to their nights together most of all. They'd rest
under a tree while the horses grazed, and Marcellus would whisper in his
ear that he loved her more than life. He'd talk of their future, that they'd
live to be old, have many children, grandchildren, they'd keep animals and
grow vegetables near the sea and he promised that every night of her long
life he'd tell her how much he loved her. Brea had never been so happy,
wrapped in his arms as he kissed her neck and stroked her hair. She was
reminded of the time she'd told Aurelia that, in her place, she'd certainly
find it easy to love her master. How right she had been! Each time she
thought of their new life together, she breathed in the belief that she could
be happier than ever, then the sad thoughts would return. There would be
silent tears for her father and for the people who had died in battle, for
Aurelia, for those she'd known in Camulodunum, and Marcellus would
kiss the tears away and urge her to think of their future.

On the fourth morning, they woke in darkness before dawn, before the
first rays of sunlight glinted beyond the fens. Marcellus covered her face
with kisses and murmured, 'It's time, my love.'

Brea blinked, hardly awake. 'Time?'

His voice was husky. 'Today, I want you to become my wife, if you will
say yes. There will be no feasting, no yellow robe, no family to welcome you
to the *domus*. But there will be me and you, and a promise that we will love
each other for eternity.'

'Of course I'll say yes.' Brea laughed, indicating her soiled green robe. 'But I'm the worst dressed bride ever.'

Marcellus was puzzled. 'What traditions do your people observe when they marry?'

Brea's voice filled with emotion. 'There's no big ceremony, no ritual to be followed as Romans do. My father and mother loved each other and wanted to be together, so they told each other so and they were wed. It is a simple contract of love. Our women choose who and when to marry. They are not the properties of their husbands and fathers, as Roman women are.'

'Then if you'll choose me, let us marry now.' Marcellus grabbed her hand. 'We'll bathe in the river. Then we'll stand together and join hands and promise each other that we will be together for all our lives.'

'Just for our lives?' Brea smiled, teasing. 'Not for ever and ever?'

'I believe we have but one life and we must live it honourably.' Marcellus sighed. He brushed her hair from her eyes tenderly. 'You are my beating heart and the blood in my veins. I feel as you do too – nothing can tear us apart, not in life or death.'

* * *

They stood quietly together beneath a tree, Venator and Bellicus grazing behind them. Brea's hair was still damp. A light mist rose from the fenlands, the first rays of sun warming the earth. Brea and Marcellus faced each other, and he took her right hand in his. Their eyes met as he held up the gold and carnelian necklace, lifting her hair, placing it over her head. He took her hand, threading the snake bracelet on her upper arm. It was too big, slipping down to her wrist. Brea's eyes were fixed on Marcellus the whole time, gleaming with love. He lifted her fingers to his lips, threading the heavy gold ring on her finger.

'We are one.' Marcellus's voice was thick with emotion.

'We are one,' Brea repeated.

Marcellus lifted her into his arms. 'Now you wear the necklace, the bracelet and the ring, you are my beloved wife.'

Brea kissed his mouth. 'I'll wear them forever – for eternity.'

He carried her to the blanket beneath the tree, placing her down carefully, his hands brushing her face tenderly. Brea wrapped her arms around his neck and pulled him towards her. She was his wife. She loved him and nothing else mattered. She wouldn't hesitate now.

* * *

They must have fallen asleep, locked in each other's arms, and they slept for some time. The sun had risen high, hazy behind the late-morning mist that clung to the fens like a cloak. Something woke Brea suddenly. She sat up, realising that she was alone, wrapped in a blanket. She looked around for Marcellus, but he wasn't there. Her vision was filled by moving vapour that shifted eerily in the sunlight. Brea struggled to her feet and called out his name.

* * *

Hanna woke up, opening her eyes to blink in the golden honey sunlight that streamed through the curtains onto the pillow. She reached for her phone. It was past nine: she'd overslept. Since the vivid dream of last night, she'd fallen into heavy slumber. She thought how strange it was that people she knew, people from her life who were important to her, had filtered into her dream and become people she'd never met, people who'd lived long ago and were important to the woman whose life she lived in her dream. It was clear now, more than ever, that the dream had been leading her to an important place for so long, and Hanna was sure she understood where it was. Today, she'd find the final piece of treasure. Hanna stretched her limbs and felt a burst of energy course through her body. Once she'd had a shower and dressed warmly, she'd go down to the woods beyond the pig field. She was sure she'd find a wedding ring there.

Twenty minutes later, Hanna hurried downstairs and sat at the breakfast table to find her mother waiting, coffee pot in hand. Stephanie's face was troubled. 'It's not like you to sleep in so late. Everyone else is outside already. Roly has his team with him – they're all metal detecting by the stile that leads to Bramble Woods. And that lovely woman Cynthia just popped in to share a cuppa with me. We had a nice chat.'

'I'll just have a quick coffee, then I'll join them,' Hanna said, accepting the mug Stephanie offered.

Stephanie was staring at her quizzically. 'She's a shrewd woman, Cynthia. We had quite a conversation. I didn't realise archaeologists had a spiritual side.'

'I'm sure Roly doesn't. He's literally down to earth.' Hanna grinned. 'But it's an interesting perspective, that the past leaves something behind that we can still feel in the present.'

Then Stephanie took a deep breath and blurted, 'You never told me about your dreams.'

Hanna saw the disappointment in her mother's eyes. 'I didn't want to worry you.'

Stephanie was visibly upset now. 'It started after your accident – Cynthia told me. That's when you began to learn all the languages, and I supported you, Hanna, but I didn't understand then. It all makes sense now. I wish you'd told me.'

'Mum...'

'There would be times you'd come downstairs as a teenager, and later on too, looking completely washed out. Just last week, I said to Paddy that I was worried you were anaemic. You've never looked like you've had a proper good night's sleep.'

'The dreams are intermittent. Sometimes they stop for ages.'

'And now you're having them again. Cynthia said they were about a Roman woman... And you walk her path in the dreams, the same one she walked in the past, that's what Cynthia explained. You feel now what she felt then.'

'Sort of.'

'And you've seen her ghost?'

Hanna sighed. 'I think so.'

Stephanie sat across the table and reached out, grabbing Hanna's hand. 'Why didn't you ever tell me this?'

'You were a single parent, you had enough on your plate. And then I left for uni and when I came back from China, you'd met Paddy, you had the wedding coming up. I didn't want to bother you.'

'I'm your mum,' Stephanie protested. 'I'd have been here for you. I'm here for you now.'

'I'm sorry.' Hanna wasn't sure what else to say.

'So – where have you seen this ghost?'

Hanna sighed. 'At the station – on the fenlands – outside.'

'When did you last see her?'

'Last night, as you drove us home.' Hanna examined her mother's expression for surprise. Instead, Stephanie seemed resigned.

'Paddy and I often say there's a creepy feeling on the road between here and Little Rymer. I hate driving home by myself... and I know Roy hates being in the pig field when the mist comes down. He'll often bark and growl, as if something's not right.'

'I've seen him do it.'

'And who else knows about the Roman ghost?'

'Ollie, Lucas.' Hanna shook her head. 'Serenity, Roly.'

Stephanie squeezed her hand. 'And now I know too, thank goodness. I want to help you get to the bottom of it all, especially if the dreams are stopping you having a good night's rest. Cynthia says you've dreamed about the necklace and the bracelet they found.'

'Yes and, Mum – you can be the first to know. There's a third piece, an engraved gold ring. I dreamed about it last night. I think I know where it is.' Hanna stood up. 'I'll get across to the field now.'

'It's been in the ground for two thousand years.' Stephanie smiled. 'It can wait until you've had some toast. Sit, and I'll make you breakfast. Then you can get your coat on and join the others.'

'Thanks, Mum.'

'I want to be a proper mum to you, Hanna.'

'You're the best. And I'm sorry I didn't tell you. I suppose you were the one person in my life who kept my feet on the ground when my mind was full of people who lived centuries ago. I'll always be grateful for that.'

'I try hard, Hanna. And we've always been close.' Stephanie smiled, a little tearful. 'Don't shut me out.'

'I won't, I promise.' Hanna's face was full of affection. 'I might ride down on Nutmeg.'

'Good idea. And I'll stay here. I'm making some soup. Ollie will be here for lunch and I thought I'd make some wholemeal bread too.'

'Sounds lovely.'

'Oh, and Hanna?'

'Mum?' Hanna saw the mischievous twinkle in Stephanie's eyes.

'You may be thirty in November and too old for your mother to nag you, but your hair's still damp and if you go out like that, you'll catch your death.'

'I'll wave the hairdryer at it, I promise,' Hanna replied with a grin, gratefully accepting the toast that her mother offered.

46

Hanna rode Nutmeg down the lane past the pig field, where Paddy and Ollie stood with Lucas, wearing waxed coats and wellingtons, examining a piglet. It wriggled and Lucas let it go, placing a gentle hand on its back before it trotted away. Roy was by Paddy's side, sitting quietly, watching.

Paddy raised a thumb, a sign that all was well, calling over, 'Good news here – the coccidiosis has completely gone. The piglets are healthy. Are you off to help the archaeologists, Hanna?'

'I am.' Hanna nodded. Roly and Cynthia stood by the stile that led to the woods, with Ralf and Toby, who were searching the area around the base of a tree with metal detectors. She called, 'Are you joining us?'

'We're right behind you,' Ollie replied. 'We wouldn't miss it.'

'Oh, I'm sure we'll find treasure today,' Hanna called over her shoulder as she encouraged Nutmeg to walk on. She met Lucas's eyes and he smiled: a moment of warmth passed between them. He seemed to feel it too.

Roly followed Ralf and Toby into Bramble Woods, heaving a heavy bag on his shoulder, watching keenly as the metal detectors hovered in a bunch of nettles beyond a tree trunk.

Cynthia was waiting by the stile, dressed in a long dress, a heavy coat and furry boots. Her silver hair waved around her face. She called out, 'I owe you an apology, Hanna.'

'No, you don't.' Hanna looked down from Nutmeg and smiled. 'It's not your fault.'

'I'm empathic. I ought to have known you wouldn't tell your mother about the dreams.'

'We're very close,' Hanna said. 'I should've mentioned it to her long ago.'

'But you didn't want to worry her,' Cynthia remarked. 'I shouldn't have said anything, but we were having a cup of tea and she was just so interested.'

'We had a long chat over breakfast. It's fine – please don't worry,' Hanna replied.

'You look very well today.' Cynthia narrowed her eyes perceptively. 'Have you been dreaming?'

'I had the most incredible dream. It was as if I was the Roman woman again, the spirit, but I saw Ollie, Serenity, and even my dad – then they became other people.'

'What other people?'

'The ghost's people. I think my friends and family represent the people she loved. I saw her spirit again last night.'

Cynthia nodded. 'You and she are so closely connected. She's certainly trying to communicate that to you. Hanna, tell me what you feel about her – when you are her, in the dream.'

Hanna patted Nutmeg's neck. The mare was calm, standing patiently. 'She loves the Roman soldier passionately. But she's sad – she's lost people who were dear to her. Then something happened that was life-changing, traumatic. And I think it's to do with the jewellery.'

'I'm sure it is,' Cynthia said enigmatically.

'I dreamed about the final piece – it's a wedding ring.'

'That makes absolute sense. Do you think our ghost lost it? Is that what she's searching for, perhaps?'

'I don't know that, but I do know where it is.'

'Oh, that's so exciting.' Cynthia clasped her hands together.

'The thing is,' Roly piped up, walking across to join them, 'what's a Roman woman doing here, in the middle of Iceni territory? And with a

Roman soldier? Do you think they got lost or were they running from someone?'

Roy bounded across, sitting smartly next to Nutmeg's hooves. Then Paddy and Ollie came to lean against the stile. Lucas stood close to Hanna, smiling up at her. She reached out and squeezed his hand.

'Didn't the Romans fight the Iceni near here in the final battle?' Ollie asked. 'Perhaps they were part of it?'

'No one knows where the battle between Suetonius and Boudicca's armies took place, except that it was somewhere along Watling Street,' Roly said.

'People have suggested many sites – it might have been in Leicestershire, on the junction of Watling Street and the Fosse Way,' Cynthia offered. 'Roly and I were just saying on the way up this morning that we'd love to do more research on it.' She glanced at Hanna to gauge her interest.

'The Romans beat the Iceni though, didn't they?' Ollie asked.

Roly was keen to explain. 'The Iceni outnumbered the Romans by thousands, but they were disorganised, without armour or strategy. Suetonius's men wore helmets and body armour and carried spears and short swords. And the Romans chose their battle site well, so that the Iceni were boxed in with nowhere to run. The Romans had ten thousand troops and there were two hundred thousand rebels led by Boudicca. The Iceni were completely obliterated.'

Hanna thought again about her dream. 'It's so sad.'

'And what about Boudicca?' Lucas asked. 'Did she survive?'

'She did, but it's believed that she poisoned herself so as not to become a Roman captive.' Cynthia looked at Roly.

Roly explained: 'Others say she died of her wounds. We'd love to do more research on Boudicca. Very little is known. I read once that Boudicca was buried between platforms nine and ten in King's Cross station in London. It's probably not true, but it would be exciting to make it one's life work to find out where she is.' He glanced at Hanna. 'Just imagine that!'

Hanna smiled. 'It would be exciting.'

Paddy pushed his hands into his pockets. 'Well, I can't stand here all day listening to a history lesson – I've got pigs to sort out and Ollie has a field to plough.' He met Roly's eyes. 'Are we going to find this treasure or what? It needs doing by lunchtime – Steph's making soup.'

Lucas grinned. 'And I have a house call to make on Mrs Rallison in Setchey. Gus the cat is terrified of coming into the surgery. It's just routine blood work, but I said I'd be there for one o'clock.'

'Then we'd better push on.' Roly grinned, pulling his hat down.

Ralf and Toby had stopped waving metal detectors. Ralf raised a gloved hand and called, 'There's nothing here, Roly. This is a big stretch of woodland to cover.'

'We won't be done by lunch,' Toby agreed, wiping his forehead on his sleeve.

Cynthia looked at Hanna. 'What do you think?'

'We need to walk down the path, to the place where you and I saw the roe deer,' Hanna said. 'We're looking for a chunky gold ring. I saw it in the dream. Our ghost lost it when she was very close to that place, I'm sure.'

'I want to hear all about these dreams you've been having, Hanna. I'm not sure what I think about ghosts, but some strange stuff happens in these parts, I know.' Paddy gave a huge shrug. 'So what are we waiting for?' He grunted. 'Lead the way, Hanna. Come on, Roy. There's treasure to be found.'

Roy barked once and was in motion, responding eagerly to the order to move. Paddy ruffled his ears.

'Well, this is exciting.' Roly patted Nutmeg's neck, opening the gate next to the stile for Hanna to pass through. He shifted the heavy bag on his shoulder to make it more comfortable. 'I hope you're right, Hanna. This could be very big indeed.'

* * *

It was quiet in the woods, the occasional crunch of twigs beneath feet, a solitary chirp from a bird high in the branches. A thin stream of light managed to filter through, and the overhanging network of leaves cast dark shadows on the ground. Tall trees rose on either side – oak, beech and sweet chestnut. Clumps of nettles clustered together around blackberry bushes, the knotty fruits in abundance. Roly and Cynthia surged ahead,

Ralf and Toby at their heels. Paddy and Ollie were deep in conversation about which fields needed ploughing as Roy scooted ahead, pausing to sniff plants.

Lucas looked up at Hanna. 'How did you sleep last night?'

'Fine, thanks.' Hanna smiled. 'I have a lot to tell you about the dream I had though. But let's find this piece of jewellery first. It's not far from here – I'm sure I know the place.'

'I'm sure you do.' Lucas stroked Nutmeg's neck. The mare answered him with a blow of contentment from her lips.

The temperature had become cooler in the woods. The leaves rustled overhead, shivering as if they were cold themselves. High in the branches, a squirrel scampered and disappeared.

Hanna glanced around and called out, 'Here. I think this is the place.'

'I certainly sense something...' Cynthia turned around to face her.

'So where shall we start looking?' Roly asked, hunched inside his jacket, his face tense with excitement.

Hanna closed her eyes. Momentarily, she saw herself in the dream, running, her legs bare beneath a green robe. She recalled crashing down a narrow track beneath a canopy of trees and falling. She opened her eyes and looked up: the same lattice of trees was overhead. Of course, they wouldn't have been there two thousand years ago. But the dream was her dream; she was being shown the place.

She pointed ahead to the exact spot where the roe deer had bounded from the shadows beyond the trees, where it had paused to gaze at her. 'Try there, just beyond the oak tree.' Hanna felt a shiver pass through her. 'I'm sure that's it.'

Ralf and Toby set to work with their metal detectors, weaving across the track methodically. Roly positioned himself just behind them, watching curiously.

Paddy turned to Ollie. 'The number of times I've walked along this path since I was a kiddie. I never thought of there being any treasure here.'

Nutmeg snorted abruptly. She raised her head, swished her tail and came to a stubborn stop. Hanna nudged her forward gently.

'The horses have never liked being in this part of the woods,' Ollie observed.

Everyone was watching as the metal detectors waved over the path, then towards the shrubs and twigs on either side. The wind ruffled the oak leaves, then suddenly there was a low eerie whine, increasing to a wail as the metal detector reacted to something beneath the surface in a cluster of teasel flowers. Roy bounded over, scrabbling eagerly in the soil with his front paws.

Roly pulled out three spades from his bag and called to Paddy, 'Do I have your permission to look here?'

'I should think so.' Paddy was fascinated. 'Dig away.'

Roly, Ralf and Toby began to dig, the hole becoming deeper and wider. Roly continued to hollow out the dark soil, piling it high on both sides, then he called out, 'I can see it. It's there, shining in the dirt – it's gold.' He was on his knees, then lying on the earth, delving deep inside. 'I've got it!'

Hanna wasn't sure what happened next, in which order the events occurred. Perhaps the sound came first, a screech of an animal from the centre of a hawthorn hedge, the red berries gleaming like drops of blood, the small branches twitching. A low mist swirled from the leaves, snaking across the ground, and she thought it formed the shape of a hare, then a running woman.

Roy growled, lying low on his belly, his fur flat. There was a cry from Cynthia, a gasp: something in the air shifted and changed. Nutmeg whinnied, bucking as she saw a moving shape. She was spooked. Ollie grasped her reins, Lucas was close by: Hanna saw them turn to her, their faces anxious, moving to her in slow motion as she fell from the saddle and crashed hard onto the ground. Then she hit her head with a thud and the world whirled away and was gone.

* * *

Hanna was standing in the pig field, wearing her own clothes, watching a woman in a green dress who was asleep on the ground, wrapped in a blanket. The sun was hazy, the late-morning mist clung to the fens like a cloak. The woman woke and she sat up, confused, as if she'd just realised that she was alone. She looked around anxiously. Thin vapour shifted eerily in the sunlight, surrounding her, separating. The woman struggled to her feet and Hanna heard her call out a name.

'Marcellus.'

47

Brea looked around nervously, clutching the blanket. She was alone. Something was wrong: she sensed it. She struggled to her feet and called out, 'Marcellus.'

Figures moved in the mist, creeping forwards, back again. Brea reached down for the sword that she always kept by her side and clutched it. Venator and Bellicus stopped grazing and turned, their ears twitching nervously. A man was suddenly visible, fighting with two more men, his sword raised, thrusting forward, and one man fell. Brea stared harder, edging backwards, unsure, as the mist filled her vision again. Then it cleared and she saw Marcellus bring his sword down hard. Another man fell, a Roman, in armour.

Marcellus ran towards Brea, his face fierce as he grabbed her hand. 'We've slept too long – we've been followed. Quick, grab your horse.'

Brea clambered on Venator, Marcellus beside her on Bellicus, forcing him forward. Then the mist lifted, and they were surrounded by ten, twenty Roman soldiers in armour, forming a circle, swords drawn. Bellicus reared once, and was still. Marcellus glanced towards Brea who reined her horse in. There was nowhere to go.

'Stay there. When you get the chance, make a run for it on Venator.' Marcellus met her eyes, his voice low.

'But—'

Bellicus leaped, Marcellus reaching forwards, and several of the soldiers fell. Brea watched, her heart thumping: her husband was a skilled soldier. She'd never experienced anything but gentleness at his hands, but now he was wielding a sword ferociously.

More soldiers sprang from the mist, and Marcellus manoeuvred his horse, lurching, twisting, fighting furiously. Brea looked on in horror as even more soldiers rushed at him, their armour glinting, dragging Marcellus from his horse, raising weapons in the air. A soldier thrust a dagger and, as Marcellus fell, swords descended. Brea's sword dropped from her fingers as she slid from Venator and rushed to him. The soldiers disappeared in the mist again and she knelt by his side. He had no armour; his tunic was already soaked in blood. She grabbed his hand, bent forward, kissed his lips and when she moved away, his expression was tender.

'You must get away, my love.'

'Marcellus.' Brea didn't know what to say. 'I can't lose you.'

'Run, and live for us both.' He attempted a smile, but Brea could see that he was in pain. 'What if we have a son growing already, a daughter? It could be, even now...'

Brea hesitated. 'I would call a boy Marcellus—'

'Our child would know peace and happiness, that is the important thing.' Marcellus closed his eyes, squeezing them against the pain that racked his body. 'You must run, Brea.'

'My love.' She moved closer, her hand on his brow. His eyes met hers and she saw that they were glassy.

'You are my wife. It couldn't be for long, but in that short time, I was happier than I've ever been...' Marcellus's eyelids flickered for a moment. He smiled; his gaze was filled with love, then he was completely still. She saw herself reflected in the mirror of his eyes. There was so much sadness there, but he no longer saw her. He was already cold.

Brea looked up. The Roman soldiers were in a circle, watching her. She seized Marcellus's sword and faced them boldly.

One of the soldiers laughed, mocking, 'What will you do with that, my lady? Stir your soup?'

Brea bared her teeth and rushed towards him, kicking high and knocking him over on his back. He fell sprawling onto the ground with a shout. She stood astride him, the sword hovering over his chest. 'I could kill you now, as easily as stirring soup.' She looked at him, the whites of his eyes, frightened as a bolted horse. Then Brea noticed the many faces staring at her, amazed.

One of the soldiers muttered, 'You are no Roman woman.'

'I am Iceni. My name is Brea, daughter of Esico and Cartimandua, wife of Marcellus Publius Julius Silvanus,' Brea declared boldly. She stepped back from the terrified soldier who was quaking on the damp soil, looking down at him with pity. 'And I could take another life, and then another, as my husband has just done, as you have just done. But what is the point of it? Too many people have died and I have seen enough of the bloodshed.' She threw the sword on the ground in contempt and took a deep breath, her heart knocking. 'No, I have done with fighting. I will leave now on my horse and you will allow me to. I have another life to consider...'

She took a step away, another.

One of the soldiers approached her and she faced him fiercely. 'You will let me go. I will return to my people on my horse.'

'A Roman horse. It can't belong to one such as you.' The man's face was scornful. He extended a hand to her throat and clutched the gold and carnelian necklace. 'And these are Roman jewels.'

'They are mine.' Brea pulled away from him, breathing hard. 'My husband gave them to me when we married.'

'You are no Roman wife,' the soldier said again, stepping forward, tugging the necklace towards him. Brea could smell the foulness of his breath. 'You are an Iceni whore.' The necklace was hauled upwards and the soldier held it in the air. 'It's worth nothing, as you are worth nothing.' He flung it away from him into the mist.

Brea felt strong hands grasp her arms. She struggled.

The Roman snickered, his face inches from hers. 'Your people were killed in the battle, your queen fled in fear. And the legate who deserted his men is now dead – we were sent after him when someone saw him ride his horse into the forest. He is a traitor – he's got what he deserves.'

Tears sprang to Brea's eyes. Marcellus had told her to live for him; he'd hoped above everything that she'd survive, that she was already carrying their child. She believed him; she'd known it as they'd lain together this morning, a few precious hours ago. There would be a new life.

She stared into the face of the Roman soldier and she saw the intention in his crooked smile. She took a breath – she could not escape, but perhaps he'd listen if she spoke to him. She summoned all the courage she had.

'There has been too much of death. I've seen those I love put to the sword. My husband...' Brea wiped her face and stared into the narrowed eyes of the Roman soldier. 'I'll kill no more.' She turned away.

She'd taken four paces, five, when the Roman caught up with her. 'You're a prisoner of the Roman army,' he sneered, and she heard the other soldiers laugh. They formed a circle around her again, leering. She knew what the Romans did to Iceni women, Boudicca's daughters, her own mother. Brea was determined that it would not happen to her.

She mustered all her strength and kicked out, biting, scratching, pushing with all the force she could manage, then she turned and rushed between two soldiers, dodging into the mist. A clump of trees was not far away; if she could reach the woodlands, she could hide in the foliage, she might escape.

She put her head down and ran as fast as she could. She heard footsteps, the clanking of armour. A soldier was just behind her. He heaved himself forward and grabbed her wrist. She jerked away and felt the bracelet fall as she hurried towards the forest, weaving between the trees. For a moment, she paused, leaning against the bark of a tall oak tree, catching her breath. She put a hand to her face and realised it was covered in tears. Her heart ached for Marcellus.

She heard the clatter of footsteps crunching twigs as they searched.

Brea panted, wide-eyed. She'd make another run for it now. She took a breath and bolted, propelling herself through undergrowth, crashing forward.

There was a noise behind her, the long sigh of something whistling through the air, then she felt a fierce pain between her shoulders and stumbled forwards, crying out in pain. Blood oozed and bubbled down the front of the green dress and she couldn't breathe. A Roman spear was lodged in her back; she fell onto the ground against the trunk of an oak tree, her arms stretched, her face in the dirt. She wheezed, but her lungs wouldn't work.

A soldier stood over her, his mouth next to her ear, his words a cruel whisper. 'You are indeed no Roman wife now.'

Brea felt him grasp her hand and tug the gold ring from her finger. There was no breath in her lungs now. The world was growing dark. In the mist, the Roman soldier was inspecting the ring Marcellus had given her. She heard her husband's voice in her ears, soft with love. '*Now you wear the necklace, the bracelet and the ring, you are my beloved wife.*'

She had kissed his mouth, she had promised him, '*I'll wear them forever – for eternity.*'

She saw the soldier fling the heavy ring into the distance; she heard the sneer in his voice. Then the last breath of air escaped from her lungs and the world around her disappeared.

* * *

Hanna watched it all. She stood, her face covered in tears, and she knew everything. She closed her eyes and stifled a sob.

* * *

Hanna opened her eyes again and looked into Lucas's anxious gaze. He was holding her hand in both of his. She blinked and said, 'I am Iceni. My name is Brea, daughter of Esico and Cartimandua...'

Lucas touched her wrist, checking her pulse. 'Hanna, don't move. You fell from Nutmeg; you've been out cold for a few seconds. Look at me.' He placed a hand against her forehead, staring into her eyes. 'Does anything hurt? Can you sit easily?'

She eased herself up, staring into several anxious faces. Ollie held Nutmeg's reins. Roy sat at her feet, his brown eyes on her. Paddy and Roly stepped forward and Cynthia crouched next to her, an expression of interest on her face. She said, 'Well, where have you been, Hanna? Some-where fascinating, I'm sure of it.'

Hanna lifted a grimy hand and wiped her face. It was covered in tears. She caught her breath, remembering. 'Our Roman wife was not Roman at all, she was Iceni. She was called Brea. She married a Roman, a legate called Marcellus. They were hunted down in the field...'

'And this is her wedding ring,' Roly said proudly, holding up a heavy piece of dull gold.

'Something sprang from the hawthorn; a hare ran out,' Cynthia explained.

'It spooked Nutmeg,' Ollie added. 'You fell.'

'I'd like to take you to A&E,' Lucas said gently. 'I think you should get checked over.'

Hanna attempted to scramble to her feet and, with help from Lucas, she stood shakily and took a step forward, two. 'I'll be fine.'

'I'm sure you will but...' Lucas wrapped an arm around her. 'Let's make sure, shall we?'

Hanna shook her head, remembering. 'You have an appointment with a nervous cat.'

'That's not until one o'clock. It's not eleven yet. I might make it to see Gus on time. If not, I'll rearrange it. Let's get you to the Queen Elizabeth.'

Hanna leaned against Lucas, walking gingerly. Her jodhpurs were covered in mud and her back ached a little, her hips were stiff, but otherwise she felt fine. Her head was fuzzy: she'd hit it hard and in the few seconds she'd been unconscious, she'd experienced scenes that had left her shaken and emotional. She felt hot tears run down her face again, and Lucas's arm tightened around her.

'What do you need?'

'You're doing everything right. Thanks, Lucas.' Hanna offered him a grateful smile. She thought of Brea and Marcellus: the images hadn't left her yet, or the intense emotion she'd felt as she'd watched. Their story still gripped her, filled her full of sadness.

Lucas guided her through the stile and into the pig field and, behind her, Paddy was muttering quietly, troubled about how worried Stephanie would be when he told her that her daughter had fallen from Nutmeg.

Cynthia moved close to Hanna and whispered in her ear, 'You saw it all, in those seconds you were out cold, didn't you? You saw everything that happened...'

Hanna nodded.

'Can you remember it?'

'Every detail.' Hanna breathed, feeling suddenly weary. She leaned against Lucas, feeling the strength of his arm supporting her, and she was filled with gratitude. She was surrounded by people who cared about her, who loved her. This was where she belonged; this was home.

And in that moment, she thought of Brea and Marcellus, of everything they had lost, and she felt truly blessed.

48

Hanna slumped in Lucas's car as he drove towards the village of Setchey. She reached out and squeezed his hand, resting her head against the passenger window. Tiredness seeped through her body and she wondered if she'd fall asleep. The doctor had been wonderful in A&E; she'd given Hanna the all-clear, but told her to watch out for any dizziness, confusion, slurred speech – sure signs to seek further medical help. Lucas had stayed with her the whole time. They had walked back to the car holding hands as she tried to explain about what she'd experienced during the few moments of blackout. He'd hugged her and told her he knew she'd been through an ordeal and she had burst into tears.

Now they were on their way to see Mrs Rallison whose cat hated going to the surgery. They drove past waterlogged fields into Setchey at three minutes to one, passing a pretty brick church, stopping outside a small bungalow in Willow Drive. Hanna expected to wait in the car, but Lucas shook his head. 'Come and meet Mrs Rallison and Gus.'

A small woman in a pinafore with white, tightly curled hair was already at the door. She beamed when she saw Lucas. 'Good afternoon, Lucas. Ar yer reet, bor?'

'I'm fine thanks, Kay. How are you?'

'Good, good, as long as the rain holds off. Oh, but I had a barney with my neighbour yesterday, being as he was playing that rock music too loud. It was a Sunday morning too.'

'And how's Gus?'

'He's a lummox, but I love him to pieces.' She turned to Hanna. 'And who's this? A trainee vet or your wife?'

'My girlfriend.' Lucas smiled. 'Hanna, this is Mrs Rallison.'

'Come in, and I'll make us a pot of tea. I'd make some toast for us all but the bread's too old, it's gone all fosey.'

Lucas winked. 'Tea would be lovely, thanks Kay.'

Hanna followed Lucas inside and sat thankfully in an armchair as Mrs Rallison rattled around in the kitchen.

Lucas picked up Gus, a handsome back and white cat, and stroked him gently. His voice was soothing. 'Right, let's check on how your kidneys are doing, shall we, Gus?' He turned to Hanna. 'He was a bit poorly last year, so we keep an eye on him. He's sixteen. It's a good age.' He raised his voice. 'Is he drinking well, Kay?'

'He and me both – I like a drop of wine afore I go to bed. People tell me I shouldn't, but I think that's a load of ole squit. What do you think, Lucas?'

'Moderation's the key, I suppose, Kay.' Lucas grinned. 'You look well on it though...'

'I do like Lucas, Hanna – you picked good when you picked him.' Mrs Rallison carried a tray into the living room and offered Hanna a cup filled with strong tea. 'So what is it you do?'

'I work in a café in Little Rymer,' Hanna began, then she added, 'and I help archaeologists sometimes.'

Mrs Rallison leaned forward. 'I read in the paper the other day a necklace had been found from the Iron Age. That's a rum 'un – it was so old and yet it's in good condition, just as it was all those years ago.'

'I found it,' Hanna said proudly. 'Well, me and Roy, our sheepdog, and a few other people. And we've dug up more jewellery since. It's very exciting.'

'Oh, I love to read all about that old stuff being discovered so close to home.' Mrs Rallison sat down, stretching out her legs. 'Well, it's our heritage, isn't it? I'm a big fan of Boudicca, you know. She was a proper Norfolk mawther. Girl power started right here in these parts, you know that.'

'All done, Kay.' Lucas had finished with Gus. He placed him down on the rug, stroked his fur and the cat purred, rushing to the window, springing onto the sill, staring outside.

'He's seen something,' Mrs Rallison remarked. 'A bird probably, or a fly. Or maybe he's seen a ghost. Since I lost my husband, he's often staring at something I can't see.' She sighed. 'He's good company, my Gus. It's short for Augustus – he was a Roman emperor, you know.'

'I remember reading about Caesar Augustus – he was the one who said "*Festina lente*".' Hanna smiled. 'Make haste slowly.'

'That's Gus's motto too. He'll live for a few more years yet. He's very wise, my Gus,' Mrs Rallison said.

'We'd better make haste.' Lucas packed Gus's blood sample in his bag. 'I think there's some soup with our name on it in Little Rymer.'

'Well, it was very nice to meet you, Hanna. And thanks for popping round, Lucas. You know how much poor Gus hates the vet's surgery. It smells of sickness and fear and animal poo. He's had three operations, you know...' Mrs Rallison walked with Hanna and Lucas to the front door. 'I don't know what I'd do without you, Lucas. The last vet was proper mean, but Gus lets you look after him, no bother.'

'It's a pleasure – I'll be in touch,' Lucas said.

'Thanks,' Mrs Rallison called. 'See you soon and keep yew a troshin'.'

'I will.' Lucas turned to Hanna with a smile. 'I'm sure Gus will be fine now.'

'One satisfied customer.' Hanna grasped his arm.

'This is exactly why I wanted to move to Norfolk. This – and now you.'

'You were wonderful with Gus and Kay.' Hanna met his eyes; there was no sadness there now, just the level warm gaze she was becoming so fond of. 'It feels like we're both coming home.'

Hanna's mind was filled with so many thoughts as she snuggled in the passenger seat of the car. It was as if jigsaw pieces of her life were fitting together; Lucas was wonderful, she was beginning to feel settled in Little Rymer, back to her roots, about to share lunch with family and friends.

She messaged her mother and Ollie that she was fine and they'd be back by two o'clock, then she lay back in the seat and closed her eyes. An image came to her quickly, the heavy gold ring on Brea's finger as she ran through the woodland, a Roman soldier hurling a spear that sighed as it slid through the air. She couldn't wait to tell Cynthia everything.

* * *

The kitchen was filled with the aroma of freshly baked bread as Stephanie ladled soup into dishes. Then they sat down to eat, nine of them grouped around the kitchen table, breaking bread, sipping water from tumblers. Roy sat at Hanna's feet, lapping water noisily from a bowl. There was a clatter of spoons as Hanna told her tale.

She finished her story in a quiet voice. 'Brea died where she fell, somewhere in the woods by an old oak tree. They threw the gold ring away – they took all of her jewellery from her and just threw it.'

'It makes perfect sense that she'd still be searching.' Cynthia nodded. 'Her husband gave it to her, it bound them together. She's been looking for it ever since. But it will be placed in the museum now. Perhaps once it's all in one place, she'll feel peaceful.'

'How do you feel now, Hanna?' Lucas asked quietly.

'A bit shaken and empty. It was as if I was a part of her.'

'I don't get it,' Paddy grunted. 'What are you trying to say? That you were this Iceni woman in a past life or that her ghost was haunting you?' He slurped soup. 'It's a bit of a funny ole tale, if you ask me.'

'We don't have to search so hard for an explanation,' Cynthia said gently. 'Let's just say that Hanna and our Iceni woman—'

'Brea,' Hanna added.

'Hanna and Brea are connected; the dreams connected them,' Cynthia explained.

'So Hanna's a medium, like you are?' Paddy scratched his head, puzzled.

'Cynthia's a psychic archaeologist – that's not the same thing at all,' Roly said.

'It upsets me, that you've had this hanging over you for so long,' Stephanie began.

'I think Hanna will be fine now,' Cynthia said calmly. 'There was a change of atmosphere in Bramble Woods after Nutmeg reared. There was a coldness before, but suddenly the air became warmer. Perhaps now Brea's jewellery is found, she will be happier.'

'I hope so.' Hanna shook her head sadly. The feeling of loss and injustice was still a tight knot in her stomach and between her shoulder blades, as if the Roman spear was still lodged there. 'What happened to her and Marcellus was tragic. They loved each other.' She reached for Lucas's hand beneath the table. 'I wish I knew for sure that she was at peace.'

'She'll let you know. It will come to you in time,' Cynthia said enigmatically.

Stephanie stood up to serve more soup. Ollie, Ralf and Toby thrust out their bowls simultaneously.

Roly reached for more bread. 'There is one thing, Hanna.'

Hanna reached for a glass of water. 'About the treasure, Roly?'

'Sort of. Nice bit of bread, this, Stephanie.' He trowelled butter on a thick slice. 'Do you remember I told you I'd applied for some funds? Well, it seems there's a wad of money coming my way to continue our research into the Iceni, and I want to ask you to join me.'

'How do you mean?' Hanna was puzzled.

'It consumes you, doesn't it, digging into the past?' Roly's eyes twinkled. 'The same as it does me and Cynthia and Ralf and Toby. We've all noticed it.'

'You're right – I love it,' Hanna confessed but she was still confused.

'Then join us.' Roly leaned forward excitedly. 'There's so much I want to find out about what happened around here two millennia ago. There's not enough information about the Iceni.'

'As I was saying the other day,' Cynthia added, 'the story of Boudicca has become a thing of legend, but the facts are scarce. We need to fill in the important gaps.'

'Plus, you have all the languages. Latin will be useful with the Roman influences in these parts, and there's so little known about the Iceni language except that it was Germanic,' Roly insisted. 'And you speak German too.'

'Are you offering me a job?' Hanna asked and she felt Lucas's pressure on her hand beneath the table. He was smiling.

'I am – a research job, working with me and Cynthia, and we can link it to a master's by research degree from Cambridge if you like.'

Hanna thought about what Mrs Rallison had said earlier: *It's our heritage, isn't it?* She nodded slowly. It would be a privilege to undertake such important research and the thought of it filled her with excitement. Her heart was in it, too – she'd known that for so long. 'I'd love to – thanks, Roly.' Hanna felt the breath leave her lungs. 'I owe it to Brea.'

'You owe it to yourself,' Cynthia said firmly. 'You've lived Brea's life for many years. Now it's time to live for Hanna.'

'Then – yes.' Hanna beamed. 'Thank you.' She couldn't stop the wide grin that spread across her face.

Hanna turned to Lucas and he kissed her. His eyes gleamed and she felt the familiar warmth. She looked around the table at the smiling faces. 'I'm so lucky,' she breathed. 'I mean – thank you, thank you all.'

Roly was delighted. 'How about we all meet again for dinner at our favourite restaurant in Cambridge next week? Bring Serenity, Ollie. We'll have a party to celebrate, all of us together and Prue and Manjeet. My team has another bright new talent on board. Welcome to the gang, Hanna.'

There was a round of applause.

Hanna closed her eyes and immediately she saw Brea in the arms of Marcellus, and she was gripped by how happy they had been, how much they had lost. She'd seize her own chance of happiness with both hands. She recalled the engraved ring they'd found this morning, the final piece, and she hoped that Brea would have some sense of closure.

Hanna was filled with excitement for the future; a research job: delving into the Iceni and their lives was such an opportunity for her – it was what she wanted. The Iceni were lodged in her heart now; Brea would always be an important part of who she was.

EPILOGUE

Hanna sat at the desk of her little office in the third bedroom at number 32 Mawkin Close, typing at the laptop. She could smell the delicious aroma from the kitchen downstairs. Lucas was making supper: it was his turn to cook. The photos on the desk in front of her reminded her how fast the last few months had rushed past. In November, Stephanie and Paddy had spent two weeks in St Lucia, the honeymoon of their dreams, although Paddy had been anxious about leaving the pigs with Ollie: he'd joked many times that he wouldn't be surprised to find them living in the farmhouse, wearing his clothes, sitting at his table, while Bramble Wood had become a tofu farm. However, Stephanie's smile in the photo standing on the beach with Paddy, their arms around each other, dramatic mountains tapering behind them, was one that warmed Hanna's heart.

Then, in February, Ollie and Serenity had married. The wedding photo showed them smiling in pale sunshine and a cloud of eco-friendly confetti outside the church in Little Rymer, hand in hand, Serenity's wedding dress snug around her just-visible three-month baby bump. Of course, she was still working, but, thankfully, she'd taken on two keen youngsters who shared her passion for trying out new recipes.

Two weeks ago, on March the sixteenth, Hanna had moved in with Lucas. She'd brought her things in boxes from the farm and he'd helped her rearrange the house. It felt strangely comforting to be back in her childhood home with him: it was theirs now; the future was theirs. Hanna smiled as she held up a goofy photograph of them both riding in the woodlands at Bramble Wood Farm on Nutmeg and Hunter, a snap taken by Ollie. Their eyes were only for each other.

Hanna read excerpts of the last paragraph she'd typed, her research comparing the lives of Roman women to that of Iceni women in the first century.

Gender in the Roman world was more intimately bound with notions of social identity... Ancient Rome prided itself on the power of its patriarchy, and was quick to condemn women who broke boundaries...

Andraste, or Andred, the Iceni goddess of war, employed a species of divination, letting a hare escape from the fold of her dress...

Hanna stared at the screen and rubbed her eyes. She was enjoying the research with Cynthia and Roly, delving into the history of the Iceni, focusing on how Roman and Iceni women's lives were so different. Brea was still never very far away, although Hanna hadn't dreamed of her since she'd fallen off Nutmeg. Her sleep was happy, restful and deep nowadays, and she was thankful.

She saved her work and stretched her arms above her head. It was almost seven o'clock. Supper would be ready.

At the table, Hanna and Lucas shared farfalle pesto, a glass of wine each and warm conversation, their heads close. Hanna was thoughtful for a while, then she said, 'Serenity said she wants to call her baby Delilah. I was trying to persuade her to choose Brea if it's a girl.'

Lucas's eyes shone. 'Brea's a lovely name.'

'My father wanted to call me Marguerite apparently.' Hanna smiled.

'Hanna suits you,' Lucas said. 'My mother said I had to be either Lucas or Alejandro. My dad wanted me called Orville, after the aeroplane inventor.' He shrugged. 'I didn't do too badly, considering.'

'Having met your mum and dad at Christmas, I'm not surprised – they are both lovely. Strong characters, though.' Hanna smiled, remembering.

'Mum loved talking to you in Spanish. It's been so long since she's spoken her native tongue.' Lucas reached for her hand. 'You'd think my dad would be better at Spanish, being born in California, but he's not really a linguist.'

'Your dad kept referring to himself as a veterinarian – he said a vet was a retired soldier. He lost me totally when he was talking about us all going to the party in fancy dress. I was thinking of going as an Iceni warrior until you told me he meant formal clothes.'

'They fell in love with you.' Lucas's eyes gleamed and Hanna squeezed his fingers affectionately before reaching for her glass of wine. 'It's not difficult.'

Hanna beamed. 'So, what shall we do tomorrow?'

'I have a free day – no Saturday routine visits, for a change.'

'Then I'll take the day off too. Drag me away from work please, Lucas. Otherwise, I'll be sitting at the laptop researching,' Hanna said. 'That reminds me, on Monday I have an early Zoom call. I'm talking to someone from the University of Warwick about Iceni weapons and coins and their latest research on female warriors.'

Lucas smiled. 'I love how this has become your life's work.'

'You and me both, doing what we love. I adore it.' Hanna put down her glass and took his hand. 'Work's not my entire life, though.'

'Nor mine. Let's borrow Hunter and Nutmeg and take them for a ride along the track through Bramble Woods,' Lucas suggested. 'It's been a while since we visited.'

'I'd love that. I'll text Ollie and Mum now,' Hanna enthused. 'We'll get up early and go out before breakfast, shall we?'

'Great idea.'

* * *

Hanna slept deeply at first, then a vivid dream came to her. She was standing beneath an oak in Bramble Woods, searching for Brea. She called her name, once, then again. Her voice was lost in dense leaves and foliage, in silence. There was a chill in the air, despite the sunlight that dappled the ground, new spring buds, blossom tumbling. A single hollow note lifted, a solitary bird's song, as a hare sprang from the bushes, pausing in the middle of a bed of bluebells watching, eerily still. It reminded Hanna of the one she'd met when she was driving back at night from Little Rymer as it squatted stubbornly, unblinking.

Hanna shivered. She found her voice again. 'Can you tell me what happened to Brea?'

The hare didn't move.

'Where is she?' Hanna tried again. 'Is she at peace? Is she with Marcellus?'

The hare stared at her with round eyes. Time stretched. Then the creature blinked once and bounded away. She was suddenly alone and a feeling of emptiness surrounded her like a cold embrace.

Hanna woke with a start. She could hear the rush of water in the shower. Lucas was up already. She clambered out of bed and reached for her phone. It wasn't yet seven, but an early-morning trek in the forest was just what she needed.

Less than an hour later, Hanna and Lucas rode Nutmeg and Hunter across the pig field towards Bramble Woods. Roy trotted contentedly in front. Through the low-lying mist, Hanna could see the pigs near their arks, grubbing in the soil.

Hanna murmured, 'It was kind of Mum to say she'd make breakfast for us all when we get back. Ollie and Serenity are coming over too.'

'Paddy wants to pick my brains about pigs' health problems,' Lucas said. 'And Ollie's keen to make more changes at the farm this year.'

He slid from Hunter and opened the gate next to the stile so that Hanna could ride through, then he led the horse into the woods and climbed back into the saddle. Roy was already scampering ahead, stopping to sniff plants.

As they continued along the path, the air became cooler. Hanna looked over her shoulder, watching the mist hover in the pig field, a shifting yellow swirl. Beyond, the trees formed a thick canopy overhead. Twigs snapped under the horses' hooves, and there was the occasional sound of a bird flapping from a branch. Leaves quivered.

'I dreamed about Brea last night,' Hanna said, her voice hushed.

Lucas turned to her anxiously. 'I thought the dreams had stopped. You haven't had one for ages.'

'I know, but I dreamed that I saw a hare in the forest. I asked about Brea. She wasn't there.'

'Was it a bad dream?'

Hanna thought for a moment. 'It was sad. We're separate now.'

The horses trudged onwards, turning the corner. Hanna recognised the track ahead, the place where Roly had found the gold ring. The path felt calm now, empty. She tugged the reins and Nutmeg paused placidly beneath the tall oak tree. Hunter stopped by her side. Roy sat obediently, waiting for the word to carry on.

Hanna said quietly, 'This is where I saw the hare.'

'In the dream?' Lucas pointed. 'Where the bluebells are growing?'

'Exactly. There were blue flowers in my dream too.' Hanna met his eyes. 'Did you know that hana means flower in Japanese?'

'Of course. That's so appropriate,' Lucas said. 'These bluebells are a bit early this spring. They thrive in ancient woodlands.'

'Don't they symbolise true love?' Hanna asked.

'I'm sure they do.' Lucas grinned. 'Bluebells are known as harebells in some parts. Some people claim that fairies turn themselves into hares to hide among the flowers. Perhaps bluebells symbolise magic? They certainly keep reappearing.'

Hanna thought about his words. 'Every year, like a cycle? Like rebirth?'

'I suppose so.' He urged Hunter forward. 'Come on, Hanna. Let's get back to the farm. It's breakfast time.'

Roy barked in agreement, springing up, following the horse's hooves eagerly.

'I'm right behind you...' Hanna didn't move. The image of Brea was still with her. She wished she knew that she was at peace.

The thick mass of blue flowers shuddered in a light wind. Brea had been in her life for so long, but it was time for Hanna to let go. It was springtime: flowers and buds were everywhere, a time for new beginnings. Hanna hoped there would no longer be a restless spirit wandering the fens. She wished with all her heart that, after almost two millennia of separation and sadness, Brea had found what she had been searching for.

Hanna pushed Nutmeg forwards, quickly catching up with Lucas, and they rode together along the track towards the farm.

A beam of sunlight filtered through the trees and a hare ran out full pelt, its legs extended, a warrior enjoying the freedom of the woodlands. Moments later, a roe deer stepped silently from shadows, watching Hanna and Lucas disappear into the distance, listening to the fading sound of their voices. It waited for a moment until they were out of sight, always alert, its feet deep in the bluebells.

A sudden breeze made the flowers tremble. The deer stood still and firm as it looked around. Then it sprang away into the forest after the hare and was gone.

AUTHOR'S NOTE

The Roman conquest began in AD 43 under Emperor Claudius and Colchester initially became the capital of Britannia. The Iceni were a tribe of wealthy people interested in metalware and horses, whose territory included present-day Norfolk, parts of Suffolk and Cambridgeshire. They made a treaty with the Romans at the time of the invasion, but they rebelled in AD 47 when the Romans attempted to disarm them.

When their king, Prasutagus died around AD 60, he left his kingdom jointly to his two daughters by Boudicca, and to the Roman emperor. Research suggests that he omitted Boudicca due to the queen's hostility towards Rome. By leaving her out of the will, Prasutagus hoped his daughters would continue his policy of cooperation. However, the Roman governor general of Britain, Suetonius Paulinus ordered Prasutagus's lands and household to be plundered by Roman officers. Prasutagus's widow was publicly flogged and her daughters raped.

Boudicca, known as Boadicea by the Romans, was outraged. She led a revolt of the Iceni and Trinovantes tribes, capturing the Roman settlement of Camulodunum (Colchester) before storming Londinium (London) and Verulamium (St Albans). She led her huge army to meet Suetonius in a final battle, which was fought in the midlands of England, possibly at place called Mancetter near Nuneaton, in AD 61.

Against the background of the Iceni revolt, I have created the character of Brea, an Iceni slave taken from her tribe in AD 47 to work in a Roman household in Camulodunum.

In the present day, Hanna returns from China to live with her mother in Little Rymer, a fictitious village in the fenlands not far from King's Lynn.

In researching this novel, I spent time in Colchester and King's Lynn, where I received a warm welcome and support from local people, including many experts at Colchester Castle. So, much thanks to everyone who talked to me about the rich history of the Romans and the Briton tribes in East Anglia.

I'd also like to thank Will Bowden FSA, Professor of Roman Archaeology at the University of Nottingham, who very kindly shared his knowledge of the Iceni, their language and lifestyle, and my agent, Kiran Kataria, who is incredibly knowledgeable about all things Roman.

ACKNOWLEDGMENTS

Thanks to my agent, Kiran Kataria, for her wisdom and professionalism. And thanks to Sarah Ritherdon who is the smartest, most encouraging editor anyone could wish for.

Thanks to Amanda Ridout, Nia Beynon, Claire Fenby, Jenna Houston, Rachel Gilbey, Jade Craddock, Susan Sugden and to the wonderful team at Boldwood Books. So many people have worked to make this book happen: designers, editors, technicians, magicians, voice actors, bloggers, fellow writers – thanks to you all.

As always, thanks to my friends: Jonno, Jan, Rog, Martin, Cath, Jan M, Helen, Ken, Trish, Lexy, John, Bill, Shaz, Gracie, Mya, Frank, Erika, Rich, Susie, Ian, Kathy N, Julie, Martin, Steve, Rose, Steve's mum, Nik R, Pete O', Dawn, Slawka, Katie H.

Thanks to Peter, Avril and the Solitary Writers, to my awesome neighbours and to the local Somerset community, especially Jenny, Claire, Paul, Gary, Sophie and everyone at Bookshop by the Blackdowns.

Much thanks to the talented Ivor Abiks at Deep Studios.

Thanks to cousins Ellen from Florida and Jo from Taunton, to Norman and Angela, and to Robin and Edward from Colorado.

Love to my mum, who showed me the joy of reading, and to my dad, who proudly never read a thing.

Special love to our Tony and Kim.

Love always to Liam, Maddie, Cait, Joey, and most of all, to my soulmate, Big G.

Warmest thanks to my readers, wherever you are. You make this journey incredible.

ABOUT THE AUTHOR

Elena Collins is the pen name of Judy Leigh. Judy Leigh is the bestselling author of *Five French Hens*, *A Grand Old Time* and *The Age of Misadventure* and the doyenne of the 'it's never too late' genre of women's fiction. She has lived all over the UK from Liverpool to Cornwall, but currently resides in Somerset.

Sign up to Elena Collins' mailing list for news, competitions and updates on future books.

Visit Elena's website: https://judyleigh.com

Follow Elena on social media here:

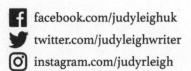
facebook.com/judyleighuk
twitter.com/judyleighwriter
instagram.com/judyrleigh

ALSO BY ELENA COLLINS

The Witch's Tree

The Lady of the Loch

The Daughter of the Fens

Boldwood

Boldwood Books is an award-winning fiction publishing company seeking out the best stories from around the world.

Find out more at www.boldwoodbooks.com

Join our reader community for brilliant books, competitions and offers!

Follow us
@BoldwoodBooks
@TheBoldBookClub

Sign up to our weekly deals newsletter

https://bit.ly/BoldwoodBNewsletter